A MIND TO SILENCE
AND OTHER STORIES

AKO CAINE PRIZE ANTHOLOGY 2021-22

Edited by Anwuli Ojogwu

With a foreword by Okey Ndibe

Abuja - London

First published in 2022 by Cassava Republic Press
Abuja – London

Editorial Copyright © Anwuli Ojogwu
Copyright of the text © of their authors, 2022
Copyright in this collection © Cassava Republic Press 2022

A CIP catalogue record for this book is available from the National Library of Nigeria and the British Library.

ISBN: 978-1-913175-52-8
eISBN: 978-1-913175-53-5

Book design by Deepak Sharma (Prepress Plus)
Cover & Art Direction by Jamie Keenan

Printed and bound in the UK by Clays Ltd, Elcograf S.p.A.

Distributed in Nigeria by Yellow Danfo

Distributed worldwide by Ingram Publishers Services

Stay up to date with the latest books, special offers and exclusive content with our monthly newsletter.

Sign up on our website:
www.cassavarepublic.biz

Twitter: @cassavarepublic
Instagram: @cassavarepublicpress
Facebook: facebook.com/CassavaRepublic
Hashtag: #CainePrizeAnthology #ReadCassava

Table of Contents

2022 AKO CAINE PRIZE WORKSHOP STORIES

Foreword

An air of history surrounds this year's edition of the AKO Caine Prize. After close to two years of global disquiet occasioned by a viral pandemic, 2022 held out some promise of restoration – a slow yet heartening reclamation of normalcy. Or, at any rate, a semblance of what was nearly lost.

It's said that life is short but art long. One proof can be found in the sheer profusion and vitality of the short story entries for 2022. The 349 submissions, and 267 eligible entries that contended for this year's AKO Caine Prize represented a record. They surpassed by far the totals for previous years.

What was the import?

For many African countries, Covid-19 was a public health and economic nightmare. Yet, by some fortuitous and inexplicable quirk, the virus did not unleash on the continent anything approaching the Olympian scale of devastation forecast by epidemiological experts.

By contrast, on the strength of this year's entries, it appears that the pandemic may have fertilised Africans' literary creativity. The marvel did not lie alone in the impressive count. All the judges – myself, Elisa Dialo (an academic, author and publisher of French and Guinean descent); Angela Wachuka (the Kenyan founder of 'Book Bunk'); South Africa's Lethlogonolo Mokgoroane (co-founder of 'The Cheeky Natives'); and the UK-based Nigerian visual artist, Ade Okelarin – were taken by the technical sophistication, stylistic poise, and thematic diversity of a fair number of the entries.

In story after story, the adeptness of touch, freshness of perspective, originality of language, and depth of insight sustained a sense of encounter with something akin to orchestral splendour. The authors hail from various geographic locations and cultures of Africa – East, West, North and South – as well as the global African diaspora. The entries are inspirited by animist, secular, Christian and Islamic ethos. Some stories are as stubborn in staking out political and historical grounds, as others are unabashed in their disavowal of such animus. Taken together, the authors represent a broad pan African tapestry. And the collective harvest is nothing short of a narrative smorgasbord. The stories are forged in a diversity of tempers and forms: mysteries, detective, noirs, the epistolary, futurism, political thrillers, experimental, the good old traditional mode.

Given the magnificent scandal of narrative riches before us, the task of selecting a shortlist of five stories proved particularly – predictably – arduous. To their credit, the judges were willing to be painstaking. They approached the task with a winsome combination of grace and patience – and a dollop of humour.

It took nearly four hours. I'd be the first to confess that the challenge of whittling down nearly 300 stories to five contenders is forbidding to the point of futility. Any group of five judges might have come up with an entirely different slate of finalists. There's certainly something inscrutable and mystical in the way any reader responds to a story.

In the end, I believe the time my fellow judges and I put into deliberations was well rewarded. I'm proud of the five stories on our shortlist: Idza Luhumyo's *Five Years Next Sunday*, Nana-Ama Danquah's *When a Man Loves a Woman*, Hannah Giorgis's *A Double-Edged Inheritance*, Joshua Chizoma's *Collector of Memories*, and Billie McTernan's *The Labadi Sunshine Bar*.

The varied soils in which the stories are rooted mirror the variety of their styles and themes. In that sense, they inhere a measure of the stupendous vastness and diversity of the broader corpus of entries. In Luhumyo's story, a woman who carries her fate and that of her community in her hair is beguiled by the duplicitous designs of Europeans out to colonise her most prized and vulnerable possession. Danquah hews a heartbreaking narrative of the tragic outcome of a love deadened by illness and toxic suspicion. In her story, Giorgis limns the intersection between fate and a reckoning with gruesome wrongs that must be avenged. In Chizoma's story, a few women come to terms with the terrible consequences of a long-ago heist of a baby-girl. McTernan serves up a tableau where desperate and dream-fuelled women must contend with their fellows and lovelorn men if they must win their fortune – or lose everything.

Placed side by side in this anthology, the stories both reveal their individual genius and intriguing thematic linkages. That revelation came to me in retrospect. But the attentive reader is bound to glean from these five stories a sense both of their profound distinctiveness and shared exploration of the themes of fate, the embodiment and contestations of memory, the ubiquitousness of duplicity in human interactions, and the fragility of love.

Okey Ndibe
Chair of Judges, 2022 AKO Caine Prize

Preface

One of the highlights of the 2022 AKO Caine Prize Workshop was watching a documentary with George Saunders, one of the finest short story writers in the world, on making a story. In the documentary he made a poignant point that 'the discontent with writing urges it to a higher ground'. This would become evident during the workshop, as I watched the evolution of the writers from anguish, hope, and then a sense of release when their stories finally took form. It is the nature of the creative process to experience torment *and* pleasure until the story is born, and for nine days, the workshop sessions were both gruelling and inspiring. I had the privilege of working with these writers, alongside award-winning writer and 2020 AKO Caine Prize shortlisted writer, Jowhor Ile, who served as the writing tutor. Together, we nurtured their ideas and helped them realise the stories that they wanted to tell.

On the topic of release: the last two years, with a raging pandemic, have been difficult ones, leaving in its wake loss, despair and isolation, and the timing of the workshop was a respite from its shackles. It provided fellowship and the sense of renewal that we all needed. The disruptive impact of the pandemic on travel was also apparent in AKO Caine Prize's decision to pilot a regional workshop by selecting only writers from the ECOWAS region. Regardless, the presence of young emerging writers and an older multi-award-winning writer only enriched the experience with their different perspectives, which will be seen in the styles and themes of the stories in the anthology. There were nine workshop participants from across West Africa: Victor Forna (Sierra Leone), Elizabeth Johnson (Ghana), Akua Serwaa Amankwah (Ghana), Kofi Berko (Ghana), Audrey Obuobisa-Darko (Ghana), Jeffrey Atuobi

(Ghana); Onengiye Nwachukwu (Nigeria), Akachi Ezimora Ezeigbo (Nigeria) and Sally Sadie Singhateh (The Gambia).

This sense of release and renewal was not limited to us the participants. Even the AKO Caine Prize workshop emerged from a hiatus since 2018 when it held the last workshop in Rwanda.

Navigating my role as editor each day of the workshop was characterised by many hours of conversations with writers to find the heart of their stories. I watched them discuss their story ideas, craft them, read them to each other, and improve on them with further critique from Jowhor. This was a hard feat as a story will only be told when it is ready to be told, and I commend the writers for their determination. One writer I worked with found her story in a thread of a dialogue between two characters in the second draft of a three-thousand-word piece. She would later discard the rest of the plot and build the story from ground up on that theme, and this eventually became *The Loan*. Some days, while working with them, I prodded for answers on the direction of a story and sometimes I offered a direction. Notwithstanding, the writers were confident in their ability to agree or object to interventions, which made the process seamless and rewarding.

There was a lot of learning, not just from the workshop sessions with us tutors, but among the writers who learned to lean on each other. They formed a camaraderie and tested their ideas among themselves, reading each other's stories, offering critique and suggestions for improvement. At the end of the workshop, the stories that emerged were evocative, vivid, and vibrant, written in multi-genres from speculative and literary fiction to mystery and romance.

Readers of the anthology will encounter themes about sacrifice, love, freedom, self-discovery, loss, all expressed in language that is visual and lyrical, bordering on the experimental. From the supernatural reconciliation between two sisters torn apart by their destructive father in Akua Serwaa Amankwah's *Sugar's Daughters* to a man who finds happiness in the reincarnation of a lost love in Akachi Ezeigbo's *Homecoming*; and from a young girl who comes of age in a futuristic world of Ghana's ancient mythology and technology in Audrey Obuobisa-Darko's *Nnome*, to a young woman who risks her life for freedom through the cultural practice of a human loan scheme in Sally Sadie Singhateh's *The Loan*, among other stories.

Beyond the workshop, the experience was well-rounded. There were other moments to engage with the community and pay it forward with visits to two secondary schools. The writers were spilt into two groups. The first group visited St. Augustine College, which was established in 1930, and the other group paid a visit to Ghana National Secondary School, which was established in 1948, both in Elmina, where they engaged the young students on writing and storytelling and listened to their aspirations.

There was also a visit to Elmina Castle once a trade settlement for goods before it became an Atlantic Slave Trade depot where the writers heard harrowing stories of the cruelty behind the capture and separation of families. In addition, the AKO Caine Prize partnered with The Writer's Project of Ghana, who organised a public event for the writers at the Goethe Institut where they read and discussed excerpts from their stories. The final night of the workshop activities came to an end with a tribute to the celebrated author and playwright, Ama Ataa Aidoo.

This workshop was memorable because of the generosity of the people we met including Martin Egblewogbe and Mamle Kabu, co-founders of The Writers Project Ghana and AKO Caine Prize Workshop alums; Professor Kwadwo Opoku-Agyemang, an award-winning poet and eminent scholar of Literature at the University of Cape Coast; Jowhor Ile, my partner tutor; and the proprietor of Elmina Bay Resort, Mr Ben Kweku Idun and his remarkable staff, who saw to our comfort in the beautiful environment. It is also in order to recognise the leadership of the AKO Caine Prize director, Sarah Ozo-Irabor, whose gentle guidance lifted the writers' spirit daily. Her famous quote: 'Give yourself grace and learn to lean on others when they give you grace' became a motivational anthem for the writers as they worked hard to meet a tight deadline.

For the last 23 years, the AKO Caine Prize has been instrumental to showcasing African talent and it is my pleasure to present to you the stories from another set of emerging talent from the 2022 AKO Caine Prize Workshop, with two additional stories by Rafeeat Aliyu and TJ Benson (both from Nigeria), participants in the 2021 virtual writer's monitoring programme. I hope you enjoy the stories.

Anwuli Ojogwu
Editor, 2022 AKO Caine Prize Workshop

2021 SHORTLISTED STORIES

Lucky

Doreen Baingana

We've been left behind. It's another morning, so we're in the school garden looking for lunch. The maize is still too young, too dark a green, but what can we do? It's not easy reaching for the long bulbs with yellowy wisps like white people's hair; the leaves cut our arms and legs with their razor-sharp fuzz because they don't want us to steal their cobs. But that doesn't stop us; the ache of emptiness keeps us going. Those who pick more will eat more, so we work as fast as we can. All around me, boys scrabble around, making the dry leaves on the ground crackle as loud as roosters. Or does it seem so loud because the rest of the school is silent?

Eh, but hunger can make you do things! Three days ago Ociti and Bosco clambered over the fence and ate like twenty hard green mangoes from the old orchard that is now more like a forest. Rumour says the owners went into exile long ago, England or somewhere. But how we laughed at those two when they spent the whole night running back and forth from the pit latrine! Laughing to cover our jealousy 'coz at least they had felt full, content, for a few hours. Envious 'coz they were brave enough to venture out of school, what with all the stories of the Lakwena rebels roaming around, and worse, the new government soldiers who still behaved like the rebels they had been for —was it six years?

This is why school has closed, and why eleven of us are stuck here; we can't go back to our homes in the north: Gulu District, West Nile. There's nowhere to pass because of the fighting. Everyone else lucky enough to leave or have relatives in the south has left. My Auntie Joyce is in Kampala somewhere, but I don't know where exactly and I don't have her phone number or anything. I tried calling my father, back home in Aboke, to ask, but his number was off, and the Headmaster —'Big Head' since his competes with a hippo's— shrugged as he took the office phone from my hands. That was it: I was staying. And yet he, whose job it is to take care of the school, took off with the rest and left us! He didn't even turn his hippo head to look back at us as the school bus rumbled out of the gate, packed full of teachers and students like onions in a sack.

Only Mr. Komakech, the mouthy maths teacher, has stayed behind with us. Even the workers have left, can you imagine? Koma, as we call him because he never stops talking, said he wanted to 'enjoy the war properly' and laughed, but it seems he's stuck here too. He can talk us to death, but for some reason, my eyes can't stop following how his large lips chew around the words like they are tasty.

Don't ask me what the war is all about: the new government army of former rebels was now fighting rebels who had been the old government army. So what's the difference? They've switched places like we did back home when we were seven, eight, those days: Ugandans versus Tanzanians and the rule was that the Tanzanians had to win because they had saved us from Idi Amin. Oh, but it was wild running through the compounds, scattering the cackling chicken, dogs barking with excitement and joining us as we scrambled through the shambas, wind whistling over and under our shouts: *Pow-pow! Got you! Die!* Shooting each other dead with stick guns, screaming, falling, then getting up, brushing off the dust and dried leaves, and changing sides. I was really good at falling in slow motion, arms and legs flailing, body jerking in the dust, like the soldiers on Bob's father's TV, which he allowed us to watch from the outside, peering in through their windows.

And here I am fighting with maize cobs, against a sun hammering my forehead. Thank God for no barber visits; at least my bushy hair is a sun shield. After picking four cobs, I turn to Ociti: 'How many have you got?'

'Five.'

'That's enough for now, let's go.'

Koma has ordered us all to stay in one dorm, 'to keep each other company,' he says. 'Birds of a feather do what?' And he cocked his head to one side like he too was a bird: tall, dark and smooth. The way he talks, you'd think we've remained behind for fun like it's a holiday at school because we like it so much. Shya! Big Head also called it a 'free term', since we aren't paying fees like he's done us a favour. As if we're stupid. Here we are, no assembly, no teachers except one, no cooks or cleaners, no sports, nothing. Free term? How about 'prison'? Ask me what prison is like and I'll tell you: whole hours, days, stretching out like an endless line of ants, filled with nothing but the same routine chores, and then sitting around staring emptily at the same few pimply faces, listening to our stomachs growl, our thoughts roaming the carefree past or a fantastic future, circling, circling to avoid the wide, flat, dry now.

To make it worse, Koma does his best to cheat us out of our 'free term'. First, he makes us get up early. 'Up, up, you don't have all day!' But of course, we do. 'Early to bed, early to what?' It's so annoying to be shaken awake by his bright booming voice and big smile as he pokes his head into our room. But also, something inside wakes up, feels good to be smiled upon by him.

'Good morning, teacher' we mutter as we drag ourselves out of bed.

Well, we sleep early because power has gone, and so what else can we do in the dark but listen to our bellies growl? Only Koma has a torch, and we use it sparingly to save the batteries. But surely we could start the morning's chores at seven, even eight, not six? After fetching water, scrubbing saucepans, floors, the toilets and bathrooms, collecting food, cooking and eating, Koma makes us sit in class straight after lunch. Not even a ka-hour of rest, how unfair is that?

'Hard work does what?'

Koma seems to look at me more than the others, so I answer louder than the rest. 'Pays, teacher.' It's as if we are having a private conversation about something else.

But pays, how? Everyone else at home is free and safe, but for us? Is it not bad enough that we're stuck here 'in the path of bullets', as Big Head so kindly put it, do we also have to be punished with class? Just because Koma loves maths —for him its meat to chew on, does he have to force it on us? For me, it's dry bone. Moreover, we're all in different classes, so it's confusing when he opens different pages of *Longman's Mathematics for East Africa*, and tries to teach us all different things at the same time.

Me, I'm not afraid of Koma; I put up my hand on our first day and asked, 'Why are we in class?' I almost added 'wasting time.'

'You boy, can't you see how lucky you are to have this extra time to revise, moreover with me?' He spread out his arms as if to show off his muscles: 'All the others are at home sleeping! No pain, no what?'

Lucky? Sure, like, if we lied to ourselves enough, we'd believe it; it would become true. Teachers! They have this thing of thinking we're foolish enough to believe what they say. Like how, in Civics class last term, the teacher droned on about how the police protect us. Really? Even a child of five knows better; he just needs to listen to the news once. We all just kept quiet and waited for the bell to ring.

Me, I can escape teachers' lame lies by going back to old Okiror's war stories. He's a mzee made of nothing but wrinkled skin and bones, who sits under the huge mango tree outside St. Mark's the whole day, back in Aboke, holding an ancient gun like a baby. He repeats stories of his glory days to us kids who hang around; adults don't have the patience. I was mesmerized as much by the stories as by how his saliva spattered from his rubbery lips as he talked.

As Ociti and I walk from the garden, our cobs held close to our bodies, I wonder what story Koma will feed us now: that the army is fighting for us —or is it the rebels? My empty belly tells me they're tending to their tummies, just like we're doing now. I can almost taste the salty chewiness we will soon enjoy; I chew my inner cheeks and swallow saliva. It helps, believe me.

Just then, on our way to the kitchen, just as we pass by the dorms, there's a bang like thunder and I bite my tongue. We fall to the ground, my mouth stinging, eyes shut tight against —what? Has the sky cracked? Silence, as though the world is taking in a deep breath. And then all the birds in the world scream and fling themselves into the sky.

'Run!'

Ociti scrambles up and takes off ahead. Koma had said that if anything happened —not that it would, he added— we should all run to the nearest building. The birds' shrieks are silenced by sharp sounds: TA-TA-TATATA-TA-TATATATA. Like that. On and on, from all around.

Somehow we reach and fall onto the dorm door, the others too, one after another, as Ociti fights with the handle. It opens; we pile in and scramble under the bunk beds. I trip on the doorstep, fall on my hands and knees into the room and crawl like a desperate lizard under the nearest bunk bed. Koma is already there, imagine, pulling in his long legs, trying to squeeze into a corner. I wish I could laugh: a whole teacher squashed under a bed! Tim also presses in: hot flesh, shoes, shorts, dirt, sweat. Bosco tries to join us.

'Go to the other one,' Koma hisses.

The poor boy has to crawl out into the open and scuttle to the next bed. We lie as still as we can, trying to quiet our panting, listening to the sharp eruptions as if they're telling us something. The bursting noise is nothing like Mzee Okiror's war stories, and I thought I knew guns. Right next to my face, the iron legs of the bunk bed are strong and straight like prison bars, but how can they protect us? I'm glad to be so close to Koma, I won't lie: his long bent limbs and warm breath are more reassuring than hard metal.

Strange, but as we hide like cockroaches, as my heart hits my chest, I feel something close to relief: *this* was what we have been waiting for all along. Finally, it has come. Everything else has been a game of using up time: cleaning, doing maths, learning how to cook, dodging bathing, ransacking the garden, what not, and then *the thing* happens, and you realise it has always been there, crouching at the back of your mind like a rat. No, it has been following me around like a pesky dog, along with every thought, and I tried to slap it away, to ignore it, but now it has stood its ground and bared its teeth.

'We won't die,' Koma whispers.

What a stupid, stupid thing to say. Typical. Now, all of a sudden, because he's a teacher, he's become a prophet? Now that he has called death out loud, won't it come? We lie there as though stuck to the floor, listening for more. Have the shots stopped? My stomach growls.

'Don't move,' Koma hisses. 'Better safe than what?'

Like I was about to do what, tour the school? One more word and I'll stamp my elbow into his calf, which is right up next to my crooked arm. His skin is dry, ashy. A strange feeling rises in me: I want to do like my mother would: rub his hard skin with Vaseline until it shines. Or maybe spit on my palm and use that. I push it away instead.

He shifts, but there is nowhere to go, and I smell him: sweet, like an over-ripe mango. We lie there: cramped, aching, painfully alert, listening to our breathing match for the longest twenty minutes of my whole life.

I shut my eyes and force escape to Mzee's stories. Ask me the name of any gun: Beretta 92, AK-47, AKM, AK-74, Type 56; what hadn't I learnt from Mzee Okiror? The deacons had tried to chase him away from outside St. Mark's, but he was a fixture like the monster marabou storks that we screamed and threw stones at. They would squawk and swop up and away, but hover in trees nearby and soon return, landing like clumsy helicopters. Mzee Okiror would aim his rifle at one of them, his eyes so wrinkled they seemed shut, gun trembling in gnarled hands. We waited, holding onto each other.

'Aaaah! They're just birds —me, I kill people!' and he stretched open his mouth with silent laughter, exposing rosy gaps, saliva dribbling, as he beat his skinny thigh.

Every single time we waited breathlessly for the shot, and every time, somehow, he fooled us, and we stamped our feet, annoyed. 'You mzee! We shall report you.'

Old Okiror made up for this by letting us watch as he opened his gun lovingly and polished it, rub, rub, rubbing each section with a dark oily cloth, holding it delicately close like an injured child. It seemed alive to me, like the metal breathed, even as it could stop breath. I remained by Mzee's side for hours in the idle holiday afternoons, long after the other boys had got bored and run off. Mzee had stories! It seems he had fought in every army: one day he would say he was with the African Rifles of World War II, fighting for the British in Burma, wherever that was; then next the colonial army had to 'pacify' the Karamajong —he said the word in English, explaining, 'you know them; they never want to be ruled by anybody, let alone whites.' That's when he came back with lots of cows and got his first wife. Then the next time he said he took part in the attack on the Buganda King's Palace in Kampala in 1966; then later he volunteered with the SPLA in Sudan in the 1980s and even later trained the UNLA to fight the NRA. When I told my mother, breathless, counting the armies on my fingers, she chewed her teeth. 'What a bunch of lies! That mzee was in Amin's army and survived it with nothing, not even his teeth. Do you think he has a brain left?'

But he had; I knew this 'coz he knew the names of many many guns, and he drew them for me at the back of my exercise book even though his fingers couldn't really bend properly. His fingers were as stiff and as hard as metal and were the same grey-black colour as if the gun itself had seeped into his fingers. Eh, but when my mother saw the pictures, the way she tore out the pages, spoiling my exercise book! Chewing her teeth juicily, she tore them into tiny little pieces, opened her palms and let pieces flutter to the ground, her eyes hard on me.

'You want to be like him, proud of having done nothing but fight other people's wars? You want to end up like him, with nothing but stories? Rubbish!'

I couldn't answer her back, of course. But wasn't she the one who always said respect the elderly? And at least *he* had been all around the world and back, so why couldn't he tell all those stories, why not?

What *is* that? A rustling, a rush like wind, louder, louder. Rain? Sounds like the steady clomp of a herd of cattle pushed to a jog fill everywhere; closer, louder, a stampede —of what? Wild animals? But from where? There's no forest nearby—

I can't stop myself, I have to see. I crawl out from under the bed. Koma grabs my foot, but his warm hand is slippery with sweat, and I twist out of it, creep up to the window, and slowly pull myself up to my knees.

'Get down, you!' Koma hisses, for once talking sense.

But the thunder calls me: I inch my head up, up, until my eyes are just above the window ledge, my fingers grasp it tight. A tremendous mass of blackness moves hugely across my eyes: Men jog forward as one, black all over: oily shiny chests and arms, black shorts, glowing arms swinging, coming from behind the classroom block, moving across the compound, towards our dorm windows and then onwards, disappearing round the building.

'Whaaaat?' My voice a scratch.

Ociti's face comes up beside me.

'You stupid boys, I said get down!'

I cannot take my eyes off the ... this gigantic swarm of black bees, no, more like a monstrous shiny-black centipede with a hundred legs. The men stare straight ahead, all of them. Light seems to bounce off their shiny chests, making them hazy like a thought you can't quite grasp.

After a long thudding instant, they are gone. And that's when I know; spirits, of course. Ociti and I slip down from the window, slump to the floor, and stare at each other blankly.

The thunder recedes, becomes an echo of itself, far off rustling, a reverberation, and then, incredibly, nothing. It's as if the spirits have sucked up all sound and left us in stillness like the first day ever. From above us streams a simple, astonishing afternoon light. Have I ever noticed it?

Snuffling, small heaves, some boy under the other bunk is crying. Tim. I can't even laugh at him. The room grows smaller, as the smell of urine and fright and sweat and light too bright to hide in expands and throbs, and all of us boys, and Koma too, hate to be so close and want to be closer.

An old memory rises of the biggest thing I had ever seen when I was four: a yellow monster as big as a house, with one giant, iron-grey chain wheel. Oh, how it roared, and how its huge rolling foot flattened everything it passed over, and how we kids cried because the devil itself had come to destroy our village! The caterpillar had come to Aboke to bring us a tarmac road. When we got used to it, how we ran around it, screaming and laughing! And how we were beaten for playing near it. And oh, when it rolled away weeks later, leaving a wide black sticky road as if leading to heaven, how empty a silence it left.

'Lakwena rebels.' Ociti's voice is high and slippery.

So that's them? The powerful, magical, spirit-possessed army? So the rumours are real? Who doesn't know the stories: the barren witch-priest with one breast, the red fire that flies out of her eyes, the bullets that bounce off them, the stones they turn into grenades, the magic oil that shields them, the rivers they walk over, all that?

'They look like how?' Bosco squeaks as he pokes his head out.

'Shut up, boys!' Koma's voice no longer booms; part of the upside-down world.

'Black, black ... black,' I whisper too, rubbing my eyes. I turn to Ociti. 'You saw?' Already, I'm beginning to doubt my own eyes and ears.

He nods, says nothing. Then I notice water, or something, trickling from Ociti's splayed out legs. I push him, but he is glued to the growing puddle. I shift away and we watch the pee crawl slowly towards the door, glistening with sunlight.

Finally, birds start calling, questioning. Koma creeps out from under the bed, and unwraps his long body, straightens, stretches, raises his arms high, as if he too is working some magic: becoming himself again: a teacher, a man. I watch from below, wanting to believe in him. With breath and doubt and whispering, we start rising too.

'Ssshh. First wait. Fortune favours the what? ... No, not that one.' Koma's low, soft voice is oddly reassuring.

He shakes out his long slightly-bowed legs and I want to wrap myself around them. As the birds continue, so sweet and normal, he walks towards the door, upright, chest open like a hero, opens it, takes that step that tripped me, out into the brilliant light, and into a loud clap, and a shriek from somewhere. The heavy thump and clumsy shape of his fall will repeat itself behind my closed eyes for years. I can see him clearly through the open door, in light that has no shame, writhing on the ground like Auntie Joyce when a pastor from Nigeria came to St. Mark's and shouted angrily at her swollen legs and feet, and she fell to the floor and squirmed like a fat but overwhelmed maggot. Blood spurts out of his mouth, a faulty tap, and he goes still. I wait for him to get up, dazed and sluggish like Auntie Joyce did.

I press my head hard into the cold floor and feel my thighs and shorts soaked in warm wetness. I close my eyes but nothing stops.

Heavy footsteps. Kiswahili back and forth, and a shoving and dragging of something heavy across the ground. The thud of boots is on the veranda, and door after dorm door is flung open. Ours, already open, is pushed, hits the wall, swings back and is held. Why did we bother to hide?

'Get out!' As sharp as that shot. 'Are you deaf?'.

Ociti is the first to crawl out, slowly, staying as close as he can to the floor.

'All of you! Outside.'

We do, like grovelling dogs.

'Kneel there. Hands high. My God, you stink!'

We shuffle as close as possible 'till our bodies touch; a mess of tears, pee, sniffling. We are kneeling before Koma.

'These are school boys, just,' one camouflage-covered figure says to another.

Their boots are caked with mud. I can't dare look up, not even to peek at their guns.

'Where are the others? ... I'm asking, are there others around here?'

We shake our heads.

'What's wrong with you; can't you talk?' One of them, short and thick, nudges Bosco, at the end of our wretched row, with his boot. 'How come only you are here?'

'They left us,' Bosco squeaks and then begins to cry for real. I peek sideways at him. He can't bring down his hands to wipe the streaks of tears and phlegm from his face. 'Boys don't what?' Koma should say.

'Stop it, you stupid boy! Useless!' The soldier laughs.

The two stride away, holding the straps of their guns firmly like handbags. Mzee Okiror's gravelly voice reminds me helpfully: AK-74.

The sun stares at us, unrelenting like we're guilty. My knees become stabs of pain, my arms too, but I dare not shift. Sweat stings my eyes, but when I close them, I feel dizzy.

Soldiers come up in small groups of two or three until they are about fifteen gathered the other side of Koma, who looks like he fell down dead drunk in red puddles. Here come the flies with a cheerful buzzing. One of the soldiers takes a black box out of his pocket and shouts into it. A kind of radio he can talk into? Old Okorir hadn't talked about that. After listening, nodding, barking back, he beckons the rest. 'We meet at the market,' Captain says. They nod, gather themselves, fling us leftover looks and stride off.

The short one who first talked to us turns and comes back. 'Your teacher?' He points at Koma with his gun. We nod. He shrugs. 'Find a way to bury him. You boys are lucky you didn't follow him out. Listen; don't even think of leaving this compound. Don't move, move around, you hear? The Lakwenas are nearby if you don't know, and they have no mercy. No mercy at all. They eat boys like you.' He shakes his gun at us and then jogs off to catch up with the rest.

Again, like the Lakwenas, the soldiers are here, and then they are not, like magic. Then why are we kneeling here, and why is Koma lying over there? The front of his shirt has turned maroon. He is not flicking off the flies that play on his face. Those lips are open, slack.

Eventually, as always, the birds start their chirping and singing again. When the sun forgives us a little, and an evening breeze starts to chill our clammy shirts and shorts, Bosco moves, and we follow him, shuffling back into our room, and creeping back under the bunks. The now shadowy smothering space is damp and familiar, and our warm smelly bodies, a comfort.

I close my eyes and see those flies on Koma's face, his eyes and mouth. What would he say? He makes no sense most of the time, but that doesn't mean flies should just sit on his face. His warm body should be here, filling up all this space. He calls me, I swear, and I have no choice, just like when I rose to the window, no choice but to believe that old Okiror would shoot: I crawl out from under the bunk again. Trembling like I have malaria, I tug a blanket off a bed, move forward on all fours, open the door, go down that dreaded step and out across the grass, my knees stinging all the way. The sun is weak now. I reach Koma, and the flies rise in unison. I wave them away with the blanket and they buzz angrily. For some reason, I want to touch his legs, and I pull them as straight as I can. They are as heavy as I imagined; they are still warm, his arms too. He doesn't say anything as I lay the blanket over him. I should go back inside, leave him alone, but I shuffle around him, my knees sinking into the soft wet ground as I tuck in the blanket edges under him, while the flies hover above.

The Street Sweep

Meron Hadero

Getu stood in front of his mirror struggling to perfect a Windsor knot. He pulled the thick end of his tie through the loop, but the knot unraveled in his hands. He tried again, and again he failed. Did he really need the tie? He guessed it would probably be easier to convince the guards at the Sheraton to let him in with one. And even then….

But he couldn't work out the steps, so Getu put the necktie in his pocket and decided to try his luck without it. Sitting at the edge of his mattress, Getu waited for the hour to pass (he didn't want to arrive too early, too eager). His mattress was on the floor in the corner, and it was covered with all of his clothes, which earlier that evening he had tried on, considered, ruled out, reconsidered, tossed aside before choosing a blue shirt (stained under the arms, but he'd conceal the stains with his jacket) and black pants. Until that day, Getu thought this was an adequate wardrobe, fairly nice for a street sweeper, but he had noticed even his best pants were worn at the hem, so he brought them to his mother.

She was busy chopping onions, and her red hands and tearful eyes gave Getu pause. He didn't want to add to her burden, but he needed her help. 'Momma,' he said, and she immediately responded, 'Later,' and walked right passed him to the garden to pick some hot peppers.

He thumbed the rebellious threads that seemed to be disintegrating in his fingers. 'Please, Momma. This stitching is coming apart.' She didn't look up from her vegetable garden, so he pressed on. 'I need to look nice for Mr. Jeff's farewell party.'

'Ah, Mr. Jeff,' she turned to face Getu and would have thrown up her hands except for the peppers resting on her lifted apron. 'Again with Mr. Jeff,' she groaned.

'I have to see him. It's his last night in Addis Ababa, and he's been so good to me,' Getu explained, following his mother back to the kitchen.

She called over her shoulder, 'Has he been good to you? What has Mr. Jeff actually done for you?'

Getu hesitated, then said, 'Mr. Jeff told me he has something for me.' He'd have said more but she was barely paying attention to him, focused on wiping the peppers off on her apron, splitting them in half, and taking out all the seeds. 'Momma,' he said.

'I heard you, it's just what is it you imagine he has for you?' Getu didn't dare honestly answer that question, his mother's ridicule primed for the slightest provocation. Ever since Jeff Johnson invited him to the party, Getu couldn't stop himself from guessing what this something might be. Over their months of friendship, Jeff Johnson had told Getu how important Getu was to him, how his organization could use a young man like Getu, and what a brilliant, keen head Getu had on his shoulders. Getu's hopes had soared as he pictured the good job he'd surely be offered. In this moment, he nearly told his mother all about the new, stable life he'd imagined, the freedom from worry that would come from the big paycheck he'd surely bring in, which would be so liberating now that the government seizure of land was creeping closer neighborhood by neighborhood. Even the Tedlu's had lost their home just a month ago, and they only lived five blocks away. But Getu simply replied, 'I just want to say goodbye to Mr. Jeff.'

'Getu, if this Mr. Jeff really wants you at his party, then he won't care what you wear.'

'But Momma, it's at the Sheraton,' Getu whispered.

'At the Sheraton, did you say?' She turned and stared at him with raised eyebrows and a sorry look in her eyes. 'It's at the Sheraton?' Her tone started high, then fell with Getu's spirits.

'Do you really think this man wants you there? At the Sheraton? He invited *you* to a party at the Sheraton? Only a man who has spent every day here having his shoes licked and every door flung open would be so unaware as to invite a boy like you *to the Sheraton*. To the Sheraton! Who is this Mr. Jeff?'

Getu didn't have the courage to reply, so she continued. 'Let me tell you. He comes, is chauffeured to one international office after another, and at the end of the night, he goes to the fancy clubs on Bole Road, feasts, drinks, passes out, wakes up, then calls his chauffer who has slept lightly with his phone placed right by his head and with the ringer turned up high so as not to miss a call from the likes of Mr. Jeff and disappoint the likes of Mr. Jeff. And then one day this Mr. Jeff invites my boy to a party at the Sheraton. At the Sheraton! They'll never let you in of course. The Sheraton? Oh, I could go on about this Mr. Jeff.'

Getu's mother had long ago formed her opinion about the Mr. Jeffs of the world. She had seen men and women like Jeff Johnson breeze through the country for decades, an old pattern. She'd kept her distance from these eager aid workers flown over for short stints with some big new NGO, this or that agency, such and such from who knew where. They appeared in her neighborhood, gave her surveys to fill out, and offered things she reluctantly accepted (vaccines and vitamins), things she quite happily pawned (English language books and warm clothing), and things at which she turned up her nose (genetically modified seeds and mosquito repellant). Without fail, the Mr. Jeffs shaped then reshaped her neighborhood in new ways year in, year out. She compared them to the floods that washed out the roads in the south of the country each rainy season carving new paths behind them, a cyclical force of change and re-creation. Each September after the rainy season ended and the new recruits from Western universities came to Ethiopia, she was known to have said, 'And now let the storms begin.'

'Momma,' Getu said softly snapping his mother out of her thoughts. 'This is a really important night for me.'

'I know you think that. But you're eighteen, and you haven't seen enough yet to know what I know.'

'Eighteen here is like seventy-five anywhere else,' he rebutted.

'Can't I talk sense into you? Is a mother's love and wisdom no match for whatever hold Mr. Jeff has over you?'

'But Momma, we need him. He'll help us save our home,' Getu said, finally owning up to that hope that had started as a little seed and sprouted and taken root and now seemed as sturdy as an oak.

After a pause that would have been enough for her to turn the idea around in her head more than once, she asked, 'Do you think he can do that?' She didn't believe in the Mr. Jeffs, who seemed predictable by now, but she knew Getu was full of surprises.

Getu held out the clothes he needed mended, and she took them cautiously. Getu followed her to the living room and watched her sew expertly. As she moved the needle through the thin fabric, she flicked her wrist, and mumbled the long list of chores she was putting on hold to take care of this task. Getu found his mood lifting as he saw her expertise with the needle and thread. His clothes looked almost new. When she'd finished, Getu took them gratefully from her, though he felt her resistance still, for she held her tight grip even as he pulled them away.

Anyone could see the Sheraton was palatial, literally seemed ten-times bigger than the presidential palace, and there were several reasons why. Of course there was the size; the Sheraton was sprawling. Also, the presidential palace was gated and tucked into a forested acreage in the city, so the structure peeked out from between the iron fencing and shrubbery. It was impossible to *behold*. But you could *behold* the Sheraton looming above all else on a hill in the city center. At night, it was spotlit from below, and with the neighborhoods around it empty or without electricity because of frequent power shortages, the Sheraton, alone with its invisible generators, illuminated that part of town each night, every night, no fail. Most importantly, the Sheraton was exclusive but not exclusionary. Some were allowed in while others were not, and this selective accessibility gave it more mystique than the palace, which was completely off limits to all but the president and his close coterie. The Sheraton created a sense of hope when it opened its arms to the few, and so occupied the ambitions of many. Inside, there were cafés, restaurants, a sprawling pool, and enough amenities to fill a hefty fold-out brochure, including a multi-DJ nightclub called the Gaslight. The Sheraton was an unmistakable presence in this city, an isle of exclusive luxury that didn't quite touch down.

Walking the long road from his home to the Sheraton, Getu carried his jacket, tie in pocket. He walked slowly so as not to get too sweaty by the time he arrived, and he walked, he practiced all the ways he'd ask Mr. Jeff for his job, his just reward. As soon as he had the courage, he'd gently bring up the matter of the job he felt was due to him. As he made his way through town, he passed burdened mules, cars trapped in traffic jams, old men and women who preferred trudging along the road to waiting for the crowded buses. Young men sat on street curb getting stoned on chat, which they languidly chewed with nothing better to do than watch the slow moving yet frenetic scenes drift by.

When Getu approached the foot of the hill that led up to the Sheraton, the buzz of the city quieted. Around this barren land, bureaucrats had erected yellow and green fences of corrugated tin to keep out any unwanted men, women, dogs, cats, and others they considered strays. It started with a single law: if a house in Addis Ababa is less than four stories tall, then your land can and will be seized. To keep your home, build! Whether there were new investors lined up or not, land across Addis Ababa was being exuberantly razed to make way for the new. Neighborhood by neighborhood, stucco houses vanished; make-shift tent homes made of cloth and rags and wood were swept away; moon-houses put up at night by leaning tin siding against a wall were tossed aside by morning.

'Who has a four-story house?' Getu's mother had shouted frantically when she first heard about the law. 'All these powers that be will get rid of everything, except maybe the Sheraton,' she had said.

Getu said, 'Be calm, I'll take care of it. We'll make it work.'

'What will we do? Of course we'll move wherever they put us. I hear they're pushing people to the outskirts of town, but how will I get to work then? I was born in this house, and why don't they just leave me alone to die here, too?'

'I'm going to handle it, Momma. You'll see. I'll make you proud,' Getu said, stepping close to his mother and rubbing her back.

'Lord, this son of mine,' Getu's mother said into her folded hands.

'There's a way,' Getu responded. 'I can get a new job,' Getu assured.

'You sweep sidewalks. What could you do with your broom and your dustbin? Anyway, who's to say that today they tell us to build a four-story house, tomorrow they won't demand the Taj Mahal. Just let it go.'

'But, Momma—'

'What did I do to end up with a dreamer for a son?'

'I could get a job with one of the international organizations. We could build a dozen four-story houses.'

'What food did I let cross my lips—didn't I forgo meat and dairy each holiday when I was pregnant? Didn't I pray enough? Every week, did I not attend church?'

'Mother, you don't understand. I have a new friend.'

'Did I stare too long at someone cursed with an evil eye?'

'I've helped him. He'll help me when the time comes. Mr. Jeff is a friend of mine.'

Up through the swept-clean land, up the hill, along the winding road, Getu walked to the Sheraton and, before he was in the sight-line of the guards, put on his jacket, and smoothed his shirt, the necktie still in a bundle in his right-hand pocket. Getu also brought a small wrapped gift, a map of the city that he bought at a tourist shop in Mercato. Getu circled where his house was on this map, and on the back he wrote his address and phone number should Mr. Jeff want to visit.

Though the sun hadn't set yet, the spotlights in front of the Sheraton were already on, illuminating the driveways and pathways outside the hotel, every inch meticulously landscaped with palms, hedges, and blooming flowers punctuating the long curving roads that all led to the five-story building and its various wings and annexes. Getu took a deep breath, and stared at the vast space. He tried to visualize walking up to the guard, throwing a casual smile, saying a quick, 'Hello, how are you?' Maybe he'd affect an accent so the guards might mistake him for one of the diaspora who lived abroad and returned with foreign wealth and connections and ease, it seemed.

He took his first step down the hotel pathway. The cement beneath his feet was spotless, as if it had just been scrubbed clean. 'Remarkable. They even kept out the soot and the dust,' Getu said to himself.

When he reached the guard stand, Getu mumbled a greeting to the two guards. One of the guards, the short one, walked up to Getu, and the other, quite tall, stepped back and began to read the paper. The guard in front of Getu was dressed in a khaki-colored suit, and wore a black top hat with gold braided trim. He casually flung his weapon over his shoulder, then looked around Getu, to his left, his right, almost through him, it seemed. 'Are you here alone?' the guard asked.

'Yes, I'm here to meet my friend Mr. Jeff for his going away party.' Getu tried to hold himself tall. 'He invited me.'

'A party, huh? Here?' The guard swayed onto his tip-toes and tilted his head back, and so managed to look down on Getu, despite being a couple inches shorter than him. 'Where are you from?'

'I'm from Lideta. I have cousins in America, so that explains my accent.' He *was* from Lideta, a small, modest neighborhood that rested in the shadow of the Lideta Cathedral. The rest was lies.

'You call him Mr. Jeff?' The guard considered this. 'Are you his servant?'

Getu shook his head. He wasn't convincing them. He'd have to think fast, and fiddled with the necktie in his pocket. If only he had stopped along the way to get help putting it on... 'I am, as Mr. Jeff says, his man on the street, his ear to the ground. I help with his work.'

'What kind of work?' As the guard walked around Getu, his heels clicked rhythmically against the ground like a ticking watch.

'NGO work,' Getu said, and seeing the guard's eyebrows rise, he kept on. 'International NGO work,' Getu stressed. He had the guard's attention.

The guard looked Getu up and down closer than before: Getu's worn clothes, his short rough fingernails, the quality of the calluses on his hands, the tan lines at his wrists, the red highlights in his hair, his muscular form, the freckles on his cheeks, the cracked skin of his lips. 'What do you do for him? A farmer, maybe? A herder? Are you his laborer?'

This was taking a turn for the worse, and Getu scrambled to get back on course. 'I help my uncles in the countryside a few times a year. A man who is at ease in the city and the countryside, Mr. Jeff says. I'm his versatile aide, Mr. Jeff calls it.'

'But what do you do?'

'He asks me questions about local things, and I answer them.'

'Does it pay well?' The guard's skepticism mingled with blossoming interest.

'It will. He says I'm important. The exact English word is "invaluable."'

'Valuable?'

'In-valuable,' Getu corrected, thinking of how to steer the conversation back to those big closed doors.

'But why you, why are you in-valuable? You don't look like you went to Lycee or the British school?'

He wished the guard would stop inspecting his clothes like this, like they were his calling card. If only he'd had another way to identify himself. 'Just think of me as a scholar. I mean, schooling-wise, I'm mostly self-taught, but I was accepted to American university. The fellowship wouldn't cover all the expenses, but this impressed Mr. Jeff enough when I told him.'

'That can't be true.'

'It is,' Getu said. And it was. Getu was still staring impatiently now at the door of the Sheraton, held open for what he guessed was a French family, and he talked faster. 'My mother says it's like a disease, but I'll read anything. Math, science, history, literature, law, politics. And I remember it, too. Mr. Jeff says it's a near-miracle.'

'Yeah right,' the short guard said, looking over his shoulder and taking the day's paper out of his partner's hands.

'You read English, of course,' he said to Getu sarcastically.

'Of course,' Getu said back. 'English, French, Amharic, German–'

The guard put his hand up. 'Just read this first paragraph.' He pointed to the story on the top left side of the paper, then watched as Getu read. A few seconds later, the guard snatched back the paper. His weapon slipped a little, and the guard hoisted it back over his shoulder, his attention fixed on Getu's eyes. 'What did it say?'

Getu recited word for word a caption about the last term of the first Black president of the U.S. and a story about the new round of World Bank loans. 'That can't be!' The tall guard came closer to see what was going on.

'This boy's like Solomon, watch,' said the short guard as he put the paper back in front of Getu. 'Read this paragraph,' he ordered.

Without needing to be told, Getu read, looked away a few moments later, and recited the column about farmland rented out to foreign corporations.

'It's a trick,' the tall guard said. 'No way you memorized it just now.'

'He works for an international NGO,' the short guard explained.

'Can you let me in, I need to go to my boss's, my friend's, Mr. Jeff's party. It would be rude of me not to, and he is an important man.' Getu said this impulsively, not sure if it was true.

'What was his name? What's your name?' the tall guard asked.

'My name is Getu Amare. His name is Mr. Jeff. Jeff Johnson. Jefferson Johnson to be precise. He introduced himself to me as Jeff Johnson, but out of respect....'

'He's with an NGO. We can let this guy in,' said the short guard.

'Is he on the list?' the tall guard asked.

'I don't know about a list. I am Getu Amare.'

'Wait here,' the tall guard said, and as he turned and pulled open the tall glass doors of the hotel, a gust of cool air sent a chill down Getu's neck while he watched the guard disappear inside.

Getu had met Jeff Johnson six months before by a bar across the street from the UN agencies. Every day at 6pm, the bar filled with aid workers, both locals and foreigners, but mostly foreigners. When Getu was sweeping the sidewalk one warm evening, Jeff Johnson and a group of other Americans stood outside smoking and talking loudly. Jeff Johnson called out to Getu and asked him to settle an old argument about the extent that 'everyday people' benefit from aid given to corrupt governments. The parking lot attendant heard this question, turned, and walked quietly and quickly away. The bouncer stepped inside, making a general gesture of being cold in the 70-degree weather, but Getu, who'd never had an audience like this before, spoke loudly. Jeff Johnson and his friends fell quiet, leaned in, and listened attentively to each word.

Jeff Johnson pointed out that as a street sweeper, Getu must see a lot in the city, and Getu said, 'Not only see, but smell, hear, and clear.' Jeff Johnson and his friends leaned in even closer. Someone asked Getu, 'What do you feel would be the most meaningful change for people your age in your neighborhood?' Getu thought about it and said, 'It's a long way to school from my neighborhood, and so I'm self-educated. Many of my friends also forgo school because the bus is too unreliable.' Jeff Johnson and his circle told Getu what a terrible shame this was, and the more they shook their heads, the more empowered Getu felt. Jeff Johnson and his circle asked for details, exact locations, number of people who would benefit, community impact, scalability. A few weeks later, a private free shuttle suddenly began stopping on Getu's block taking passengers from around where Getu lived to the closest grammar school. Getu could hardly believe his eyes, like he'd conjured it up himself with his fingertips. Jeff Johnson saw Getu soon after the shuttle began running, and listened as Getu praised the deed, which would make a big difference in the lives of his neighbors. 'Team effort on this one,' Jeff Johnson deflected. 'You know, we could use a man like you in our organization. It's important to know what the man on the street thinks about what we do. You'd be an asset to us. Look how much you've already done.' The words rung in his ears all that night as Getu imagined a new life for himself with those new friends, their salaries, their style, their access, their influence.

That experience left an impression on Getu, and the relationship that developed over daily discussions outside the bar during Jeff Johnson's cigarette breaks was the most significant in Getu's life so far, Getu thought. Through their discussions, Getu was able to magically engender new textbooks for the local library; a water-well near the contaminated stream where he'd often seen people drink; a seminar series on prenatal care, which Getu hadn't suggested, but had approved. After each new program, Jeff Johnson would tell Getu, 'We're a dream team. We'll be *running* this show in five-years.' Getu couldn't imagine not saying goodbye to Jeff Johnson on his last day in Addis Ababa, and he trusted Jeff Johnson—with all his powers—would come through for him somehow, now that Getu was the one in need.

Getu was still waiting for the tall guard to return when he caught a snippet of conversation between two women and realized one seemed familiar to him. 'I wouldn't trust Jeff with my book collection,' she'd said. 'He'd probably end up giving it away.' The young woman was pink with sunburn and was applying aloe to her shoulders.

'Or misplacing it all,' said the other woman who was walking slowly while looking at herself in a compact and opening a tube of lip-gloss.

'So then I don't know why you'd let him borrow your car,' said the first woman, putting away her tube of gel.

'Because,' mumbled her friend, who paused to apply the gloss, then smiled into her compact. 'But he does always mean well, that Jeff,' she said, pursing her lips, walking up to the door of the Sheraton without casting a glance at the guard station.

Just as the short guard held open the door, Getu approached the woman with the pink sunburn, and he called out, 'Madame!'

'No change, sorry, honey,' the woman dismissed. The short guard heard this and shook his head; he knew Getu wasn't a beggar, and clearly disapproved of the woman's words, for regardless she should have blessed Getu, invoked some higher kindness if her own did not compel her to give.

'Madame, it's me, Getu. I'm Mr. Jeff's aide. His man on the street. I think we met by the bar outside the UN...'

The young woman looked at him for a moment, and said, 'Of course, Getu.' She leaned in to kiss him three times, as was the custom, but the spark of recognition never entered her eyes. Getu could smell the scent of the aloe gel, subtle, like a broken blade of grass.

'Madame, forgive me, but I don't know if I ever got your name,' Getu said bowing slightly.

'It's Patricia,' she said. 'Pat. And this is a friend of mine Lisa, Lis.' She gestured towards the other woman, who also leaned in and kissed Getu on the cheek, left, right, left. The two women reached into their purses and pulled out their business cards, which Getu took, memorized, and put in his jacket pocket. Pat worked with a management consulting firm, Lis with a multilateral.

'We were just going to see Jeff now,' Pat said to Getu.

'I wish I could join you. Mr. Jeff invited me to his farewell party, but the guards are asking a lot of questions,' Getu said, trying to look inconvenienced but not desperate.

'Come with us,' Lis said, then linked her arm with Getu's and boldly walked through the door, passing the guard, who smiled as Getu entered. Inside, Getu, Pat and Lis were searched, and Pat and Lis tossed their bags on the scanner before walking through the metal detector.

Pat turned to him and said, 'Entering the Sheraton always feels like going through airport security, don't you think?'

Getu nodded, but he had never been inside, nor had he flown, either. He wiped his shoes several times on the doormat as he stood by the scanner. The guard there asked him to take off his jacket and put it through the machine. He hadn't planned for this, and wished he had asked his mother to help wash away the stubborn sweat stains on his shirt. He took off the jacket using a rigid motion, keeping his elbows tucked into his body, then walked through security without swaying his arms. He put the jacket on again using the same constricted motions.

But Getu quickly forgot about his jacket or the stains. Such insignificant things could hardly compete with the opulent gilding, glass, and marble that surrounded him, and the colossal fountain in the center of the lobby. The polished clientele wore colorful clothes from West Africa and India, or the grey and black geometric shapes of New York or London. Getu inched as close as he could to Lis and Pat, and followed them as they led him through a kind of abundance he'd never seen before. The air-conditioned lobby opened in front of him with its high archways, its shining floors, its multitude of rugs that would have had to be folded in quarters to fit in his bedroom. Overcome and transported into a world that seemed to swallow him whole, Getu couldn't sense himself.

Pat's loud laughter broke his trance, and she threw her arms around two tall men and a young Ethiopian woman. Getu was introduced and handed three new business cards from Pete from DFID, Chuck from OECD, and Nardos from OHCHR, and he trailed the group, almost stepping on their heels as they made their way downstairs to the Gaslight.

The party was a blur at first. Pat declared she was going straight to the bar to start a tab, and the others followed leaving Getu to wander on his own. After fifteen minutes, Getu found the man-of-the-hour, and when he saw Getu, Jeff Johnson quickly came over, and shouted, 'You made it! You came.'

'Yes, of course. I said I'd come. It's your farewell,' Getu said and embraced Jeff Johnson, who wore a grey suit, dark brown hair shaggy and loose, a departure from his usual combed-back style. Getu noticed Jeff Johnson had his tie untied around his neck. 'You couldn't tie it either?' Getu said.

'What?'

'Your tie–'

'Yeah, after a long last day, I had to loosen the grip, you know.'

'Yes, mine's in my pocket,' Getu said, and mimicked his host, throwing his tie around his neck and letting it hang loose like an untied scarf. Getu then took the small gift from his pocket, and handed it to Jeff Johnson, who seemed to appreciate the present. 'I love maps,' Jeff Johnson said half opening a crease, then folding it back up.

'That's my home, here,' Getu said, unfolding it all the way, pointing to the circled spot. 'It has been in my family a long time,' he added, wondering if he'd still be living there the next time Jeff Johnson came to town, if there was a next time. He began to ease into his ask, saying, 'I wish you could visit. I know we've talked about it—'

'I've really meant to,' Jeff Johnson said, and put the map carefully in his pocket.

'Next time,' Getu said, adding, 'I might have to get you a new map then, though, with all the changes in the city.'

'Yes, I bet when I see you again, you'll be living in one of those big new houses. I'm not worried about you, Getu.'

'Really? I'm quite concerned....'

'Hope is the greatest asset a man can have, you know,' Jeff Johnson said, then trailed off distracted by a group who passed to wave hello. 'Anyway, I really think with a little optimism a guy like you—intelligent, kind, driven, and articulate—can do anything he wants, if he puts his mind to it.'

'Do you really think so, because—'

'Hey, Jeff, there you are!' Pat was standing with Lis, Nardos, and a tall red-haired man with square glasses. Jeff Johnson introduced Getu to Toni from AfDB, and others who made their way into and out of the discussion. Getu collected business cards from a roving editor, a strategic specialist, a starlet and her agent, a relief worker, and a freelance philanthropist.

'Can I buy you a drink?' Jeff Johnson asked Getu after a lull. Getu was about to direct the conversation back to his home, but talking over a drink seemed like the best approach.

'Oh, let me buy you one,' Getu said taking out his wallet.

'Oh no, they're overpriced here,' Jeff Johnson said, and flagged down the bartender. 'Can't allow it.'

'It's the Ethiopian way. You are a guest about to go! You must let me.'

'Okay, if it's a cultural thing, I guess I'll have a beer,' he said to the bartender, 'Just a draft. Local.' Getu ordered water. Jeff Johnson was absorbed in a heated debate, so when Getu got the bill, no one was paying attention when Getu realized that the water cost more than the beer, and either way, he couldn't cover what he owed. Getu thought of his mother, and her insistence that Mr. Jeff's world was not his world, even if they shared a city-code. Still, here he was in whatever world this was, and someone had to pay. He began counting his money discretely under the bar; somehow he'd misjudged by a factor of ten. Getu leaned toward the bartender, and without knowing what he was going to say, found himself whispering, 'Can you put this on Miss, on Pat's tab? Patricia Walcott, Pat. She's getting this one.' The bartender nodded without asking any questions, and like that, Getu wondered if once in, he was operating within

a new system of trust. Whereas in his life, establishing those
bonds required quite a lot, especially around money matters
(too much to lose), here, an unfamiliar nonchalance seemed to
permeate. He took a chance, and ordered himself a beer, just
one, on Pat's tab, too.

A fog machine was positioned in the corner of the room, and
small spotlights and stage lights dotted the trance-like Gaslight
with glimmering blue, purple, and white. The atmosphere
disoriented Getu and as soon as he walked away from the bar,
he realized he'd lost Jeff Johnson again. Getu ran into a few
people he had met in the past through Jeff Johnson, but for the
most part, he walked around the party looking for the host,
introducing himself to one guest after the next as 'Mr. Jeff's
man on the street,' which others found endearing. He hopped
from conversation to conversation gathering business card
after business card from employees of all kinds of organizations
(PEPFAR, GFAR, DADEA, ICSID, ILRI, USAID, UNFPA,
UNESCO, UNICEF, UNDP, UNECA, IDB, IFC, ICTSD, FAO,
WIPO, OIE, WTPF...), memorizing them, putting them in his
pocket in careful order. He was pulled onto the dancefloor as
he followed Mr. Jeff's trail, dragged upstairs where he heard Jeff
Johnson was by the fire pit gorging himself on tibs, but Getu
didn't find him there, either. From time to time, he touched
the business cards in his pocket, fingered them, played with the
stack as he made his way through the maze of a hotel. He finally
found Jeff Johnson by the swimming pool in the back sitting
with a group, and went over to his host. Just as he arrived, Jeff
Johnson stood and announced it was almost time for him to go.
The night had snuck by and Getu still hadn't asked after his job.
He'd have to be direct, risk being awkward about it, or miss his
shot completely.

Jeff Johnson said goodbye to his friends and left them at the
pool, but Getu insisted he'd walk to the gate. Jeff Johnson said,
'You've been a good friend to me, Getu. A gracious host, my
man on the street. I'm lucky to have met you.'

'Thank you very kindly. About that, I—'

'It's like I always say, we really could use a man like you on the team.' Jeff Johnson spoke all his familiar lines.

'Then hire me,' Getu said, pointing at himself and finally voicing what had been on his mind the entire night, if not their entire friendship. 'Hire me.'

Jeff Johnson laughed gently. 'I know, right? Exactly. I wish I could.'

'Then do!'

'Oh, Getu.' Jeff Johnson looked at Getu, and seeing his serious face, turned serious, too. 'I'm sorry, did I give you the wrong….did you think…?' Getu listened very closely. Jeff Johnson took a step back, a look of clarity descended. 'I think you've misunderstood somehow. I'm just a junior staffer, so obviously…,' he said as if that explained it. 'I mean of course I'm hoping this assignment will lead to a promotion, but you know…'

'But you know people. I'm counting on you,' Getu said, his voice was tense though he tried to sound casual. If he'd misunderstood, hadn't he been misled?

'You can do so much better. You don't want to work for these guys. There'd be no culture fit, I don't know, they all have their own—'

'Culture fit?' Getu almost heard his mother's voice come back to him, 'They'll never let you in,' she'd chided before. Getu said to Jeff Johnson, 'I could be a guide, an interpreter between your world and my world.'

'They already have guys like me as interpreters, so to speak.' Jeff Johnson's sympathy only sharpened his authority.

Getu's mother's voice practically rang in Getu's ear. 'Ask him the difference between an interpreter and a thief,' she would have said.

'I have other skills,' Getu explained. 'I'm a trained street sweeper. I'm good with directions. I'd make a top chauffeur.'

'Getu, I'm afraid you've somehow been misinformed,' said Jeff Johnson, avoiding Getu's eyes.

'But didn't you say you had something for me? And what else could it be, all this talk of working together?'

'Did I say that? Yes, I guess I was just, not being literal,' and Jeff Johnson furrowed his brow and started to walk quickly towards the gate. Getu walked sort of next to him, sort of behind him trying to keep up.

'Oh, a joke,' Getu laughed uncomfortably, walking quickly, trying to sound friendly, but wondering what to do next.

'No, it really wasn't, but I can see how you'd take what I said...' Jeff Johnson said stopping.

Getu lifted his right hand out towards Jeff, and said, 'Well, I was just joking with you, too.' Getu imagined his mother's voice again, this time aimed at him. 'When someone slithers out of a tight spot by saying they're just joking, they're not just joking. Never let anyone get away with that. Never do it yourself.'

Jeff Johnson awkwardly approached Getu's outstretched hand, and shook it quickly. 'Still, I wish I could, Getu. I don't know how this happened. I really wish—'

'I really wish, too.' Getu didn't know what else to say, watching this vague but powerful expectation unravel before him.

'Stay optimistic, Getu. Things will work out for you. I'm sure of it. For a guy like you.' Jeff Johnson had so much passion in his voice, so much hope and promise that Getu almost felt ashamed by the impossibility of his situation. 'I'm sorry. I'm so sorry.' He felt like he was saying this to himself, his mother, Mr. Jeff.

'For what?' Jeff Johnson asked.

Getu didn't know why he suddenly felt so guilty, but he also felt he was meant to. 'I'm sorry for everything,' Getu replied, then added, 'Thank you for everything.'

'No, thank you for everything. I'm sorry for everything,' Jeff Johnson responded.

Getu composed himself, pushed away thoughts of his mother, their house, the enchanted future on whose doorstep he had briefly lingered. Had he made a mistake, and if so, when, how? Or was his mother right, had he misplaced his trust, believed too much in these elusive words. He'd wanted to save their home, but he also wanted to be an exception, an exception to the rule that he'd seen proven over and over again that someone like him could be so easily swept aside, his home cast aside, his dreams cast aside. He wanted to prove his mother wrong, but more than that, he wanted to prove everyone wrong, the whole set-up wrong, the whole system that marked him from birth, and placed him at the mercy of the powerful, relative as that may be.

Getu thought about this as he walked Jeff Johnson around to the side exit, and said a rushed goodbye, parting words, some combination of 'Good luck' and 'Take care' back and forth a few times. A line of blue and white taxis circled the gate like a moat around the property; like so many, they, too, were not allowed to enter. Getu watched Jeff Johnson get into the first one, and as it sped away, the line inched forward. Getu waved until Jeff Johnson's taxi was out of sight, and Getu imagined it twisting down the road, down the dark hill, past the empty lots, the barren slope below. Getu pictured his house leveled, nothing left in the city but the huge spot-lit structure looming beside him, its tinted-bulbs attracting his gaze again, captivating his attention like gleaming jewels, and Getu wondered if somehow he could still collect on what had turned out to be an illusion of a promise. For wasn't a door still left a little ajar?

Getu adjusted his tie that hung loose around his neck, then walked up to the entrance of the Sheraton. A new set of guards was standing there.

'Can we help you?' one asked blocking his path, the other ignored him.

Getu didn't flinch. 'I just stepped out for a minute,' Getu said to the guards. Getu felt the thick stack of business cards in his pocket, and pulled out the fourth from the top, carefully removed it, and handed it to the guard. 'My name is Elias Isaacs with the W.H.O. I'm an interpreter here to meet a client.' Getu spoke with ease, and he was ushered in, the tall glass doors flung open.

The Giver of Nicknames

Rémy Ngamije

Prelude.

When we were clowns, children, and things – before we
sprouted personalities, individual hopes, and collective guilt;
before we reconciled all aspects of our conflicting beings – there
were four Donovans at our school: Donovan "Donnie Blanco"
Mitchell, the rapist; Donovan "Donnie Darko" Manyika,
the fastest kid in our phrontistery; the short-lived Donovan
Latrell who, hoping to be called Donnie Brasco or DL when
he realised there weren't enough Donnies to go around, was
called Fatty; and Mr. Donovan, our English teacher – Mr. D
for short.

1.

Donnie Blanco was this white kid with colonial money
all the way to Diego Çao's arrival in Namibia. His parents
had mining interests deeper than Dante's inferno, sat on
numerous companies' boards, and owned game farms as big
as provinces, panoramic swathes of land with wild sunsets
lacking only in the absence of Meryl Streep and Robert
Redford to give them their *Out of Africa* romance. Because
they paid some of their taxes instead of caching them in
Caribbean mulct havens, the Mitchells – Los Blancos – were
considered Namibian model citizens. They were allowed to
add their billionaire's two cents to any damn topic: Sir Ken
Robinson's TED talks; border security and the movement of
people, pandemics, and dreams; social media, climate change,
or the nutritional requirements of the modern corporate go-
getter. Los Blancos even prescribed parenting methods for

raising future moguls. Their money had bestowed upon them prophetic status; I was a nonbeliever. To me, all Blanco's parents had was money – they knew how to play the rigged capitalist game the same way my uncle always made himself the banker whenever we played Monopoly. In everything else, especially in their son, who I still refer to as the rapist to this day because he is, I found them woefully inadequate. I despised the Blancos because of their privilege. But I especially loathed them for their ability to co-opt my poverty into Donnie Blanco's coverup.

***

In addition to his presence at our school – the top one in Namibia – Blanco's parents believed traveling was the best education. Our parents, mostly middle-class folk who stressfully and strenuously financed our stints in private school, believed education was the best education. Unlike Blanco, we were parvenus trying to acclimatise to the rich air of lush lawns, changing rooms with showers (and hot water which flowed unto the world's ending), and a computer lab with more Apples than the Garden of Eden. We weren't collecting passport stamps like the rest of the philatelic travellers with diplomatic passports who made up the rest of the student corps – we were academic workhorses with one job: to keep the test scores high and our parents happy and gloating with their sacrifices. Blanco and his ilk provided the necessary posh veneer which permitted the fees to rise and spike each year like a Six Flags rollercoaster. While we were clocking into and coining out of the lone video game arcade or shuttling between onerous weddings and sweaty funerals in towns so small Google Earth never bothered to give them coordinates, Blanco was hitting up forty countries before he turned fourteen. He'd smelled the hot rubber of the Monaco Grand Prix and posed with Christ The Redeemer. Our English teacher, Mrs. Braithwaite, who gloated over Blanco's globe-trotting essays, always marked down our writings, using her socially distanced red pen to tell us we needed *more traveling in them, broader horizons, higher skies, and a keener sense of adventure.* Basic Bs and discouraging Cs are what you'd get if you hadn't been on a first-class British Airways flight to Amsterdam or Basel. Blanco had A-plussed his way through English because he'd seen the Alps, the Andes, the Rockies, the Hindu Kush, and the Himalayas. We were told our *compositions barely rose above sleep level.* All we wrote about was the calefaction of days in the North, the sand in the South, and the repetitive stories our *oumas en oupas* told us when we were condemned to stay with them in the long December holidays.

The year I dubbed Donovan Mitchell as Donnie Blanco, his family had taken a tour of the Spanish-speaking world. They'd passed through South America and finished off in Spain, a country they'd visited for what must've been the sixth time. He went on about the *guapa* girls of Ar-*he*-ntina and Chi-*leh,* the Colombian *culo,* and did a lot of *hombre*-ing and *muchacho*- ing about all the friends he'd made in Me-*hi*-co. He returned from Spain with signed football jerseys from Madrid and Catalonia's top teams – the souvenirs we envied most (we really didn't give a shit about the landscapes in his descriptive essays, which Mrs. Braithwaite insisted on reading aloud) – and kept telling the rest of us untravelled *campesinos* to pronounce Bar-*the*-lona properly. Understandably, we were annoyed by this fucking *pendejo.* I, being a much sought after merchant of humiliating sobriquets, the fast-mouthed comeback kid who could roast the devil over his own coals, was assigned to Blanco's case. I took my duty to follow in Carl Linnaeus's scientific steps, to formalise teenage taxonomy in such a way that class, neighbourhood, physical deformities, or crippling insecurities were easily denoted, quite seriously. If my previous work in getting Naomi 'Naai-Homie' Nakwafilu (it was one moment of indiscretion, but one too many), Daniel 'Lying Den' Shikongo (that one explains itself), Layla 'Refu-G-Unit' Madioka (shame, she wasn't a refugee, but we didn't know anything else about Congolese people), and Gottlieb 'Gone-Arears' Hendricks (poor kid was always out of school because of late school fees) to become popular nomenclature – even teachers used Pirra, Peeta, and Blackimon, to differentiate between the Canadian, Namibian, and Ugandan Peters then Donovan Mitchell would've been an easy case.

Only, it wasn't. Blanco's parents directly or indirectly employed most of ours. And we knew it. We didn't want our mammas being called into HR offices and our families being put on the streets because we'd taken liberties with playground banter. We didn't know if corporate retribution played out that way in the real world, but we didn't want to fuck around with our families' well-beings. I wisely settled on Donnie Blanco. He thought it was because he was white. It wasn't. It was the safest and slyest thing we could call him. Because the Gini coefficient allowed us to outnumber Blanco ten-to-one, and because we were so mad at this boy who had enough money to insult us in foreign languages, Donnie Blanco stuck.

It was petty but sweet revenge.

You see, for all his money, private tutors, and his mother's unchallenged and unconstitutional tenure on our school's PTFA, Blanco was *el imbécil supremo.* He'd been passed through every grade because his parents signed extravagant fundraiser cheques. Our heavily endowed Catholic school which ran from pre-primary all the way to the twelfth grade, true to form with its finances shadier than a clerical scandal, wasn't immune to Blanco money. After the not-so-small matter of Donnie Blanco forcing himself on Aliyanna, and our school's principal, my mother, his parents, and Aliyanna's agreeing to keep quiet about it, I Sherlocked the web of Mitchellin patronage: there was a correlation between Blanco nearly failing the seventh grade and our library's newly minted computer wing; the spiffy senior chemistry lab equipment capable of testing for a Nobel Prize or two followed his entry into the eighth grade; the patchy, sun-smacked grass on our soccer field gave way to expensive and evergreen astro turf in the ninth grade; and in the tenth, after the rape, Mitchell Education Foundation scholarships were handed out to every overachieving student like communist pamphlets in the Soviet republics. Our first- *and* second-string basketball, hockey, netball, and soccer teams attended once rare out-of-country sports tours to Botswana, Zambia, Zimbabwe, South Africa, and Mozambique thanks to the Mitchell sponsorship and PR machines for the rest of his tenure at our school. In class, everyone's test scores were read out in ascending order – to keep us competitive, we were told – but Blanco's tests were placed face-down on his desk, top secret, classified, and way above everyone's pay grade. While the rest of us did our best to earn the grades needed to discourage our parents from looking for cheaper schools, we watched Blanco grade-surf each year. We found some comfort in knowing Donnie Blanco was white as snow, rich like whoa, but dumber than daaayuum.

Only later would the full gravitas of the name I'd given him become apparent and abhorrent. Even now, I wonder if the person who names the monster shares the blame with the one who flips the switch to release the lightning-charged current. I still feel like if I'd been braver and called him Why Boy (because we couldn't fathom a reason for his existence) or Needle Dick (since he was such a prick) things would've turned out differently.

Maybe not.

It's my experience that money alters destinies forever. Kismet for chaos is for broke people. The rich just send karma back to the kitchen if it comes out under or overcooked.

In the principal's office, I'd explained what had happened after basketball practice to the convocation of parents. I thought I was on the road to being an A-grade whistleblower like Daniel Ellsberg or a conscientious objector with a million dollar-grossing biopic from Steven Spielberg soon to be declared.

I told them what I'd seen: *Donnie Blanco raped Aliyanna in the boys' changing room.*

You'd think SETI, with its satellite ears scanning the sound of silence from the outermost reaches of the solar system, would've

detected the hush which descended on the room following my
testimony. You'd be wrong. There was no reticence.

Money talks.

—*Hmm. Did she try to push him away?*

—*And was it a firm no or a coy no?*

—*Are you sure it was my son and not someone else?*

—*Are you certain? A boy could go to jail here. Do you understand*
that? You must be absolutely sure.

I *Boston Legal*'d my cross-examination.

Yes, Mr. Bla—I mean, Mitchell – she tried to push him off.

It wasn't coy, Mrs. Mitchell – it was pretty robust. (I hate to admit
it but I was rather pleased that I knew what coy meant.)

It was Donnie Blanco – sorry, Donovan Michael Earl Mitchell, sir.
I'm telling you the truth, Mrs. Mitchell. It was your son.

Then came a question I couldn't answer.

—*What were you doing while all of this was going on?*

Everyone leaned forward in their chairs.

—*Am I to understand you saw all of this and did nothing?*

—*You certainly sound like a man of action. Omission or negligence*
would surely offend or implicate someone like you.

I turned to my mother. She looked at me, frightened by this
new line of enquiry from the Blancos who shared a look I
couldn't fathom. Mr. Van Rooyen, the principal, slitted his eyes
while Aliyanna's parents' eyes scoured my face for any evidence
of complicity.

I... err... I...

—*Yes?*

I didn't do anything, Mrs. Mitchell.

—*Really?*

(Since then I've equated Mrs. Mitchell's uncrossing and re-
crossing of legs – without any Sharon Stone shenanigans – as
the quintessential sign of moral indignation and disbelief.)

Err, Mrs. Mitchell, I was, err, too shocked.

—*But you're sure the girl was being raped?*

Err, yes, sir.

—*You don't sound too sure now.*

I'm sure, ma'am.

I looked at my mother. Her dotted dress held her gaze in its lap.

—*But you didn't do anything.*

No, sir. I was too surprised.

—*Seems highly improbable to me someone can be aware that such a crime was happening but do nothing about it.*

I...I...I'm doing something about it now, ma'am. Mom?

She kept quiet.

I wonder if there's a statute of limitations for shame. I've never forgiven her.

I'd walked into the boy's changing room after being dismissed from practice by our coach. I'd dissented when he prescribed suicides for every missed layup. (*This isn't Remember the Titans, coach. You're not Denzel!*) In one of the showers, Blanco's buttocks peeked over his red shorts (he'd been excused from the team's fitness training for fatigue) as he thrusted into Aliyanna's pulled-up skirt. I, coming across this scene, this after-school activity which made everyone blush in the sexual intercourse module during school hours, had been thoroughly startled.

What the—!

They turned at the sound of my intrusion to me. I pivoted quicker than Michael Jackson on a concert stage and walked out. I went back to the court's bench, shamed (and scared) of being a witness. Ten or fifteen minutes later, Blanco came out of the changing rooms and strutted towards the school's gate. He climbed into the shiny Audi waiting for him. Maybe five minutes later Aliyanna exited the bathrooms, smoothing down her hair, wiping her face. She looked around the basketball court. In the cursory contact of our eyes I understood the difference between an instant and a moment, something Mrs. Braithwaite struggled to explain to us in our literature class: an instant is blinked away, forgotten so quickly it's barely registered, but a moment spills past its temporal occurrence – *a moment has consequences*. Aliyanna walked towards the gate and waited for her parents to pick her up in their significantly less shiny Toyota Corolla.

Only later, as I sat outside the school's gate waiting for my mother, did I realise that a moment can be slowed down, panned around like a three-sixty degree bullet time shot to reveal nanoscopic details you miss in an instance: the biology and physics of penetration had been explained to us, but what had happened between Blanco and Aliyanna lacked the chemistry of consent.

I recalled his hands wrestling her wrists, her legs looking for purchase on the floor, pelvis trying to push him off, him telling her it was *okay and that they'd agreed.*

I remembered her saying *no, no, no.*

Mr. and Mrs. Blanco were wrong. I had done something: I'd walked to Mr. Van Rooyen's office and barged past his receptionist to report Blanco.

Within the hour, me, my mom, Aliyanna and her parents, and all the Blancos were outside the principal's office. The parents went inside. Aliyanna, Blanco, and I were to be seated apart and wait to adduce our evidence. The gruff and confused receptionist kept muttering about having *a family to attend to even if no one else did and, really, this was above and beyond her duties.* Blanco pressed buttons on his razor-thin flip phone while Aliyanna's knees rubbed against each other with nervous friction. She avoided looking at me.

Aliyanna was called upon first. Blanco and I defiantly stared at each other before he broke the deadlock with a dismissive shrug of his shoulders and returned to his phone. My spine steeled. Blanco was going down.

He was called in as Aliyanna walked out. The two of us sat opposite each other, avoiding all the moments our eyes would make. The recently vacuumed carpet, with its circular whorls of fibres sucked against their grain, seemed a point of interest for her.

I went in last.

—*You said you heard my son saying they'd agreed to do "it". Is that correct?*

Err, yes, Mrs. Mitchell, but I'm not sure what they agreed to do.

—*It certainly wouldn't be the first time teenagers have regretted their choices halfway through something.*

I understand, Mr. Mitchell. But she said no.

Mr. Van Rooyen inhaled in what seemed like a business-like manner and thanked me for my asseveration. I waited outside as Aliyanna and Blanco were called back in. With night slipping under evening's covers, the receptionist grumbled some more. The door opened twice, once when the boxy printer and copier churned out a sheaf of documents the principal collected quickly before returning to his office, and the second time, when Aliyanna's family walked out, followed by my mother, the Blancos, and Mr. Van Rooyen.

Everyone, except the receptionist had a moment.

Mr. Van Rooyen broke the pall by saying he was glad *that bit of confusion was ironed out hehehe these things happen you know with all of these teenagers together hihihi bound to happen hahaha yes always bound to happen hohoho.*

Aliyanna's parents nodded to everyone, her head remained bowed. Blanco stood with his boredom weighed on one leg, the other foot-tapped his impatience. Mr. and Mrs. Blanco shook everyone's hand. When it came to me, Blanco's father squeezed my hand too hard while his mother, whose hand was soft, said it was wonderful to hear of my academic, cultural, and sporting talents from the principal.

—*He's a fine boy.*

My mother looked from Mrs. Mitchell to me and concurred.

—*By the way, I'm sure it's just playground nonsense, but why do you call Donovan "Donnie Blanco"?*

(I've never heard anyone physically use air quotes with their voice while their hands remained crossed in front of them, Cartier carats counting the seconds.)

It's just a nickname, Mrs. Mitchell.

—*Hmm. Of course.*

The principal ahem-ed and said such tomfoolery would surely stop and ahem-ed some more as he ushered all of us out, into the parking lot, and into our cars. Aliyanna's family drove away first, out towards the flat suburbs of flattened incomes where we were also bound. The Blancos made for the hills.

On our way home, I asked my mother what had happened.

—*It's been sorted.*

She kept her eyes on the road.

What does that mean, Mom?

—*It means it's been dealt with.*

A whetted tone sliced through her voice, signalling that *something* was *res judicata* – decided, settled, and final, certainly not something she wanted to discuss with her sixteen-year-old. The only time she used her silencing voice on me was when I asked about my father: *Your father is just that, your father. Not my husband and not a parent. There isn't much I can say about him.*I could never get more out of her. Whoever he was, wherever he was, whatever he did – all of these were secrets my mother held firmly within herself.

Dealt with how?

—*There's no need to bring this up again.*

She didn't look at me. She said it to the road in front of us, driving us away from a past she didn't want discussed again.

Bring what up? That Blanco's a rapist?

—*I don't want you saying such things in public. Is that clear? I said it's been sorted.*

Mom.

—*Listen, you have to understand that I work for these people. They've offered to pay your fees. And hers.*

Mom!

—*Yes?*

She said no.

My mother turned to me. In the instant between her engaging the indicator to turn right her mask slipped for a moment. I saw Aliyanna in her face. I saw my father's absence.

—*I know.*

2.

Before Donovan Mitchell became *un archivo en blanco,* Donovan Manyika joined our school in the ninth grade. He immediately became the top student on our competitive campus. He was Zimbabwean and everything Blanco wasn't: smart, quiet, and the poverty scholarship kid financed by the Mitchell Education Foundation. Manyika knew every African country's capital city, currency, and lingua franca, excelling at everything on the sports field and in the classroom. He Tenzing Norgayed our school's reputation to the top of every maths and science olympiad, general knowledge quiz, and running the home stretch of the relay in athletics meetings, making up for everyone else's lost time, dishing out disappointment and embarrassment to all he passed en route to the finish line. Whenever Manyika's name was announced at our annual prize-giving ceremony everyone applauded loudly. His success was our success, and given how hard he had it nobody envied his achievements. The price of his brilliance was unrelenting hardship – he single-handedly looked after his three brothers and two sisters (also MEF scholars) who were then making their way through primary school, filling in their older brother's footsteps and collecting every bronze, silver, and gold star in the teacher's cupboards. Even though Manyika had our collective respect, I called him Donnie Darko to let him know gravity was a bitch and affected all men equally.

Donnie Darko stole my title: Onion Marks.

When I arrived in the third grade, I didn't make friends easily. I couldn't speak English, Afrikaans, or German. I was shunned. The first couple of weeks were hellish. No Kinyarwanda, no Swahili, not even a smattering of French – in each class I was surrounded by incomprehensible noise. I was a tropical orchid in welwitschia country. Slowly, and with much laughing from the other children at my pronunciation, my larynx picked up some of the common tongues. The only period I enjoyed was physical education. The other kids might not have understood my words, but they knew exactly what my body said whenever we lined up for races:

—*I'm too fast for you.* (Bang!)

—*You can't catch me.* (Five metres!)

—*I can let you catch up now.* (20 metres!)

—*I can let you gain a yard.* (45 metres!)

—*I can even let you think you're going to win this.* (60 metres!)

—*But I'm just too fast for you.* (Finish line!)

I earned their respect because children, like most people, are drawn to visceral elemental forces like earth, wind, water, fire, strength, beauty, violence, and kindness. They admire and fear speed.

My speed made friends slowly and enemies much quicker.

From the first moment I crossed the finish line in first place I felt Blanco's hate on my heels in second place. Thus far, he'd been the fastest third-grader around. After me, he was another obsolete white boy. I didn't fully understand what I'd snatched away from Blanco until it was taken away from me by Darko. Being Onion Marks made you top dog of the *ludus*, a reputation recorded in the ledgers of the school's history. The fastest runners in each grade were awarded silver onion-shaped pins which sparkled on blazers, letting ordinary *plebeians* know they weren't governed by the normal laws of the *Pax Slowmana.* You bragged like few others could. *No need to cry, man – it's just Onion Marks, bro.* With Blanco's head already struggling to stick with the pace of third grade maths and reading, I stole the sense of selfhood he'd made for himself with his feet. He became slow in more ways than one.

There's no honour amongst thieves, and this is how the story of black-on-black crime goes: you're the sigh of speed at local and regional level, unable to compete at nationals because you aren't a citizen. You focus on destroying the track at provincial meetings, letting everyone else who goes on to represent their country at international competitions know the immigration laws granted them an unfair head start. At the hundred-metre dash in the ninth-grade you and Blanco stretch in the fast fourth and fifth lanes, eyeing each other. His new running spikes claw the track's surface; your worn-out ones pinch your toes. You take your starting position and inhale once, twice, three times. A vision of yourself crossing the finish line in thunderous glory jumps the gun ahead of you. All you've got to do now is chase your dream down the track. Your name is chanted in the stands.

Onion Marks!

Get set...

His name is Donovan Eloterius Manyika.

He runs barefoot.

All you know about him thus far is that he's the new kid. His heels wink up and down as he sprints in the eighth lane, with you straining to catch him. You're rugged from the sprint and breathless with disappointment.

You watch as Manyika has his skinny arm lifted in the air. '*ONION MARKS!*

You catch Blanco's eye.

A moment.

Only one of you has lost the race: he's still Donovan Mitchell. Donnie Blanco. Rich. Slower than you.

But you aren't Onion Marks anymore, the title that made you untouchable.

You're just a second-place shit-talker.

Blanco smiles at you.

3.

Fatty insisted on being called African-American instead of black. He got faux-mad when we called Namibian Coloureds *Coloured*. He couldn't accept things were different on the continent, that whatever black people called themselves in Chicago, Oakland, or Detroit was none of our stick, but here, at home, *in the motherland* – which is what he called it – we had the right to discriminate and differentiate between ourselves as we saw fit. There were blacks, whites, Afrikaners, Coloureds, Basters, Indians, Chinese, Asians, and foreigners (basically, Zimbabweans and Angolans). No amount of Martin Luther Kinging us into disinterested boredom would make us judge people by the content of their hidden and undisclosed characters when the colour of their skins made it quite clear who they were and weren't.

I shouldn't have called him Fatty. But I only realised this later after he committed suicide. We didn't know casual hazing was a leading cause of death in American teenagers. We assumed a return to Africa would bequeath him a thick skin; a hide so tough it couldn't be penetrated by our tick bites of bad humour.

—*Hey, Fatty, your country needs to leave the Middle East the way you need to leave vetkoeks the fuck alone.*

—*Yeah, Fatty, we know – you're African American in the Useless of A, and maybe that's a badge of honour where you come from, but around here you're just American.*

—*For shizzy. Around here you're just another Fatty From The Block. Keep quiet.*

Fatty had arrived at our school in the middle of the eleventh grade, taking Aliyanna's vacant seat in our classes. The previous year, Aliyanna's parents had decided to move her to another school, not as good, but far away from the scandal they feared might've erupted if she stayed on. They needn't have worried because my mother had promised me everything had been worked out by the adults, everyone was happy with the solution, and everyone, Aliyanna included, thought it was for the best she transfer to another school. My fees had been paid up until the end of the twelfth year of my school career. Our fridge at home filled with food from Spar instead of Shoprite. My mom bought herself a new car and copped me the freshest AND1 kicks. Maybe, I thought, skipping onto the basketball court and shimmy-shaking to applause from the rest of the team, it really was for the best. I was still young. Guilt clung to me as briefly as my Axe body spray – I was sweating hormones all the time, erupting into young adulthood, and revelling in my status as the tormenter of the uncool and unpopular.

—*Now lookahere, Fatty, I've got a philosophical question: if a Big Mac disappeared from a restaurant plate in Atlanta but you weren't in the country, did you eat it?*

Besides losing Aliyanna, our old English teacher, Mrs. Braithwaite, had decided to move back to England for fish and chips and to avoid *the crime in this country I swear to god this whole continent has gone to the dogs I should have moved when Zimbabwe happened.* (Back home, she found tikka chicken to be the new national meal because how about them Indians?) Mrs. Braithwaite was an okay English teacher: heavy-handed with the Dickens; oblivious to the fact English wasn't many people's first, second, or third language; decided the range of your linguistic ability based on the first essay of the year regardless of subsequent improvement; and reluctantly conceded Darko wrote better essays than Blanco even if the former hadn't been to the Taj Mahal or the Sidney Opera House. When she told us she was leaving, I hoped our workhouse days were over. Fatty hoped we'd get an American teacher – a viable hope since part of our school's success was having a roster of teachers whose diversity was only rivalled by the UN General Assembly. We didn't have an American, though, so Fatty, with his fanatical belief that whatever came out of the US was better – even though we knew this to be untrue since we had him as proof – hoped we'd get some Frank McCourt-esque English teacher.

—*Fatty, as the abdominous fifty-second state in the United Slaves of America, and the preeminent nigga on all things emancipatory, dietary, and otherwise, do you think our new English teacher will prescribe Huckleberry Finn as our course reader?*

Huckleberry Finn was prescribed. But our teacher wasn't American; Mr. Donovan was from Liberia – or 'Little USA' as Mr. Chikoti, our Malawian physics teacher called it in one of our classes, chuckling at his own little joke. 'Okay, now Fat – Latrell – please calculate the force needed to...'

As Mr. Donovan read out roll call in his first class his eyebrows lifted.

—*Three Donovans in one class?*

Donnie Blanco, Donnie Darko, and Fatty.

Mr. Donovan fixed me with a disinterested look which said he'd met a thousand versions of me before.

—*Right.*

He finished ticking names off the register, acquainting them with their corresponding raised hands and faces.

Here.

Present, sir.

Yo!

He put the list down.

—*Okay. Let's begin with some housekeeping rules. First, if you're a clown and you believe your job is to make us laugh with foolish shenanigans then by all means, feel free to leave this classroom. I don't like clowns. I think they're a waste of good makeup and an unnecessary source of fear. If you're a child, and you think you need more maturing I suggest you go home and take that issue up with your parents. I don't know how to deal with children. My classroom isn't a day-care for spoiled children.*

We all sat up, hushed, curious. This was a peculiar introductory soliloquy. Mr. Donovan looked at me directly.

—*And if you consider yourself to be a thing, incapable of being respectful towards me, yourself, or your fellow classmates then beware: things exist to be used, once their utility has been expired they're put in the bin. If it's your high duty and supreme destiny to be used and binned please save me the trouble of crumpling you and tossing you into the wastepaper basket.*

Mr. Donovan and I stared at each other, both of us seeing who'd blink uncle.

I looked away, seething, vowing to find some way to crush this man who embarrassed me in front of the whole classroom.

—*Good. So we'll only have, let's see, Mitchell, Manyika, and Latrell, and all the other government names on this list. You can call me Mr. D for short if you want. But that's it. Does anyone see a problem with this arrangement?*

No one did.

—*And you, the giver of nicknames, any problem?*

No. No, problem, sir.

If there's one thing Mr. D got wrong in that classroom it was to make it a safe haven for Fatty. While I might have been stripped of my power during our nigger-infested readings of *Huck Finn* Fatty's life was a misery before and after the bell rang. He was Fatty from the moment he stepped out of his father's Mercedes-Benz in the morning until he was fetched in the afternoon. That one hour with Mr. D was the only time Donovan Latrell was addressed with dignity.

You know what?

I plead the first, second, third, fourth, fifth, and every other amendment under the sun for everything we said to Fatty. We didn't know any other way to be. We were masters of all things group-y: group-think, group-speech, group-walk, group-slouch, group-exclusion. If I thought something the hive vibrated with the same idea and if we were unconscious about Fatty's depression then I sure as heck wasn't woke to whatever he felt and how it affected him.

He shot himself one Friday evening. His younger sister found him in his bedroom.

When we were told the news on Monday morning in our register period, we all looked at Fatty's empty desk in the front desk, wondering if we were implicated in his death as accessories to cruelty. There were no jokes that day. No wisecracks. No roasting in recesses. Group- recrimination pushed us apart to our individual thoughts and actions, fracturing and sundering us to our own paths and ways of being.

When the card of condolences was passed around our classroom, I alone had no message to write. I just signed my name and passed it on.

Our English classroom was especially grave. Mr. D had liked Fatty – he read a very convincing Jim and had scathing opinions about Huck Finn and people who distanced themselves from wrongs by claiming refuge in groups. (Honestly, when I think about it all, Fatty was subtexting us the whole time.) Mr. D didn't teach that day. He seemed deflated. He put us in groups of three and sent us to the library to research *King Lear* which was our next set work for literature. I was with, yep, Blanco and Darko.

In the library, the three of us didn't talk to each other. Blanco and I had never shared space so closely since that day in the principal's office. He quit the basketball team which meant I didn't have to in order to avoid him. With him not being the Pinky to my Brain in our hateful duo, we never had to wonder what we'd be doing every night: I'd do my best to complete my homework and he'd continue snacking on the world. In this way we'd coexisted – him with his friends, and me with mine. The only time I had to deal with Blanco was when he handed me the baton after running the back stretch in the relay so I could round the corner and give it to Darko, our unbeaten Onion Marks, who then blitzed the shame stretch and brought us the gold. Besides our collaborative efforts to share the podium with Darko, Blanco and I had no other interaction. I'd been cautioned by my mother not to upset him or do anything which disturbed the bedrock of our newfound easy living. To dispense with any need to talk to him, I mumbled my willingness to look up succession controversies in England. Darko said he'd look into mental illnesses. Blanco chose what I deemed to be the easiest topic on the list Mr. D had given us: costumes and dresses of the Elizabethan era.

—*Should be easy to wrap myself around that.*

What can I say? We were foolish clowns in the circus of life, our teenage-hood was a ringmaster who whipped us through hoops and hopes. In another year we'd have to choose what we would be for the rest of our lives even though in the preceding seventeen we had no idea what anything was about. I interpreted Blanco's words as a slight against me, as an accusation for my part in Fatty's suicide. My stomach boiled. My words bristled. I easily substituted the weight of Donovan Latrell's suicide for the tangible, assailable mass presented by Donovan Mitchell.

Or easy for you to get under, Blanco. You know, with you being a rapist and all.

—*What are you talking about?*

We were petulant children. We needed to be raised. For many of us that wasn't happening at home, so we discovered ourselves in the wildness of our wit, our ids served our egos, shielding us with reflexive name-calling and character assassinations which we considered to be part of our basic programming. Later, of course, these things would be knocked out of us. We'd learn about ourselves, about each other, about other people.

But not yet.

I looked at Blanco, desperate to hurt him, to let him know that I knew he wasn't blameless and could never be.

Aliyanna.

Blanco's eyes narrowed.

—*What about her?*

We were still away from being people. We were things.

We moved through the world, guided by our own utility.

What we didn't respect, we binned.

She said no.

Darko was confused. His eyes ping-ponged between us as we swatted the onus of guilt between each other.

Blanco laughed loudly.

The whole library looked up at us. We were shushed by the librarian. Blanco took his time dialling down his volume.

He leaned in conspiratorially.

—*So did Fatty.*

This Little Light Of Mine

Troy Onyango

In the silence of the dark room he finds his voice but realises he has forgotten how to use it. He clears his throat and tries again, opening his mouth wide as if yawning. Warm air liquefies before him and he blinks twice then half-closes his eyes. He gropes in the dark, tapping the side of the bed and finds his phone. The light from the screen is blinding and he turns down the brightness. He opens one app, closes it, opens another, closes it. He puts the phone back on the bed, screen facing down. The room is once again dark. A sound makes his hand dart, by reflex, and reach for the phone. He hesitates then taps the screen. He sees the message and his voice comes alive with a sob, tears flowing freely from his eyes, fire burning under them.

It is only when his alarm rings that he stops crying. He presses the back of his hand on his face and wipes away the tears, feeling the shame of having an outburst because of a text message from another stranger he will never get to meet. He pulls himself up on the bed, presses his legs together, and slowly lifts them towards the edge of the bed. He lowers them. The right foot touches the floor first, then the left. He lets them stay on the cold floor, hesitant to make the next move. The alarm rings again. He remembers: *the medication helps with the pain.* And although the pain he feels now is not in his leg, he hopes the doctor forgot to mention that the drugs also help with heartaches.

Every rejection, however it comes, is a memory; a way of remembering how he ended up here. A conjuring of the events leading up to the 'I love you. I really do. But I have to move on with my life. I don't want to be, uhmm, what's the phrase, held back by all of *this*. I'm sure there'll be someone else for you.' And: 'I don't want to break your heart. That's why I'm doing this over the phone.' And then: 'Just let me be. We had a wonderful three years, I know. But there is more to life, Evans. I have to go.'

It is too late to lock it all out. He remembers the prolonged beeping sound on the phone.

The silence of the other side.

He grabs the chair by its wheel and pulls it towards him. The thin wheel rolls backwards slightly.

With one rehearsed move he lifts himself off the bed—his weight resting on his arms—and onto the seat. He breathes slowly and bites on his lower lip leaving teeth marks.

The lights flick on and he switches on the television too. He skims through the channels, trying to find a distraction—something to keep his mind off the silence of his house. The silence reminds him of things he'd rather not remember, things he wishes he could forget, things that only cause pain when he'd prefer to feel nothing. On the television, a man's with a voice sings about love or something to do with it. He switches off the television, because that, too, he prefers not to hear about.

A sound from his phone, he picks it from the bed.

A new message:

—*Hi.*

—*Hey, how are you?*

—*Im good. What you up to?*

—*Nothing much tbh. Just at home. You?*

—*Well, my friends and I are going out. In Westie. Wnna come?*

—*I'd love to. I can't.*

—*Why not?*

He wonders whether he should tell this stranger he used to go out every weekend, that he used to love dancing on Fridays and Saturdays. He wants to be honest but honesty has brought him nothing but rejection and loneliness. And so he wonders whether he should reveal he cannot go out anymore. He needs his chair to move around, he remembers the previous message: *Omg!! You are a cripple? Sorry but I don't do cripples.*

Instead:

—*I just don't like going out.*

—*Oh it will be fan. Just come. We'll go to Brew then Havana. *fun*

—*Next time maybe. Why don't you come over we hang out. Maybe watch a movie?*

—*Lol. Most movies are boring. I liked Black Panther though.*

—*So you are a Marvel nerd?*

—*Whats that?*

—*Nvm. Anyway, I'm gonna go to sleep. It's late.*

—*Ok. Maybe I can come over after the club. Kitu 3am.*

He doesn't notice the silence in the room, the way it takes up space, like a thing capable of being inflated. He doesn't realise his hands are trembling. It has been more than two years since the accident, since he started using the chair. This is the most time anyone has given him on this app.

—*3am is late but I can give you my number and you call when you wanna come.*

—*Ok. Im a bit tipsy and really horny btw.*

—*Me too.*

—*Really? When was your last time?*

—*Two years.*

He wishes there was an un-send option. Like words spoken in a conversations it is impossible to take them back. He shakes his head and thinks himself a fool.

—*No way! That's a long dry spell. Lol.*

—*Yeah. I had a bad breakup with my ex.*

—*Wah! Sorry bout that.*

—*It's alright. It's just I've been looking for a meaningful connection with someone. Not just sex but someone genuine.*

—*Yea. Me too. People are so dishonest out here.*

—*Sorry. Gotta go. My friends say the Uber is here.*

—*Ok. I'll just leave my number here and you can call me later.*

The silence rushes back. He closes the app, opens YouTube, and plays some old school dancehall. He shakes his head and shoulders. His legs are still, like they are not part of his body, like they refuse to belong to him. He tries to move them. They are heavy. He winces at the pain. He squeezes his eyes shut and the sound fills his head: glass breaking; metal ramming on metal and flesh alike; tyres skidding on the wet tarmac as the driver tries to step on the brakes; men, women, and children screaming; rain pouring from the open sky like a curse; someone's phone playing *this little light of mine, I'm gonna let it shine* for the child on her lap; his mother's voice asking him what time he said he'd be home; other cars hooting; onlookers saying how stupid the driver was to try and overtake a lorry in the Salgaa stretch while drunk; ghosts screams from people who died on that same road.

He opens his eyes.

On his phone screen, a sinewy man with thick, jet-black dreadlocks falling to his shoulder sings about how much he loves pussy, and walking around Kingston's streets looking for somewhere to put his cock. A woman dances besides him and bends for him to rub his crotch against her back. He is short; her behind rubs against his stomach instead. His voice was meant for anything else, not singing. When he 'sings' the veins in his neck nearly burst. The woman dances, compelled, perhaps by economic circumstances, to be in the video.

3 AM.

He has not slept at all. He wheels himself to the kitchen, opens the fridge and picks out a tub of what he thinks is ice-cream. His last visit to the supermarket was more than a week ago. Since the chair he has avoided public places lest he meets his friends from days before and they ask him—with a look of pity and dread—what happened to him. He has also stopped going to church or work—his office job at the IT firm allows him to work remotely. He misses going to the movies and wonders how soon the new Marvel movie will be available online in HD.

He moves to the sitting room and finds the window open, a gentle breeze billowing the curtains. He watches it until the wind stills and wonders with irritation why the cleaning girl left the window open. He tries to close it but the latch is too high. Outside, he hears the sound of cars rushing past and a dog growling then howling. The moon smiles upon him, the stars are diamonds pinned to the sky. He tries to close the window again and fails. *Is it time to move to a new house that accommodates his current disposition?* He heads back to the bedroom.

Two new messages:

—*Hey. Saw your number. You still awake.*

—*Hi, I am awake.*

—*My friends just left. Can I come over?*

—*Sure.*

—*Can you pay for my cab? I'm broke aki.*

—*Take an Uber. I'll pay when you get here.*

—*I don't have Uber. Just Mpesa me. I'll get regular taxi.*

He has doubts, but he does not think anything could go wrong with this person. Maybe luck has finally smiled upon him. He wonders if now is the time to admit he uses a wheelchair. He decides against it. The admission has cost him so much and he has paid for it with loneliness.

He sends the money. When he tries to send his location he notices his number is blocked. He shakes his head and curses aloud for being so desperate he did not stop to think. He tries to call the number but it is switched off. He wheels himself to the bed and throws himself off the chair onto the bed. His legs dangle over the side. He wants them removed, cut off and taken away. He hates their betrayal. He hates the driver who caused the accident and ran away, who is probably driving another bus full of unsuspecting passengers. He cries himself to sleep.

When he wakes, his room is filled with a blinding sheet of light. He presses his face against the pillow and remembers a deadline for work—his phone tells him it is three hours away. He closes his eyes and rubs the erection pressing through his pyjama pants. He picks up his phone and opens Pornhub and finds something he likes. The act is short-lived. He closes the browser with disgust, annoyed by the wet patch on his pants.

He lies in bed, silence all around him. He wonders if the cleaner will show up today.

He gets out of bed and drags himself to the bathroom, his purple towel draped on his shoulder. This is the highlight of his day—when he can display a sense of independence and shower by himself. He looks forward to it, unlike those first weeks when his mother camped at his house and cleaned him thrice a day. It was her way of showing concern. He wishes it had not been a reminder of how helpless and child-like he was. His mother was not bothered, she would laugh loudly and say: 'Now you are embarrassed when I am the one who bathed you for the first nine years of your life.'

Birds outside his window sing, not privy to the sadness he feels.

He perches on the toilet seat and kneads his stomach as if to jumpstart his bowel movement. He holds his knees and hears the splash, a stone thrown in a pond. One of the side effects of the medication: he does not shit with ease. Another stone drops in the pond, he breathes with relief. He wipes himself, flushes the toilet, and opens the shower. The jet of water splashes on the darkened scars on his torso and rubs soap over them, massaging gently, begging them to go away. They are like war marks, the wounds caused by the shards of glass entering and exiting his body, as he lay on the tarmac surrounded by strange faces, his lower half still trapped in the wrought metal of the car, waiting for an ambulance.

His phone beeps. He fights the urge to get out of the shower with foam still clinging to his armpit hair and pubes. He finishes his shower, ties a towel around his waist and walks slowly towards the bed, leaning on the wall more heavily for support. He winces at the pain but he tells himself pain is a necessary part of the recovery process. He remembers those are not his words but the doctor's.

He does not check his phone. Instead, he dresses in loose-fitting sweatpants and a grey t-shirt and sits at his desk. He works, an Afrobeat mix in the background. A song he has not heard in a long while comes and he remembers how he and his ex loved dancing to this particular song. When the chorus comes on he remembers: 'Listen, Evans I love you so much and I will never leave you.'

He switches off the music.

He works in silence.

Two hours later he emails his boss to report his finished work. He cracks his knuckles, the popping sound makes him smile. He leans back on the chair and stretches, spreading his arms wide until his shoulder have some bit of strain. He moves to the bed and finally checks the message.

—*Hey, it's me. Sorry about last night. I didn't mean to block you.*

—*Why did you do that?*

He wants to add an angry emoji but leaves it.

—*I don't know. I'm sorry.*

—*I can send back the money.*

—*No need. I just thought you were honest at least. You could have just told me you needed money instead of conning me. It was not nice at all.*

—*I dint con you. That's why Im saying I can send back the money.*

—*You can keep it. Don't text me again.*

—*Pls don't say that. I have told you Im sorry.*

—*Can we meet up?*

This is the point he thinks things should end, the point he should walk away, and, maybe even delete this app. However, since the accident and the break up—*the desertion* as he thinks of it—this app has been the window through which he can see the dating world, perhaps his only hope of meeting someone who will accept him and fill the absences in his life. Although he has been unsuccessful on so many occasions, he knows at some point the world will hand him *something*. In the bleakness of everything around him, he chooses to cling to a strand of optimism, something he never really had before. But then those days the world was at his feet, he had all the attention he wanted, and he could go to a club in Westlands and come back home with whomever he wanted.

He is filled with a longing, a yearning to go back in time and live a life where he did not board that bus, where he did not phone his mother and say: 'I have never spent Christmas away from home. I will be there on the 23rd.'

And then there are other longings too, that cannot be ignored or pushed aside with the wave of a hand.

—*I don't think we can meet up. Let me be honest with you, I was in an accident a while ago, and I now use a wheelchair.*

—*Oh. Your photo doesn't seem like you are disabled.*

—*It's an old photo. Taken about three years ago.*

—*Oh ok.*

He knows what *that* means. He knows that form of brevity that is a substitute for silence. He has seen this response so many times but still the finality of it shakes him. He puts the phone down and goes to his computer. He goes through the folder of his movies and wonders whether to re-watch *Who's Afraid of Virginia Woolf?* or *A Streetcar Named Desire.* He ends up watching an animated film instead. Halfway through, he feels tired and falls asleep on his desk.

Dreams are the worst part of his day because in his dreams he has to confront what he is afraid of the most. He has a dream in which he is standing in the middle of a black river that looks like a road and cars are zooming past him at bullet speed. One of them goes through him and then another and he feels a slight pain when they do that but it builds up as more cars do the same until he is on his knees. He sees his mother telling him to get out of the way but his legs cannot move so he stays kneeling down until, at last, his ex appears and tries to stop the cars.

He wakes up from the dream shaking. Beads of sweat cover his face, his back is drenched in sweat, and his fingers tremble as if he is feeling cold. He calms himself and remembers the doctor always telling him to count backwards—ten to one.

Ten...nine...eight...

A notification on his phone.

Seven...six...five...

Another notification.

Four...three...

He breaks the counting and picks up his phone. It is a message from his service provider asking him to donate towards the Safaricom Marathon for the Lewa Wildlife Conservancy. He remembers when he took part in the marathon three years ago, and how the sun was hot and he was sweaty and sticky as he ran the dusty high-grassland roads. He had told himself that he would take part in the marathon every year for the cause. All that changed after the accident. Now he only wishes he could walk again. No aspirations to run marathons or climb Mount Kilimanjaro or do a trek along the sandy beaches of the coast. None of that. Just be able to walk from this room to the next and the next. And to dance again. He wishes for nothing else but a time when his life was whole and he could go wherever he wanted to whenever he felt like it. He realises now that he had never thought of it as a privilege, that simple act of putting one foot forward followed by the next. He had never stopped to think of what life would be if he had been born without that privilege. Now he embodies that reality and sometimes he finds himself wondering what he did to deserve this.

Nothing. He answers himself. He knows that, as difficult as it is to admit, life happens that way, every single day, and the fact that it is not one's reality does not mean it does not exist.

He decides to go out and get some fresh air. He feels suffocated by the silence in this house, and often finds himself regretting the decision to reject his brother's offer to move in with him. He regrets shutting down the proposition from his mother to have someone else come in to take care of him. He was used to his freedom—absolute, uninhibited freedom—and he knew someone else staying with him would mean an end to that. Back then, naturally, he had not come to terms with his new life in the chair.

Outside he wheels himself on the concrete slab that was added to his veranda when he was discharged from the hospital. He goes around the house twice, looking to see if any of his neighbours are around. No one seems to be in the vicinity so he goes back into the house and sits in the living room, consumed by the terror of silence and loneliness once more. He goes to the bedroom and picks up his phone. He checks Facebook, Twitter, and Instagram to while away time but there is nothing of interest going on them. He has not uploaded any photos of himself on any of the platforms since the accident. He wonders if he should close them down.

After an hour, he finds a response to the earlier conversation:
—*Hi, sorry I went silent. Was a bit busy. Anyway, what you up to?*
He responds: *Nothing much.*
—*Wanna meet up today?*
—*Told you I can't.*
—*I can come over.*
—*I'm okay with that but I hope you are comfortable with who I am.*
—*Yup. Im cool.*
—*What time?*
—*10.30pm*
—*That's a bit late. Maybe 8.30?*
—*I'll try.*
—*Let me send you my location.*

He hopes the fact that there has been no request for money this time means he has finally found a genuine connection. He pushes the previous events aside and tries to focus on the fact that this is the first who has agreed to meet him since he got on the app. Even though it is still a few hours away he phones the cleaner and asks her to come over and tidy up. He tells her he will pay extra if she comes right away.

When she arrives he has tidied his desk and tells her to clean the kitchen even though there is not much to clean in a house where barely any cooking happens and there is rarely a visitor. She polishes the surfaces, he nods to show his satisfaction. His body feels awake, he wheels himself around at a pace she has never seen him move before. When she is done he pays her and thanks her for coming on such short notice.

Afterwards, he calls Domino's to order two large pizzas. As he waits for the delivery he has a second quick shower. He puts on a pair of black sweatpants and an orange t-shirt with black sleeves. He rubs some cologne on his neck and wrists. He checks his phone every ten or so minutes and wonders if time has slowed down to frustrate him. He plays some music to distract himself but he does not listen to it.

At 8.30 PM he wheels himself to the living room and waits near the door. His heart races and he can feel drops of sweat form on his back. The t-shirt clings to his skin. He counts.

Ten...nine...eight...

He checks his phone.

Seven...six...five...

Still no message.

He dreads the thought of getting to one without a call or a knock at the door. He closes his eyes and tries to make the time move faster. He hears the music coming from his computer. He does not recognise the song. He waits by the door telling himself to keep calm and wait until 9 PM.

He notices the window from last night is still open, but the air is so still and the curtain stays unmoving.

He did not remember to ask the cleaner to close it.

A Separation

Iryn Tushabe

On the evening before I leave for university in Canada, I sit on the terrace of my childhood home watching Kaaka, my grandmother, make lemongrass tea. She pounds cubes of sugarcane with a weathered pestle. She empties the pulp into a large pot and tops it up with rainwater from a jerry can the same olive-green as her A-shaped tunic.

I step down from my bamboo chair and stride over to her. I lift the heavy pot and set it on a charcoal stove smouldering with red-hot embers.

'Webare kahara kangye,' Kaaka thanks me in singsong Rukiga, the language of our birth. She comes from a generation of Bakiga who sing to people instead of talking because words, unlike music, can get lost.

I smile and sit back down in my creaky bamboo chair to read a copy of National Geographic that a British photographer sent me. His photograph of a troop of gorillas in my father's wildlife sanctuary is on the cover of the magazine, and the accompanying article quotes me blaming the Ugandan government for refusing to support our conservation efforts.

'I hope I don't get in trouble for this,' I say.

Kaaka laughs the sound of tumbling water. 'You flatter yourself if you think the fierce leaders of our republic have time to read foreign magazines.'

She chops fresh lemongrass leaves on a tree stump, sniffing the bits in her hands before tossing them into the pan. The simmering infusion is already turning the light yellow colour of honey and will taste just as sweet. As the herb steeps, a citrusy fragrance curls into the evening like an offering. Kaaka fans the steam toward her nose and inhales noisily, closing her eyes to savour the aroma.

'The tea's ready,' she says a short while later, rolling out a mat woven from dried palm fronds. She sits on it, legs outstretched, hands clasped in her lap. This is how it has always been with us. Kaaka makes the tea. I serve it.

I pull the sleeves of my oversized sweater over my fingers and lift the pan off the stove. With a ladle, I fill two mugs. I give Kaaka hers and sit down next to her, blowing on my cup before sucking hot tea into my mouth. Its sweetness has an edge.

'You'll do very well in your studies overseas.' There is finality in her voice. When the invitation from the University of Regina's Anthropology and Archaeology Department arrived months ago, I showed her saying I would go only if I had her blessing. 'You'll acquire some new knowledge and a whole world of wisdom.'

'I'll be home for Christmas,' I tell her now.

'Yes, you will. Something to look forward to.'

Three weeks later, I'm standing by my open living-room window looking down at the street, watching people go about the business of living. I arrived in Regina, Saskatchewan, on the tail end of summer. The August heat has turned my apartment into a sweltering cavern. Mr. Stevenson, the silver-haired professor who met me at the airport, will be supervising my doctoral research. He also found this Munroe Place apartment for me. I can't seem to say the street name right, though. Is it Monroe as in Marilyn Monroe, the deceased American actress? Or moon-row like a row of moons?

Two teenage girls walk by sharing a blue slushy. The one with a thick mass of coffee- coloured hair takes a sip and hands the cup over to her friend, whose short hair is tinted the bright pink of a well-fed flamingo. Sticking out blue tongues at each other, they double over in laughter. They're wearing high-waisted shorts so short that when they bend, I glimpse the lobes of their flat-flat buttocks.

Dark clouds have gathered above the high-rise across the street as though getting ready to pounce. But the sunlight pierces their serrated margins, turning them into silver beacons.

The sound of my cellphone jolts me. The call has a Ugandan country code.

'Kaaka!' I shout into the phone. My elation keeps her name in my mouth longer, making it last.

'Harriet, it's me,' my father answers, his voice loud and strident. A call from Father frightens me a little. Always, I phone him. It's never the other way around. His preferred medium of communication is email – lengthy reports with headings and subheadings. The last one had an index and a couple of footnotes about his observations of infanticide amongst chimpanzees in Kibale Forest, our sanctuary's rainforest home. Did I know that contrary to previous observations of infanticide, deadly aggression in chimpanzees is not a gender-specific trait?

'Are you there, Harriet?'

I brace myself. 'I'm here.'

'It's about your Kaaka.' Father's voice suddenly acquires an uncharacteristic softness. 'She has died.'

He likes directness, my father. And sharp things. He has a prized collection of spears and *pangas* in his office that he says our forefathers carried with them when they migrated from Rwanda many centuries ago. In this moment, his words are a machete that cuts me to the core. I feel empty as though the part of me that's most substantial has left, leaving me hollow. Only skin and bone.

My hand goes limp and slowly falls from my ear until finally the phone hits the carpeted floor. I can still hear Father, but his voice is now muffled and distant, reaching me as though through a tunnel. I lower myself into the dining chair that has found a permanent place by my living-room window. I finger the cowrie shell necklace around my neck, wishing to go back in time before having this knowledge, back in time when I felt whole.

Time passes and it doesn't. Father's faraway voice through the phone stops, and silence eclipses the room. How long have I been sitting here, lost? He'll be worried, want to know I can be strong.

I hear the ping of email arriving. It's from Father. Kaaka went missing the evening before and when she didn't return by nightfall, he put together a search party. A game ranger found her body lying among the moss under a tree canopy behind the waterfalls.

'It was lucky he found the body when he did, before some wild animals got to it. That would have been gruesome,' Father's email says. I wonder about the moment my Kaaka became *the body*. Did it hurt? Or was it peaceful?

Outside, the dark clouds have huddled closer together, blocking out the sun. Then slanted lashes of rain beat down from the sky, battering my windowpane like they want into the apartment.

I pull on my sneakers and fly down the stairs, a caged bird let loose. I run toward Wascana Lake, a path shown to me by Mr. Stevenson. Gaining speed, I part grey sheets of rain as hot tears run down my cheeks. Every few minutes, bolts of lightning fire up the black skies followed by a ripping sound like a great big cloth being torn down the seam. I splash through silver puddles pooling on the concrete lip of the lake. I want so badly to go back home.

'I'll have more tea,' Kaaka says on the evening before I leave for Canada. But when I refill her cup, she sets it on the tree stump behind her, next to the Kerosene lantern radiating amber light into the dusk. She fishes a lilac satin bag from the deep pocket of her tunic and presses it into the palm of my hand.

'Hold onto these for me, will you?'

The bag's contents clink together as I loosen the string tie to reveal cowries, their porcelain surfaces gleaming like sea-polished rocks. Kaaka stretches herself out on the mat, looking up into the stars as though she hasn't just offered me an everlasting memory. This ninety-year-old woman who raised me would have given me the shells on the night of my wedding to wish upon my marriage the strength of the Indian Ocean. Except I haven't brought a suitor home, and at thirty years old I've turned into an old maid.

'Have you also given up on me ever getting married, Kaaka?'

'Not at all,' she says, still looking up into the indigo sky dotted with millions of stars, her hands forming a pillow underneath her cloud of grey hair. 'I know you will get married. This is just my way of telling you that your worth isn't tied to marriage and procreation.'

I try to undo the knot in the necklace I wear, the one I inherited from Mother after she died, but it won't loosen. It seems to have become tighter as the years have gone by. I keep tugging and pulling until eventually it loosens and comes apart. Mother had only six cowries on her necklace. Adding my new six makes it fuller, heavier. I'll be an old maid with twelve cowries around my neck, which is rare.

The light from the lantern makes shadows of the wrinkles in Kaaka's mahogany face. Lying there on the mat, she looks solemn as if trying to untangle knots from an old memory. I'm struck by how tiny she is, how little space she takes up on our mat. She reminds me of a stub of a pencil worn with its work, the best of its years shaved away.

My mother was a dressmaker. In my head, I have an image of her sitting behind her sewing machine on the front porch of our cabin, a yellow pencil sticking out from behind her ear. As the pencils shrunk, she'd shove them into her puffy hair. I always imagined the tiny pencils getting lost in that thick hair, getting trapped in its tangles, no way out. I wanted to save them but Mother never let me touch her hair.

'I can't remember her face,' I say, lying down besides Kaaka. 'Mother's face. The contours of it have faded.' The realization, saying it out loud, hurts my chest. What kind of a daughter forgets her mother's face?

'You're the spitting image of her,' Kaaka says. 'Look into a mirror anytime and hers is the face that looks back at you. You have her voice, too. Sometimes I hear you speak and I think, Holy Stars! My daughter lives inside my granddaughter.'

I was eight years old when Mother succumbed to the poison of a black mamba. That's when Kaaka came to live with Father and me. (Grandfather had left her years before to go live with a much younger woman.) On the day of my mother's funeral, Kaaka told me that Nyabingi, the rain goddess our tribe worships, had called Mother into the spirit world. She wanted me to understand that my mother still lived on, only now her physical presence was lost to us. I didn't tell her that her explanation was cruel, that it only made it harder for me to grieve for my mother.

'Tell me again how she died,' I say, willing myself to accept her view of death, that it births one into a form of oneself bigger than life and visible only to the living whose eyes have grown eyes.

'You know how it happened. If you still have to ask, it means you doubt.'

I'm a primatologist. I believe in verifiable, quantifiable data and logical explanations of the world. I was born in a cabin on the edge of a river and I see connections everywhere. I bridge between species, places, and time. I was six years old when I first learned the names of all the birds in our sanctuary, from the little Bronze Mannikin to the imposing Shoebill. I wrote them down in a notebook and recited them to tourists from Europe and North America like a morning prayer. I was ten when a baby chimpanzee hooted and purred his way into my heart. When we found him, Father and me, he still clung to his dead mother's leg. A poacher had shot her and left her for dead. It was then that I decided to study non-human primates, to try and protect them from humans.

'But how do you know for certain that Nyabingi took her? How do you know if Nyabingi exists?' I hear myself ask Kaaka.

'Because her spirit has visited me every night since she passed on. That's how I know.'

This is brand new information. I don't know how to respond to it so I lie there quietly, too many questions hanging in the air above me.

The day after Mother's funeral, Kaaka packed a picnic. She sat me down by the river and said, 'Repeat after me: My mother has been ushered into the spirit world.'

I repeated the phrase because she'd told me to, not because I believed it.

'Say it with conviction,' She pleaded. 'I'm certain of it the way I know that the moon is the moon and the sun is the sun.'

I wanted to believe her. Really, I did. But when the customary week of mourning ended and I returned to school, I told anyone who asked that a snake which moves faster than most people can run, whose venom is so potent and fast-acting that only two drops of it paralyzes its victims, killing them within an hour, which has a head the shape of a coffin and a mouth blacker than the chimney of a kerosene lantern, struck my mother twice. Trying to get away from this snake, she fell into the nameless river that runs through the sanctuary, and the river spat her out at its frothy mouth where it feeds the swamp. That's more or less what Father had told me. The rest I had read in his big book on snakes of East Africa.

'Our dead are always with us,' Kaaka is saying now. There's a hint of suppressed anger in her voice. 'You must always remember this.'

'I know but—'

'Why is it impossible for you to believe in a world whose existence you can't explain?' Kaaka speaks over my objection. 'You are smart enough to know that just because you can't see something that doesn't mean it's not there.'

A sort of electric hush charged with the loud singing of crickets sits between us. In the distance it creates, I probe the walls of Kaaka's theory of death, walls that are warped and distorted and never hold up whenever subjected to reason. But

I suppose gods don't listen to reason. I suppose gods go about doing whatever they want even if it means leaving a trail of orphaned children and childless mothers.

'She just materializes at the foot of my bed like an image from a projector,' Kaaka says. It takes me a moment to realize she's talking about Mother's spirit. 'Except it's obviously not just an image because she tidies up in my room. She walks around picking my tunics from the floor and folding them and putting them away in my wardrobe.'

'No!'

'She talks to me, too. It's a kind of wordless communication like the hum of the forest. It took me a while to understand it, but now I do.'

I want to ask her what else Mother has told her, but I don't. If she wants to, she will tell me unbidden. And after a moment's silence she does. Kaaka wants me to know that mother's spirit has promised to escort her over to the other side soon, very soon. She wants me to be prepared for this possibility. I'm not to worry, though, she warns. I'm not to cry. This is the ending she desires. It's what she's always hoped for. I should want it for her.

'Will you come back and visit me?' I say, all of my sensible questions having deserted me. 'When Mother takes you, will you come back to me?'

'If you want me to.'

I don't know how long I've been running when a dog's bark stops me short in a dimly lit back alley. He's a large black dog with a rumpled coat like the skin of an elephant. A white picket fence overrun with vines separates us. He scratches at it with his paws before giving up and turning away from me.

The rain has let up, but I'm still dripping wet, cold to the bone. I resume running to generate warmth. A bearded man with a long whip of braided hair down his back is standing outside a convenience store. He yells his sexual desires at me in an alcohol- induced drawl. I run. When we are scared, time

slows. I'm running so fast it feels as if I'm standing still and
everything around me is a blur. It seems incredible to me now
that an hour or so ago I thought staying in my apartment one
second longer might kill me. And now that I've strayed too far
and don't know how to get back, I want, more than anything,
the safety of its concrete walls.

I see a street sign up ahead, Cameron Street. The houses on it
look alike, old and eccentric. I run up to the closest one and ring
the bell by its purple door. My heart is beating sorely against
my ribs. My throat is burning.

'I'm lost,' I tell the middle-aged woman who opens the door.
Waves of chocolate- coloured hair frame her long face. 'May I
use your phone to call a cab?'

'Come in, come in,' she says, pulling the door wide open.
Then looking up a narrow staircase, she shouts, 'Ganapati!'
Her accent is East-Indian. Her body emanates warmth and the
sweet smell of jasmine. She offers me a large towel from a linen
closet.

A man comes down the creaking stairs wearing a frown
on his face. His white slacks are folded up at the bottom like
someone at the beach who wants to wade into the water
without getting their clothes wet. When he sees me, he tilts his
head at a questioning angle.

'Weren't you about to leave?' the woman asks him but doesn't
wait for his answer. 'Can you drive this young woman to her
home so she won't be swindled by a cab driver? Their fees are
exorbitant, aren't they?'

I nod my head yes, even though I've never taken a cab.

The man introduces himself. He says I can call him Ganesh.

I put his name on my tongue, toss it around my mouth, and
push it out between my teeth. I once knew a man with the
same name. Ganesh. He stayed in one of our guest cabins at the
sanctuary for three months. He wrote poems in jagged cursive
all day long. In between bouts of writing, he walked around
on calloused feet, touching Kaaka's honeysuckles, cutting
his fingers on her roses, sucking up the little beads of blood.

In the evenings, he sat cross-legged outside the cabin and recited his day's work. Kaaka and I listened to him in blissful incomprehension.

I shake Ganesh's hand, and a symphony surges through my brain. His face glows as though he's lit from within. My body is in love with him, this stranger named for a god. It bends toward him like a vining plant to light.

'I love your necklace,' he says.

'Thank you. The cowrie shells are a gift from my grandmother Harriet. I'm named for her. My name is Harriet.'

'A beautiful name.'

Ganesh opens the passenger door of his blue sedan for me. He turns a corner onto 13th Avenue, and soon we are cruising down Albert Street. The shimmering surface of Wascana Lake is lit with fiery shades of gold and red. Where did I lose my way along this lake? Can we outrun fate?

'Here we are,' he says, pulling up in front of my apartment building. 'I'll walk you to the door.'

I want to tell him that he needn't. That contrary to prevailing evidence, I'm quite normal. That running too far and getting lost was really the universe's doing, not mine. But I hear how alien this self-defence sounds in my head, how lacking in logic, and I let him walk me to the entrance of my building.

We stand at the door and I awkwardly fumble around my wet pants, feeling for which one of its many pockets hides the key. Finding it, I hold it up victoriously, evidence that I'm not crazy, not completely. But mad people probably think that they are the normal ones – everyone else is insane and should get help.

'I better get going then,' he says. But he doesn't leave. We stand at the door as though held together by something outside of ourselves.

'Would you like to come in?' I ask.

'Sure. But I can't stay long.'

Inside my apartment, Ganesh offers me the details of his life like a present. He left India five years ago to attend a music residency at the Regina Conservatory of Performing Arts, and then he decided to stay afterwards. Now he's a pianist with the local symphony orchestra. The woman is his aunt. She owns an Indian restaurant downtown, and he dines with her every Sunday. Would I like him to make us some tea? What kind of tea do I have?

'Lemongrass. I have dry lemongrass.' I pull open a kitchen cabinet to find it. 'I brought it from home in Ziploc bags. In cut-up bits. An airport security officer wanted to toss them into a garbage can.'

'Why?' Ganesh says, his hazel-green eyes wide with surprise.

'He was worried I might try and plant "whatever this stuff is" on Canadian soil.'

Ganesh's laughter is the warm colour of hope. I excuse myself to change out of my wet clothes. When I return to the kitchen, Ganesh is tossing a fistful of lemongrass into a pan with water. As the lemongrass boils, its fragrance fills my apartment with the sweet smell of home. I close my eyes and inhale its aroma, remembering a time so recent yet so irretrievably gone.

Ganesh takes a sip of the tea and purses his lips; the taste hasn't lived up to his expectations. He sets the cup down on the kitchen counter and scribbles his phone number in my day planner that I left open after breakfast.

'You'll call me?' he asks.

'I will.'

'You promise?' His high-pitched voice sounds like pleading.

'I do.'

On the morning I leave for Canada, Kaaka puts her hand on my back and leaves it there as she accompanies me to my father's beat-up Range Rover, caked with mud. We stand on the passenger side. I drape myself around her small frame, breathing her in, letting her clean scent – the smell of soap just unwrapped from its package – cleanse all the fissures of my soul. I transform my body into a plaster mould and imprint her on it, creating an impression of her on me.

'Christmas will come quickly,' she whispers. 'We'll see each other very soon.'

When she lets go of me, I have a sinking feeling like I have fallen out of time.

I'm sitting in my living room drinking the tea Ganesh abandoned. Without sugarcane syrup it's bland, like a cheap, watered-down version of the real thing. But the aroma is potent and breathing it is restful.

I sink deeper into the couch, dropping my head over the backrest like someone getting their hair washed in a salon. And that's when I feel it – a hand on my shoulder. The sensation is real enough for me to jump up, terrified, but all I see behind the couch is an unadorned wall the colour of dry bone. And yet my shoulder carries a memory of the hand, its familiar smallness and warmth. Suddenly I'm filled with a lightness of spirit and aware of the irreplaceable joy of this moment, what it might mean. Are my eyes growing eyes? I'm open to all that is possible.

2022 SHORTLISTED
STORIES

Collector of Memories

Joshua Chizoma

Mother made me a collector of memories. She taught me that we carry our histories in sacks tied around our necks, adding to their burdens as years lengthen our lives. Each time she told me about the night she found me, she added to my collection. We'd be in the middle of watching a movie and she'd go, 'Do you know you did not cry the first two weeks I brought you home? I was so scared you were dumb.' Or, 'I can't believe you like custard now. As a baby, you only tolerated pap, hot pap like this that did not even burn your throat.' She'd then launch into a narrative punctuated by laughter, pausing only to confirm some detail from her sisters or to disagree with them over one.

Over the years, I learned that she found me on a new year's eve, right about the time the harmattan cold was just picking up, but not boil-water-even-for-doing-dishes freezing yet. That I was wearing a yellow pinafore, swaddled in a blanket that smelled of talcum powder, and that there'd been two different earrings in my ear lobes. I also learned that she found me in an empty carton—a Cabin Biscuit box, she added later.

She reached into the air to pluck those memories whenever she wanted to throw jabs at me about my skin, or my face, or my penchant for eating Cabin Biscuits. However, the first time we had that heart to heart, it had been because of a fight she had with our neighbour, Regina.

We lived in a compound where the houses were spread so far apart as though to pretend it wasn't a public yard. The two-bedroom bungalows squatted in a semi-circle, huddled together like American football players before take-off. It surprised everyone that the landlord who'd had the good sense to build each bungalow separately, would then do something as foolish as making the toilets, shared one to three bungalows, communal. The toilets were often the cause of quarrels. The fights were about who did not flush the toilets well (and left it for their slaves to flush abi?) or who used only one sachet of detergent to improperly wash the toilet (shey those of us that wash with two sachets na fool we be?) or who lost the shared key and was taking their time replacing it. This last reason was the cause of the fight between Mother and Regina.

Regina's son had lost their own key. They'd asked us for ours and had been sharing it with us before the boy, a whole twelve-year-old dimkpa, lost our own key too. Mother had had to suffer the indignity of asking our other neighbour for their key any time we wanted to use the toilet. That day, she made me practically run from school because she was pressed. When we got home, she was about to grab the key when she remembered that it had still not been replaced. Instead of going to ask our other neighbour for theirs, she headed for Regina's house, her handbag still slung over her shoulder.

Regina's church's house fellowship was in full swing when my mother knocked. The tenants had had meetings about these evening fellowships because the attendees sometimes forgot that Regina's parlour was neither their church auditorium nor soundproof. That day, Regina first sent out her son to tell my mother to come back later. When Mother refused, she came out herself.

She wore the face of someone who was being courteous on the pain of death.

'Ah, neighbour. What is this thing that cannot wait for me to finish listening to God's word?' she asked, retying her wrapper laboriously.

My mother told her she was sorry to interrupt but that she wanted to collect money for the new key.

'Ah, I no get plenty money here. In the evening na me go come find you. Abeg, no vex.'

But Mother insisted. She was firm and malleable at the same time, using the tone she used when telling the obnoxious parents of her pupils that, no, she would not go to their house to conduct lessons for their children, they'd have to come to hers. And it worked, because Regina went in and came out with the money scrunched up in her fist.

Perhaps, it was the way Regina gave her the money, almost throwing it at her, that my mother had had to clap the air to catch the notes. Or maybe it was not really the money that was peppering her, maybe my mother just wanted to be petty, because as she turned to leave, she gave as a parting shot:

'Do I blame you? Is it not because I am sharing a compound with an illiterate like you?'

'Don't even come for me. O gini di? Who does not know children make mistakes?' Regina shouted.

My mother could not have aimed her punch lower. Everyone in the compound knew Regina's story and how she'd clawed her way from poverty.

'If your world is complete, go and fetch water with a basket na. Nonsense and nonsense.'

'It is okay,' her church members said. They were standing on her verandah; an emergency recess had been called, no doubt.

'Leave me. Every time she will be carrying face for somebody like say na she better pass. She thinks we do not know her shameful secret. If I open this my mouth for her eh, she will pack out of this compound.'

When my mother heard this, she dropped her bag and every pretence of civility with it.

'You see that thing you want to say, you must say it today oo.'

She clapped her hands together and came to stand in front of Regina, pushing her breasts onto her face.

'E pass say I pick child for gutter? E pass am? Oya, talk na?'

Regina did not respond. She was probably too shocked to. Even I had not expected the drama to take such a swift turn.

'Good. I think say you no dey fear.' My mother turned around then and saw me. Her face became a mélange of conflicting emotions: anger, shame, remorse. But anger won. She grabbed me and said, 'Who asked you to follow me?' Although she hadn't asked me not to.

That night she bristled with anger, and even grading papers did not help. Eventually, she dropped the pen and called me to her side.

'Chibusonma, come here,' she said.

I walked over from the sofa to the single chair she was sitting on. She shifted and I squeezed in with her. She stroked my arm, and I could feel the flames within her tempering, losing their rage.

Aunty looked up from her phone, and Chidinma paused the movie she was watching, trapping Ramsey Nouah's face on the screen.

'It is better you hear it from my mouth,' she began.

It was one of those things you knew. The way yes was yes and no was no. They were definites, and I could hold them to my breast, my history. That night, my mother did not romanticize the idea that I was an abandoned child she had picked up. She said it in a matter-of-fact way, like she was teaching me to memorize numbers, like she wanted me to know just for the sake of it. As I grew older and recognized that bricks and sticks sometimes are no match for words, I was grateful. Because after that day I realized how things could shape-shift if you had no sight. Snide remarks and snarky jokes found context and became decipherable. But because my mother did not burden my story with the weight of shame, I had none to spare. Even beyond that, I was hemmed in on every side by love, from my mother and her two sisters. Their love cushioned the effect of the taunts from the other children, fashioned me an armour that bricks and sticks and words could not penetrate.

Rhoda, whom everyone called Aunty, was the oldest and had a hairdressing salon. Her sisters did not go to her shop.

They said her hands were 'painful', although they made sure it was only the walls of our house that heard them say so. She loved 'living' and was the one who bought the TV and paid for the light bill. Each time the bill came, she'd divide the sum and remind her sisters each morning to contribute, placing her share on the centre table so 'everyone could see she had done her part'. Seven out of ten times she'd eventually go to pay it herself, gaining monopoly over the TV remote and daring anyone to change the channel even when she fell asleep watching Super Story.

Chidinma, the middle child, sold recharge cards and phone accessories. She was the most generous of the three, the one with the least savings too. They used to say, 'Except Chidinma does not have, that's why she will not give you. If she has money and you have a need, forget it.'

Mother was a primary four teacher. She taught the class for years, even when she got her teacher's training certificate, even when she got a university degree through distance learning. She refused to leave for another class. Her name was Florence, but most people knew her as 'Aunty Primary Four'.

Mother mothered me exclusively when it came to meting out punishment. Her sisters would tally all my infractions, waiting for her return so they'd bear witness. At the end my mother would respond, 'You mean she was this stupid, and you did not beat her?' incredulity lacing her tone, after which she'd drag me close and give me a whooping herself. But apart from this area, the three sisters fed me their different flavours of motherhood. It usually was Aunty who bought me clothes and made my hair every weekend. Saturday evenings she'd bring out the kitchen stool to our corridor, spread her legs, and trap my body within her warmth. Sometimes it was a whole family affair, with Mother shining a torch and Chidinma separating and handing out the attachments. I did not have the luxury of protesting her painful hand. It was enough that I debuted a new hairstyle each Monday morning. Pain was a small price to pay.

Chidinma bought me the UTME form for the polytechnic I ended up going to. I'd written JAMB the first time and failed. When I wrote it for the second time and failed again, Mother did not say anything. I knew she was beginning to think that the first failure was not a fluke. I passed the third time with a small margin, and Chidinma bought me a form for the polytechnic.

That day, she called me to her shop, brought out the papers, and in a voice that entertained no arguments said, 'Fill this thing, my friend.'

I stared at the paper on the table. None of my friends went to the polytechnic. Who would? University students were the *shit*. They returned home only during the holidays, bamboo stalk thin and sporting lingo that included 'projects' and 'lectures' and 'handouts'. They got away with many things, especially those who went to schools with ear-famous names like the University of Ibadan and the University of Nigeria. Plus, everybody and their nannies knew that it was the 'not-so-bright' students who settled for the polytechnic.

I considered my options for a while. They weren't many.

'I am going to live off-campus. I will not be going from the house,' I said.

'Okay,' Chidinma replied. We both understood it was a bargain. That was a compromise she could take to her sisters.

I started dating Chike in my final year, four years ago. He was a customer care agent at a mobile phone company and had once helped me do a SIM card welcome back. Chike was affable and took the job of being a nice person very seriously. He was the kind of person who would never refuse going the extra mile but complained while doing the task. Good-natured complaints about how it was taking his time or how he was tired, in such a way that it was not really grumbling, seeming almost like a normal conversation.

I moved in with him after graduation. By that time, I had spent so many weekends at his place that the one time I did not come home on a Monday, Mother did not bother asking me what happened. It was like a natural occurrence, like night giving birth to day or weeds sprouting in the rainy season. One day I was living with my mother and her two sisters, the next I was going from Chike's house to the bank where I worked.

Every time he mentioned marriage, I packed my bags and went to Binez hotels down the street. The manager knew me and usually assigned me the one room with good netting on the door. Chike always came for me after two days or so; the longest he'd stayed without me was seven days. The last time he came to pick me, he had been dripping with righteous anger and asked me whether it was not time to stop my childishness.

Whenever I think of it, I wonder if I hadn't moved in with Chike, if my attention hadn't been consumed by that puerile drama we were intent on performing, whether the events that followed afterwards would have been different. Whether I would have caught my mother's sickness earlier, or more appropriately, traced its root and found its cure. But like a hen, I took my eyes off Mother for a minute—such that I was unaware of how dire things were at home the Friday Aunty and Chidinma visited me at work—and a kite swooped in.

That day, I was wearing a new Ankara dress. Chidinma sat on a plastic chair in the reception area and Aunty came to stand before me, speaking to me in snatches while I attended to customers. In between clearing withdrawal slips and receiving deposits, Aunty managed to tell me to come by the house in the evening for an urgent matter and I was able to feign that the most pressing thing then was the zip of the new dress cutting into my back, and not the scary reality of what it meant for my aunts to visit me at my place of work to summon me home.

In the evening, I stopped on my way home to buy bananas, then remembering that Mother preferred oranges, I bought those instead. Then, in order not to offend the seller, I decided to pay for both.

The light was on when I stepped into the house. Mother was lying on the couch in the parlour. The room was thick with gloom such that even though the light was on, it was as though the darkness was winning.

'How is she? Is she getting any better?' I asked.

My aunts shook their heads. It was odd how they just sat down doing nothing. I placed the items on the table and sat at the foot of the couch Mother was lying on.

'Chibusonma, your mother has something to tell you.' Aunty's words sliced the silence.

Chidinma went to Mother and helped her up.

Mother stared right ahead, mute.

'You will not tell her now? What is wrong with you?' Chidinma said. 'You don't want what is holding you to leave you eh?'

Mother shuddered, as though the words actually made physical contact with her. I was quiet. The spectacle, it seemed, was for me.

'See, Chibusonma, there are some things I've not told you about the night I found you.' Her voice was low, but I listened nonetheless, my ears sharpening to pick up stray words.

'Yes, it was on a new year's eve, and Pastor Gimba gave a powerful message that day. I was still tingling with the power when I saw you at the dump. Or rather, heard you. That in itself was a miracle given all the New Year bangers going off that night. But it wasn't at Crescent Street. I went to the church at Faulks road. We had a combined service that night.'

'How are any of these important kwanu?' Chidinma interrupted.

'Keep quiet,' Aunty said.

Mother gave a deep sigh.

'Chibusonma, I did not find you. Your mother was around then. I took you from her,' she said.

I stood rock still and let the information wash over me.

'She'd given birth weeks before and did not let anyone touch the baby. She even chased the police away when they came. That night she was so tired. When I came by, I told her I'd hold you small, and she said okay. Then she fell asleep. I took you and left.'

She rushed through the story, barely pausing to take a break, suddenly seeming to be in a hurry. When she was done, she was winded and had to lay back down.

'Why was she at the dump?' I asked.

'Your mother was a madwoman. She was not by the dump, really. She had a small shack that she stayed in.'

'I see,' I said. 'So, you lied to me?'

'Technically, it was not a lie,' Chidinma said.

'All my life I thought that my mother abandoned me. That maybe she was one of those careless girls who threw away their babies. Wait, so you stole me from my mother?' I said.

'I am sorry,' Mother said.

'You erased my mother? What am I supposed to do with this information now?'

'I'm sorry.'

'Chibusonma. We felt it was for the best,' Aunty said. 'What your mother told you was for the best. Would you have preferred the truth? That a madwoman is your mother?'

'You probably would have died from the cold or caught an infection or something,' Chidinma added.

'You don't know that,' I said.

'You don't know that too,' she returned.

I felt ganged up on. And then my mother said again, 'I am sorry.'

'Why are you telling me this now?' I asked.

There was a shift in the mood. It was as though the sisters were waiting for something else.

'Before I took you.' She paused and a film of terror slipped into her eyes. 'Your mother said that if I didn't hand you back that I will always know no peace.' She looked away. It was the end.

Aunty took over.

'Ever since my sister became sick, I told her this thing was spiritual, but she did not listen. Now, after three tests, nothing nothing,' she said.

'Look at her. She has been like this since morning. But thank God for Pastor Gimba. He got a revelation from God that your mother offended someone, and she needs to make peace,' Aunty continued.

'How?' I asked.

Chidinma brought out a folder and handed it to me. Their actions were like a well-rehearsed choreography, like actors on a stage acting out a script. I flipped through the content.

'We've managed to trace your birth mother. Her family house is in Nkwerre. They came and carried her from the dump after a while. We believe she is the one your mother has to make peace with,' Chidinma said.

That night, after I came back from Mother's, I cried when Chike spanked me. He became even more scared when I asked him to make love to me gently. He was fidgeting as though it was our first time. Eventually, I had to climb on top, controlling the rhythm of the thrusts myself.

I woke up the next morning to the sight of him holding a tray and wearing a nervous smile. I sat up and held out my hand for the tray. He'd made pap and fried plantains.

'Sorry, I could not go to buy eggs,' he said.

'No problems,' I said, biting into the plantains. They were well done, and I was surprised.

'So, about yesterday, what happened?' He came to sit beside me. He didn't know what to do with his hands. He kept them on the bed for a while, then touched his collar.

'Just go.'

'Why? You don't want to talk to me?'

'Just go abeg. I'm not in the mood,' I said.

He got up, smoothened his shirt, and left.

On our way to Nkwerre, Chidinma got into an argument with the driver. She thought he was driving too fast, to which he'd replied that she had no business telling him how to drive his own car. I wanted to reach out to smack Chidinma. I did not understand how she had space in her head to notice other things,

like how the seats were cramped—she complained about that—
or that I used makeup—she didn't think that was appropriate.
And how could she have a problem with the driver's speed?
Wasn't speed important to us?

When I asked them that morning how they knew the
particular place we were going, Aunty said, 'We've been
planning this thing for a while now, Chibusonma. Let's just go.'

'How about my mother, is she not coming with us?' I craved
a fight, an outlet for the nameless emotions broiling within me.

'No,' Chidinma said.

'We will still go again,' Aunty added, a little cheerily. 'That
time, we will go with a lot more of our people.'

Chidinma came to me and took my two hands in hers. Her
eyes held such kindness and love that I felt my rage buckle.

'Nne, I know that you are angry, and you should be. But can
you postpone your anger one more day? Just after today you
can be angry all you want. Can you do that?'

At Ngor Okpala, Aunty bought me a packet of plantain chips,
handed me a handkerchief when I started sobbing, and placed
my head on her shoulder. No words were exchanged.

The house we went to had a huge bird on the gate. The bird
split into two when the gate was opened. The inside of the
compound was swept clean. The patterns the broom made on
the ground was beautiful. It had rained the night before, so the
ground still retained enough moisture to make sweeping less
arduous and more like a process in making art.

A group of people sat on the verandah—men and women
whose generations were far removed from mine. A man broke
away and went straight for Aunty.

'You must be Rhoda,' he said in perfectly enunciated
English. 'My name is Peter. I am the person you have been
communicating with.'

Aunty bowed a little.

'Is she our daughter?' He asked. Aunty nodded, smiling
broadly to emphasize the good news.

'Oh, welcome, our daughter.'

He came and gave me a swift embrace. Several women came out to hug me, as though I'd been declared safe for communal interaction. They held me with an air of familiarity that surprised me. I was led to a seat. They sat around me, smiling and asking questions I didn't have to think about before I answered: what school I went to, whether I was married, if I knew I had my biological mother's nose.

A hush descended when one woman came out from the backyard. Her hair was shaved to a crop and she wore a gown that hung off her shoulder, revealing the strap of a black bra. She had on a static smile, not widening into laughter or extinguishing into a frown.

She came and pulled me up and hugged me. When I looked up, I noticed that more than one woman had tears in their eyes. The woman walked with me back the way she came.

At the backyard, she brought two seats and placed them side by side. She told me that she sold tomatoes at the market and lived here with her brother's family. She was a member of the Legion of Mary and loved going for the Latin mass. She shaved all of her hair because relaxers made her scalp itch, but she wore wigs when she went to church.

She talked and I listened, noting that her life revolved around the church, maybe a little too much, and that she did not ask me anything about myself, this woman that was my birth mother. Some of the women sat nearby, listening too as though they were not familiar with the details she was sharing.

'I know what you are thinking, but I am fine now. I take my medications dutifully, and I go for my doctor's appointment whenever I have to,' she said after a while.

I reached out and flicked lint from her gown.

'It is manageable. Not everyone dies from dementia. That is what my doctor says I should call it, dementia.' She laughed. The women shifted uncomfortably in their seats.

'My mother—'

I began and then paused. I had not considered that there would be a need to call my real mother anything other than

Mother. The woman did not respond. I continued, 'My mother tells me you said something to her the night she took me from you. She said you told her something dangerous would happen to her if she took me.'

Her face remained free of ripples. She still looked up at me as though expecting me to add something.

'I want to know what it is. I want you to forgive her.'

'I can't remember. Is she sure?' she asked.

'Yes, she is.'

'I can't remember. Things upstairs are jumbled up.' For a moment, the smile slipped, and I saw something that looked like fear lurking beneath the mask.

'Okay. But I think you should maybe forgive her.'

'Okay, I do.'

I sighed, exasperated.

'Maybe you should do something, like a ritual?'

'I don't know,' she said. 'Oya why don't you kneel down and let me pray for you,' she said.

I kneeled. She placed her hands on my head.

'May the curse pass over you. I forgive your mother.'

When I lifted my eyes, she was smiling. It was the same smile she had on before. It seemed like mockery now. Aunty quickly looked away when I stood up. But in her eyes, I'd seen prayers.

That evening, a petulant expression sat on Chike's face when he came in. He walked around, his displeasure as imposing as a billboard, but I ignored him. Finally, when we were in bed, he asked, 'Where did you go today?'

'Somewhere,' I replied.

He sighed.

'My people have found a woman for me. Since you are not ready,' he said.

Even though I'd noticed the steady exodus of his clothes from the closet, it still stung to hear him say it out loud. I was briefly scared. What if he left and I discovered that I actually loved him? What if I told him I was ready to marry him now?

'I hope she knows that you like getting pegged?' I said instead.

'I don't like getting pegged,' he said.

'And all these sex toys, better carry them with you.'

He said nothing.

'Your new bride, you think she'll like being tied up, or she'll rim you well? It did take me a while to learn how to do it.'

'Just stop.'

'Plain vanilla sex, imagine how you'll miss me pegging you.'

I started laughing. He swung over and climbed on top of me. He placed his hands around my windpipe.

'I don't like getting pegged. If you tell people that nonsense about me, I will kill you,' he snarled.

Around midnight, when my phone started ringing, it caught me awake. By then, I was busy rearranging the contents of my sack of memories, deciding the ones that would stay and the ones that would go. It was futile. Even though my mother's betrayal ran deep, I knew which version of that night I was going to hold on to.

'Answer the call na or turn the phone off,' Chike grumbled and then grabbed the phone and said, 'Aunty.'

The ringing stopped, his hands still stretched out to me. It started again, and Chike placed the phone on the bed.

'Are you really going to leave me? Did they really find you another woman?' I asked.

'Jesus! What is this? What is going on?' Chike said, alarm stark in his eyes.

I did not respond. Instead, clouds gathered and a noisy deluge fell from the sky of my eyes. Frustration and anger flowed downwards, accompanied by an unlearned dirge I didn't know I could manage. My voice grew hoarse, and Chike left the room, but the phone wouldn't stop ringing. Aunty called, Chidinma called, and I let them. My tears were helplessness made flesh, an attempt to stretch time's finiteness and leave unchecked possibilities. Because I knew that on the other side of that phone was maybe a prayer unanswered.

When A Man Loves a Woman

Nana-Ama Danquah

Every morning for the past five days, Kwame had woken up next to a corpse. Well, technically, Adwoa had not yet become a corpse. She was still a fully breathing, flesh-and-blood human being; but there was no way, in those first few lucid moments, that Kwame could have known this. So each morning he'd lean over, position his lips right next to Adwoa's ear, and whisper in a voice rough and gravelly, an odd mixture of fear and sleep: 'Good morning, my love.' And then he'd wait, the fear twisting his intestines into a tight bow of pain.

Each morning she'd return the greeting—meaning, of course, that she was not dead.

'Good morning, sweetheart,' she'd mumble, turning to face him, her eyes wide open, the hazel pupils shimmering with life. She'd then softly, softly, place her lips on his, making him remember why he loved this woman with all his heart. And making him regret, at least momentarily, his decision to end her life.

Had this been before 'the illness,' as they still, for some reason, called his bout with cancer, Kwame would have received her kiss as the invitation it was. He would have pulled Adwoa to him and they would have made the sweetest, most tender love. That had always been their way, their ritual. Before breakfast with the kids, before the obligatory daily discussion about the details of each person's day, then the school drop-offs and the long work commutes, before anything else, there had always been that—their love. It was elemental.

He sincerely believed that those lovemaking mornings had kept them together for twenty-five years. It wasn't simply the sex; it was all that informed it, defined it, drove them to it. Some couples observed date nights or planned regular week-end getaways as a means of checking in, making sure they were still in step. For Adwoa and Kwame, their time together each morning did the trick. It confirmed anew that they were still each other's priority, that even with all the things and people vying for their attention they still chose to greet every single day in each other's arms. And it was in that embrace, their passion spent, that they planned and dreamed, declared their commitment to one another. Their mornings brought to the fore a certain vulnerability, one that spilled over into the rest of their interactions, made them more willing to compromise, to forgive.

Kwame desperately missed that intimacy, especially now that they'd returned to Accra. And yet, whenever Adwoa inched her body closer to his and slid her hand inside his pajama bottoms, he immediately recoiled and pulled it away.

Adwoa suffered from hypertension. Hers was not an extreme case. She was thick, about a dozen kilos over the recommended maximum weight in the 'normal' range on the chart posted in their doctor's waiting room in America. Kwame had always dismissed that chart, believing those markers were meant for non-African women, those who were built without fleshy thighs and full, round butts. That theory, however, had come crashing down when he'd seen the same chart in one of Dr. Agyekum's examination rooms.

Even though Kwame thought Adwoa looked fine the way she was and didn't need to lose a single kilo, he did think that she could eat a little healthier; they both could. His weight also fell beyond the 'normal' range on the male version of that chart. He had a paunch. It was not exceedingly large, the size of a slightly deflated soccer ball, and perhaps would not have been too noticeable on a taller man, but on his five-foot- eight frame it stood out.

They were both fairly sedentary. Before the illness, when Kwame was still working full-time, he met with clients in the mornings then spent the afternoons writing letters and briefs and motions. As a bank executive, Adwoa also spent most of her days at her desk.

'The uneducated live longer,' she often joked, 'because honest work is corporeal. We should have become farmers. Each degree we've earned has probably taken ten years off our lives.'

Before the children arrived, Kwame and Adwoa hadn't been so formal about meals, not during the workweek. They'd eaten heavy breakfasts—kenkey and fish—and packed their lunches. Dinners were more spontaneous. Sometimes they ate out at restaurants. Other times they prepared a bowl of gari, opened a tin of sardines, then threw some habaneros, a tomato, a sliced onion, and a pinch of salt into the blender and made fresh pepper to complete the meal.

On the weekends they ate like royalty. Like most people they knew in the small Ghanaian community of Washington, DC, they ate food from back home. Every other Sunday, they would take their old white cabriolet, the first car they bought in America, and drive to one of the African groceries in Northern Virginia. There, they would stock up on all the ingredients they needed to make jollof, kontommire, tinapa, apɔnkyenkrakra. Then came the kids—Henry and Ama, their oburoni children— one almost immediately after the other.

Try as Adwoa and Kwame did to stay true to their culinary heritage, by the time the kids started school, their home had successfully been assimilated. It became, quite essentially, American. It was pizza on Friday nights; popcorn and double-scoop ice cream cones on Saturday afternoons; and brunch consisting of scrambled eggs, bacon, and pancakes after church on Sundays.

Whereas the excess weight, lack of exercise, and heaping platters of heavily salted french fries did not appear to have any obvious adverse effects on Kwame's health, with Adwoa they contributed to a constantly elevated blood pressure. Whenever she made an effort—started walking daily and eating healthier—her body rewarded her, and their doctor followed suit by reducing the dosage of her medication.

Adwoa made significant progress after Henry and Ama went off to college. They did away with the requisite family dinners on weeknights. Kwame invested the additional time in his law practice. Adwoa did the opposite: she cut back her hours at work and started taking various classes at the local gym—Zumba, Pilates, kickboxing, yoga. Before long, Kwame could tell the difference in her body during their morning lovemaking. She was stronger, had greater endurance, and, above all, showed more confidence. She moved her limbs with the grace and agility of an athlete. It made him self-conscious. He sometimes wondered what she thought of his body, which was still soft and sagging. Was she repelled? He wanted to ask her but couldn't bring himself to display such weakness in the presence of her newfound strength, so instead he'd turned the question into an accusation.

'Pretty soon,' he said as he entered her one morning, 'you'll trade me in for a younger model, some fit macho man you'll meet at the gym.'

She arched her back, received him with her entire body. 'Never,' she moaned. 'I will always want you. I will always want this. You are my everything.' Done with their morning lovemaking, they lay facing each other. She gently took his hand, laced their fingers together, and whispered, 'Till death do us part.'

Kwame stared at her, and everything he saw brought him joy—her short-cropped hair, mostly pepper with traces of salt scattered throughout; her wide smile and perfectly straight teeth, the result of years of orthodontics; and that smooth butterscotch skin he so loved to caress. He wondered how he'd gotten so lucky. All of his male friends had girlfriends, women other than their wives, women who supplied whatever was missing in their lives—laughter, excitement, romance, attention, sex. He had Adwoa, only her, always her. He didn't want or need anyone else.

Right then, Kwame had a fleeting image of her at his funeral, inconsolable, wailing to whomever would listen that she prayed the Lord would take her too because she could not live without him. Her grief was palpable. It nearly moved him to tears to imagine she loved him that much. He blinked hard to clear the image, then leaned forward and kissed Adwoa's forehead, which was still moist with sweat, and repeated, 'Till death do us part.'

'Homicide by suicide' is a term that Kwame coined while reading an article in his doctor's waiting room. He didn't even know what magazine it was in because someone had torn the cover and first few pages off. The article was about the number of deaths that occur every year as a result of people inadvertently taking the incorrect medication. It was some ridiculously impressive number that he had since forgotten, though he'd immediately told himself the real number was probably much larger.

According to the article, pharmacies sometimes mislabel prescriptions, giving John the pills that were meant for Jane. Also, with so many new medications, many of which sound similar, there is the issue of simple human error—a patient is handed a prescription bottle containing a month's supply of zolpidem, a sedative, instead of Zoloft, an antidepressant; or Fosamax, which slows bone loss, instead of Flomax, a prostate medication that makes it easier to urinate. Though the names are similar, the medications usually look nothing alike. Still, as noted in the article, that is not the point; most people do not stop to look at what pill they are taking. They just trust that what is in the bottle is what is supposed to be in the bottle.

For the better part of a year, Kwame had been taking Flomax, yet no matter how hard he tried while reading that article, he couldn't picture the pill. Was it round or oval? Was it white, blue, pink? He didn't like to think of himself as average. He was hardworking and exemplary, and the life he'd led reflected that. He'd chosen an intelligent, beautiful, and loyal wife. Their children were bright, award-winning; they attended Ivy League universities.

And yet, in this instance, Kwame had to admit that he'd been as clueless and careless as the average person. Every day, he'd opened his pill bottle, shook a tablet into his palm, popped it in his mouth, and swallowed. He'd done it all by rote, mindlessly. He could have very easily caused his own death. The thought of it made him shudder. Then it occurred to him that this was the perfect way for someone to cause another person's death. 'Murder by suicide,' he whispered.

My goodness, he thought, *I have to tell Adwoa.* She'd be just as alarmed by the realization that she had also been absentmindedly swallowing her medication, then she would laugh at what she called his 'lawyer brain.'

'Why must you always find criminality in everything?' she always asked. '*Ehbeiii!* If I didn't know you were such an honest man, I would fear you!' Then the two of them would laugh.

But he never told Adwoa about the article. By the time he'd arrived home, there'd been more pressing news to share. For nearly a year, Kwame had been under the impression—the illusion, really—that he suffered from benign prostatic hyperplasia (BPH), more commonly known as an enlarged prostate. That day at his doctor's appointment, after reading the magazine article, he'd learned that he had prostate cancer. That was the news he'd carried home with him.

There were tears. There was anger, confusion, disbelief. There were more trips to the doctor. More tests, more interpretations of the results. A second opinion, a third, and a fourth. They all agreed: it was cancer; it was aggressive; it had most likely not spread, but the gland needed to be removed immediately.

After the diagnosis, they made love every morning with a fervor that was almost bestial, as though they were two feral animals who'd just found one another. She was often late to work. He'd altogether stopped going into the office. They spent every morning making love as if their lives depended on it. They made love in the evenings too. Adwoa no longer went to the gym. After work, she would come straight home. They'd have dinner delivered, eat the food in bed, then tend to another, more primal hunger. He loved that her body was growing softer, that the angles of her face and shoulders and hips were smoothing and rounding, becoming curves again. He dreaded the day when he would no longer be able to enjoy them like this, when he would not be able to explode the whole of his love and joy and longing for her.

'They're going to turn me into a eunuch,' he cried the day before his surgery.

'Don't be so dramatic.' She laughed. 'The doctor said that after you recover, you'll eventually be able to do everything again.'

'Not everything,' he sighed.

'Everything except ejaculate.' She kissed him on the lips. As though it did not matter. As though it were nothing at all. She did not understand.

Kwame wanted to die at home.

He wanted to take his last breath in Accra, surrounded by the sights and sounds that had ushered him into this world.

He knew he wasn't dying. Not yet, at least. But the illness had brought him face-to-face with his mortality. His body had never before failed him, but he knew that while this failure was the first, it would not be the last. It was the beginning. No matter how long it took between that beginning and the inevitable end, Kwame knew that his body would only continue to fail him.

Their time in America was supposed to have been brief, only until they'd completed their education. But then they'd had children and decided to stay, only until the kids started school. And then it was only until the kids reached high school. Only until he'd built the practice up enough to sell it for a mint.

Only until they could start collecting Social Security because, after all, they'd paid into the system. Only until they finished building their perfect retirement villa. Only. Only. Only.

It was time. They'd agreed before the surgery. As soon as his wounds were healed, they would go home.

They'd rented a house in a gated community, just behind the new American embassy in Cantonments. 'That mighty building,' a taxi driver had called the embassy. And he was right, it was. Kwame resented it. He resented America. He had come to associate it, however irrationally, with the illness, the failure of his body, the disappointing state of his manhood.

They'd been building a house in Prampram, about an hour outside of Accra, right by the ocean. There, they could wake up in each other's arms and listen to the roar of the waves. For five years they'd dutifully sent Kwame's younger brother, Fiifi, regular remittances so that he could oversee the construction. He would send them updates, e-mails with detailed descriptions of what the contractors had accomplished. Sometimes he'd include pictures. They'd hoped that once they were on the ground, actually living in Accra, they could speed up the process and be able to move into the house within a year. When they finally repatriated, what they discovered, instead, was that their retirement villa was nothing more than an empty plot of land. Fiifi had been lying. Believing that they would never actually return, he'd been pocketing the monthly remittances. Not even a single brick had been laid. Fiifi's photos were of a nearby home, one that belonged to white expats. This one detail, the fact that the home Kwame had been envisioning himself and Adwoa in actually belonged to white Americans, somehow made his brother's betrayal hurt all the more.

'It'll be all right,' Adwoa assured him. 'No use getting angry. The plot is still ours. We can still build the house. I'm sure we'll soon realize that there's a blessing in this somewhere. We're alive, we're back home, and we're together. That's all that matters.' His wife was ever the optimist. And because he loved her so much, he allowed himself to believe her.

Even so, he couldn't summon optimism. Thankfully, nothing else caught them by surprise. Kwame hated surprises. Their life back home fell easily into place. They'd been smart about their savings and pragmatic with their plans. They maintained a modest existence, one that easily exposed them as the returnees that they were—no full-time driver, no live-in help. They shared one vehicle. If it was gone, the other made do with a taxi. They shopped for their own groceries and prepared their own meals. Once a week, a young woman, Mawusi—an Ewe name meaning 'in God's hands'—came to wash their clothing and clean. It was the beginning of a new life, their new life. He sincerely looked forward to living it. Still, he could only feign optimism; he could not yet feel it.

Weeks passed. Months passed. Kwame's body continued to fail him. His American doctor had told him it would take time. His doctor in Accra had echoed the same words. Neither had been able to tell him how long, to give him a concrete number, something that he could hang his hopes on.

The surgery had, predictably, disrupted their morning routine. In the first few weeks of his recovery, he'd slept in late, drowsy from the pain and the medication he'd been given to relieve it. Adwoa took excellent care of him. She tended to his every need while single-handedly organizing their move. By the time they'd settled comfortably into their home in Cantonments, he was feeling much better. The pain was gone, and he was anxious to move forward. But try as he did every morning when Adwoa greeted him with a kiss, those beautiful eyes expressing a specific yearning, he could not rise to meet her desire.

Every morning they tried and tried, and there were many days when, for a few moments, Kwame reached the level of 'almost.' Half-cocked. Almost ready. Almost able. Almost the man he'd once been.

'Be patient,' his doctor advised. 'These things take time.' In all other ways, his life was perfect, even idyllic. Kwame had reconnected with Mr. Johnson, his best friend from childhood. His name was Kojo but everyone called him Mr. Johnson in crèche; whenever an adult had asked him his name, he would respond, 'My name is Mr. Johnson.'

Growing up, Kwame and Mr. Johnson lived in the same compound. They'd spent their entire lives side by side, from crèche to primary and secondary schools. They'd both married their sweethearts, the first girls to whom they'd pledged their hearts. In many ways, Mr. Johnson felt more like a brother than Fiifi.

While Kwame and Adwoa had attended university in America, Mr. Johnson and Naadu stayed in Accra to complete their studies. They'd later moved to London and had three children, all girls. When their children were young, the couples vacationed together once or twice. The men stayed in touch throughout, but as both of them left the logistics of family vacations and such to their wives, and the women did not share as close a bond, those few instances never turned into a tradition.

Naadu was killed in an accident. At the request of her family, Mr. Johnson brought her body home for the funeral and burial. When it was all done, he saw no reason to return to London. The children were busy creating their own lives, and without Naadu, there was nothing there for him. He figured it would be easier to remain in Accra. He'd been living there for nearly a year when Kwame and Adwoa returned.

Several times a week, Kwame would meet Mr. Johnson at +233, a popular jazz club, to talk over drinks and music. On the way home, Kwame would sometimes stop at the Cantonments roundabout. It was a mile or so from the entrance to their housing complex, and a popular gathering spot for prostitutes. He would pick up one of the women and drive her to a secluded spot on a nearby side street. He didn't consider it cheating. It was, in his mind, a therapeutic exercise. What else would he want with a common whore?

When he was with Adwoa, the weight of his inability to perform, to please her as he had for so many years, was crushing. With the whores, there was no tenderness. There was no expectation, no disappointment. There was only a straightforward transaction. Be that as it may, his body still continued to fail him.

Adwoa started going to the gym again. At least that's what she'd told Kwame.

'I feel like I've let myself go,' she'd said. 'I want to get my body back.'

For whom? he wanted to ask, but didn't. 'I love you just the way you are,' he said instead.

'Our birthdays are coming soon,' she whispered, as though revealing a secret. 'I want to be able to slip into something sexy.' She grinned and winked. He smiled politely, then turned around and walked away.

They'd been born two weeks apart, he in late October and she in early November. This year, they would both turn fifty-three. He imagined that by their birthdays, he'd be back to normal. He hoped that he could whisk her away on a small trip to someplace romantic like Mauritius or the Seychelles. He wanted to reclaim what the illness had taken away from them. But that was nothing more than a fantasy. Already they were in the last days of September, and he was still unable to make love.

'You know, there are many other ways to make love besides penetration,' his doctor reminded him when, during his appointment, he complained for the twenty millionth time about his dysfunction. 'I've found with my patients that sometimes their attitude makes a huge difference. Positivity can lead to progress.' The doctor's comment made him feel ashamed of himself. Right then and there, he decided to try harder, not to change his situation, but to make the best of it.

After he left the doctor's office, he drove to the gym at the Air Force Officers' Mess. It was on the other side of Cantonments, and it was where Adwoa and, it seemed, every other returnee and expat worked out. If she was done, he thought the two of them might go for lunch at the Buka in Osu. As he drove into the complex, he noticed Adwoa and Mr. Johnson sitting together at a table in the outdoor social area. They were talking and laughing, so deeply engrossed in whatever they were discussing that they did not notice him drive in, turn, and drive back out.

When Adwoa came home that afternoon, he asked about her morning, whether her time at the gym had been productive. He assumed that she would tell him about running into Mr. Johnson and fill him in on whatever they'd been discussing.

'Oh, it was good,' she said while stripping off her sweaty gear. 'I ran into Ama Dadson. We spent some time catching up. She's started an audiobook company.' Ama was an old friend of theirs. She'd attended Wesley Girls' Senior High with Adwoa. 'I'm going to have a shower; do you want to join me?' she asked.

'No thank you. I'll probably have one later this afternoon, before I change to meet Mr. Johnson at +233. Would you like to join us?'

'That would be nice,' she said, walking toward the bathroom, 'but I'm going to let you boys have your fun. Give Mr. Johnson my regards. I'll be out in a minute so we can have lunch.'

That evening while having drinks, he asked Mr. Johnson about his day.

'I was in Tema all morning, some small meetings about a project,' he told Kwame. And in that moment, Kwame realized that something was going on between his wife and his best friend.

Adwoa and Mr. Johnson met nearly every day. Kwame had started looking at the call logs on her phone and reading her text messages whenever she was in the shower. He knew the times and locations of their meetings.

I can't tell you how much this means to me, she'd texted him one day.

This is just what the doctor ordered, she texted another time.

Does he suspect anything? Mr. Johnson asked once.

Not a thing. He doesn't have a clue.

He was confused by the casual cruelty of this woman he thought he knew so well. How could she press her lips against his every morning, tell him how much she loved and wanted him, and yet sneak around with his best friend and then laugh behind his back about how he didn't even have a clue?

And Mr. Johnson! Of all the women he could have chosen to replace Naadu, why his wife? Why Adwoa? They'd been friends for nearly a half century. Kwame had shared his most intimate secrets with him. He'd even told him how inadequate he'd been feeling since the surgery, how he'd not been able to make love to Adwoa.

During the times when he knew they were meeting, he wondered what Mr. Johnson was doing to her, how he was touching her. He wondered if she'd ever worn her gold and blue waist beads while she was with Mr. Johnson, if she'd ever pleaded with him, in that near-growling voice, to do things to her.

Sometimes when Kwame pictured them together, he would come closer to achieving an erection than he ever had since the surgery. This only confused him more, made him angrier. It hurt to think of the pair.

The pain was unbearable. Kwame simmered in it all day, every day. He thought it might kill him. He even considered killing himself, but he decided, no, he would not give them the satisfaction of his death. He would kill *them* first.

Since Adwoa and Mr. Johnson believed that he was clueless, he saw no reason to let them think otherwise. He continued the charade that was their relationships, greeting Adwoa every morning as though they were still in love, being buddy-buddy and having drinks several nights a week with Mr. Johnson.

He planned to take care of Adwoa first. He remembered that article he'd read at the doctor's office, before his diagnosis. He now believed that it had been an omen, a sign of things to come.

One night, after some drinks at +233 with Mr. Johnson, he stopped at the Cantonments roundabout to speak with the whore who sometimes serviced him. He asked her to buy him several fentanyl tablets. He needed a powerful opioid. And with the influx of counterfeit pharmaceuticals from China and India, it was pretty much guaranteed that any drug purchased in Accra through unregulated sources was lethal.

The following evening, he stopped by the roundabout again to pick up the fentanyl. He went home and deposited a single tablet in Adwoa's bottle of hypertension medication.

Every evening that week, as they got ready for bed and Kwame watched his wife take her medication, he believed that the tablet she was swallowing could be the one that would end his suffering. He believed that while they slept, that tablet would make its fatal journey from Adwoa's stomach to her small intestine to her liver, which would immediately empty the chemical compound into her bloodstream, sending it to all her other organs, including her heart—her deceptive, ungrateful little heart.

The anticipation was so stress inducing, Kwame could hardly sleep. That whole week, he was a disheveled, bumbling wreck. He was racked with guilt, fear, satisfaction, anger, sorrow, and, more than anything else, sadness. Each morning she survived, it made him regret his decision to kill her even more. He didn't want to do it. It made him sad to think that his marriage, his perfect union, had come to this. But Adwoa had left him no choice.

The morning of his birthday, she'd not woken up easily. He shook her shoulder several times, greeted her loudly, and nothing. He started to cry. He was crying so hard, he looked like he was convulsing.

'What's wrong, sweetheart?' Adwoa asked. At first he thought he was hallucinating, but then she sat up, reached over, and started wiping the tears from his face.

This made him cry even harder. 'I'm sorry,' he wept. 'I'm so, so sorry.'

'You have nothing to be sorry for,' she said. 'We'll get through this. I love you.' She leaned over and kissed him on the lips. 'Happy birthday,' she sang.

'Kiss me again,' he insisted. She did. 'And again.' His love for her flushed out every other emotion he'd been feeling. What had gotten into him? She meant everything to him. What kind of life could he have without her? How could he ever face their children again? As soon as he was alone, he'd remove the fentanyl from her bottle of blood-pressure medication.

'I love you,' he told her. 'I love you more than anything.' And as he was telling her this, he felt himself becoming aroused. His doctor was right—what guides the pleasure of lovemaking is the love. There are ways to work around whatever is lacking.

'You might hear some commotion downstairs,' Adwoa told him as they were getting out of bed. 'I asked Mawusi to come this morning to prepare breakfast for us. I was up late last night organizing your gifts and making sure she has everything she needs.'

'You didn't have to do that.'

'I wanted to. It has been a difficult year for us. I know you've been having some challenges recovering from the surgery, and we're going to have to make some adjustments. But I am so grateful that you are alive and still with me. I thank God for your life, and I want us to celebrate it.'

He felt like a terrible human being, the worst on earth. He was so ashamed of himself and his selfishness. He turned and started walking toward the bathroom so that she couldn't see his tears. 'I'm going to have a shower. Will you join me? I'll say my thank-yous in there.'

'I'm right behind you,' she called out to him. 'I couldn't fall asleep last night so I took a sedative. I don't like mixing medications, so I didn't take my blood-pressure tablet. Just taking it now.' A pause. 'Here I come.'

He heard her footsteps. Then she stopped.

'I . . . I don't feel . . .' He heard her fall.

'Adwoa!' He ran into the bedroom and picked his wife up from the floor. He carried her in his arms and hurried down the stairs, screaming for Mawusi. When he got to the bottom, he saw Mr. Johnson, then he saw his parents, who lived all the way in Cape Coast. He saw his doctor and Ama Dadson and various other old friends.

'SURPRISE!!!' they yelled at him, blowing bazookas and throwing confetti in the air.

He stood there looking at them, all the people he loved most in the world, staring at him as he held his wife's limp body and listened to her breathing turn shallower and shallower.

A Double-Edged Inheritance

Hannah Giorgis

Meskerem didn't believe in fate.

Fate was one of those silly things her Orthodox aunties whispered about in their singsong voices, starry-eyed and full of desperate, ill-advised hope for something, anything. Fate was for people who had abandoned control, the last refuge of the weak and uninspired. Fate was for women who didn't know any better.

So when the call came from back home that the aunt who had named her—the great-aunt who shared her birthday— had died, she felt no grand cosmic realignment, only a churning grief, the kind that empties out your stomach and makes unseasoned mincemeat of its remains.

Almaz had loved Meskerem with a kind of uncommon, unreasonable fervor that bordered on desperation. From the moment she first learned of her youngest niece's pregnancy, the stern woman had softened her heart for the child no one else wanted. This child would be born into blame; this child would need protection.

The whole family had recoiled in performative horror as news of Tigist Negash's pregnancy snaked through their networks. Tigist, the youngest and brightest of seven girls, was the beacon on whom all their hopes had rested. She'd received the highest marks in her class at Kidane Mehret, a future engineer whose first semester at Addis Ababa University had been so impressive that her professors called her mother on several occasions to insist she consider sending Tigist abroad to continue her studies.

It was Tigist who had turned their offers down with a sudden, furious anger. The flash in her eyes was quiet, a lightning-fast break from the pools of warmth with which she normally saw the world. She didn't want to leave—Addis Ababa was home. What could exist beyond it? She hardly left Amist Kilo. Quiet and pious, Tigist spent all her time studying or following her *emaye*.

Until, of course, she met Robel.

Robel Girma smelled like whiskey and freshly printed birr. It was nauseating at first, his scent so strong it knocked Tigist off balance when their shoulders bumped against each other in Shiro Meda one early *kremt* day.

'*Yekirta, ehitey,*' he'd whispered through a crooked grin that sent her head spinning. He reached down to help her up, gold rings on three of his calloused fingers. '*Asamemkush? Be shai le'adenish?*'

She'd been shopping for *gabis* that morning, nervous about her first night in university housing. Her oldest sister had moved back home after her husband's disappearance, carrying two children with a bad back and a broken spirit. Tigist's room in their mother's house soon became the children's playground, their constant tugs at her *netela* a consistent interruption to her strict studying regimen. But still, she loved them. And so she planned to spend more time on campus, burrowed in the libraries. That would have to do.

Almaz was a literature professor at her niece's university, a stoic career woman who lived alone in an apartment tucked between Siddist Kilo and embassy row. Sharp and poetic, she prided herself on her pragmatism—even and especially when others told her she didn't behave like an Ethiopian woman should. Almaz wanted Tigist to take her professors' advice and leave; she didn't understand why a bright young girl would want to stay in Addis tending to her family when the world was calling. Almaz had never taken much interest in her nieces and nephews, but she found housing on campus for Tigist the moment she heard the girl insisted on staying in Addis Ababa.

'Don't thank me,' Almaz had said, less a demure platitude and more an agitated demand. 'Please, *ebakesh*, just meet people who do not live inside your books or your mother's house.'

Tigist had been thinking about her aunt's directive as she shopped for *gabis*, pressing them against her face. They smelled strange and dirty, unlike the *gabis* her mother had washed meticulously each season. None of them were soft enough; none of them felt like home.

When Robel Girma bumped into her, Tigist Negash stopped thinking of home.

Girma Woldemariam never wanted his son running around with some common girl in the first place.

Girma was the Ethiopian army's most respected general, and he had a reputation to uphold. Robel could spin lies to these college girls all he wanted, but the oldest Girma son did not have time for romance—and he certainly couldn't be seen walking around Siddist Kilo with his hands intertwined with some girl from a *balager* family no one could name. Robel had business to attend to: his final year of law school was coming to an end, and his father wanted him to spend more time accompanying him to work. His path had been forged for him, and all the ungrateful brat had to do was show up.

All he had to do was stay away from distractions.

When Tigist told Robel she felt sick, fingers fidgeting in her lap as she sat across a table from him at Enrico's, he joked that the cake must have gotten to her. She shouldn't have eaten it during *tsom* anyway, he insisted, before noticing a quick flash in her eyes.

'Are you sure?' he asked quietly, the words hanging in the thick air between them. He didn't bother repeating himself. He knew.

Girma smelled the fear on his son the moment Robel walked into his office the next morning.

'What did you do?' the general barked, pushing Robel into the carvings in the oak door that listed his military honors in Ge'ez.

Robel shrank, his voice cracking as he tried to relay the information. His head spinning, he explained how the girl had come to feel like home. He wanted to do this right, he insisted, eyes trained on the floor.

'I love her,' he whispered, his attention suddenly turned to the row of rifles hanging above his father's desk. They shone with a menacing gleam, crafted to be beautiful even in their violent precision. Robel gulped as the last word escaped his lips, a foolhardy attempt at pulling it back into himself.

Girma laughed, a throaty snarl that rose from the pit of his stomach. Spitting at his son's feet, he growled two words, each its own sentence: 'Fix. It.'

Turning to walk away from the trembling young man before him, the general mumbled something in Amharic through gritted teeth. Reeling from the encounter, Robel could hardly hear what escaped his father's lips, but he didn't need to.

'Or else I will.'

* * *

When Tigist woke up in Tikur Anbessa Hospital a week later, her nurse did not address her. Instead, she turned to Almaz, who was reading Baldwin with heavy eyelids in a wooden chair beside her niece's reclining bed.

'She's awake,' the nurse announced plainly, meeting neither the woman's eyes nor Tigist's. 'Maybe she'll talk now.'

Almaz had been sitting in the cold room with her niece for seventeen hours. Each second had felt longer than the last, but she didn't dare sleep. The thin girl lying in the bed looked more fragile than Almaz had ever seen her. She was gaunt, broken. With her body a maze of tubes and plaster, Tigist was lucky to be alive. The doctors had regarded Almaz with concerned eyes when they asked about her niece: Who would want to hurt someone so young, with eyes so warm? What could she have done to earn a beating reserved for prisoners of war?

'*Teseberech*,' Almaz heard herself telling Tigist's mother when she could finally access the phone in the hospital's graying lobby. 'She fell down the stairs on campus. I am here with her now. The doctors said not to worry.'

Before racing back toward Tigist's room, Almaz spun a toothless lie she knew her sister would not question until the girl recovered. 'She was racing to class. *Beka*, she missed a step and so she fell. That's all.'

'I'll pay for it,' she'd added before hanging up abruptly as she caught sight of the clock. Tigist might be awake now, and Almaz had no time to argue with the girl's mother over money she knew her sister did not have. Tigist needed her aunt; everything else could wait.

'Tigist? Can you hear me? Almaz *negn*,' she offered tentatively when the girl's eyes first opened. 'You . . . you fell, *lijey*. But you will be okay.'

The girl tried to move toward her aunt, but the IV yanked her back. Eyes bloodshot and filled with tears, she strained to move a bruised hand toward her stomach. Her breathing quickened, her body tensing. Turning her gaze downward, Tigist whispered: 'They can take me, but not my baby.'

She couldn't lose this baby, not to the swarm of uniformed men who'd descended upon her. She blinked back tears as images of their terrifying grins played themselves back on an infinite loop.

'*Babiye!*' she'd screamed as the first man pinned her arms back so another could kick her so viciously that she lost consciousness. The word came back to Tigist as a whisper now. '*Babiye.*'

Almaz sighed. 'Why didn't you tell me? We could've fixed it. This would never have happened.'

Almaz had known her niece was gallivanting around the city with some general's son. She'd warned the girl not to get too close. Powerful men were dangerous, their lust for dominion more potent than any love they might claim to feel for a woman. Powerful men enchanted easily, but their affections waned with all the grace of poison.

By the time Almaz saw the two of them together, waltzing around Shiro Meda in search of a second *gabi* for Robel's room, she knew it was too late. This boy, half teeth and half arrogance, had gotten under her niece's skin.

It did not matter to the girl that the boy's father was a man whom her aunt spoke of only in hushed tones. Almaz had called her that evening, whispering into a pay phone near Meskel Adebabay with fearful contempt: 'The only thing that boy's father loves more than his son is his power, Tigist. Do not stand in his way; you will be trampled.'

The memory of those words filled the space between Almaz and Tigist for hours, the silence punctuated only by the staccato beeps of the machines attached to the girl's body.

Robel had never defied his father before. Mischievous as he was, the boy had never transgressed beyond disobeying orders regarding his schoolwork or telling white lies about khat.

But when Robel ran up three flights of stairs at Tikur Anbessa and saw the girl he loved fighting for two lives Girma had tried to extinguish, his resolve ossified. He didn't want to walk in his father's footsteps if it meant this.

Breathless and full of youthful indignation, he laid his head in Tigist's lap as she slept. Terrified, Robel had waited behind the hospital until he saw Almaz leave. She'd stormed out of the hospital after Tigist had fallen asleep, presumably to tell her superiors at the university that she would not be teaching class the rest of the week.

In Almaz's absence, Robel cried thick, heavy tears into Tigist's lap. He pressed his head against her stomach, praying for some sign of life as he knelt against the edge of her bed. The girl looked gray now, her skin purple in places where he'd once worshipped its brown richness.

His face a gnarled mess of tears and shame, Robel did not move when he heard Almaz's footsteps approach. He knew she would be enraged at the sight of him. He knew she had a right to be. Still, even the jolt of her heel nearly puncturing his thigh could not match the blunt force of the words Almaz flung at him upon seeing that he'd sneaked his way into Tigist's room.

'How dare you touch her? Her blood is on your hands already!' the woman heaved at him as the girl lay sleeping. 'The best thing you can do for her is forget about her. May you and your father carry the shame of your sin until Satan calls you both home!'

Robel whimpered. Wiping tears from his face with scratched, ashen hands, he made a simple plea: 'Let me fix it. Let me keep her safe. I will sacrifice my happiness to keep her alive.'

When Tigist landed in Washington, DC, she asked the first Ethiopian cabdriver she saw if she could use his cell phone to call Almaz.

The rest of the family had stopped speaking to her, content to pretend the foolish pregnant girl now leaving for America had never existed at all. The days preceding Tigist's flight all seemed like a blur now. Only one thing stood out to her amid the dizzying sequence of packing, pain medication, and rushed goodbyes: Robel had never called.

Dialing Almaz's number as the cabdriver smiled at her for two seconds too long, Tigist wished more than anything that she could apply her family's miraculous power of memory erasure to Robel. If it weren't for Robel, she wouldn't be standing here alone, cold and vulnerable. If it weren't Robel, she would still be home.

When her daughter was born months later, Tigist again called Almaz. 'She came early,' Tigist said simply, looking down at the child whose eyes already mirrored her own.

The baby had not been due for another four weeks, but Almaz smiled when she got the call in the late-night hours of September 11. *'Meskerem ahnd, ende!'* she'd laughed. *'Ye Meskerem lij naht,'* she mused before the line disconnected. *'Ye Meskerem lij.'*

Exhausted and alone, Tigist resolved then that she'd never tell this dangerous miracle of a child about her father. *Girls are already born into a world of heartbreak,* Tigist reflected. *It's best not to saddle this new life, this new year, with details of the pain that runs through her blood.*

* * *

Meskerem was a brilliant, preternaturally insightful child. As a result of her mother's sacrifices and her great-aunt's blessings, she grew up with the two women raising her from opposite sides of the Atlantic. Their love buoyed her through childhood and adolescence, their faith in her a guiding light.

Meskerem didn't learn that her great-aunt shared her birthday until her sophomore year of college. Tasked with writing about a woman who inspired her, Tigist's only child chose to call Almaz, the woman who had carried them both. Almaz comforted Meskerem when the girl asked why God had let her mother die alone in a car accident while she had been away taking classes earlier that year. Almaz told Meskerem story after story of Tigist's engineering brilliance and the family's hopes for her education. Their calls lasted hours, each one longer than the last. Meskerem delighted in learning more about her family, even if her great-aunt had no answers about the death of her father. It was the only balm she had, the only time she didn't feel alone.

Talking to Almaz made things make sense for the first time in Meskerem's life. The quiet, sullen young woman smiled a little easier. She walked into class feeling more excited than bored. Still, when all her classmates spoke passionately about their aspirations to embody the spirits of women like Eleanor Roosevelt and Susan B. Anthony, Meskerem suppressed the urge to laugh. She had learned of bravery and brilliance that made these women pale in comparison, and she couldn't wait to overshadow their foolhardy presentations.

Standing in the front of the lecture hall wearing only black, except for the yellow Meskel flower pin attached to her combat boots, Meskerem presented the details of her research: a woman named Almaz Gessesse had been born into a poor family in Addis Ababa and became a prominent literature professor; a woman named Almaz Gessesse had found a way for Meskerem's mother to come to America after her husband had died mysteriously (in the war?); a woman named Almaz Gessesse had come all the way to America to hold her after her mother died in a car accident; a woman named Almaz Gessesse had named her after the month in which they were both born.

Meskerem was working on her doctoral thesis when the news came of Almaz's death several years later. Exhausted and angry, she'd yelled at her boyfriend for waking her from a much-needed nap just to answer a phone call.

She saw the *+251* pop up on her Viber app and immediately sat up in bed, her whole body an electrical current. Why would someone whose number she didn't have be calling from Ethiopia? She hadn't been back in years—she only spoke to Almaz.

A solemn voice asked for Meskerem Negash, then said simply, 'Almaz is gone.'

The last time Meskerem had been in Addis Ababa, she'd stayed with Almaz the whole summer. She was young then, a voracious reader about to start high school. She spent weeks cooped up in Almaz's small apartment near Addis Ababa University, reading Baldwin and Fitzgerald and the Brontës. She'd accompanied Almaz to campus and sat in the back of the classroom while the professor taught, eagerly absorbing new phrases in Amharic. After class, Meskerem would beg Almaz to quiz her on the material she'd learned.

The two of them walked through Shiro Meda together for hours, buying whatever they pleased. It had been their first destination the morning after Meskerem's first night in Almaz's apartment, when the visiting child had woken up shivering. Almaz had laughed at the American girl for being so cold in such light *kremt*. 'Isn't it freezing in your country?' she'd joked before suggesting the two take a trip to the market to grab another *gabi*. Meskerem had never been so excited to shop.

The chaos of Shiro Meda calmed Meskerem in a way she couldn't explain, even to Almaz. She wanted to lose herself in its alleyways, let herself become anonymous amid a sea of people focused on anything but her. The road felt endless to her, the paths themselves as plentiful as the bounty sold there.

Yet during this trip, Shiro Meda felt like a cage. Even as the sun shone on her shoulders, Meskerem felt cold. She'd walked from Almaz's apartment all the way to Shiro Meda in search of a distraction from the upcoming funeral processions, headphones in her ears. This place wasn't home without Almaz. When she finally reached the market, she was horrified. Where was the charm she'd romanticized all these years? Before she'd seen freedom and excitement, whereas now she saw only the bleak repetition of commerce. Vendors seemed sinister, shoppers selfish to the point of revulsion.

Meskerem walked toward the first seller whose makeshift booth held a selection of *gabis*. Dust and sun in her face, she tried to force a smile on her face when she made eye contact with the vendor. He stared back at her with a mixture of pity and irritation.

'What do you want?' he asked roughly as she stood silent in front of his display. She walked away, unsure if he'd even been asking about merchandise.

With Almaz's favorite songs blaring in her headphones, Meskerem was the last person to notice the general approaching. Shiro Meda had slowed from its usual frenetic pace, shopkeepers and tourists alike pausing to marvel at the tall man with the stunning smile.

'General Girma!' a child squeaked as he raised his hand in salute, running into the middle of the road. His mother scooped him out of the way moments later, and the general looked straight through them both.

General Robel Girma had not been to Shiro Meda in years. Shiro Meda was for poor tourists and even poorer locals, he'd told his son Elias. But today was different. Today he had learned of Almaz Gessesse's death. Today he was thinking of Tigist. Eyes fighting back tears behind his reflective aviators, the general walked down the road with determination.

When all 6'1' of him barreled into a young woman and sent her careening onto the ground, the general didn't apologize. He was not a man who apologized. He simply adjusted his sunglasses and kept walking.

But the girl caught up to him a moment later, pushing his shoulder from behind. The shock prompted him to remove his sunglasses as he spun around to face her, forgetting for a moment that his eyes betrayed the very anguish that had brought him to Shiro Meda that day.

Meskerem opened her mouth to chastise the gruff man who'd knocked into her. She didn't care that he was in uniform. She did not owe some soldier her loyalty; she certainly did not owe him the skin on her knees. He turned to face her, and she was certain in the split second between her push and his pivot that he would hit her.

Robel did not hit the girl who'd pushed him. He grabbed her face with his calloused hand, rings imprinting themselves into her cheek, the second he saw her eyes. They were warm, sad. They went on for days.

They looked so familiar.

* * *

The next time Meskerem went to Shiro Meda, she needed gifts to send back to America.

She'd promised her boyfriend she would return after taking care of Almaz's funeral, but weeks later the thought of leaving her great-aunt's flat caused her anguish. She could hear the irritation bubbling up in John's voice every time he asked why her trip had been extended a week, and then another week, and then another. She missed him, but John would have to wait. She hoped a set of paintings from back home, maybe some jewelry or a *netela* for his mother, would help ease his anxieties. Day after day she went to Shiro Meda, telling herself she'd keep going until she found the perfect gifts to make up for her absence.

Most days, Meskerem just walked to the market. Passing the campus where her mother had studied and her great-aunt had taught became a soothing ritual, a way to bide the time while she delayed her trip back to America. Each day, new people greeted her along the road, but it was the familiar faces who punctuated her path. When she walked past the embassies, important-looking men took stock of her all-black attire and asked who she'd lost. She didn't know where to start, so she'd laugh and tell them, 'No one.'

One morning, Meskerem sacrificed this curious anonymity for something even more peculiar: a sense of direction The general came to pick her up in his truck, having promised to steer her toward the things she needed to see. In the weeks leading up to Genna, the market was even more busy than usual. Diaspora returnees with stories less tragic than Meskerem's flooded its streets with their fast-paced strutting and their embarrassing Amharigna. A group of them gawked at her as she hopped out of a military truck they'd only seen in movies. Shopkeepers stared as she stood next to the man who'd been driving: she was General Robel Girma's daughter, and she was no longer a secret.

Chickens ran around her ankles, and Meskerem laughed. This wasn't quite home, but it was something like it. The general (she couldn't bring herself to call him 'Dad,' not after all these years) picked out some housewares and 'manly' art for John ('*Habesha aydelem?*' he asked, raising his eyebrows. Meskerem raised hers back; the general wasn't allowed to ask those questions yet). He insisted on paying for the gifts then and later for pastries from

Enrico's, and Meskerem protested only once in the grateful, facetious way all Ethiopian children do. Meskerem walked back into Almaz's apartment that afternoon feeling lighter. She placed John's gifts in a drawer near Almaz's bed, taking care not to upset the balance of the dresser's contents. She wanted to leave before Genna, she decided. She'd already missed Christmas with John in the US, and the prospect of bypassing the awkwardness of the Ethiopian holiday by going back to the States seemed perfect. The general was friendly, but he was not yet family. Leaving would be for the best. It would be like Christmas had never come at all.

She nodded to herself, pacing around the bedroom after grabbing her laptop. Yes, this was right. She would head to the nearest Internet café and buy her ticket now before having dinner at the general's home. It would be easier that way, to let go of all the pleasantries at once. There would be no fight over how long she should stay, no obligatory suggestions that she and his other children get to know each other.

Meskerem had settled into the kitchen easily, cooking herself *shiro* and *kik alicha* almost nightly. The bedroom had taken longer; for the first four nights, she'd slept on the loveseat in the living room. When her neck protested violently, she conceded, eventually rummaging through Almaz's closet in search of the outfits that most reminded her of the woman whose spirit still moved through the space. But it had taken weeks for Meskerem to let herself open the door to Almaz's office—the space felt sacred, like the source of her brilliance. She knew it was the space her great-aunt had cherished most.

Meskerem opened the door slowly, like she might still be caught. She walked to the bookshelf instinctively, hands grazing the spines of the books she'd read here as a teenager and the many that had been added in the time since. Pausing to sit at Almaz's desk for a moment and let the scent of their pages wash over her, Meskerem noticed a thick piece of paper sticking out of the same Baldwin novel Almaz read every year. Almaz had treated *Giovanni's Room* with more tenderness than she treated most humans; Meskerem knew she would never shove a random paper into its pages so carelessly.

Pulling it out slowly, Meskerem braced herself for what she immediately sensed would be something she shouldn't see: *WE WILL FIND HER THERE. WE WILL FINISH WHAT WE STARTED.*

Meskerem stared at the thick, torn sheet. She turned it over, searching for any sign of its origin. The script itself was nondescript, the English letters resembling *fidel* in the way every Ethiopian's handwriting did. Sighing to herself and unsure of what to do, she stuffed the sheet into her pocket and ran out the door.

The general lived in a massive house near the American embassy, the kind that dwarfed all buildings in its immediate area, not for practicality, but to make a statement. When she was younger, Meskerem had walked past these houses and scoffed at the arrogance of the people she'd imagined living inside their walls. What kind of people built monuments to their own grandeur?

Meskerem had been uncertain what to wear for dinner, but she knew nothing she'd packed was right. She had no intention of wearing any color other than black, so she settled for the same black jeans she'd worn earlier that day at Shiro Meda. They still smelled of dust, chickens, and children. She grabbed a top from Almaz's closet, a blouse she'd always loved. It still smelled of Almaz's perfume. Dior.

The family was pleasant enough. The general's wife didn't seem to have a name or many original thoughts. His son, Elias, stared at her from across the table, asking repeatedly why she didn't play video games. He did not call her 'Sister,' and for that she was eternally grateful.

When the house staff cleared up after dessert and the general's wife retired to her parlor, Meskerem asked to see her father's office.

The two walked the two-kilometer path talking mostly about why she still smelled of the market. She may not have been ready to call him 'Father' yet, he insisted, but surely she could at least try to act like a general's daughter. The thought bothered her, but Meskerem tried to laugh anyway. The sound of her ambivalent chuckle reverberated off the trees lining the road.

'I think John will really like the *jebena*,' she offered. 'I don't make coffee, but he loves it. I told him about it before I came to dinner, and he sounded so happy,' she said, unsure of what compelled her to add a lie.

The general was pleased to hear his suggestion would be adored, even if it was by a man he'd never met. He reveled in the feeling of being needed somehow. When he opened the door to his office, he offered Meskerem some whiskey. Turning away from her for a moment, he walked toward his desk to pour from the decanter he saved for special guests.

'Usually this is for diplomats. Or colonels. Sometimes kings even,' he said, back still turned. Meskerem stared at him in this environment, suddenly struck by how harsh his consonants sounded when they echoed among all the oak. The door was so heavy, the chairs so tall. She didn't belong here.

As the general moved toward her, Meskerem slipped her hand in the pocket of her jeans and pulled out the piece of paper.

'Do . . . do you know what this means?' she stammered, shoving the sheet toward his face, filled with rage.

The force of her movement caught him off balance, and he fell to the floor. His glass crashed down with him, shards embedding into his palm as the whiskey mixed with his blood. Meskerem screamed at the sight of the blood, then started to crouch toward him until she saw the look in his eyes.

He knew. He had to know. He'd known all this time, and he'd never called after her. He'd known all this time, and he'd never stopped any of it.

Pressing down on his palm to extract the glass, Robel started to choke on his own words. They came tumbling out rapidly, his heaves interspersed with thick tears that only served to intensify Meskerem's anger. She hovered above him as the general told her everything, her body shaking. Robel's blood seeped into the paper as he spoke of his father's threats, and she snatched the sheet out of his hand. Turning toward the door, she noticed Girma's name carved into the oak frame. This had been his office too. This is where he had made the decision. This is where her mother's life had been wagered. She knew then that they could never coexist, that the general had a debt to pay.

Robel tried to steady himself and stand again, calling after her. '*Babiye*,' he whimpered, stumbling as he rested one palm against the desk where his father had drawn up the plans to have Tigist killed.

'*Babiye*,' he repeated, finally resting his weight against the desk where he'd begged for her life to be spared, for the baby to live.

'*Benatish*,' he whispered, stretching the bloody palm out to touch her shoulder.

She turned to face him quickly, her body moving with an untrained agility more frightening than his own.

Meskerem's eyes were the last thing Robel saw before she reached the last rifle Girma had left him. They were warm, sad.

They looked so familiar.

Five Years Next Sunday

Idza Luhumyo

My locs are just shy of five years. They flow, like water. They are fluffy and black. They are dark. I forbid anyone to touch them. I use a black scarf to cover them. And how they coil, and how heavy they are, weighing me down with the expectations of my quarter. We are in the fourth year without rain. A sack of maize is gold. Water is divine. Here is a lesson we have learned: there is thirst and then there is thirst. And believe me when I tell you that we don't remember it, a time when we did not know such thirst, such dryness inside our mouths.

It is an afternoon when Neema calls me to her side and hands me two hundred shillings for the ten-litre jerrican of DWL water. 'Go to Jumaa's shop,' she says. 'His prices are better.' As security – 'You never know,' Neema says – she sends my brothers to the shop with me. They are to flank me, like bodyguards. We walk in silence, having never exchanged more than a few sentences in our lives. They don't even use the cups I use, these brothers-mine, not even the house slippers I wear. When we get to Jumaa's shop, I stand under the awning and wait my turn. My brothers fall back, mock-fighting each other, sniggering, doing whatever it is teenage boys do when they are caught between too much time and too little space. Then one of the coins I have in my hands falls. I bend to pick it up. My scarf falls to the ground. My hair is out. There is a gasp, not mine. When I stand straight, he has my scarf in his hands, and his mouth is open. A white man. Stocky, sunken eyes; something parched about him. And not the thirst we all have, having known no rain in the past three years. Something neglected, something dry and dead, as if from childhood. What in him needs watering?

'Your hair,' he says. 'Beautiful.'

He reaches out to touch. He stops short when he sees the hard glare in my eyes. 'I'm sorry,' he stammers. Everybody knows it, he is Zubeda's mzungu. What business does he have going around touching people's hair? Out of nowhere, Zubeda herself emerges. Her eyes on me are daggers. She pulls him away. Mzungu wangu, the eyes say. Jumaa, the shopkeeper, laughs and laughs. 'You've confused mzungu wa wenyewe jamani,' he says to me. I don't laugh. The white man has gone with my scarf. Open to the world, my hair is heavy.

The next day, he is at my father's door, the white man. I smell him before I see him, my eyes peeping through the grille of my bedroom window. My brother, the younger twin, goes to call my father. And then: 'Pili,' my father calls out. I shuffle to the sitting room. The man is seated on the couch. Still, that parched look about him, as if something is empty inside him, as if he is looking for anything – *anything* – to fill him up. His eyes are still on my head.

'I brought your scarf,' he says.

I look at him.

Baba speaks for me. 'Thank you,' he says.

A large smile on Baba's mouth. Not once has he ever smiled at me in that way, sat me on his lap, eased and teased me out of a cry. But now? A wonder. And then Neema. Hearing about it later, after the white man has left, his eyes still on my hair and my father's eternal laugh still clinging to the air, she will walk into my room, smiling, saying: 'I hear you have a new friend.' I will say nothing. In my head, I will hum the shock, and then the joy. How is it possible that she who has avoided me all my life is in my room, on my bed, talking to me about this hair that she fears so much? For years, she has not allowed me to call her mother. 'Call me by name,' she says to me, when I forget and call her Ma, as my brothers do. She has never forgiven me for choosing to become a caller, for growing the rain in my hair. So Neema I say, whenever I want to catch her attention. But today, a different song. She is smiling. She is calling me her kichuna. She is touching my hair, gently pulling at the scarf, saying: 'Maybe you should stop wearing those scarves on your head.' The shock, yes, but the joy. Ma, I want to say over and over and over again. That smile she gives me; I don't want to lose it. So I promise to do it, just so I can look at her as my brothers do and say Ma.

About a week later, I come from the market and he is there again. My father and brothers are in the sitting room with him. All of them – they giggle, they laugh. In the kitchen, Ma is busy. The smell of garlic and ginger and dawa ya pilau sizzling in oil. Lemons. It is not Christmas but haki-ya-nani, isn't this Christmas pilau? Tena complete with the pilipili ya kukaanga? Passion juice freshly squeezed. On the kitchen floor, the bales of maize flour and wheat flour, the jerricans of Pwani Oil, the packet after packet of Mumias Sugar. She sees me and smiles, then frowns. She tugs at the scarf on my head.

'I thought we understood each other,' she says. 'Go remove it.'

He doesn't take his eyes off the hair the entire time. He says his name is Seth. I don't believe him. He looks nothing like a Seth. He is not alone. Next to him is someone who shares the colour of his skin, her eyes the saddest things I ever saw. She sits next to him like a child admonished, a little girl asked not to squirm, to sit still and not make a nuisance of herself. Everyone seems to be having a grand time. Except me and her. She has a thin red line for a lower lip, a defiant forehead, and eyes that seem to be pleading for anything (or everything?). We sit through my parents' laughter and my brothers' sniggering and the silent eating of the pilau served in my mother's Christmas utensils. The TV is on. My father talks about the three-year drought. Shakes his head. Blames the government. The white man grunts to my father's monologue, eyes on me. Later, they leave

the sitting room to us, Ma leading the woman away. Her name
is Honey. Ma laughs, says: 'Honey, what a name.' When they
leave, Seth and I sit in silence. He is a strange man. Something
thirsty about him.

'I have to say again,' he starts. 'You have such beautiful hair.'

'Thank you,' I say, my mind thinking about honey, how it
sticks, how it never goes bad, how it … tastes.

He cannot stop touching the hair. Sniffing it. The sacks of food
to my parents, they keep coming and coming. Then my parents
have an idea. They pull Seth aside, speak to him for hours.
Money changes hands. Soon, my parents open a shop at the
front of the house. They put Jumaa out of business.

'There is no need for rain,' they say. 'No need for you to cut
that hair.'

They smile. Ma smiles longest, strokes my hair. 'Our blessing,'
she whispers.

They become plump, my parents; they struggle to walk.
Months pass. My hair gets closer to the five-year mark. The
drought thickens. Seth leaves Zubeda, settles into being with
me. When he talks about my hair, stroking it, there is a choke
in his voice. Business for my parents is booming. The money is
coming in fast. They put the other shopkeepers in the quarter
out of business. They bless the drought. They call me to their
side.

'No need for rain,' they say.

My brothers, they nod, agreeing. Now they speak to me,
telling me about their lives, their exploits in school, their antics.
When they stop attending classes at Mombasa Aviation, no
one admonishes them. There is money in the family business.
Seth's name becomes hallowed. My hair is a small god.

There are cars parked outside the house. My parents dig a
well, install a pump, sell the water in twenty-litre jerricans at
absurd prices. Sometimes thirty times the price. Sometimes

fifty. My brothers, they start drawing up the plans for shops two, three, and four. My parents put something away for my brothers' dowries. Ma starts to read books. To buy lifestyle magazines. Sunday afternoons she spends at Mombasa Resort, stretching out on a beach chair, now staring at the ocean, now with cucumbers on her eyes. They start to spend time at the sports club, attending piano recitals and plays. My father gets a subscription for *Newsweek*, the *Times*, *Reader's Digest*. They think about buying the Swahili house next door. They will knock it down, put up something to go with their new personalities. They talk about the new house. It is right there in their minds, clear, concrete. There is so much culture in it: a record player emits New Orleans blues; potted plants jostle for sunlight by windowsills; heavy mauve velvet curtains block the light outside; large paintings draw their guests' attention from the white coral stone walls; Persian carpets drink in the sounds of dailyness; the cypress furniture matches the deep brown of the mvule wood in the ceiling; the windows go from ceiling to floor; and the kitchen, glory of glories, opens out to a vibrant colourful garden, complete with a small pond, where the ducks – not meant to be eaten, mind you – mind their business and sway their lives away.

I turn twenty-three. Only a couple of weeks to the five-year mark. Ma is anxious, asking me at least twice a day: 'No need for rain, sio?' Soon, we will be entering the fifth year without rain. On Citizen TV, the experts from Israel are talking about how their own country is a desert, but look what they have done. My father smiles at me. His smile is a wink. 'No need for rain,' he mouths. It has become his song. He laughs. I laugh with him, calm him, reassure him.

Seth rents an apartment by the beach. Sometimes, to switch things up a little, we go to hotel rooms. He has money. He has whims. And yet, he looks like he is stuck, waiting on something.

Night after night, he hangs his torso across the balcony rail, holding an unlit cigarette in his hand. He stares at the water.

'Your parents think I am just another mzungu,' he says one night.

'No, they like you,' I say.

'They don't like me,' he says. Then turns to me with a smile, hard. 'They like my money.'

'But I like you,' I say.

'No,' he responds. 'You like Honey.' Then he walks away.

He has friends. They are loud. They stare. They ask whether it is okay to reach out, touch my hair. It is just hair. And yet, 'I have never seen such hair,' is what they say. 'It's so ... natural,' they say. 'Real.'

They shudder. They are almost always men. But sometimes, there are women too. No, not women. A woman. Honey. Of course, it is not her real name. None of them, including Seth, use their real names.

She has anxious eyes, Honey, a sweet smile, and a wild pretty heart caught up in a lost cause. On the wrong continent. I feel like I could like her and still keep my wits about me. I catch her staring at me. When our eyes meet, we laugh. We've been looking at each other all night. She is from Belgium by way of Iran, she says, when we finally start talking. 'Same as Seth,' she says. I cannot locate Iran on a map. I don't believe her. Still, I forgive the lie. There is something about her that calls out to me, some sadness, some grittiness, some stoicism in the thick of things. She looks like she has seen the other side of the world, seen it inside-out, or outside-in, and, for that reason, has come to expect very little from it.

And yet.

That unguarded softness, as if she would yield to the slightest tenderness, to the first person who walked up to her and asked her real name, asked how she was doing, yaani, *really doing*. I want to scoop her up and save her. She keeps staring at me. I am unable to look away.

Another night. Honey pulls me away from the party of laughing men and asks whether I smoke. I shake my head, say no. Still, I accompany her outside.

'They are all obsessed with that hair,' she says. Flicks the cigarette ash, takes a drag. 'You must be tired of it.'

I smile, say nothing.

'Have you ever thought of cutting it, selling it?' she says.

I scowl. 'Sell my hair? Why?'

She catches the scorn, bounces it back to me with a scowl of her own, followed by a shake of her head.

'You African women wear our hair all the time,' she says. 'Do you ever see us surprised?'

I finally get it. She is in love with Seth. Beyond herself. And so out of jealousy, or that perverse need to maim that which one loves, I say: 'I don't even love him, you know?'

She looks at me long, hard. She frowns, takes a drag of her cigarette. It's the first time I have seen pure calm rage. Then she says: 'Of course you don't. Do you think wazungu are stupid?' She is tapping her head as she says this. 'That we don't know it's all about the money?'

Her eyes are ablaze. But I know defeated anger when I see it. I play my cards as I want, hurt her as deep as I can. 'Even if I were to leave him,' I say, 'he still will not come to you.'

'We both know it's that stupid hair,' she says.

She grinds the cigarette butt with the soles of her feet. She is barefoot.

Love burns.

Another party. She stares at me all night, so I follow her outside when she steps out to the balcony. She smokes the first cigarette in silence. She offers one to me. I take it. She is different today, tender.

'What happens when you cut it?' she asks.

'Honey, why are you so obsessed with my hair?'

'Because he loves it.'

'Will you love anything he loves?'

'Stop changing the subject. Tell me what happens when you cut it.'

'You will not believe me,' I say.

'Try me.'

Here is what will happen, I want to say to her. It will rain, like it never has before. There will be anger. And even though the fear of thirst – and death – is strong, the fear of those who have the rain in their hair is stronger. So the men will come to me as soon as someone alerts them. It will probably be the twins who do it. The men will hold torches of fire in their hands. They will strip me of the colour, the red and the black and the white in the kisutu my sangazimi left behind; then the red studs I wear on the lobes of my ears; and even the blue slippers I will have on. I will be barefoot in my banishment. They will wrap me in black cotton cloth, dyed the night before, the black barely clinging to the fabric. It will work. I will feel so black inside. Bleak. My parents and siblings, they will stay in the shadows and watch me jump over the fire. The fire will be the test, the exam. There are two worlds, the men will say, during the speech before the fire. The world to the right of the flames, and then the world to the left of the flames. Safety is in these worlds. My parents, my siblings, the men – they will stay at the edges and watch. I will take my time. Then I will jump and fall right into the fire. From the edges will come the sounds of righteous vindication: my father's yelp, my siblings' clapping, the men's stamping of feet. My mother will be quiet. Someone will scoop me up like a baby, ready to banish me to the quarter of witches, where all women who have the rain are sent. Someone else will begin the chant. And when I say everyone will join in the chant of mtsai, mtsai, mtsai –everyone including my mother and my father and my brothers – believe me.

But I don't say all that to Honey.

'Rain,' I say instead. 'It will rain.'

'Oh. So you are one of those women, the callers?' Honey says.

The expression on her face, something has come home to roost.

'Yes,' I say, guarded.

'I've heard of them,' she says, moving closer to me. 'Who did you get it from?'

'My father's sister,' I say. 'My sangazimi.'

She is standing close, maybe too close, to me. She smokes in silence for a while, staring intently into my eyes. They are so intense, her eyes. Urgent, with the franticness of quick calculations. Her hair is a pixie cut, the bangs falling over her eyes. She has a round face. Her dimples are something difficult to forget. When she smiles at me, I feel rewarded. She lights a second cigarette. She says: 'How old is your hair?'

'Five years next Sunday,' I answer.

'You mean this coming Sunday?'

'Yes.'

'So you are ready, ripe?'

'Yes.'

'Will you do it?'

'My family says there is no need.'

'But it has not rained for years.'

'Yes.'

'You owe it to your quarter.'

'Maybe. I'd have done it. But my family likes me now.'

'Have they never loved you?'

'Not quite. It's the hair. They feared it.'

We fall quiet. Honey smokes another cigarette. Then another one. I watch her pull in with her mouth, then sigh out the rings of smoke.

'I don't love him, you know,' she says, after another stretch of silence. She is talking as if she has resolved something in her head. 'It's just, he is like an addiction. There are people like that. Addictions. You don't ever forget them, unless someone else comes along to undo the spell.'

We go quiet for a long time. A long time.

Then I say *fuck it,* and I break the silence. 'Has someone come along?' I ask. 'To undo the spell.'

She smiles, Honey. 'Yes,' she says. 'And she has the most amazing hair.'

I smile.

'Just hair?'

'No, not just the hair,' she says. Then she smiles again and says: 'She is also a caller. Says she got it from her sangazimi.'

I smile back at her. We stare at each other. The smoke from the cigarette, it rises to the sky, which is where I think our hearts are. In love, sky-high.

Sunday.

If you can imagine the buzz of bees, incessant, then you know how the men sound. They are everywhere, the white men: on the couch, standing by the window, even on Seth's treasured writing desk. There are two men on the carpet, their palms cupping whisky glasses. The men have a wet and icy look in their eyes, that shimmer that comes after a gulp of one or two servings of good whisky. Seth has the best stuff. Smooth, like a problem easing away. He has a smile on his face when I get in. I shut the door behind me, shuffle out of my slippers. He gets up, comes up to me. Then Honey emerges from the kitchen. I stare at her, but she won't look at me. Her lipstick, red, is smeared at the edges. As if she has been fighting something, or someone, with her mouth.

'Hey,' she mutters in my direction. Then a frown, as she makes her way to the couch. I nod at her and sit on the couch with Seth. He pulls me up, sets me on his lap. He hands me a glass of whisky. We drink in silence. I can feel the eyes of the men on me, on my hair. The air is loaded with the heaviness of something unsaid.

Honey is stretched out on one of the sofas. She is staring at us. Then she gets up and comes to where I am. 'Come,' she tells me. 'I want to show you something.'

We walk down the hallway and stop at an abstract painting suffused with various hues of blue. Before I can wrap my head around all the colour, Honey lifts the painting and pushes the wall. It is a secret door, opening into a large room with white walls. And black skin.

'Seth likes the walls white,' Honey says. 'He thinks it's the perfect backdrop for the display of black skin.'

There is something soft in how she talks about Seth, something like how mothers talk about the errant ways of their spoiled children.

And how much skin there is. Acres of it. The women on the wall are all black, African. And they all have dreadlocks. There I am, with an entire corner wall to myself, as I have never seen myself before. Most of the photos have been taken surreptitiously; this is the first time I am seeing them. The hair is the focus. I can almost feel the camera walk all over for me. There is no part of my body that is not there. But the hair, my coils, they dominate everything. I stare at the wall in silence. Stunned.

'You see?' Honey says, the tenderness from that night back in her voice. 'He only loves the hair, not you.'

'I know that,' I say.

'Then cut it. He will lose interest when you do. Then we can be together.'

'But my family...' I start.

'No,' Honey says. She moves closer to me. Her hands on my shoulders are fire. We are already so close to each other but I want to move closer, to bridge whatever distance is between us: two women from different parts of the world yearning for things that we are yet to name, to baptise. 'I have money. Your parents will not care which mzungu gives them the money. I'll keep them happy, okay?'

I stare at her.

'Okay?' she asks again. Her hand is now on my cheek. Her gaze is intense, scorching. I look away, but her hand on my cheek gently draws me back. 'Trust me, okay?' she says. 'Cut it and everybody wins.'

I do it, right there in Seth's house. I go to the kitchen, I rub the edges of two knives against each other, I put the edge of a knife to my coils. Honey sticks around until I am halfway through. She keeps looking outside, reporting on the gathering of the clouds, the darkening of the day, the flight of the birds. 'Rain is coming,' she whispers. 'Keep going.' She leaves the kitchen before I am done. She will wait for me in the living room with the others, she says. 'So that it doesn't look like it was my idea.'

There is only one word to describe the sound of rain after five years: magical. I am lighter. My soul, my head, even my voice. I can feel the wind on my scalp. But the anger, I can feel it too. Somebody will tip the men. They will come, torches of fire in their hands, looking for the one with rain in her hair. They did it to my sangazimi and her sangazimi before that. But I will have Honey. I will get to her before they get here. And then we will run away together.

I cut the last coil. Outside, thunder, then rain. I walk out of the kitchen. I walk into the living room. It is empty. No Seth. No Honey. No men. Outside, the rain keeps falling. I call out Honey's name. My voice is a plea answered by an echoing silence. The rain outside is deafening. Then the lights go off. I switch on the torch on my phone. I go to the main door, open it. And that's when I see them. I count five men. They are holding torches of fire, chanting mtsai, mtsai, mtsai. Then I see something – someone? – moving behind them, gliding away, like a snake. The pixie cut is unmistakable. In one of her hands, the coils of hair, coiling and coiling and coiling.

The Labadi Sunshine Bar

Billie McTernan

The Labadi bɔɔla collectors drive around town from as early as four or five a.m. during the week, bandannas covering their noses and mouths, barely keeping the smell of days-old bean stew from being caught in the back of their throats. Their tinny music rings from the wagon, piercing through the area, attracting customers, an alarm for those who have yet to rise and begin their day. As the minitruck circles around, residents, like dutiful ants, scuttle to the roadside to hail the crew with bags of refuse. After a few hours the truck is full. Often the driver dumps the waste at a landfill site on Mortuary Road, close to the Korle Lagoon. Everything from fridges and mattresses to car parts and cholera can be found in it. After paying a fee to the minders of the landfill, they drive off. And as one job ends, another begins. The salvagers take charge of the refuse. They wade through the junk to make sure there is nothing of value left to rot away, then set the junk alight; flames burn through the rot, licking the stench-filled air around them.

It's not uncommon to find dead bodies there: men and women, young and old, surface. The blowflies and maggots always find them first, crawling around lips and poking out of nostrils. The salvagers groan, hand on head. What happened to these people for their bodies to have ended up in this fill? Bankruptcy? Divorce? Depression? Betrayal? A makeshift burial is given, a short prayer spoken: *In life, in death, O Lord, abide with me.*

But they end it there. No need to get the authorities involved. After all, no one wants to be suspected of a crime they didn't commit.

When Priscilla arrived in Circle, along with all the other travelers venturing into the city, Accra became real. It was loud and obnoxious with cars, commuters, and hawkers vying for space. As the passengers from across the country poured out into the bus station from vehicles big and small, layers of the city's stress settled onto their skin.

Before leaving Aflao, the busy border town between Ghana and Togo, some of the girls had advised Priscilla to look for work in Labadi.

'Osu busy o. Dey get plenty Liberian girls for there,' Gifty said, gnawing on a chewing stick. 'Dem fill de place.'

'Abeg no go East Legon. Too much police wahala,' Yomi added.

'Labadi town dey between Osu and Labadi beach,' Gifty continued. She spat out wooden splinters from her chewing stick. 'You go still find obroni for dat place.'

By way of Ghanaian beaches, Labadi is fairly unremarkable. In fact, it was quite dirty, the ocean gray with accumulated filth. Priscilla was directed to Madam Joanna, one of those older women with a perpetual *I am not amused* face, the mouth poised ever ready with a quip should you step out of line. Her darkened knuckles were a telltale sign of regular skin-bleaching rituals. Her hair was shaved low and she wore large gold-hoop earrings, gold bangles, and a collection of necklaces. Her chest heaved in the tight mid-length floral dress she wore.

More was more for Madam Joanna.

'Good afternoon, ma,' Priscilla greeted.

Madam Joanna, while in repose on a sun lounger, shifted her eyes from her diary toward Priscilla. She peered at her over her sunglasses. The young woman was tall, and she wore her hair in long braids that fell down her back. Her eyes shone.

'Yes?'

'Please, my name is Cici. I am looking for work. I was told you can help me.'

Madam Joanna raised herself from the sun lounger in a bid to create balance between her and the towering Priscilla, who, she noticed, made no attempt to reorder the space between them. 'What can you do?'

'Well, I have experience, ma.' Priscilla adjusted the bag so the strap sat firmly on her right shoulder, then ran her hands down her midriff and adjusted the waistband of her skirt where it dug into her skin.

Madam Joanna understood.

During the day, Madam Joanna set up her kebab stand on the beach in front of her bar. All her servers were girls and roughly the same age. Some were slim, others were thick and round. There were short girls and a few taller ones. All were fairly attractive.

Cici would fit right in, Madam Joanna concluded. Madam Joanna offered to set her up. She could live with the others and pay Madam Joanna a portion of her earnings. There was space at the house since one of the girls had recently moved on.

While washing plates at the beach a week later, Cici asked a girl she came to know as Kukua what happened to the previous tenant; she received a shrug in reply. Then a few minutes later, the girl said: 'Sometimes it happens like that, a girl just leaves.' Kukua sighed, her shoulders rose then fell. 'And that girl, Chrissie, she was my friend. She didn't even say bye.'

* * *

Of all the chores involved in her work, it was cutting onions that Priscilla hated most. As a child she would often get scolded by her mother for her haphazard chopping skills. The pieces would be all different sizes, as if she were waging a fight with the onion and the chopping board, the knife her weapon. And then her eyes would sting, as though bees had planted themselves in her sockets. But she would continue to chop and slice, averting her gaze, using only her sense of touch. When it was all over, the onion would be in pieces, but in a way, so would she, with tears streaming down her face. She could never tell who came out as the victor of these confrontations.

When customers arrived, Cici's fingers would still be stained with the odor of onions. Madam Joanna said some of them liked that. One regular would give her ten cedis just to sniff her fingers and that would be it. It wasn't too much to ask, she supposed, but some days she resented the work, feeling as though she'd taken a step backward. These new customers were really no different from those she used to receive at the border: truckers with slabs of cement on their trailers and crates of dollars, euros, and pounds hidden between them; travelers with just one bag in tow searching for work along the coast, looking for some comfort for a night; and immigration officers. The pay was a pittance and she'd gotten tired of that life, particularly the officers, the pretend 'big men' with false bravado, who were always answering to someone else. Although now she was getting better pay, she was eager to reach higher heights. A nice apartment, a car, trips to Dubai. She wanted more.

It was Wednesday, the day Mr. Boakye would almost always come to the beach with two or three of his employees, usually the younger ones, to drink a couple rounds of Club beer. He would then order some kebabs for the 'boys' to chew on, before heading off to the nearby Labadi Beach Hotel where Madam Joanna would be waiting for him in their regular room, cleaned up from the day's beach debris.

This had been their routine for over fifteen years. They were much younger then. Those were the days before the hair at his temples completely gave way to his balding scalp, admittedly later than most men. She would tease him about it, but secretly enjoyed watching the granules of sweat cling to his last remaining follicles during sex. She told him that once. Soon after, he began shaving the whole thing off.

Having Mr. Boakye as a client was a smart move that saw her open the bar in the first place. She prided herself on that move, on him. She had specially imported sun loungers and umbrellas—the type you see on beaches in the south of France, the supplier told her—and a regular stock of the most popular foreign brands. Mr Boakye's connections rarely failed. She called her place the Labadi Sunshine Bar.

The business had changed since Madam Joanna first started working and then taking in girls. In those days it was mostly the Ghanaians who used her services, but in the last ten years there were so many more Europeans, Americans, and Arabs that came to Ghana with all kinds of demands. But Madam Joanna liked to think of herself as a flexible person, able to change with the times to keep her head above water. And like any good businessperson, she learned how to keep the police at bay.

On any given day the crowd at Jokers built up quickly. Priscilla and the other girls spent late nights at the club. Men came to meet women, and women came to make money. Couples sat outside smoking and people-watching over beer and Smirnoff Ice. You could always tell the new girls. The ones who were more used to wearing slippers than stilettos, knees knocking as they walked. Inside, Jamaican dancehall had women bent over, legs straight, the strobe lights catching the twists and turns of bum-shaking on the dance floor. Groups of young men would shout in chorus to American hip-hop anthems, hands tightly gripped around bottles of liquor.

The Brits and the Europeans, who prided themselves on the fact that they worked on the country's oil rigs, were often drunk and obnoxious. The Indians would sit quietly by the pool tables, watching intently as scenes unfolded before them. The Lebanese were also seated, but with a confidence the Indians lacked; after all, this small space in Labadi belonged to them. And of course, there were the Africans. Besides the regular

Ghanaians there would be businessmen from Nigeria, Côte d'Ivoire, Cameroon, South Africa, Kenya, and others too.

Priscilla quickly discovered that learning a few words in a prospective client's language helped him warm up quicker, and earned her a few extra cedis for the effort. The other girls had advised that she stick with the whites; they were usually only in town for a short while so were prepared to spend more. Best to find the ones who were on their own too. Avoid large groups.

Madam Joanna warned the girls not to get too close to the clients. 'Love can be dangerous,' she'd say. But love was never an option for Priscilla. Why have love when you could have freedom? Love was what kept her mother pregnant; recycled promises and pleas for forgiveness always inevitably led to a new baby. Love was what made her grandmother, who'd lived her whole life in the village, keep a decades-long hope that her childhood sweetheart would return to her after his studies in Accra, and then later Europe as a young graduate, to make 'an honest woman' of her. Love was what kept her aunties serving Sunday after-church akple and soup to their drunken, hot-tempered husbands who left them with Saturday-night bruises. If there was one thing Priscilla had learned in her short time on this earth, it was that love can slow a woman down and hold her back.

That's why she had left home for Aflao, and then Aflao for Accra. Labadi was a good step for her, closer to the life she felt she deserved.

Priscilla took her time getting ready for the night. She wanted a hot bath, so she boiled two pots of water on the stove to fill up her bucket. She lathered her sponge so thoroughly it became a cloud in her hand. This was her time. She allowed herself to feel her body with all its dips and crevices and folds. It was hers. It was important to affirm this daily, to make herself remember. Because, before long, some man might attempt to make her forget.

It was Friday. The sun had just laid itself to rest and Labadi was easing into the night's life. The sounds of Afrobeats, hiplife, and reggae blasted through the neighborhood, sliding through the louvers, filling the room, and bending the walls until the entire space became a bubble.

Two girls from the beach ambled into the house. 'Good evening,' they said in unison.

'Evening,' she mumbled back. Now that they were here they would disturb her.

'You hear say dem deh find annuda person for Dansoman? Weh dey cut am up. Commot ein breasts and tinz.'

'Kai! All dese sakawa boys, na demma rituals b dat.'

Priscilla had heard stories about women going missing after picking up customers on the roadside. The rumors went that groups of young men would abduct these women and make sacrifices for their online fraud activities. The connection didn't really make sense to Priscilla. They were cutting up people? What did they do with their body parts?

'I need some girls for a party,' Mr. Boakye said as he got up and reached for the checkered shirt he'd laid carefully on the office chair by the desk. It was the type of shirt afforded to CEOs; those lower on the chain of command tended to opt for a safe white or blue. 'I have a new group of guys coming into town,' he added, pushing his arms into the sleeves of the shirt. 'I need to make sure they are comfortable as they settle in.' Mr. Boakye left the top button undone. He had remained slim after all these years, rebuking the bulk of the 'big man.'

'Okay, how many?' It was Madam Joanna's turn to dress. Unlike Mr. Boakye, time had settled on her stomach, molded by the loss of babies that weren't permitted to stay.

'Ten should work. And Jojo, they should be fine too. Strong. Healthy.'

It had been awhile since Mr. Boakye had called her Jojo. She hadn't realized how much she'd missed it.

'This one is serious business. A lot of money can come.'

'Of course, darling. I will arrange for it.'

'And you will come. To keep an eye on them. Nothing can go wrong.'

'I will make sure everything runs smoothly for you,' she purred.

'For us,' Mr. Boakye corrected. He put on his suit jacket and kissed the crown of her head.

'For us,' Madam Joanna repeated.

* * *

'Give me a Savanna,' Priscilla said to the barman at Jokers, who silently obliged. She generally had a rapport with the waitstaff and often got free drinks until someone offered to buy her one. But this was not her guy, so she'd probably have to pay for this one.

'Eight cedis.'

She reluctantly handed over the money, picked up the bottle of cider, and took a sip. After a quick scan of the room, Priscilla observed a few regular faces. Tina, the po-faced girl who came to her aid last week after an altercation with a taxi driver; long-legged Hawa, who swore that her incense was a sure way to get clients up and out in less than ten minutes; and Serwaa, the girl who never came out on Saturday nights, because she needed to be up early for church the next morning. She didn't want to get too close to the other girls. Yomi and Gifty had told her that Accra was not like Aflao. 'Na so everybody dey carry dem matter,' one of them had said. She nodded at Tina before returning to her drink, tapping her white acrylic nail on the side of the bottle, tracing lines between the sweaty droplets.

'Can I take this seat?' a voice from behind asked.

Priscilla turned to face a tall white man. His hair was gray and spiky; she imagined it might prick her if she ran her hands through it. His mustache looked just as sharp. His skin was blotchy, not yet used to the sun, she assessed. He wore cargo trousers and a pastel-green shirt, tucked in and belted. She put him in his fifties.

'Oh, yes. Of course,' she replied.

'So what's your name, pretty lady?'

'Cici. Yours?'

'Stuart.'

'Akwaaba, Stuart,' Priscilla welcomed.

'Medaase,' he responded in Twi. 'Do you like to dance, Cici?'

'Yes, I like to.'

'Let's dance.'

Cici dreaded dancing with the white customers. Their arms and legs were never in sync. But this guy smelled expensive, even if he didn't look it. So Cici took the lead, leaning herself into him, guiding his hands around her hips and thighs.

'We don't have to stay here, you know.'

Priscilla didn't like going to her customers' hotels. Most of the time it was obvious she was working and she preferred to be more discreet. Now, anyone who knows of the Grace Jones Hotel knows that it is a place for short times. Priscilla frequented it often enough for management to keep a room reserved for her—room 102.

'What would you like to do first?' Priscilla asked.

Cici was getting too comfortable, Madam Joanna thought. Once they start to get comfortable they start to lose respect. And that was one thing she would not stand for.

'Cici!' Madam Joanna yelled from her front porch, clipping her toenails with concentration and precision.

'Yes, ma?' Priscilla rushed to her side. Although she was getting tired of living under Madam Joanna's roof, she was still far from being able to live in an executive apartment in Labone. The ones with the preinstalled kitchens with glossy cabinets and counters, and floor tiles you could see yourself in. For the time being, she had to do as she was told.

'So you've been with that same man every day this week again, ehn?'

'Oh. Yes, ma.'

'Don't forget what I told you. You are here to work.'

'Yes, ma.'

'And Cici, your rent and repayment will soon be due.'

Priscilla was growing accustomed to Stuart's company. She'd not had such close contact with one customer so intensely before. He was actually quite polite and kind, not something she was used to. This had to mean something. If she was smart, she could get some good money from him, enough to rent a nice apartment and maybe even start her own boutique for women's clothing. She'd always felt she had a good eye for fashion. She could travel to Dubai and China to buy bags and shoes and dresses; it would be a good business. This could be her chance. And if he was smart, she could be his forever.

'She reminds me of you, Jojo,' Mr. Boakye reminisced. 'From back in those early days.' He took a sip of the translucent brown liquid, whiskey probably. The ice was melting in the tumbler. His eyes followed Priscilla as she poured glasses of nondescript alcohol for a group of guests. She made a joke and they all laughed. The man with the mustache, laughing longer and harder than the rest, placed his hand on her back and kept it there a moment.

'She's sharp, like you were.' He leaned in and placed a hand on her shoulder. 'Ambitious. I want her.'

Madam Joanna's skin pulled to a tautness. The time had come again, she thought, mistaking Mr. Boakye's intentions.

Madam Joanna hadn't received any clients for several years, not since she started taking in other girls. Mr. Boakye was all she had left. He was more than a client. He was all she had.

'Hmm?' Mr. Boakye pushed.

'I can arrange it for you,' she whispered. 'You don't worry.'

'Wonderful.' Mr. Boakye got up and walked over to speak with the crowd that was being entertained by Priscilla. Madam Joanna felt her stomach contort into a hollow cave.

In room 102, Priscilla and Stuart were wrapped in each other's arms. It had been like this for weeks. Sometimes they would go for a drink at a spot on one of the other beaches in town. They'd even eaten dinner together a few times; it was Priscilla's first time tasting Chinese food.

Stuart lifted himself from the pillow and rested the side of his head on his hand. He poked his chin over Priscilla's shoulder. 'Cici baby, I might be able to stay here with you for longer. My time is getting extended,' he said gleefully.

'Stuart, I need to get out of here.' She turned to face him.

'What's going on, baby? Talk to me.' His wet breath on her lips made her nauseous.

'I just have some trouble, that's all. And I need to fix it quick.'

Stuart sat up. 'Okay, okay, what do you need? What can I do?'

Madam Joanna sat by her bedroom window listening to the praise and worship songs her church neighbors would carry for over an hour. Their haunting voices always filled her with melancholy and memory.

Hold Thou Thy cross before my closing eyes; Shine through the gloom and point me to the skies.

Heaven's morning breaks, and earth's vain shadows flee; In life, in death, O Lord, abide with me ...

As the singing came to an end she picked up her diary and flipped through it. Three months. Tomorrow it would be three months since Cici arrived, and she was still waiting for her money. Madam Joanna didn't like to feel as though the wool was being pulled over her eyes. She would not be made a fool of, she affirmed. She provided a good service in this business. There had been enough waiting around. Madam Joanna stuffed her feet into her slippers and marched to the Grace Jones.

'Where is Cici?' Madam Joanna barked at the receptionist.

'Erm,' the receptionist held his breath, 'I'm not sure, madam.'

'What of the white man? Have you seen them? Where are they?'

'Maybe check her room, madam.'

'Her room?'

Madam Joanna rushed down the corridor to number 102, her will moving faster than her body would allow. She banged her fist against the door, her bangles clanking with every thump. 'Cici, open this door! If you're not careful I will deal with you, ehn!'

After several moments, Cici opened the door.

'So you people are together again.'

Madam Joanna regained her composure and looked past Cici to Stuart, who sat on the bed with his pale legs poking out from the cover. As he stood up, Priscilla backed into the room and sat on the bed. Madam Joanna and Stuart locked eyes, then both turned to Priscilla. The air shifted.

Madam Joanna had noticed Priscilla when she first arrived at Labadi Beach. A lonely, pretty little thing who walked with a slight air of arrogance afforded to the young. She seemed plain, but that was good, she'd be easy to work with. Before Priscilla had even approached, Madam Joanna could tell she wasn't new to this game. She would keep an eye on her if she was going to work. A girl like that could bring in good money, and there were high-bidding customers to appease.

The day after Madam Joanna went to the Grace Jones Hotel to look for Priscilla, it was almost business as usual. The kebab stand had been set up. The bar was stocked. The girls were chopping up slivers of gizzard and goat meat. But Madam Joanna wasn't there. Cici was. Making directives, as the body of the previous owner of the Labadi Sunshine Bar washed up into the Korle Lagoon.

2022 AKO CAINE PRIZE WORKSHOP STORIES

A Mind to Silence

Elizabeth Johnson

The creaking sound was how she knew it was happening. The hand would reach for hers and guide her out of bed into the cutting cold of the night. The grass always felt like her mother's needles, scattered on the sand, left to defrost. It was the leaves that soothed her. Forming human-like shadows against the walls so that when the coarse, trembling hands let go of hers, she would feel she was not alone. The first time it happened, she was three, maybe four. By six, she had learned to not ask questions, cry or breathe too heavily or else a thick object would find her body. The episodes happened in intervals. On some nights, it was a hand to her cheek, sometimes in her eyes, a strangle long enough to quell her screams. She learned to keep her eyes shut in the inky darkness of the night. Somehow, keeping her eyes closed made everything seem further than they were, so that by the time the butcher knife started to strike, it sounded like fading claps from the church in the distance. When the shuffling began, she would imagine they were dancing feet in the church, and when the shovelling began, she would imagine the men mixing mortar on her way to school. When the warm thick liquid touched different parts of her face, she ignored the smell and imagined it was holy water from the priest's aspergillum. By the time she was twelve, she would have her first period and smell it. That was how she knew the difference.

Hypnopompia. That is what the psychologist called it. A state of consciousness leading out of sleep. Schizophrenia, haemophobia, DRC, dream-reality confusion as a result of borderline personality disorder.

***

Albert was a good man. He was good to Ese, took her in without question when she left the church with nowhere to go. He never mentioned what he thought: that she was a delusional, crazy liar who never got past the childhood phase of living in imaginary worlds. The first day they met, she was in desperate need of a place to stay. Their eyes locked immediately, and he spent the first few seconds in the bar forgetting about everyone else. He was not the type of guy to walk up to a girl. He did not have to. The ladies came to him, taking in his full chest and enjoying how they felt small under his gaze. They stood in seductive ways to accentuate their assets as the scent of his woody perfume took over their senses and their imaginations went wild. He walked up to her offering a drink and she immediately pleaded into his ears for some food and a place to sleep. Their eyes met again, he observed her for a while, contemplating his decision and then he took her hand, leading her out of the noisy pub. In the quiet of the night, he sat listening to her. She explained her situation with desperation. Pastor Fred, her pastor and guardian for the past five years, tried to have his way with her. Being denied, he went into a frenzy declaring that if he could not have her, no one else would. She had been under his care since she was sixteen, but that night as she watched him burst out in anger and call her a mentally unstable person whom no one would marry, she knew she had to leave. The next day, while Pastor Fred prayed for the many women lined up to see him in his office, she packed and left Winneba for Accra.

A few weeks later, the pastor would track her down and pay them a surprise visit, demanding that she return to Winneba with him. She refused, the men grappled and she started to scream. That was Albert's first encounter with her. The pastor fled, and Albert called Kwabena, his best friend in medical school, to get anti-tremors medicine, force it down her throat and watch as she fell into deep sleep. The next morning, he woke up to find her vehemently scribbling and immediately identified the opportunity that had fallen into his lap.

Albert believed he was a good man. He also believed that every human was dysfunctional in their own way. It was the reason he understood why his father, who had a drug problem, cut him off when he found out he had been involved in some quick money business. He had a good eye for art and dreamed of building a gallery space in Accra. The money from the quick business was meant to set him up as an art agent and collector. It was drug money, but it was enough money to establish himself. Ese was his redemption.

He thought she was a lovely girl, sweet, soft spoken, distrustful and determined to be normal. He was still struggling to make her realise her obsession with proving her madness was a futile journey. 'One can never be rid of problems.' He had lived with a cheating mother and a father with a drug addiction. But, regardless of her tender personality, Ese was also stubborn, insisting that knowing that the things etched deep in her memory were real or her own imagination would help her move on in life.

He was in love. It was not part of the grand scheme of things but in the process, he had fallen for her. He had gotten used to having someone in his life, someone he cared for. Someone who wanted to be with him. For so long, he filled the void created by his parents with one-night stands, drink, drugs and late-nights out in noisy pubs that helped him avoid how lonely he felt. Until Ese came into his life.

But he could not spend the rest of his life with her because she was also deeply troubled. He had to remind himself that she was a means to an end. A goal that took time and dedication; in this case five good years. He compensated himself with the idea that soon, all her work would be his. That was why, as he stared down at her new art work, he knew it was time to make that call.

***

When the call came, Ese was adding the final strokes to her last painting for the day. *Turquoise Blood*, she named it. The painting was of a deep vast space of sea and sky. The sun was a bloody red that left fading reflections of itself on the clear water, deliberately blurred out by the delicate white strokes of a rising wave. Glancing over at the Caller ID she allowed it to ring. It was her mother calling. She imagined the woman placing the call. Her small dark self, now round and wrinkled with age, sitting by her sewing machine trying to reach her daughter.

They barely spoke. Not when she lived at home, not when she moved out and not when, despite Albert's disapproval, she visited home a month ago. For the two hours of her stay, she had sat in the same spot watching her father, a withering image of himself, sitting on his favourite chair holding a rosary in his left hand. They were never a religious family. They. were. never. a. family.

She watched her mother in a trance spinning the balance wheel a bit too hard, humming loudly as if to outdo the sound of her sewing machine. She was so focused on her machine that when Ese was telling her goodbye, she did not hear. When she realised her mother would not hear her, she looked over her shoulder to glance at her father. He was staring at her from the corner of his eyes. His rosary now hanging loosely on his leg. Maybe he was asleep with his eyes open. She opened the door and closed it gently behind her.

'Aren't you going to pick your phone?' Albert asked, his tall self, walking out of the kitchen and into the dining area where she stood painting. He placed the two plates of food on the table gently, careful not to make any noise that would upset her. 'It's my mother,' she whispered. He nodded, acknowledging what that meant. Drawing her to his side, he freed the paint brush from her grip, silently praying that he would not have to handle any situation. He loved how she fit perfectly into him, like a jigsaw. He took in the gentleness of her afro curls, the rise and fall of her gentle breathing, the smell of paint and perfume mixed up. In an oddly familiar way, it was comforting. They had been making good progress with her art and her stability. Her palms were trembling. They were both used to this. The trembling. The screaming that lasted hours, the sweating, the vomiting during her period, the sudden need to get home because some sounds upset her, the random calls from strangers to come pick her up, the dreams, the need to rid the room of non-existent metallic smells and her inability to cook because the smell of raw meat or fish made her nauseous. 'I am here,' he assured. 'I am here, just pick the call. We will pick it together.' He placed the phone in her now loosened grip and she put it to her right ear.

Ese—

They heard the voice.

Ese—

Ese—

Ese your father is dead. Funeral is soon. He left you some things, pass by.

***

He spent the last few hours of his life in agony. In the morning, he woke up exhausted and with a parched throat. From her corner in the dining room, she watched him taking slow and deliberate steps around the house. He groaned and bowed forward from the pain in his stomach as he leaned on the wall, his hands gripping his midriff with each step. Outside, he stayed a little longer in the backyard where the pungent smell was heavy, before making his way back inside to sit on his coach, holding his rosary close to his heart. In the afternoon, she promised him some herbal tea to ease his pain. From the kitchen, she listened as he groaned from his daughter's room, where he spent most of his afternoons. She took her time to make his tea, stirring and stirring until the extra dose of rat poison and sugar blended well. Satisfied, she carried the cup to him for what she knew would be the last time. Then, she returned to her sewing machine and continued to sew until she heard the thud.

The woman smiled at herself, taking her sweet time as she made her way to the room. She stared at the body of the man she once loved dearly; the love that turned her into a blood-seeking vengeful woman. The girl could not be protected now.

***

The drive to Winneba was a long bumpy one with a few stops so that she could catch her breath, get something to eat and wait as Albert made a quick business call. They were thirty minutes away from her home now, having spun around Winneba roundabout and into its main road. Albert was driving, both hands on the steering wheel, keeping his speed at a steady pace. Occasionally, he would look over at her to make sure she was fine. She did not know how to feel about it. About the death, the trip, staying under the same roof with her mother. A woman she barely knew.

She thought about her father. Why did he not object when she asked to go live in the church for a while? Why did he never bother to ask why she was not coming back home? Why did he stop hugging her and tucking her into bed after the first night? Why did his coarse hands never lead her back to her room? Instead, he let her scream until she blacked out. Were these memories real? She wanted to ask him, or were they all just in her head?

When Albert advised her to try visualising her feelings, she did just that. She saw a small faceless woman looking down at nothing, her heavy shoulders slouched towards the ground. The mood was grey with splashes of black and dull off-white. She was trying to feel the pain born out of loss, but all she felt was the loss of never knowing why things changed the night the memory started to come to her. He stopped tucking her into bed. Stopped telling her the stories which he sometimes drew for her so that she could see what a Kaaka Motobi looked like. She felt Albert's fingers wrap around her left hand and her body started to relax. Closing her eyes, she imagined the fresh soft wind as a veil over her face. It is what she missed about Winneba, the fresh sea breeze, the slower pace. The space. Accra had heaviness in its air and no room to move. It also had too many people with many more problems on their shoulders.

She was four years old again standing with her eyes closed, the warm liquid fresh on her face. She could almost taste it. She opened her eyes abruptly, staring over her shoulder to see that she was truly here with Albert on her way to her home. Ese would have preferred Albert to stay at home, but he insisted on coming. It was the least he could do. To make sure she was safe and to be with her as she navigated this hard time. 'It would surprise you how much more troubled people are,' he had assured her the night before, when for the eighth time she had failed at convincing him not to embark on this trip with her.

Albert caught her stare and gave her a reassuring nod. 'Take the next left,' she ordered. Eyes back on the road, he made a careful turn into the rough, road junction. It was a sharp curve, and he was trying not to dent his car with the useless cement blocks piled up at the corner.

He did not know what he was doing but he could not bear to see her alone, especially in these times. The call had slowed things down; he considered this the last good thing he would do for her. So, here he was driving for over three hours from Nungua to Winneba, his right hand in her left as they rounded yet another corner, leaving a shadow of trees behind them. His mind drifted to the woman behind the voice he had heard in the past few days. This trip was good for him too. He convinced himself that it was a good way to establish that Ese was truly troubled and none of her childhood experiences were real. It also gave an opportunity to meet the woman he was leaving her with. He hoped that what he had concluded about her was the truth.

'Here.' Ese pointed to the house. A large, old duplex building in the suburbs, surrounded by several trees and an untended garden filled with blades as tall as maize stalks, sitting on a vast expanse of land. It had a small wooden gate in between huge stone walls with a long driveway leading to the house. It looked like wealth. 'We are here.' Ese announced. He gave her hand a tight squeeze and got out of the car.

***

The woman that greeted them at the gate was nothing like the voice on the phone. She was rotund, dark and wrinkled; her eyes were friendly and welcoming. The woman kept her eyes on Albert, her smile almost too wide, the white of her eyes more pronounced thanks to the smooth darkness of her skin. She wrapped him in a warm motherly hug. 'Welcome to my home.' Then she held him away at arm's length, her short hands on his broad shoulders, taking him in. He noticed the dried blood stains on the apron she wore and the fat rolls of brown and black thread that danced in the apron's pocket. They reminded him of Ese's colour pallet when she painted those disturbing and blurry images of home. 'Let's go in,' she beckoned.

The woman took Albert's hand, guiding him into the house with Ese following behind, keeping a good distance and closing the door behind her. Once seated, she started small talk, laughing at how much he smelled of the city—musky sweat, car fumes and weariness. It reminded her of the smell of her husband, she said, a young tough man sitting in the passenger's seat of his father's meat truck, his muscles chiselled in the way that young men at the gyms aspire to. That was the first time she set eyes on him and she'd made decision then to make her way into his life. 'The butcher's son,' she laughed. The last few words came out as a whisper. There was a silent pause. Then the woman smiled at Albert again. She told him the room was ready and that she had picked her best bedsheets for him, careful to dust the fan blades before fitting the sheets. She disappeared into the kitchen abruptly, as if suddenly remembering some unattended business. He looked over to find Ese seated behind him at the dining table. She smiled a knowing smile and when the woman reappeared from the kitchen, she had only one cup of water on the tray.

***

On the fourth day after their arrival, the couple sat in a poorly maintained chop bar to catch a quick meal before heading back to the family home. Albert watched as Ese cupped the last morsel of fufu in her bowl, bits of the goat light soup dripping back into the bowl 'What are you thinking about?' Ese asked, studying Albert's face. 'The funeral is tomorrow,' he answered. Sitting up from her bowl, Ese leaned into the plastic chair, took a deep breath and nodded in agreement. She placed her left hand on her stomach and rubbed it gently, before waving away the house flies hovering on their table, because the fan above their heads was not enough to keep them away. He turned to his own thoughts and wondered about how to leave. He still did not have a plan.

Watching the last piece of meat swimming in his now curdled goat light soup, he remembered the woman's food. On the day of their arrival, the warmth of home-cooked food greeted them as soon as they settled in. Ese had warned him about the food at home but when the woman offered, he considered it rude to decline. On the third day, for dinner, he accepted a full plate of jollof rice and fried goat meat, sitting on the dining table with the woman to keep her company. Ese was sitting on the couch facing the dining table watching him with an intense glare. It was not that she was a bad cook, on the contrary she was amazing. It was just the meat. The woman observed him while they ate. The meat was tough, almost leathery and black in the middle, it made him wonder what kind of meat it was. When the woman was not watching, he picked a piece of the meat and drew it to his nose, and it registered a sudden unpleasantness. It smelled stale, almost rotten, reminding him of the smell of an open wound. He dropped the spoon and felt his stomach churn. He glanced at the woman.

The house made him nervous. On their second day, the woman barged into the room with two cups of tea. `I bring you something warm to drink, Albert,' she announced, smiling as she raised her cup to her small lips to take a sip and sat on the bed. Goose pimples appeared on his forearm. What if she had walked in on him naked? She spent the time talking about her husband: about his work as the owner of a butchery, how he had given up his many cold stores in Winneba and how he had decided to sit in the house doing nothing until his dying days. She sounded annoyed. Albert pretended to fall asleep and heard her pick up the cups. When Ese walked into the room, he jumped to his feet and locked the door, making a mental note to keep it locked until he left.

That evening, at the dining table, he felt an unsettling pang in his belly, the food churning as it made its way up his throat. He rose to his feet to dash to the bathroom, but he vomited all over the table. The woman did not bat an eyelid.

He wanted a way out.

Full and satiated from the meal, Ese thought that Albert was distant. He was spending less time with her and more time with her mother. Last night, after she had mopped up his puke from the table, he sat quietly in his room and mumbled on the phone when it rang. When he did try to make conversation, he asked what her father left her. She did not like the ease with which he warmed up to her mother, a woman he knew she despised. She also did not like how he closed up anytime something in the house made him nervous. She loved him, even the parts she did not understand—his obsession over her paintings, his impatience when she was slow to complete an artwork, his disinterest in her family and now his sudden bond with her mother.

'Do you think I lied to you?'

Albert looked at her with surprise.

'No Ese, I believe you.' He looked her straight in the eyes when he said it.

'I don't believe you.'

'Why not?'

She did not want to tell him about his behaviour. Instead, she washed her hands, signalling that she was ready to leave. Albert did the same, careful not to splash water on the table. He got up to leave.

'Everybody has doubts. Ese, life is too complex not to.'

He reached for her hand, she stretched out hers and he pulled her to her feet.

'I will have to leave for Accra,' he announced.

'When?'

'The morning after the funeral. Early drive to beat the unpredictable Accra traffic.'

'Are you leaving me?'

'Just to conduct some business,' he lied.

She felt the loss then; what she should have felt for her father.

***

The woman sat on her creaking bed, the box on her lap. It was an old wooden box with nothing particularly interesting about its exterior. She held it closely to her ears, shaking it gently to make sense of the content in it. He had left her a good fortune, the house and the damn box. She stared at the box with disdain, wondering what surprises it held. She was certain that the girl would come for her father's funeral and make it easy for her, but she had shown up with a man. Ese must have told him about the house because she had caught him observing the walls with intensity. He was particularly interested in her husband's paintings, there were several framed and hung around the house. Once, she had caught him staring at a painting of a man carrying a baby, with two women in the background. He looked nonplussed, throwing glances between the woman at her sewing spot and back at the painting. When she asked him if he paints; rather, he told her about his interest in art.

Eight years they had tried for a child. She ran to hospitals, quack preachers and medicine men. Her husband, Mensah, went to his cold stores every day, and returned home with chunks of meat. One night she went to get a glass of water in the kitchen for her dry throat and under the dull rays of the light bulb in the corridor ceiling, she caught her husband's shadow slipping into *her* room. From that day, every time he told her he wanted to stay up a little longer to watch TV, or left their bed to quench his thirst in the thick of night, she listened for soft footsteps and the creak of a door opening down the corridor. One day, she returned home, and he told her he had sent Adjoa home to attend to an urgent family matter. Adjoa, whose father repaired watches and her mother sold bofrot from a glass case at the market to feed their ten children. Adjoa, who appeared at her doorstep, malnourished, at sixteen, gifted by her mother to reduce the number of stomachs to feed. Adjoa, who worked hard to please her and blossomed under her care.

Adjoa, who brought into their home a child that was not hers.

She loathed the child. Mensah carried her in his arms like she was the most precious thing he had ever possessed, and she began to store her rage in jars.

He refused to stop visiting her room after the baby, almost brazen with his newfound confidence. On the day the jars could not take more of her rage and exploded, she found them in bed in the afternoon, when she returned to collect her spool of threads that she forgot at home.

She felt numb, walking to the kitchen for the knife, allowing her feet to lead her to the child's room, the child who was the root of her discord; the child's cries beckoning the two lovers to see her holding it so tight in one arm, and a sharp boning knife in the other. A mother's love pushed Adjoa into the blade's sharp tip and the blade into her heart when she tried to collect her baby. Then the woman, stimulated by vengeance, stabbed at any part of the girl she could find first, her blood splashing on her face. That was when she tasted it. The warm thick blood, its metallic yet earthy taste sparking wildfires in her brain, making her feel alive again. So, she slashed and slashed until there was no more screaming. Trembling, Mensah had snatched the child – who was screaming at this point – away from the woman before she did the same to her or him. But he had stood in a pool of his own urine as he watched the love of his life cut into a million pieces.

Nothing was the same after that. Their relationship, her cravings, and her need to taste the girl's blood. But he would protect her by offering the blood of others who showed affection to her. First, it was the gardener, then the young boy that picked up plastic around the house, her husband's younger brother, and on, until it was hard to keep count of them.

The woman opened the box and saw a bunch of rushed illustrations. There were many of them, paintings of odd things she had no interest in. Why would he leave her these strange things? She wondered.

The door in the hallway swung open with the voices filling up the emptiness of the day. She heard Albert's voice, the slow footsteps of Ese. She glanced through the illustrations again as fast as she could. The box was willed to Ese and there was nothing that proved that Adjoa was the girl's mother, or anything that led to the events of the night. She shut the box sharply and made her way outside.

**

The funeral was a sad one with only ten attendees: Ese, her mother, Albert, the priest, four pallbearers and two helpers from the cemetery.

Ese was relieved when the pastor said the last prayer and poured a handful of sand onto the lowered casket. She was watching from a distance to avoid the shovelling of sand into the grave from getting to her. She watched as an elderly grave digger picked up the shovel and started filling up the hole. Her mother was standing by Albert. Her short hands wrapped around the elbow of his left arm, his right hand tucked into his black trouser pocket. They looked like mother and son bidding farewell to a loved one as they watched the grave fill up slowly. She said a little prayer for her father and watched as Albert walked over to her. He was leaving for Accra the next morning, an important meeting that could not wait. One that would change both their lives.

**

The woman changed out of her mourning clothes and was back at her working desk turning the balancing wheel as loudly as ever. She was humming to herself. Albert was getting under her skin. She yearned to feel his slowing heart close to her ears; the thought of it made her feel alive again. He was beginning to be a bit too pushy. At the funeral, he asked her what Ese's father had left her.

'Just a box with papers,' she replied to him, 'I will give it to her tonight.'

'Is that all he left her?' he asked.

She smiled up at him, unwrapped her hand from his arm and started walking towards the pastor, when she saw Ese in the distance. Albert loved her like Mensah loved Adjoa. Sometimes, she caught a glimpse of his handsome face staring at Ese with such tenderness that it made her chest hurt.

In the car while he drove them home, she sat in the back seat. She noticed him stealing quick glances at her from the front seat rear-view mirror as if uncertain of her. She had overheard a bit of their conversation in the church. He was leaving the morning after the funeral without her, so she could collect what was bequeathed to her. He expected her back in the city after the weekend.

Spinning the balancing wheel with a ferocity, the woman smiled to herself. If only he knew.

***

The next morning, Ese woke early to clear her head. It was the morning of Albert's departure. She picked up her medication and made her way to the door to catch some air. She needed to clear her head. Last night, he snuggled with her longer than he had done since their arrival. He asked her if she had finally spoken to her mother about her inheritance. Her answer was no, and he did not say anything but pulled her closer to him whispering how much he would miss her.

Albert was all packed now, ready to leave and never to return. She watched as he packed his luggage into the boot of his car, smiling as he did. She noticed the urgency in his movements. She was sitting on the porch now. He walked up to her. 'I love you,' he confessed. She knew it was true. He kissed her and gave her a hug. Looking into her eyes, he smiled down at her. 'See you shortly?' he asked. She nodded and looked away. Closed her eyes to listen as he opened the gate and drove off.

She retreated to her room. The woman had stepped out and would close the gate whenever she returned. She would spend the time in the garage rummaging for things that would help her remember more from her childhood.

***

He was halfway to Accra when he made the abrupt U-turn. Cursing at the drivers who cursed at him, he sped his way back to Ese, all the while wondering what he was doing, why he felt the way he felt for her. The urge to protect her, to continue to do good by her even though it could cost him his dreams. They could both leave and drive straight to the agent or just go home and continue their lives together; despite her insanity, despite his flaws, despite it all.

Barging into the house he started to call out for her, panic in his voice. He looked for her in the room, kitchen and where he had left her sitting on the porch. She was not there. He found himself in the woman's room where he saw the little wooden box on the floor next to the bed. There was a canvas with its edges sticking out. He caught glimpses of wild colour. Albert picked up the box and flipped through the unframed paintings in the box. There was an image of a woman with a cleaver in her hand with splashes of blood like a river; there was a painting with trees casting shadows on the wall and stars in the sky; there was one with a beach, vast blue sky and sea. The last one was of a little girl hiding behind a tree, blood trickling down her face. He was staring down at Ese's eyes and saw the same fear that looked back at him that morning when he had bid her farewell.

He did not know what hit him. He was too stunned to turn around; he let go of the painting, which dropped to the floor. He could feel his left trapezius drop as the pain registered. He was barefoot and until now had not realised how cold the tiles felt under his feet. His shoulders burned and his head began to feel light. Albert felt another slam on his head and felt the world move from side to side. Droplets of his blood stained the canvas of a beach, vast blue sky and the sea. As he fell, he kept his gaze on the waves as his body crashed to the ground, his last thoughts were of crumpling paper, the agent who would meet his absence, his father, his art gallery, Turquoise Blood. He thought of Ese last before he blacked out.

***

Ese dropped the heavy piece of wood in her hands. She shivered and trembled in the cold. The scream from the main house made her jerk her head up from the box she had been rummaging through. She was surprised how fast the day had gone, noticing the darkness of the clouds through the small window that allowed air to circulate in the garage. She could not move. She took deep breaths to suppress the screams erupting in her belly. She closed her eyes. She was four. The creaking sound was there again and she listened as the footsteps got closer. Her tears blurred her vision now, but she could feel her body moving towards the door. There was a warming presence with her. She felt it more than she could see. She was four again in the darkness being led out. She began to scream.

The familiar scream brought him back to consciousness. Albert opened his eyes and the weight of his own body left him breathless. He was in severe pain. He saw the woman seated on a rocking chair, the box on her lap. She smiled at him, pestle in her hand. Ese's screams were getting louder. He could see her curled up into a ball screaming and pulling at her hair. He wanted to save her, but his head throbbed. The screaming was getting closer or maybe he wanted it to be so. The woman got up, pestle in hand. His eyes followed her as she raised it as high as she could. He watched the pestle come down. One more blow to the head and he would be gone. With the last strength he had, he reached out for the woman's ankles and pulled her towards him. She lost balance letting go of the pestle, her hands scrambling for something to hold on to in the air. She yelled as she fell on her back. He pushed himself to his feet, took the pestle and hit her.

The door flung open.

***

When she felt the warm liquid all over her face, she knew it was blood. The fresh blood of a human losing the warmth of life. She opened her eyes and stopped screaming. The air was cold and the silence between them was filled with the sound of the howling wind beating against the windows. 'Grab the body and follow me,' she commanded. A terrified Albert mustered strength and did as he was told, dropping the pestle and dragging the small lifeless body. In the natural light of the night, he could not make her out so well, but he listened for her footsteps, dragging the weight with him out of the house to the large wild garden behind the house. The long blades of grass reached his torso and the weeds pricked under his feet, piercing his skin.

She stopped walking and he let go of the lifeless hands. The spot they stood in had a pungent smell and the moonlight hit the wall so that the leaves from the plantain trees formed shapes that looked like an observing crowd. He could not see well but he could tell she was bent over searching for something behind the trees.

A shovel.

A butcher knife.

She dragged the body closer to the spot. That was when he knew it was about to happen. He closed his eyes so that he wouldn't see when the cleaver started to strike. He imagined her scribbling with a ferocity on the drawing papers that always made her fingers bleed. When the shuffling began, he imagined the sounds of paint brush strokes on canvas and when the shovelling began, he imagined the sound of crumpling paper. When the thick warm liquid touched his face, he imagined it was red paint from the top of her brushes. The metallic smell made him bend over and retch until his insides hurt.

She led him back inside the house, both trembling. They sat in silence on the bed in her room, holding hands, their clothes stained red. Albert squeezed Ese's hand. Ese squeezed Albert's hand too. Silence engulfed the room, but she felt okay.

Everything would be okay, now.

Nnome

Audrey Obuobisa-Darko

Onyankopɔn is a woman. And a man. And everything above and in-between. Akuba says Onyankopɔn kissed the tips of His fingers on the sixth day and sculpted these bodies as worldly vessels for our spirits. Why do we call Onyankopɔn just 'He' when Akuba says that all of us were made in the image of God – all the men, all the boys, all the women, all the girls, all those people who don't quite look like either men or women but rather cut-and-paste versions of each thrown together?

Why do we reduce Onyankopɔn to only 'He' when I see God in that video of my mother, with her full body that flows like emerald water, and silvery-black locs that cascade down her arched back till they kiss the point where her buttocks greet her waist? You should see the part where she wields her *tumi*, when she closes her eyes, and her locs dance and rise about her like living, breathing things, when they weave themselves together to form the shape of a stool, when the stool appears in the sky above, when her hair wraps around it and sets it down on the ground. I see Onyankopɔn in Asante from my class; his body glows like the sun on God's happy days when he Fades from one place and Reappears at another. Onyankopɔn also looks like the man-woman person Da warned me to stay away from, with their body that can bend, and shift into different forms of being other than human. But when Onyankopɔn made me, They did not make me well.

'You should have never been born.' My father's words are pressed down into the crevices of my brain. I see them on the walls, I see them in my dreams, I see them each time I lift my cursed hands to wield my *tumi* and nothing happens.

A familiar mechanical sound licks my ear as small voxels bind to one another above me. The strong beams burn my sleepy eyes. The hologram forms and my virtual assistant, Akuba, squeaks to life. 'Good morning, Nnome. It's 13 am, Friday the 42nd. Your first class begins in fifty-two solar minutes, after which you—'

'I'm not going.'

The map to school appears on the hologram and Akuba calls out the coordinates of the trajectory. She issues a command to the portal spawn device, and the portal begins piecing itself together. 'Simulating your father. Create in ten, nine, eight—'

'I said I'm not going! You've forgotten what today is?' My voice cracks. Horror washes over me in a thousand solid waves. I run my fingers through my hair and down my face, my hands quivering, my body weak. Tears pour down my face.

'Today is Friday the 42nd,' Akuba repeats.

The sound of heavy footsteps grows louder. My door swings open. 'Nnome.' My father stands at the door, his voice heavy, his eyes empty.

'Da.'

'Get out of your bed.'

He walks toward my workshop table, which is cluttered by the workings of a struggling inventor and sets a colourful paper bag on it. It has 'Happy Birthday' written across it in bright pink. He notices the hologram suspended in the air and wrinkles his nose. I stand beside the partly built portal. The *Adinkra* symbols carved in its mahogany frame gleam against the holographic lights – *dɛnkyɛm*, the crocodile, for adaptability; *aya*, the fern, for endurance. My portals look good, but they'll never be as good as those made by my father's *tumi*.

'What is this nonsense?' He points a large, hirsute hand at the portal.

'It's... it's one of my inventions, Da. I made it... like the gateways you make. I've been... I've been working really hard, and now I can simulate your *tumi* with techno—'

'No matter what you do with these toys of yours, Onyankopɔn denied you *tumi*, and you can never be like any of us.' He walks towards me and stops short when my face is only a few inches away from his chest. I raise my eyes to meet his. They glisten; he's been crying too. His lips stretch into a smile, one that does not reach his eyes, and he says, 'Happy birthday, my dear.'

'Tha-thank you, Da.'

He picks a confetti blower from the paper bag. 'Tell your talking thing to play a birthday song.' I issue a command to Akuba, and *Happy Birthday, Happy Birthday* fills the room. Mirth fills Da's eyes as he breaks into dance around me, spraying confetti on my head.

'Whose birthday is it?' He shouts over the music, dancing.

My voice does not know me anymore. 'Mine.'

Da cups a hand over his ear. 'Hm?'

'Mine.' Guilt sits heavier and heavier, on my shoulders, pushing me into the ground where wastrels like me belong.

Something flashes in his eyes. 'And whose death day is it?' He continues in his jolly dance, capering and frolicking as if *Happy Birthday* is the most melodious song in the universe. His movements are more frantic, more exaggerated.

I open my mouth to respond, but I cannot speak. Thoughts spin in my head till everything in my vision spins. I open my mouth to speak, but my words meld into one another, one wave of a wail.

Da stops dancing and looks at me. He steps closer to me, the mirth lost in his eyes, and lowers his voice. 'Whose death day is it?'

I take in a deep breath. 'Ma.'

'And who killed her?' His face is even closer to mine now, his breaths long and hard, and hot against my face. His eyes bore into mine, mocking, provoking.

I bow my head. 'Me.'

'That's right! If it weren't for you...'

'She would be alive,' I continue, my voice barely a whisper.

He takes a cake out of the paper bag. He rubs his palms together until blood begins to flow from his fingertips and onto the floor. I've watched Da many times when he Creates – weapons, cooking pans, jewelry, portals – but I can never get used to the sight of his blood. He closes his eyes and draws the shape of a knife in the air with his finger, and the blood moves at his command, hardening till it becomes a knife.

I pick it up without question and cut a slice and put it in his hand. I tip my head back and open my mouth. He stuffs the cake in my mouth, and I lick his fingers, sugar and blood interlaced, like I know how after all these years. He steps back and watches me, a satisfied smile on his face as he admires the work of his hands: a trembling, frightened, guilty me.

'Happy birthday, my darling,' he says, and walks out of the room.

***

'I want to see the dead,' I said to Mrs Sankara, my teacher, six solar months ago.

She batted her eyelids. 'Hmm?'

'No, not like that,' I laughed. 'My project. To apply to the Academy. I want to develop something to help me see into a dead person's past life. My mother's past life.'

I told her about Ma, how I knew nothing about her beyond that video card I stole from Da. I did not add that the next thing Da told me was that she killed herself when she saw she made me, that she chewed the umbilical cord and strangled herself with it, that Da walked in with a smile on his face, and when he saw her, and he saw me, he lifted me and slammed me against the wall, that I refused to die. I told her about Da, how he never said much about who she was, how he shut down whenever I asked, how I want to help him cope with his grief somehow.

'Nyansa Academy is the place for brilliant minds like yours, Nnome. That's where all the greatest inventions you can think of were made by our ancestors – Kobi, Ansah, Diaka – and sent out into other universes beyond Alkebulan,' Mrs. Sankara said when I was eleven solar years old, and pausing to look at me with tender eyes, added, 'where there are more people like you without *tumi*.'

She sparked a determination in my heart that day and it grew more and more afire six years forward with each page I turned, each machine I made, functional or faulty, every birthday I endured the taste of sugar and blood on Da's hands till the year came when I was old enough to apply to Nyansa. 'If I can get in, Akuba, I can leave this godforsaken house. I can change all the worlds. Especially for people out there like me, Akuba! And I can see Ma.'

My room is a riot. My bed, the floor, the tables, the shelves, they're riddled with old textbooks with tired, dog-eared pages, metres and metres of conducting wire, metal scraps, batteries, glass, laser monitors, screws, acoustic modulators, analog amplifiers, and heaps of crumpled paper thrown across the room in utter frustration. It's been like this for many solar months, yet with each iteration, I feel farther and farther away from getting the chip right with the application deadline to the Academy coming closer and closer.

'Nothing is working!' I slam my fists on the workshop table, sending screws crashing to the floor. They roll around in circles. The terminal on my screen is filled with endless lines of error messages in an ominous red.

'Kafra, Nnome. You've made significant progress. Just keep trying, you're almost there,' Akuba says.

Akuba and I have come a long way from the moment she was only an idea in my head, to the moment she said her first word. In between those moments were the days of studying fuzzy logic and neural networks till my brain folded into itself. The day Mrs Sankara shouted, 'Eureka!' when the natural language program ran with no bugs, and she asked Akuba the time, and Akuba told the time. The day I smiled for the first time in forever after integrating her into all my machines. The day I gave my hologram device to Da to try Akuba out, and he

Created a boulder and smashed it over and over and over again till Akuba's voice glitched and disappeared into the shards. The day I made a new hologram device and brought her back to life.

'Akuba, run a diagnosis. What else do I need?'

'So far, everything looks good. The surgical droid for the implant procedure is ready, good job. The chip is better, the electrode wires for the transmission are thirty microns wide now, so that's perfect. The program is syntactically correct, but the data you have on your mother is simply not enough to satisfy the conditions in the brain interface functions. You need more—'

'Shhhh, Akuba.' I slap my thigh, a little harder than I mean to. I turn to face the small, round hologram device, as if I'm seated face to face with a real person. Akuba is nearly a real person to me. 'Right now, we only have Da's video card, right?'

'Right.'

'And everything else we know, Da told me, right?'

'Right.'

My face breaks into a smile. It feels unusual, but I let it linger. 'And surely, Da has some of Ma's belongings kept somewhere, right? Even her clothes? We can use anything of hers?'

'I believe remnants of her spirit could be somewhere. If we can find any part of her, or anything she might have worn, we should be able to translate her biotic composition data into something useful for your program. I have been trying to suggest this to you, but—'

'What's the time?'

'26pm'

I smile wider. 'It's almost time to clean his room anyway.'

'Nnome!' Da's voice rings through the walls from across his side of the house. Disgust strokes the wrinkles on his face when he sees my cleaning droids hovering behind me as I walk into his room. 'What is this?'

'I-I designed them not so long ago, just to make cleaning easier.'

He groans, waves a dismissive hand at me and walks out. I quickly press the buttons on the cleaning gadgets to start work as I think of where to begin my search. The machines scurry about, wiping dust off shelves, pulling sheets taut. Da never allowed me into his room until recently, and I never asked. I wasn't sure what to think of it, when I first saw his room, the grey paint on the walls, the low lighting, the floor drowning in scraps and scraps of unfinished Creations, no pictures on the wall, no human warmth in it.

The hover broom gets stuck trying to sweep under the large bed. It makes a loud whirring sound as it keeps knocking against something in its way. I go down on my knees to dislodge it, and I see a dark brown box obstructing it. My heart knocks hard and fast with iron fists against my chest as I drag it out, looking over my shoulder every other second.

The box is heavier than it looks. There's no lock, and it has the eerie feel of having just been touched. My fingers rummage through it with hunger. There's nothing much of note: old, dusty books, unfinished iron carvings, wooden handles broken off knives he Created. I pick everything out until there's only a piece of cloth spread out on the bottom. It's only when I lift it, and the vile smell of something dead and rotten slaps my face, that I realise I've been holding my breath. Bile crawls up into my mouth and I jump back. My heart stops hammering against my chest. Before me, wrapped in a strange, protective sheath, beside a knife covered in old, darkened blood, lies an umbilical cord.

***

'Once upon a time—'
  'Time time.'
  'There was a woman—'
  'Woman woman.'
  'She had a baby in her womb. When the baby came out, its face did not shine. What does that mean?'
  'Onyankopɔn did not bless it with *tumi*.'

'Good. So the woman was sad when she found out what she had made. And she chewed the umbilical cord and ended her life. Riddle riddle.'

'Riddle.'

'Why did the woman die?'

'Because of the child whose face did not shine.'

'And what is that child?'

'A curse.'

'And how do we say that in our language?'

'Nnome.'

'Fantastic. Open your mouth for your cake now. Happy eighth birthday, Nnome.'

***

I used to beg Onyankopɔn to sever me from this body, this hundred-pound cage of girl; to put my spirit in another vessel whose face shone at birth, or leave me to wander in the realms where none of these mattered.

Surely, this isn't the image of you? Not these hands that bring forth nothing. Not this tongue that tastes the maleficence of a father. Not this being that kills a mother. Not this godforsaken excuse of a human being.

Every night before my birthday, Onyankopɔn and I warred on my bathroom floor, when I slit my wrists to cut ties with my body, when They shut the gates to the realms above and shoved me back inside this vessel of flesh and bone, of strife and woe.

Why did you allow Ma to do it, then?

I stopped fighting when I turned ten, when Mrs Sankara said she saw something in me, something better than *tumi.*

'Nnome, it's your turn,' Mrs Sankara says. She's seated next to the other members of the school board. They wear bored looks on their faces, except for Mrs Sankara whose eyes are illuminated as I walk onto the proscenium, my hologram device in hand.

'For my Academy application, I've invented chip technology that can help one see into the life of a dead loved one and have a closely simulated experience – like you're there with them. My mother died very early in my life, and I never got the chance to know who she was, so this is a project inspired by that.' I instruct Akuba to switch through the presentation on the hologram.

The teachers look on with blank expressions. I clear my throat and proceed. 'Data about the person whose life you wish to simulate is collected and encoded onto the chip. The input machine reads the sample placed on it, and I have developed an algorithm that analyses these inputs and encrypts them onto the chip. The sample could be anything, videos of them, audio tapes they recorded, clothes they wore, even bio samples, like their hair or nails.'

Or umbilical cords.

'And what happens after that?' Mrs Sankara asks, her eyes wide, her body on the edge of her seat.

I smile faintly. 'The implant procedure will be done by a surgical bot, which I have also built. The probes of the chip are connected to pathways that control your vision, emotion, and hearing. You may begin or end the simulation just by thinking it.'

'Is your work ready for a demo session tomorrow?' That's Mr Bansah, the talent scout from Nyansa Academy. The others remain disinterested, slumped in their chairs.

'Yes,' I tap the back of my head, 'the implant procedure has already been done on my brain, and I've run a few unit and system tests.'

'Good job. See you in the final stage.' He turns to Mrs Sankara and gives her a nod, and she squeals and leaps from her chair.

Da is in my room when I arrive home, his broad back hunched over my workshop table. Dread wraps its fingers around my heart, ripping my heartstrings. He turns to me when I step into the room, his eyes filled with an emotion I have never seen before. The umbilical cord dangles from his hand.

'Da I—'

'Are you mad?' Sweat slides down his face and soaks his shirt. His hands tremble as he clenches them into fists and releases them, clenches and releases. His eyes are bloodshot. Tears well up and flow into the river of perspiration running along the folds of his face. He paces back and forth, past my workshop table, running his hands through his hair in a frenzy. 'You always ruin everything, you always ruin everything, you always ruin everything.'

My voice takes its leave like it knows how, when Da arrives. Words scrape my tongue, questions, but nothing comes out. Tears stream down my face, and I put the back of my right hand in my left hand, pleading.

'I'm sorry for touching your things, Da. I just … I'm making something. For the Academy… Remember Nyansa? I want to go there. And– And, look!' I rush towards the table to show him my work. I lift the scanner with trembling hands. 'This will help us experience Ma again, Da. I've already tested it. I've already seen some things. Oh, no wonder you loved her so! But the umbilical cord … why do you … why did you keep it?'

Da's eyes turn vacant as I ramble. He stands frozen and stares at me, tears still coursing down his face, his chest heaving like an animal. His lips come apart slowly. His voice is soft. 'You've seen what? You've seen what?'

'I …' My legs are stuffed with droves of fear, riveting me to the ground.

He lunges towards me. 'You've seen what?!' He rubs his hands together faster than I've ever seen him do. Blood gushes out of his fingers with the might of a million waterfalls. The crimson fluid forms a great pool around our feet, but he doesn't stop. His palms grate into each other till they're a canvas of black and blue. The bloods seeps under everything on my bedroom floor. He swoops his arms in large motions in the air, drawing a shape I cannot read. As the blood comes together, hardening up, my spirit falls apart, melting down.

The thing he Creates is ugly, a large mass of spikes and hammers bound together. He lifts it with immense strength, screaming, and drops it on my table. The desk caves in down the middle, swallowing everything on it – my coding devices, the implant droid, the scan machine – all my life's work, the testimonials of my self-worth.

'Please stop ... please stop ...' My knees give away and I fall to the ground. Akuba's voice glitches inside the hologram device on the bed, panicking. Da dives towards it and flings the weapon. I leap onto the bed to shield her, but it's too late. The weapon strikes my head, the impact tossing me against the wall, where I strike my head again. As my consciousness drifts away from my body, I see my father sitting on the floor, his body rocking back and forth like a baby as he cries into the umbilical cord in his hands.

***

I don't know where I am. This body isn't mine. It's small, too small for me. A sharp pain burns through my head as I pry my eyes open. This place is strange, the white walls, the small bed, the bookshelves, yet there's something familiar about it. There's a broken table to my left, all sorts of things crushed and broken under it. I hear heavy footsteps coming towards the door. It swings open.

My heartbeat stops. 'Ababio?'

My husband freezes in his step. Confusion clouds his face. His wrinkles are numerous now, his hair gray. 'Nnome, what did you say?'

'Who's Nnome?' I try to get off the floor, but these small legs, they fail me. 'Ababio, is that you?'

He takes a step back. 'Whatever games you're playing—'

'Ababio!' Shock gives way to fear, and then to rage. Memories flash before my eyes. The first cry of a baby, the hatred in his eyes, the rough hands on my neck, the heavy blows on my face, the gleam of a new knife, the slam of something against the wall, the gnashing of the umbilical cord under his teeth, the chill of a blade against my neck, the heat of my spirit fizzling into the afterlife.

'Why did you do this to me?' I step forward. He steps back again. 'What did I ever do to you, Ababio?'

His face drips with sweat, his eyes wide, scared. 'Adowa, I didn't mean to. I didn't mean to. I didn't mean to.' He falls to the floor and puts his hands on his head, trembling, like a frightened little boy.

A sharp pain sears through my head again. I feel pulled away from my body, and a heavy blanket of darkness falls over me as my consciousness drifts.

***

'How long have I been unconscious, Akuba?' My head throbs with a wild pain. I touch the back of my head, where the chip was implanted. A large scab of dried blood falls on my fingers.

'There's something I need to show you,' Akuba says, a humanly concern in her voice. The hologram device hums as it launches a screen. She plays back the incidents from the moment I arrived home and saw Da in my room.

'What's happening?' I stand up and point at the hologram. On the screen, Da cowers on the floor, and I tower over him, yelling. 'What was that?'

'The chip. Something is wrong.' Akuba pauses the video. 'When your father struck your head, the impact dislodged the wall.'

I cannot breathe. 'What wall?'

'The firewall that prevents your mother's core biotic data from taking control over your body. So this,' she plays the video, 'this is your mother taking over. We had all the data we needed from the umbilical cord to reactivate...'

Akuba's voice drifts farther away until it's only a faint echo in the distance. I feel removed from myself again, like I'm somewhere far away. I observe my body move, but I do not have control. Suddenly, I sense myself flung forward.

I yawn. 'What just happened?'

'You dissociated again.'

'So my mother ...'

'Yes, she came to the fore.' Akuba rolls the rest of the video. My mother, screaming through me at her killer. My father, sinking into his gorge of lies, and deceit, and evil, and evil, and evil.

I grab my hair and tug it till my scalp burns. Akuba is saying something about calming down, but I can't hear her clearly as my screams reverberate around the room. I'm drowning in a pit inside me, an abyss in the shape of my father.

I carry my broken inventions and run out of the house. Past the children in their compounds marvelling at their newfound *tumi*, past the homes that never let me in, past the man-woman who always tried to tell me something, but whom I always stayed away from because Da said so. I run, and run, and run towards the school.

A scream cuts through the air, stopping me in my tracks. It's coming from the town square. The gong-gong floats in the sky, calling everyone out of their homes. The streets fill up with people rushing towards the square from all directions. I follow them, my heartbeat a metronome to the rhythm of my running feet.

The people crowd around the centre of the square. Some put their hands on their heads and wail. Some shout '*Tufiakwa!*' and spit on the ground. As I approach, everyone steps back and makes way for me. I fall to my knees when I see what they see.

'Da!'

I switch.

'Ababio!'

I switch.

In the heart of the square, on a stake that gleams like the sun on God's happy day, hangs the lifeless body of my father by an umbilical cord. Blood surges from the tips of his fingers with the might of a billion waterfalls, but it doesn't harden.

The Loan

Sally Sadie Singhateh

i

Beep!

The audiobook's battery is almost spent. Only five circles left. I turn the volume down slightly to conserve the battery life as the narrator's euphonious voice continues to flow distinctly through the miniature speakers. Her tone is warm and easy with just a hint of huskiness.

'And so, the land that was once divided by seventy-seven warring kings, chiefs and nomadic sect leaders was finally united in 1734 by Bello Sanusi.

However, the Dampho Chronicle, and the most reliable of TAK's historical markers, paints Sanusi as a nomadic scholar and philosopher, fluent in numerous dialects – traits that enabled him to mobilise and band together the warring leaders in just under six years against their common enemy. The Chronicles also indicate that, prior to 1500, the indigenous people of Vastlen lived a secluded life. They tended livestock, hunted, fished and farmed. Some travelled south of Vastlen's borders to trade with the Feefi Clans with whom they shared similar customs. In the early sixteenth century, exploring merchants from the west, north and east of Vastlen landed on its shores to barter goods and discovered the abundance of resources on the land.

Concessions were made with the more viable of Vastlen's leaders to mine charcoal, gold, copper and diamonds in exchange for spices and fabric. Merchants and other businessmen followed, seeking wealth to build their own lands and enhance their lives, with no care for the consequences. The demand for more Vastlen wealth amplified and soon the indigenous people were being forced to work in the mines to increase output.

Realising the strength, prowess and intelligence of Vastlenians, those from across the oceans returned with ships and, with the help of rogue Vastlen leaders and rival merchants, began to seize men, women and children by force and transported them to work on their own lands. Resistance by the Vastlenians was met with harsh retaliation and by the mid-eighteenth century the continent had lost over half its population, either through forced labour oversees or village massacres.

Led by Sanusi, envoys were dispatched to negotiate a deal with the oppressors. But their attempts at brokering peace were met with deaf ears, leading to a brutal war that lasted thirty years. The scales were uneven for the Vastlenians, and many lost their lives. By the late eighteenth century, Sanusi – then close to eighty years old – recruited the young and vibrant expert war strategist, Nya Walli, to train a handful of men in war tactics. These men systematically targeted, ambushed an—'

Beep, beeeep!

The battery blinks three circles! I click on a button hastily to move forward in the documentary. The narrator continues.

'And finally, the insurgents were able to fight back, driving the outsiders off Vastlen and back to their own lands across the ocean. The destruction on the land was immeasurable and the leaders who emerged after the Savannah War began to rebuild Vastlen. By majority vote, Nya Walli was elected the first True High

Organiser of Vastlen – known today as THO – aided by other leaders who fought in the war.

By 1790, THO Nya Walli had sealed off and secured all major borders around the continent and commenced mining operations in what is today the Gundo Kingdom. He established a foolproof self-governing system that allowed every kingdom on the continent to be governed by its own leader, the Chief. With the aid of a democratically developed schedule, the system ensured that every seventy-seven years, each elected Chief was given the opportunity to serve as THO for one year. This union of kingdoms marked the birth of The Affiliated Kingdoms, which has progressively become known as TAK.

Experts in different fields of progress soon began to emerge and by the early 1800s, the first Takyans ventured outside TAK's borders. But the rest of the world had changed over the centuries and destitution ruled many of the lands. THO Kain Garba opened the borders in 1822 to refugees, who brought with them diseases and crime. Unemployment rose. Housing and living space became a problem. To curb the surge of refugees, THO Sera Konziabo instituted the renewable Pass System, which allowed non-Takyans to remain in TAK. By the turn of the century, foreign trade had increased, and investors settled in, but many small Takyan businesses were being pushed out. The borders were soon sealed again to prevent a repetition of the 1521 invasion. Many non-Takyans left.

Beep, beep, beeep, beeeep!
The battery has only one circle remaining. I hit the forward button once again to hear what comes next further along.

Those who chose to remain in TAK worked as domestic help, factory workers, farmers, vendors and street cleaners, receiving enough wages to sustain them. Many non-Takyans were invited to live with their employers. Some had families in these households and their children continued serving their employers.

I fast forward.

The wages of non-Takyans have since been dropped and their movement restrictions tightened, forcing them to remain indoors unless given permission in the form of a signed and dated pass to move about outside of their hom—'

Beeeep! The audiobook's screen goes dark.

ii

I return the audiobook you loaned me this morning to your shelf, battery depleted. To be caught with the device by any member of your family means trouble for both of us – a risk you have taken, time and time again.

I finish up my tasks in the bedrooms on the third floor and put the cleaning things away. Reez might need help with the vegetables for lunch. The sprint in my steps glides me down the stairs, one flight at a time, as my fingers trail along, practically caressing the handrail of the long black – almost obsidian – wooden balustrade. I stop on the first landing where the split staircase becomes one flight of steps that tapers out and downwards towards the front door like the wake of a wedding dress. A pretentious staircase, your mother likes it.

I'm about to descend to the ground floor but stop short with one foot hovering above the first step of the bottom stairs. Voices. Getting closer, Soosie's speaking.

'–as far as I know, sir, but I'm sure we can manage.'

'Well, it has to be either Jay or Sai,' Master Bai says in his unpleasant, guttural voice. Why isn't he at the office right now? 'Even though the loan is important to the Marsas, I cannot afford to let you go. You're far too valuable.'

Soosie was twenty years old when she started managing things around the house – which is the same age that I am now. Life has thrown many wrongs at Soosie. Aged thirty-five, she is petite with a drawn and pale face, but her eyes are alert and full of kindness. She is patient and diligent in her work. She keeps her shabby clothes clean and pressed and knots her headtie above her forehead and not at her nape, which is how servants are supposed to tie their heads. A rock, if ever I saw one

Their voices are below me. I retreat a step backwards, blending into the shadow cast by the large, dark brown cupboard standing close to where the main flight splits up to the right. From my hidden post on the second landing, I have a clear view of the main hall and front door.

'I understand, sir. We'll shift things around as soon as I know which of them will be the loan.'

As you know, Behqu'a, it is not uncommon for homeowners to loan us out to other households when they need us. It is like loaning your neighbour a vacuum cleaner or a water hose. But, being loaned out is much more than that. It's the only opportunity we get to experience something close to a vacation. Of course, the work is always there, but the change of environment, the new faces, the different smells and unfamiliar dynamics in the people's relationships tend to break the monotony of our daily lives. I wish I could tell you how badly I need this opportunity; how badly I want your parents to choose me for the loan, but I cannot trust anyone with my plans.

My attempt to get back to your bedroom is thwarted by the arrival of your half-brother, Amat. He's still in grade school and comes earlier than you and your sister, Ami, who are both in university.

Two hours of waiting and then he finally leaves for religious studies. I hurry back upstairs, pausing on the topmost landing, on the third floor. My eyes swivel to the left, then to the right of the short passageway, chancing a glance behind me, just to be sure that I'm alone. A deafening pounding fills up my ears. You know how anxious I get sometimes.

My knock is quiet and hesitant, my nerves unable to settle. The doorknob is cold as I turn it and push. *Silence.* My nerves settle with the slow exhalation of my breath that I have been holding in all this time. The room is empty. The gods are on my side – you choose today to forget your VisionPhone, dubbed Vizpho, at home.

A few swift steps, a quick snatch from your bedside table and I flee, your Vizpho burning fiercely against my breast. You once told me that the cemented walls have watchful eyes, so Lord forbid I am found in your room when I'm not cleaning it and when you are not home.

I am safe again inside the bedroom I share with Jay in the servants' small flat in the backyard. It is a tiny room with a tiny window high on the wall, almost reaching the low ceiling. The two straight-back wooden chairs, two single beds and a few awkward looking shelves nailed to the wall containing most of our possessions, give the room a crowded look.

It is not a room I am proud of or care about, though it has given me shelter my whole life, ever since Soosie found me next to a dumpster outside Killi Bantamo Temple. I was a scrawny little thing with no lineage, half submerged in a muddy puddle, squealing but ignored by those passing by. I was barely six months old; not much younger than Meeka is now.

I sit on my bed, alert. I know where everybody is right now, but my ears remain strained. My eardrums are stretch like an evening shadow to hear an ant's footsteps approach. I turn on the device.

Cheep, cheep, cheep, cheep, a jarring sound like the chirping of a cricket. My impatient glance on the smooth video screen suddenly brings up the welcomed image of Mo's familiar face.

A Neanderthal brow meets a balding hairline. 'Sai!'

'Mo! Listen, I can't stay long. I've got to get Behqu'a's Vizpho back before he returns from university.'

You don't know Mo; you have never met him. Yet, I told you about the day I first met him. Soosie could not collect the curtains from the tailor and had sent me to get them instead.

Remember how upset you were when I told you about the boys who yelled at me disparagingly, *haram*! *haram*! and laughed as I walked past the train stop? But I hardly heard them because I was soaking in the rays of the sun as it pomaded my skin in ways that I could never have in my prisoned shelter. I even told you how I had to run all the way back home before my bladder exploded and you laughed. I told you so many things about that day, but I did not tell you about Mo.

He followed me after I left with the curtains. I did not know him, a bulbous man with black skin and a squat figure, adorned in a black tunic, navy blue slacks and black fez hat. He told me his name – a distrustful name. Then he mentioned Ray and my shoulders eased down. He was Ray's older brother on their father's side and had recently arrived in Capital City on some errands for his homeowner. The two had not seen each other for over a decade.

He wanted to know about his brother. I told him about the five of us and how we lived and took care of our three-storey, amber roofed, brick house, with its white wooden soffits and weathered but sturdy mahogany and oak front door. I made sure that he knew how much I didn't like living in that house and how desperately I wanted to get away from my life. I've never told you this, but I despise living here, even with you in it.

He told me about the colonies on the autonomous Islands of Mataha where non-Takyans live freely and, oh my! Those honey coated words caress the eardrums. Life is not easy on the Islands, but the people are free – they can make their own choices and have a life of their own. He knew a way off TAK and has been trying to get this message to Ray for over a month. He was going back to the Congg Kingdom in a few days and wanted me to take the message back to Ray. He wrote down the details of a Vizpho on which I could reach him, which I hid in my panties. The paper still has that acrid, yellow urine stain on the corner because I could not take it out before reaching the toilet.

'Is everything all right? Is Ray all right?' Mo asks.

'Everyone's fine. A loan request has been announced. I heard Master Bai telling Soosie about it earlier today.'

An in-drawn breath on the other end of my screen. 'Then the time has come.'

My head bobs up and down. 'The time is here.'

'Then do what you must. In a few days, some of us are relocating to Virtue, a small island west of where we've been living since we arrived at the Mataha Islands, but I'll start getting things ready for you as soon as we are settled.' His high forehead creases. 'Good luck, child! Keep me informed when you can. And please be *careful*.'

To *not* be careful isn't an option. I have come too far to be caught now by the TAKPOLs. These law enforcers are the main reason why none of us dare to venture outside our houses without a signed and dated pass from our homeowners.

Mo's image disappears from the screen, and I head back to the main house. Time resets. I throw more agitated looks around me. Another tentative knock on your bedroom door. It opens this time. My brain works fast.

The corners of your lips curve attractively upwards, but your eyes narrow ever so slightly. I've always found your face pleasant to look at, something I wasn't able to do at the start because we don't look homeowners in the face. But you are different. You're not much older than me, only by two years, with your clean-shaven hair cropped short except for a long, thin, braided strand of hair on each temple, hanging down past your broad shoulders. It was about a year after we met that you told me your hairstyle is worn by young men going off on their own for the first time, and in your case, you were leaving to start university in a few months.

'Sai! I wasn't expecting you until tonight.'

Your arms are warm and tight, your kiss generous, your scent intoxicating. Your hand is on my head, sliding slowly downwards towards my nape as you slip off my headtie. A thick mane of ash-blond, almost white hair falls loose. Untamed, wavy tresses settle unevenly across my shoulders and down my back. My hand finds one of your braids and my fingers twirl loosely around it, feeling the slightly rough texture of your afro hair.

You pull back. Charcoal eyes meet sky blue ones for a moment. You flash me a sheepish grin and step aside to let me come in. I lower my eyes immediately, but only because my guilt will tell you my crimes if you look into them long enough. I don't want to hurt you, but the lies come naturally to me these days.

I take your Vizpho out from my breast pocket and hand in over to you with my hurriedly concocted explanation. And because you love me, you always believe my lies. And because we now have a child together, I can manipulate you even further.

It is not uncommon for one of you to take one of us as a lover.

Soosie's daughter, Jay, doesn't have a father. But the fact that her swarthy, olive skin never burns in our harsh sunlight and her dark hair is less manageable than even my unruly tresses or Soosie's auburn hair leaves a question that hovers over my head like a thundercloud.

It's interesting how certain words can direct one's thoughts to something else. I am reminded of the fierce thunderstorm that had been raging on the day Soosie informed us that the previous owners were leaving and that your family was joining us in a few weeks. It was on that same day that I learned that your father works in Government, at one of the highest levels, and he had children close to mine and Jay's age.

I knew you liked me the first time you came to see me. It was Prayer Day and you had just returned from the Temple with your family. As you shuffled your feet, you told me that you'd misplaced your audiobook and had I seen it. I told you no, sorry, I had not, and you muttered something about taking another look and left. That was a few days after you moved into the house. Do you remember that day? We were so young then, only fifteen and seventeen.

A few weeks after that, you came to apologise for your brother's behaviour when he pulled off my headtie to see the colour of my hair. This time, you stayed longer and talked to me. You ignited my appetite to read the stories you have read and written. You listed a number of books and authors I'd never heard of before. But then, why would I have? I'm not a privileged child. I've never been to school.

You spoke about how hard your father works to keep the family comfortable, yet he disregards the comfort of the servants, and how with some courage, you would tell him exactly what you thought about the current government and its treatment of non-Takyans. You told me your birthday and asked me for mine, which was in fact less than a month away. My head soared up to the ceiling when you found me in the kitchen on my birthday helping Reez peel the potatoes for the evening stew he was preparing, and awkwardly thrust something into my hand. I replied: 'I can't read.'

That was the beginning of our friendship. The next two years brought us closer. Soosie grew more anxious about us. I could see it on her face and in the way her cat-green eyes followed my every movement when she thought that I was not looking. Do you blame her? She was worried because she had been where I was, she knew what was coming yet she lacked the power to protect me from it.

I didn't mind though because Mo and I had a plan. I wanted what was coming. I *welcomed* it. Do you remember your summer break from university last year and how eager I was when you made love to me for the first time? How tenderly you held me and kissed me when you took my virginity? Do you remember when Meeka was born?

Soosie was scared of course; incomparable to the gusts of fumes bursting out your parents' and stepmother, Mother Sien's, ears, first when I got pregnant and then when Meeka was born. You told me that you loved me just after Meeka was born and I told you that I loved you too. Then you promised to take care of us, which you have, and I'm grateful. I hope you will still remember your words one day. At six-months old, our daughter's 7.5kg plays deadly havoc with my lower back as I go about my daily chores. A good child. A lot like you. These days, she usually sleeps, satiated, after using my nipples as scratching posts for her teething gums, leaving them throbbing painfully. My innocent beauty. Obviously, there is no question of marriage between you and I, and Meeka can never live in the main house or claim you as a father, but I hope she will know who you are someday.

  Because, as you know, I am not one of you. My job is to see to your needs and that of your siblings. I clean your rooms from 8 am to 2 pm I change your sheets and dust your rugs. I put away your carelessly discarded clothes, underwear, socks, books and other personal items. I tidy up your wardrobes and place your shoes on the racks, toes facing forward. I sweep your floors and wipe your furniture. In your bathrooms, I fish out clumps of wet hair from your sinks and shower plug holes. I often wonder about how much hair one person can shed a day. I wash toothpaste splatter off your mirrors, while a tiny bit of bleach and a hard bristled brush keeps the tiles flawlessly white. I also run errands for you and your sibling when you are back for the day, and your voices begin to make demands. Your voices. Every day.

'Sai! Bring me a glass of water!'

'Sai! Clean those shoes for my event this evening!'

'Sai! Go and tell Jay to iron the clothes I need for tomorrow!'

'Sai! Take all this stuff downstairs for me!'

'Sai! Clean up this mess!'

'Sai! Sai! Sai!'

It hardly ever stops.

Your voices are like gravel in my head.

Soosie knows how to give me respite sometimes. She sends me to the market. You know how much I like going to the market, it is full of everything you can want – from food stuff to fabrics, furniture, accessories, beauty products and livestock – all stacked or perched or hung or lined up or grouped on stalls, on shelves, in boxes and jars, and in pens, depending on the product. It is a rich place to be in. Everything is affordable at the market and people are happy. Capital City is thriving. Life is good, but not for people like me or Soosie or Reez or Ray or Jay.

We work. Our parents worked, and so did their parents before them, and so on, to serve those who occupy the houses we live in. Your daughter's back will break like mine one day. Her graceful fingers will bend and creak a few years after she starts working – talons that would make an old crone proud. Her eyes will not see or know the features of your face, and it eats you up inside. I see it sometimes. Forgive yourself. There's nothing you can do.

I find Soosie in the kitchen taking stock of the content in the pantry by the backdoor. The kitchen. My sanctuary. My hideout. The only piece of the house I call mine. My eyes delight with every glance at the teal blue walls. Bright orange tiles layer the lower half of the walls, a conflicting beauty to the high white ceiling, now stained with mud, ochre, grey, and dirty white linings. I give you the lingering aromas of Reez's cuisines, clinging to the ceiling and floor, and swirling up into my nostrils like ghostly bouquets of stalagmites and stalactites.

Reez smiles over his shoulder as I walk in. He has an ugly, wrinkled face, beetroot from spending all day over sweltering pots for the past forty-six years. The conspicuous disfigurement on the right side of his face and neck makes him uglier. According to Jay, the homeowner living here when Reez was a young man threw boiling oil at him during a disagreement over a meal he had prepared for her. Despite his pleas, she'd refused to give him a pass to go for treatment. He'd tended the injury himself using herbs from the backyard. It healed after several months but left him this horrific scar.

'You've done it again, Reez! The peanut butter stew smells wonderful!'

He flashes me short, tobacco-stained teeth and goes back to stirring the pot.

I amble over to my surrogate mother. My voice is casual. 'Soosie, I heard you talking about the loan this morning. Any news of who is going?'

Soosie does not look up from her task. 'Sorry, love. I haven't heard anything yet.'

The urge to persist is strong but I don't press further. Instead, I nod and move to Meeka's cot at the far end of the kitchen to check on her. Drunk on mother's milk, she's still snoozing peacefully. There's always somebody who can keep an eye on her in the kitchen.

Later that evening, Soosie comes to our room to inform us that Jay will be going on loan to the Marsas. I have no words to describe my disappointment. I go outside for some air to clear my head and plot my next move.

The following morning, we all hear Jay's screams of anguish.

Early this morning, while feeding the two goats, one ram and few chickens we keep in the backyard, Ray discovered most of the white sheets that Jay had slaved over during the night covered in bird droppings, egg yolk and some black sludge that no one could identify. Ray's green thumbs can make anything grow in the backyard, but his skills do not extend to stain removal. I watch him set his boyish, weather-beaten face in a determined expression, troubled brown eyes hard with concentration, brown hair waving gently in the light warm breeze as he tackles the sheets for the second time with a brush to appease the inconsolable Jay.

I am very fond of Ray. He is the big brother I never had. You see, his tongue was cut off at a Penalty Ceremony when he was just fourteen because his previous homeowner had accused him of telling lies. He was also separated from the people he's lived with his whole life, including his brother Mo, and sent to our house. I was only ten years old at the time, but I felt very sorry for him. You know how much I disapprove of this cruel practice. We watched one on the television once, you and I, and I was appalled when the hands of a non-Takyan youth were chopped off for stealing herbs that could help his sick sister.

Now, this business with Jay's sheets is very unfortunate. I had promised to iron them this morning so that she would have enough time to get ready to be at the Marsas' by midday when she was expected. Now she cannot go, of course. If Ray does not succeed, she would have to do whatever it takes to make sure that Mother Sien's prized sheets are white again.

As it turns out, the bird nest at the top of the pear tree with branches hanging over the washing line had fallen during the night. Half of its contents had landed on the sheets.

Still, no one knows what the sludge-like thing is.

iii

The Marsas could well be your family – same house structure, same upper end of Capital City. The Master works at the same ministry as your father. He has sprouted three children and displays a pretty, bejewelled wife on each arm.

Meeka and I live a quiet and partially secluded life in the back yard with the rest of the servants. We eat and we sit with them but there is a lack of camaraderie between them and us, which I find puzzling and sad all at once. Meeka cries a lot, with her chubby arms stretched out as if reaching out for somebody. Perhaps Soosie or Jay.

The idea of me going on loan upset you; that I was taking Meeka, annoyed you. Yet, you must know that at her age I cannot leave her behind. But I feel guilty because you enjoy being with her so much in the evenings. I wear this guilt like a sock every day as I go about my chores, keeping my head down and trying not to rub the mothers the wrong way. Here, I serve the bickering Mother Haja and querulous Mother Ooly whose covetous and excitable personalities can only be censored with material possessions.

I saw Mother Haja's case full of jewellery. She leaves it lying around carelessly in her room unlocked, but safe in the knowledge that none of the servants will help themselves to a piece. She is especially attached to a pair of dangly gold earrings shaped like teardrops, which she wears only on special occasions. I have been left alone in her room twice already. The last time I was in there, I handled the jewels and put one or two on to see how they fit.

I have kept my head down, yet the TAKPOLs are here for me, just over two weeks after I joined the Marsa household. I am terrified.

Why have they come at night?

Meeka! Panic slides up my throat. I have to get to Meeka!

Bright lights everywhere. I am blind. I'm being silently but brutally man-handled off my bed. No time to change out of my nightwear.

Where *is* Meeka? Why can't I hear her?

Why *won't* they say anything?

I am now floating out of the room I share with Meeka and two other servants. My feet are nowhere to be found. My mind is fuzzy; my surrounding is blurry like a smudged mirror. Fresh, cool air caresses my face, bare arms, bare legs and bare feet. Sand interlaces with my toes. Sharp stones acupuncture my soles.

The Marsas are standing with a large group of gawking spectators.

I feel a cool hard metal surface as I am flung into the back of a waiting vehicle with TAKPOL written on the side in huge characters. The Marsa family continue to stand on the curb, gaping as the vehicle moves away and I see them retreating, until they are out of sight.

I lower my lids and keep them shut. I comfort myself by believing that Meeka is being cared for by one of the Marsas' servants. In despair, I begin to cry.

I gaze out the barred window in front of me in time to see the Penalty House towering before me like an ominous shadow, dark grey and foreboding. Its double turrets, three stories high, loom high against the backdrop of the early morning sky. Just past those turrets is the Enforcer's Hall where all public punishments are carried out, and each crime has a specific punishment.

Terror grips my chest as I stare at that menacing hulk of a building slowly gliding past my view as the vehicle takes a left turn, aiming for its entrance. Given the timeframe, I know it's silly, but I can't help wondering if you've found out what's happened to me and when you're coming for me.

They leave me in a tiny, windowless cell for the rest of the day, as far as I can tell. Somebody's just brought me some doubtful-looking drinking water after several hours of being locked in here, and I'm grateful.

Ray comes with Soosie to see me.

I don't know how much time has gone by.

Her eyes and nose are bloodshot. As soon as they heard, they took permission from your mother, got a signed pass each and rushed over.

No, Meeka is still at the Marsas, but they will get her back soon.

Poor Soosie. Dear Soosie. Her lips quiver as she tells me what I've been waiting to hear; what I've been *dreading* to hear.

But strangely, I feel calm as I take in the news.

More time passes. Shadows lengthen and shorten as the candle wick burns down slowly. The door opens again, and a stern-faced man enters, trailed by two other men in less decorative outfits. He's an envoy of THO Crisa Phaal – the overseer of the Penalty Ceremonies – the judge, jury and executioner. He is here to formally charge me for the theft of one pair of gold teardrop earrings belonging to one Haja Marsa. There is evidence that points to my guilt. My hands will be hacked off at the wrists in four days.

I look down at my shaking hands and giggle without control. I take consolation in the fact that you will come for me just like you promised.

You come the morning before my punishment. I must look like a shrivelled up sultana. My tongue is slimy sandpaper and food is the slug that glides down my throat. Putrid vomit stinks up the corner of my cell. My appearance, my stench, they don't put you off. My fears ebb somewhat as you hold me against you. I'm relieved that Meeka is now safe and back home with Soosie. I hope Ray is milking Goat's breasts fresh every day for my little angel.

'Don't worry,' you tell me, 'everything will be all right.' Your reassuring lips convince me. 'Hang on tight. You'll be out of here by this afternoon.' But they refuse to let me go. Your frustration and helplessness seep from your pores – their crooked fingers constrict my guts as the true implications of my actions catch up with me and the terror on your face unsettles me. Had I not thought this through?

If this all fails, Behqu'a, I am sorry.

You leave, forehead furrowed, no doubt exploring every possible solution. But you take back with you my plea to seek out and speak with Ray as soon as you get home.

Then once again, I'm smothered by the sunless three by four room – its heat, its foulness and its closing walls emitting the fears of previous inmates. Time has no meaning in here. But I wait, latching on to the prospect of seeing Meeka again soon, of seeing you again soon, of attaining what I've been planning these past five years.

iv

There will be grave urgency in your movements and speech when you come for me. You won't say much but will lead me out of the unguarded cell and onto the vast, sweltering courtyard. It will be too early for dusk, and I'll wonder why nobody is around and how you managed to pull off this magic trick. But the questions and answers and explanations and regrets and apologies will come later. My priority will be to get Meeka.

Your car will be standing just outside the main gate, and you'll usher me inside. Then my breath will catch, my body and mind will invigorate as the excited 'ahahah ahahah!' babbles of Meeka fill up my ears. I will yank her out of Ray's arms, clasp her gently against my breasts, inhale deeply. Her scent will rejuvenate me, the softness of her body against mine will comfort me, her incessant babbles will give me hope. But your anger and disappointment will dampen my bliss. For by then, Behqu'a, you would have already known something of what has been happening these past few years, and I will finally reveal it all to you.

You see, Behqu'a, you are my ticket to the Mataha Islands. Your father's position, security clearances and wealth can get us out of the house, out past security checkpoints, out across the border and out into the far north. I've seen his credentials. I sneaked into his room and snooped through his things whenever I was upstairs cleaning your rooms. Soosie and the others were too busy with their own demanding chores to suspect anything.

At first, I wasn't sure if my plan would work. But when you came to see me in my room that first time, I was convinced it would. I had to make sure you wanted me to the point where you'd do anything for me. I don't have an education, but I am smart, observant and pretty. I *could* read a little by then but pretended not to know a word, which brought us even closer together. I know that my fairness and blue eyes are attractive to Takyans, and I saw the way you looked at me. So I played my part and made you love me. Then I waited for the right moment to act.

What was the right moment? You will ask me, and I will tell you that I didn't know at first. It was Mo who suggested the loan, which would get me out of the house so that I could get arrested. I know it sounds insane, but we agreed that the only way you would sacrifice your home, your family, your fortune, the life you've always had was if Meeka or I were in danger of getting hurt. I couldn't commit a crime at our house, you see, I could not incriminate Soosie and the others.

I will tell you about Mo and how he and Ray have been helping me. Remember your stepmother Sien's sheets? Ray. His remorse over hurting Jay nearly gave us away that day. The black sludge was slime that he made using corn starch, water and black paint. He showed her how to clean them the next day by using both freezing and heating methods.

Did I take those earrings, you will ask? Yes, I did. I flushed one down the toilet and hid the other among my things, where it was found by one of the servants. The only glitch was the arrest happening before I could take Meeka home to Soosie.

I will exhale a lengthy sigh, procrastinating but not for too long. I'll tell you that it's now time to talk about Meeka. Then I'll say: from the start, I'd planned to have a child with you and use it as a pawn. You see, Behqu'a, I thought I would despise you like I despise all of your kind. I also had intended to hate any child we had together. But I fell in love with you too and having Meeka was the best thing that ever happened to me. I'm sorry you feel deceived, that I couldn't trust you, couldn't confide in you. And I'm sorry that you have lost everything because of Meeka and me.

This journey has been long, scary and lonely, and I'm bursting with the guilt of betraying the trust of a mother who loved me unconditionally, a disfigured cook who was a father like no other, and a dark-skinned sister who comforted me when I wept at night. I am damaged by the guilt of selfishly abandoning my family to slavery so that I can be happy, and the pain of never seeing them again.

So, please Behqu'a, don't hate me. I am already riddled with enough guilt and pain.

You will not smile but your shoulders will relax, and your eyes will soften. We will cross the border together, the four of us. We will take a boat to the Islands of Mataha where Mo is expecting us. There, we will be safe to raise our daughter under the open blue sky and run freely on the soft fresh grass and swim in the warm clear waters of the Mediterranean Sea.

They Will Fly with Blooded Wings

Victor Forna

We begin with a fable

There is an old story of a devil who walks out of his forest home and lures a girl away with his beauty. His height. His skin. His smell of loam and flowers. His chest. His jokes. His stories. His touch. His gifts. The girl, against the words of friends, against the questions in her heart, follows the man, and marries him by the old River Sewa that meanders behind the town. Her parents support their love, gifting the couple with fruits and rice and clothes. But, after their marriage, their unity, with every step the man takes towards his forest home, he starts losing pieces of himself, a falling of the mask. The girl's heart crashes into her toes. She wants to go back but can't find her way through the towering palm kernel trees. The man's feet, which she loved to kiss, become brown spiders that dance into the night. The man's legs, which she caressed as if searching for miracles, become flies—a dark constellation buzzing around the girl. The man's chest and neck become silent white maggots that puncture the earth. Only his head remains when they reach his forest home the next evening. His skin melts and falls away, his banana yellow skin. The girl holds a bleached skull in her hands, in the end, stuck forever in the devil's forest home. In some versions of the story, the girl still roams amongst the red trees, searching. In others, a boy, a child, swoops in, fearless and tender, and saves the girl with nothing but a cutlass in his hand. There is also a version where the girl learns how to fly and saves herself.

Then

He hit her for the first time on the last day of Harmattan, January 2013, a few months before the fangs appeared, before the scales started growing on his forearms, dandruff-like.

She looked at herself in the bathroom mirror, at her blackened eyes, at her swollen lips, at the history of violence he had written on her body, and she wanted to leave. But she also glimpsed on her body the ghosts of his love for her, the ghosts of his kisses at 3am. on mornings she couldn't sleep.

(And sometimes the ghosts of all we were, the memories, were the reasons we stayed with these monster-things.)

And that was why she stayed.

And that was why when he came back from the office, from his work as a geologist, at 9pm, with their son dreaming on her back about flight, she spilled herself at his feet.

She begged for his forgiveness. Because it had to have been her fault that he hit her; something in the way she said a word, a phrase, something in the way she moved her eyes, something in the way she added salt to his cassava leaves.

Wordless, he walked away.

Every tap-tap of his shoes against the earth, against the universe, was a dagger to her heart. He left her on the floor, on that maroon carpet he bought so long ago from a marketplace in Morocco.

She cried.

But she stayed, and she stayed, and she stayed.

Now

The house does not dare breathe when he returns from the night.

He parks his red jeep in the middle of the compound.

The doors of the house do not dare creak as he opens them, nor the table he props a bottle of beer on, nor the chair he sits in for awhile before lumbering off to bed.

In this pinching silence, she hears a sound: her son plucking the strings of his new guitar. One by one by one. She rushes down the stairs, heading for his room. He should know better. But it's already too late. She lets out a thin and weary sigh. She watches from the corridor.

Her husband crawls into their son's room. He crawls on all fours. There are scales on his wrinkled forehead. He has vertical slits for eyes, blinking, blinking, blinking. He snarls. His fangs glint at the touch of the weak light overhead.

Her heart crashes into her toes.

Her son's smile fades, suddenly, on seeing his father; a smile a god has just remembered to erase from the world.

—Papa, please, I am sorry I woke you.

The monster-thing slaps at the boy with his jagged tail.

A scar on the boy's cheek reopens. The boy scurries to a corner. His fingers fumble over his bleeding face. Please. Please. Please.

The monster-thing crawls closer to the boy.

He lifts his tail and strikes again, and again.

She hesitates, then inches forward. She enters her son's room. She dares. That's enough! Let him go. She reaches to touch the back of the monster-thing. That's enough. Does this make you feel strong? Go and do this with men your size.

He turns and faces her, all she hoped for, head tilted and twitching. His movement is graceful through the air. In a flash, he nails her on the floor. She doesn't fight, numb. His mouth latches to that space where the neck meets with the clavicle, like sky and sea.

He sucks her blood.

The house breathes, exhales.

A small moment of calm.

She doesn't see her son go into the kitchen.

But she sees him return.

So much rage in his nine-year-old eyes, the downward curve of his brow.

He sprints towards them.

— No!

In the boy's hand, there is a knife.

Then

A friend forced her to come along to River Number 2 that lonely December day. How had she been in the city for almost two years and still hadn't visited River Number 2? There, she met him. They walked past each other, he in his early twenties, and she, just turned eighteen. They smiled. Their eyes shifted along their bodies. Not love at first sight, but they both felt a tingling in their hearts, a fluttering not quite butterflies. So, when they met a second time that same day, and he came up to her, she did not walk away.

All through her days in university, he brought her provisions: milk, cocoa, sugar in blue boxes, cereal, bread, butter, cheese, when she had no one to give her a leone. She said yes to him, at last, that evening, third year, when he walked through the rain to bring her a novel she needed for her lectures the next morning. Chinua Achebe. Yes. Yes. Yes.

He was into rocks; she was into poetry. He, melancholy-hearted and she, talkative and dramatic on most days. He tended gardens, dug the earth, made new life; she baked, found meditation kneading dough, the smell of yeast. He went for walks on long and winding roads; she stayed in, reading long and winding books. They both jogged and preferred to do it in the morning. They both played video games. They both hated dancing. He only watched movies in black and white, or Nollywood movies; she hated both, but joined him those Saturday evenings, head on his chest, listening to his heartbeat.

When her grandma died, he let her cry onto his arms. They sat on an unfinished structure made of dark wood at Lumley Beach. Pigeons, brown and grey, dotted the distant horizon. She cried for her grandma because she couldn't tell her how much she meant to her. He gave her the silence she needed to grieve, playing gently with her braids, like the breeze from the sea.

On other nights they would talk and talk and talk about films, and books, and gods, and god, and magic from ancestors, and his rocks and her poetry and how the entire universe existed between them, and the family they were going to make someday. They never wanted to get married. She cited from a story she once read – too romantic for marriage – and he agreed, but they were married in November 2007, at Syke Street, in a church dedicated to Saint Anthony.

The morning their son was born, he couldn't stop looking down at him and crying. His hands trembled. I love you, she said. I love you, too, without the too – their private joke – and I love him, he continued, laughing through his tears.

(How did we become these monster-things, hurting the ones we say we love?)

Now

The monster-thing swivels just in time, and he is like a flame in her tear-glazed eyes.

She does nothing. She doesn't hold the monster-thing down, pull back his head and show the world his neck, so her son could stab deep into it, into a vein.

The monster-thing fists the boy's chest. He snatches the kitchen knife from his grasp.

Still, she does nothing. She doesn't slap the monster-thing. She doesn't dig her nails into his skin, no matter how pointless it could have been.

The boy falls, breathless, like a leaf, onto the floor. There, he whimpers.

She catches her son's eyes.

He doesn't look away.

— Mama, he mouths, help me.

She does nothing. She doesn't hurl her body over her son. She doesn't become a shield that saves him from the wrath of the monster-thing.

— You think you're grown now? You can fight me now? He says, as he crawls towards the child. His forked tongue licks the air.

She does nothing. She doesn't plead on behalf of the boy, from the floor, that's our son, that's our son, that's our son, don't hurt him anymore.

He towers over the boy.

— Why, papa, why?

— Because you deserve it, says the father to the son, we get what we deserve.

She struggles to get to her feet, because of all the blood she lost when her husband sank his fangs into her.

She sways.

The monster-thing pins down the boy. They breathe heavily.

The boy wrestles, kicking, scratching.

— I'm sorry, I'm sorry, the boy mutters. What are you doing? No. Papa.

The monster-thing wields the knife in his hand like a butcher, like a god bent on rewriting the flesh. He chops off fingers on the boy's left hand.

—You think you can fight me now?

Three fingers on the floor.

Pointer. Middle. Ring.

The boy flails, screams, shrieks, holding one hand in the other.

The pain, the pain, he passes out.

The monster-thing crawls away, returns to his lair, to his dark room.

On the floor, she cradles the unconscious boy, in her quaking, flower-like embrace.

As she wraps her dress around his bleeding hand, she spots goosebumps on his neck, on his shoulders, right down to his back, almost like places where feathers once were, where feathers should have been.

He needs a hospital.

She needs to do something. Why has she been here so long?

Then

When he began turning into this monster-thing, in April of 2013, it was the fangs that first appeared in his mouth. Through a grin, he showed her his new teeth one morning, like a child might show an art piece to their mother in bad lighting. A slap. Sweltering with rage over the colours of the bedsheets. She vetted the new formation: long, sharp, and red. She should have run away that morning—but she made him breakfast instead, bread with scrambled eggs, almost dancing, and served him coffee in his favourite white cup with the stars along the sides, and kissed him, and told him not even fangs could set them apart.

Now

She tip-toes up the stairs.

With each rise towards his lair, her heart screams louder.

Her right hand hovers over the golden handle of the door. Contact, cold. She opens.

She enters his room.

No longer *their* room.

—I need the keys to the gate, she says. I need the keys to the car. He'll die. He needs a hospital.

At first, he only answers with grunts, with his mouth turned down.

Shed-skin huddles on the floor. The stench rising, rum, rot, bitter in her eyes.

Then, into the silence, he says, through cigarette smoke, let him die.

His words. His words bring back that primal pain she felt in May of 2010. The pain that hung around her groin, her back, her sides, as she pushed an entire universe into the world.

Let that universe die.

Desperate, she lunges towards the book-strewn table where the keys to freedom, to life, await.

Then

She grew tired of the fangs two years after they came. Fangs to scales to hooves to eyes rimmed with crimson. She grew tired of his late nights out. She grew tired of his drinking. She grew tired of his coldness. She grew tired of how he drained her blood, how his fangs demanded to be fed. She grew tired of swollen lips. She grew tired of swollen eyes. She grew tired of being afraid of a person she was meant to love.

—I want to leave him, she said to her mother one day, between spoons of rice.

—Hmm?

—It's all becoming too much for me, Mama, she says, the stew colourless on her tongue. I have lost so much of myself.

—No.

—What do you mean no?

—Transformation is nothing new to us, her mother replies.

—Mama, look at all these scars, look at all these scars where he bites to suck my blood, and lashes me. I tried. I tried. I'm tired. Nostalgia and ghosts are no longer enough to keep me there. Do I even love him?

—Shut up.

—Mama.

—A man will be a man. You, as a woman, must endure. Must sacrifice. Think about how far you've come. Think about your son. Think about your age. You're no longer a child. Go home. Take care of your husband. Did I not teach you well? Do you know how much your father put me through? But did I leave? Answer me. Don't look at me like that.

—I will die in that house one day. You will find my body, I swear. You should see my son, Mama. He has gotten so timid. Doesn't even dare touch his guitar when he comes home...I wish Granny was here.

—You like exaggerating. You don't just leave a marriage ... everything will be fine. It will get better.

(And sometimes the imagination of all a person could become, the hope of better, better, better, was why we stayed with these monster-things.)

Now

She doesn't even get close to the table with the keys—his tail slaps against her face.

The world spins, as she falls.

—Our son will not die because of you.

She stands, gets up.

—My son will not die because of you.

He keeps hitting her, over and over, with his tail, over and over, beating her, until she is all tears and the perfect portrait of defeat. He wins. She can't hold herself up anymore. She lies on her side, on the skin-covered tile, sweating, crying into her hands, silent, silenced, and cowering without hope.

Then it happens so quickly. She hears the call, piping notes, and lifts her head—a giant silver eagle, demanding to be gazed upon, has entered the room.

It comes in through the open door, beating its wings, again and again. Its talons are sharp, ready for war, for battle. The bird circles around the chandelier on the high ceiling, cutting the soft light.

It hurtles downwards, to attack the monster-thing.

She sees its brown eyes, in a shivering moment, and she knows, at once, this bird, this giant silver eagle in the half-dark, is their son.

And his presence as a bird makes a forgotten echo of her grandmother bloom in her, a resurfacing of a sunken thing.

Back home in Sumbuya, in the evening, as the farmers returned from their plots of rice, her grandmother braided her hair. She sang into her strands of how she could transform into an eagle, that there was a magic that slumbered inside her spine.

—Can I fly too? asked the girl, five or six years old.

—Maybe. It runs in the family. But we forget. There are things that will try to hold you down, people, places, time. You must never let them, child.

—Granny, teach me the magic.

—Everything that will learn how to fly someday, must teach it to itself.

—Show me.

Then, her grandmother showed her. She forgot everything.

How did the boy, at nine, teach himself to fly, like his great-grandmother the eagle? This boy, always on about his guitar and music, this daydreamer. She had been so focused on her husband's transformation into a monster-thing, that she missed her son's transformation into the freest of things, the most beautiful. So strong he has become, so vast are his wings. But is it not known that pain, that the need to uncage himself, could set a boy into strides grander than the lengths of his legs? The severed fingers could have been the last push. What will our bodies not do for solace?

She watches with awe, at the boy as an eagle, she watches. A smile dares on her bleeding lips.

—Don't fight for me, she almost yells. Don't forgive my betrayal, my inaction. Go on, fly away, and own the sky.

But the boy as an eagle fights the monster-thing.

Son versus father.

Blood on his beak. Blood on his wings. Maybe the blood is the boy's, maybe it is the mother's, maybe it is the father's. A family unable to tell where the hurt of one member begins and that of another ends.

They fight.

They dance.

Their fight goes out into the compound.

She chases them. She squints, to see in the blue moonlight.

Is her husband trying to run away?

The boy as an eagle descends from the sky. He dodges the whipping tail of the monster-thing, familiar with the history of its movement, the history of its hate. His beak catches skin, but the monster-thing doesn't bleed.

The monster-thing stabs at his eagle boy with his limb, sending him staggering backwards through the air.

The fight weaves for a long time, back and forth, and back again.

Fearless, the boy as an eagle darts forward, talons outstretched. This time, he lands firm on the monster-thing. He plucks out an eye.

The monster-thing yelps, a shattered howl.

The boy as an eagle plucks out the other eye.

The monster-thing flails wildly, screams, turning in circles, like a dog after its shame.

The boy as an eagle beats his giant wings and floats in the air. He could fly down and cut a vein that would end the monster-thing forever.

She notes his hesitation.

Maybe, the boy thinks of kindness—to give a thing never offered to him.

Heart throbbing, she waits for him to decide.

Next

They will hold hands in the woods behind their house. She will breathe in, breathe out, breathe in, again. The smell of her husband's blood will reach for her nostrils, like a phantom limb trying to destroy a lover one last time. But she will not flinch, her new feathers over her landscape of scars will not rustle.

— Yes? she will ask her son. Is this how you do it?

He taught her a thing she couldn't teach herself —how to fly, how to be free, how to leave ghosts and pointless hopes behind.

—Yes, he will answer, and glance back one last time.

And they will run, run, run, mother and son, and they will leap into the night air, reaching for the sky, reaching for the stars, and they will leave all their hurt behind, and they will fly with blooded wings.

We end with a fable

There is a story, a newer story, a lesser-known story, a story not to be trusted, the account of a man who walked into the forest-home of a devil in April of 2013. A man lured by the beauty of a rock through the trees, as he searched for a hole into the underparts of the earth. A rock almost, but not quite, covered with yellowing leaves. The man stood in front of the stone, mouth agape. How could the inanimate remind him of his mother, of his wife, of his son, of everyone he had ever loved? He also saw in the stone a likeness of his father—that man of sorrow, that man so miserable at loving him when he was a fledgling child. He reached out his hands, through space, to touch the god. Boom. Explosion. A thing not meant to be caressed by mortal palms. The story could then tell us that the man died in the white explosion, no trace of his soul or body to be found in the aftermath, torn from the fabric of existence. The story could also tell us that he lived, the man, that he went home early, that he showered, that he ate fruits, that he read one of his geology books, that he watched the news, that he rustled his son's hair and tucked him to bed, that he made love to his wife from 8:00pm until they could no longer know the borders of their bodies, that he woke the next morning and found fangs growing in his mouth, over his canines. The story could also tell us none of this was true, that the man had always been a monster, that monsters weren't always justifiable things.

Trial By Fire

Onengiye Nwachukwu

Kariba sits in her favourite chesterfield chair. She turns around to view the clock on the wall behind her again. It is 7:29pm She wishes time would move faster. A smile flashes across her lips at the sound of a honk outside. She lifts her head to peak through the open louvres. It is not the grey vehicle she hopes to see. She sits back, sighing. There is a stool positioned in front of the sofa opposite her. There is a food warmer made of stainless-steel on top of it, a bowl of water on the floor, and a neatly arranged pile of china plates as well. She looks at the clock for the umpteenth time. It is 8:00pm.

***

Kariba has had a tough life. Nathan and Furo Lawson, her maternal grandparents, raised her when her mother decided to leave for the city in search of a better life, when she was just three. The man who got her mother pregnant, Levi, a local pallbearer, strongly denied the pregnancy. They had other children who Kariba could have gone to live with, but they agreed it would encourage their daughter's recklessness if they did. So, she was stuck with her grandparents.

They adored the little girl and gave her their time and affection. Most nights, after dinner when the stars were out, Kariba and her grandma would lay a mat on the ground, spread a piece of cloth over it to keep them from catching a cold, then lay together under the sky. Nathan would drag his cushionless chair close, so he could sit beside them, then he would narrate a folktale to Kariba, one with a lesson, which he often revealed to her after the story. Other times, Furo would be the one to entertain with stories of the tortoise or lion. Sometimes, they would sing songs, talk about the stars and moon, then go to bed. Sometimes, Kariba would fall asleep before the end of the story and Nathan would carry her and tuck her in bed.

***

Kariba is about eight years old now and one night, while she is asleep, she has a strange dream. In the dream, she is crying and chasing two babies. She is calling out to them, wailing at the top her lungs, to not go any further and return. The dream is bizarre: the babies are only in diapers, yet they run at a pace that Kariba cannot catch up with. They run until they arrive at a place on the path where a giant wall blocks the road. The top of the wall goes far up into the skies. There is no way around, but the babies run right through the wall like it is not there. Kariba arrives at the wall seconds after, still crying, she pushes it, like it is something she can bring crashing down with physical strength, but nothing happens. Then Kariba throws her hands over her head and sits on the ground, crying even more loudly now.

The night outside is still, the stars glittering up above, the moon, shy and absent. Only the creaking of crickets and that distinct ribbit of frogs pierce the silence. Inside the room, there is a dim glow of flickering light in the corner, it cuts through the blackness of the night casting slanted shadows on the wall – of a chair and a mat that is positioned upright. It looks like the image of a weirdly-shaped monster on the wall. There is loud snoring coming from the adjoining room. The room is silent until there is a faint cry.

'No! stop running. Come back, come back please!' The voice grows louder into a passionate cry. Furo is jolted awake. In her sleepy state, she does not know where she is or what is happening, for a moment. Then she shakes herself out of her daze and what she sees next frightens her: Kariba is pushing against the wall in a corner of the room with her eyes shut.

'KB! KB! Kariba open your eyes.' She commands as she lightly slaps her, several times, across the cheek to snap her awake. When she opens her eyes, the child is confused. Nathan stumbles into the room, only wearing his loin cloth around his waist.

'Erebo, what is happening here?' he asks, confused.

'It is Kariba. She had a bad dream.' She holds the child's face in her palms, examining her.

'Please you people should go to sleep. And try to be quiet for the rest of the night if you can. I am too tired.' Nathan instructs as he stumbles back into the room from where he emerged.

Furo smoothens the bed as she urges Kariba to go back to sleep, and she falls asleep a few minutes later. Furo does not sleep immediately, she is disturbed. Kariba's behaviour was a bit odd, but she dismisses the event as an isolated one that will probably not occur again.

Nathan and Furo run a small kiosk in front of their house, where they sell essentials such as tea, milk, sugar, sweets and a few other items of little worth. The shop is scanty and barely earns them any profit. They cannot afford to send Kariba to school, but the girl does not despair. Every day, when she wakes up, she sweeps the compound and keeps the house clean. After finishing her chores, she sits with her grandma until the other children start to return from school. Then she goes out to play with them, not going too far from the house. Furo draws her close when she is in the kitchen preparing meals. 'One day, you will get married and have a family of your own. It is important that you learn to manage your home now so you will be a good wife and mother.'

The strange dream did not occur again, and everyone forgot about it, until one night, when Kariba is ten. Furo awakens in panic and sees the little girl pushing against the wall as before. She moves swiftly to grab her and shake her awake. Nathan arrives, and this time, he does not leave, instead, he sits on the chair in the room and asks Kariba to narrate this bothersome dream to them. After, they have sent Kariba back to bed. He goes back into his room, sits on the floor and just stares ahead, into the dark, into nothing, deep in thought. *What could be happening to this child? What does this dream mean and why does it afflict her so?* Later, he goes back to sleep, resolving to pursue the matter at dawn. Meanwhile, sleep eludes Furo. The similarity of Kariba's two episodes raise more questions. The child said the same words as she cried, even pushed at the same spot on the wall. *Why would an old dream reoccur after two years?* She also resolves to get clarity when Kariba wakes up.

The next morning, while Kariba is busy outside with chores, Nathan and Furo sit together to deliberate over what they should do about Kariba's dream. They agree to speak to Kariba again and maybe pay Adaka, the seer, a visit if the dream occurs again. After Kariba narrates the sequence of her dream, Nathan is no closer to understanding it. *What could this all mean?* He is not a superstitious man nor is he religious, but he is aware that the recurrence of a particular dream is ominous. He did not arrive quick enough to witness Kariba pushing the wall, but the sound of her crying, that awful and passionate cry worried him; it almost scared him.

Months pass without an episode. Things appear to be back to normal in the Lawson household. They keep a watchful eye over her. Even Kariba is becoming free-spirited, she has made more friends and she is allowed to go to their houses, and they are allowed in the Lawson household too. One day, while she is loitering at the docks waiting for her friend Angela, who has gone to buy some snacks for them, a boat arrives and a man descends with his wares and sees Kariba. He stares at her like he is studying a book. She catches his gaze but feeling awkward about making eye contact with a stranger, she looks away. Her curiosity gets the best of her, and she looks at him again. He is still staring – his brow furrowed, a scowl on his face and a creased forehead.

Kariba is standing by a shop waiting for her friend near the dock. The man walks to the shop, and says, 'I want to buy groundnuts, how much do you sell?'

'Ten and twenty naira,' the shopkeeper replies.

'Give me one for twenty naira then,' he says, handing the seller a twenty-naira bill.

He has decided to talk to this little girl and her parents, whoever they might be. He cannot afford for her to flee, or it will create the difficulty of going into the village to search for her. He must pursue this matter now. That is the problem that comes with his gift, the urgency. The gift of séance has been as much a bane and as a boon in his life. It is a gift to share in the joys and agonies of the people whose lives he sees into.

Then he wheels around and walks the short distance to where Kariba is standing.

'Little girl, what is your name?'

'Kariba is my name.'

'Do not be afraid, I have not come to hurt you but warn you: something bad is going to happen. I may need to talk to your parents. What are their names?'

Now, Kariba is even more afraid. Just at that moment, Angela arrives at the scene.

'Good afternoon, sir,' Angela greets, but the stranger only acknowledges her with a quick raise of the hand.

'Can you take me to your parents? I must see them now if I can. I need to discuss something important with them.'

'Okay sir,' Kariba responds, afraid, 'let us go.' She begins to walk homeward with a confused Angela, and the stranger in tow, who follows quietly.

When they arrive at the Lawsons' residence, Kariba goes inside to inform her grandparents of what has transpired and her grandfather comes out first to see the man whom he recognises as Adaka George, the popular seer.

'Adaka, good afternoon. I didn't know it was you. I was coming out with an intent to berate the person who has scared my grandchild,' he said.

He offers him a chair to sit and a cup of water.

'Nathan, I am sorry about the way I approached your grandchild. The situation called for it. Perhaps, I could have done it differently, but I didn't have time to plan. Anyway, I am here because there is calamity afoot in that little girl's future. I see some grimy hands tugging at her and rubbing her face. That child is going to need all the assistance she can get. Has anything strange happened in her life lately?' he asked.

'Yes. She has had the same dream, two years apart. It has troubled my wife and I, and we even agreed to see you should it happen a third time.' He sends for Kariba and Furo, and Kariba narrates the dream to Adaka, who tells them that Kariba is destined to only birth two children and those are the two children she is chasing in the dream. But she is also destined to bury those children. That wall she sees in her dream represents death and it keeps the living sequestered from the dead. The babies go through the wall because they know they belong to that world. Kariba cannot go through because she is not of that world.

'God forbid.' Furo protests loudly as Adaka is interpreting the dream and draws the attention of everyone. 'Not my child,' she says.

'Quiet woman! Let the man speak.'

'This is what I see about this child. Her soul is troubled.'

'Adaka, I have heard what you have to say. But I have a question. What can be done to forestall this impending tragedy?'

'To be honest Nathan, I do not know. I only see and interpret the message. I do not recommend or dispense a solution.'

'Okay. I suppose we will have to find one elsewhere. Thank you for everything.' Adaka gets up and leaves.

Kariba is afraid and weeps. Furo takes her away to comfort her. Nathan remains where he is a while longer. After a while, he rises, picks up his cane and exits the house.

***

Kariba sits alone on the bed. She has not gone outside to play with her friends for four days now. She has been crying since the seer's visit. She hardly eats. Furo has assured her that they will do everything in their power to find a solution to this.

One night, a few weeks after the prophesy, Kariba has the same dream. This time, Nathan reveals in the morning that he has consulted Akaso, the village deity, and her oracle will perform a ritual at the house later that day.

Akaso's oracle arrives at the house. He chants and pours libations in the name of his deity. He hands Kariba a white gown and instructs her to change into it. A hen is slain, the blood emptied on Kariba's head while she is kneeling in the centre of a room, amidst more incantations. After this ritual, Akaso's oracle informs them that Kariba is clear now. They will need to perform another ceremony, but this one puts her in the clear. She has no reason to be afraid anymore. But days after the ritual, Kariba has the dream again.

***

Kariba is fourteen years old. She has been subjected to several blood sacrifices by this time and her grandparents have spent so much money on goats and chickens. The dreams are no longer as frequent, but they still occur. Kariba is convinced this curse cannot be reversed. She is never going to start a family like other girls.

By December that year, people start to troop into the village to celebrate the festivities. Kariba is thrilled to be meeting friends who she only gets to see this time of the year. She goes to the beach for a carnival one day. There is music and entertainment for everyone to enjoy. Someone bumps into her from behind, she turns to see a young man who apologises. His name is Dagogo. He is funny and she likes him, so she introduces him to her friend Angela, and they spend the rest of the day together until it is time to go home. The three friends are inseparable throughout the holiday. At the end of it, they escort Dagogo to the docks to board a boat. It is the beginning of a great friendship. Whenever Dagogo visits, the three of them are always together. Their parents get to know each other and approve of their friendship, especially Nathan and Furo, who hope that it will give Kariba comfort despite her hardships.

One day, Kariba tells her grandfather that she wants to learn to make clothes. If she cannot get an education, at least she can learn a skill. Nathan agrees. Two days later, he gives her the money from his savings to pay for three months of sewing school. She shows so much dedication to her craft, graduates with flying colours and is rewarded with a sewing machine. Kariba continues to perfect her skill until she becomes one of the best seamstresses in Buguma.

***

Six years have passed since she met Dagogo. Kariba has matured into womanhood; she is twenty years old now. Men begin to woo her, but she does not consider a relationship with any man; she is only focused on herself and business.

Kariba has never visited any other city; she has spent her entire life in Buguma. Dagogo tells her that work as a seamstress would be more profitable in the . He suggests she move to the city and stay at his place until she has enough money to get one of her own. His suggestion makes sense, because she only makes a few clothes a month in the village, and the designs pose no challenge. Kariba is ambitious, she has been a seamstress for over six years, and desires to be successful. When she informs her grandparents of her intention, they are not convinced at first. But with time, she makes them see reason and they agree, with the promise that she will come home often to see them. She and Angela cry when she tells her she is moving to the city. When the day comes, she leaves the house at 8:00am and boards a boat. The ride is one hour long. She marvels at the city when she arrives, it seems so big and crowded with vehicles. She has a book with the address of Dagogo's residence written in it, and with help of strangers, she finds the house. Dagogo gives her a warm welcome.

Months after her arrival in the city, Kariba rents a shop, which doubles as the house where she will live. Dagogo works as a technician at Newclime. His office is not far from her shop, so he sees her on weekends or sometimes, after work. He is the only person she knows in the city. All the time they spend together has made him fall in love with her. One day, he tells her about his feelings, but she rejects his advances, telling him it is a waste of his time. He knows about her situation, but he does not care. He just wants to spend the rest of his life with her, he tells her.

'Why would you want someone like me when you can have any woman?' She asks.

'I have known you for years now and you are the best woman I know, that's why.'

'We can be married, even if we do not have kids. I just want to be married to you,' he adds.

After months of persistence, Kariba agrees. She knows she is in love with him too. He is a good man and since he knows about her problems and still wants to marry her, that could augur well for them. She goes home to inform her grandparents. They are thrilled but also have doubts, but she assures them he knows about the curse, and they give their support and blessing.

Before the wedding, Nathan informs Kariba of a strong Juju man in Alabama, a nearby village, who has promised that he can reverse the curse. She is not convinced, but he appeals. She knows he wants the best for her, so they plan for the trip. When the day arrives, the sorcerer gives her a cream to apply every night just before she sleeps. He tells her it is to ward off the evil spirits. He buries a goat whole afterwards, with promises that the curse has been reversed. A week later, she weds Dagogo.

Since her marriage to Dagogo, the dreams have ceased. She is not sure the curse is lifted yet because it appears too easy. Her husband has faith that it is, but he supports her decision not to have children. But after three years of marriage without the dreams, she is optimistic and wants to have children. She wants to reward her husband for being supportive. They try for a child, and she gets pregnant. Her husband is so happy that he does not let her even carry her own bags. He hires a domestic helper for the house chores and he handles any other tasks. Kariba does not even make clothes the entire time she is pregnant. After her full term, she delivers twin boys, without any problems. The babies are certified healthy by the doctor, so they return home.

They name them Nimi and Omie. She breastfeeds the boys when they are hungry, and her husband makes sure she lacks nothing. One evening, while alone at home, she feeds them. When she is done, she places them in their crib and runs to the bathroom to take a shower. When she returns, she goes to the crib to play with them but only Omie is responding; Nimi is dead. She screams and when her neighbours gather in her home, all she says is, 'I just fed him.'

Dagogo tries to comfort her; they still have a baby. Her shock lasts a long time after the death of Nimi, so Dagogo brings Furo to the house to temporarily care for the baby until his wife recovers. Kariba is filled with fear and paranoia after the death of Nimi. She remembers her dreams. She thinks she has done everything she can, yet Nimi died. She is determined to fight for Omie to survive even if she must trade her life for his. Kariba becomes overprotective of Omie. She tries to control every aspect of his life, but she cannot tell him why things are this way.

Omie is a good and healthy child. He performs well at school and is competitive at sports. He receives awards as the most outstanding student through every level of education. After university, he gets a good paying job in the oil and gas industry, and he is a dedicated and responsible staff member. His parents want him to marry quickly; he understands that he is an only child, but he is not in a hurry. He understands his mother's anxiety, but he refuses to be controlled. As a child, as soon as he learned to speak, he held his own opinions.

Omie meets a girl when his company sponsors them to take a joint mandatory course, which they are to attend with staff from another company. They sit together and he finds himself attracted to her. 'My name is Omie,' he says as he takes her hand and shakes it. 'Jessica,' she replies. Before the course is over, they are good friends and enjoy each other's company. Soon, they begin to date. They date for almost a year, and they know they are perfect for each other. He decides that he will ask her to marry him.

One evening, Kariba is invited to a church vigil by her neighbour. She agrees to attend. It is a miracle service with deliverance from all forms of affliction. *She has tried witch doctors and sorcerers, and none have worked. What does she have to lose if she attends this miracle crusade, she thinks?* She attends with the neighbour and does not enjoy the service. There is too much shouting, and she does not understand the proceedings. When she hears the pastors asking people with problems to come to the altar, she joins them. When it is her turn in the queue, she explains her problem. The pastor prays for her and when the service is over, she is taken to the head pastor who puts her on a long fasting and prayer routine. She is hopeful and accepts the challenge because she will do anything to keep the hand of death away from her child. She has made one mistake before due to her misguided feeling of euphoria; she is not about to repeat it.

Dagogo has travelled to Abuja for work, so Kariba is alone at home. She fasts for three days without food and water, along with three-hour prayer sessions daily. She asserts in her heart that nothing will happen to Omie. On the third day, after her prayers, she calls her son Omie at a pay phone; she has not heard from him in days.

She dials his office number.

'Hello, good afternoon, this is NAOC dispatch, please who is on the line?' A female voice replies.

'My name is Kariba Braide, please may I speak with Omie Braide, I am his mother?' She replies.

'Okay. Please stay on the line while I connect you to him.'
'Hello Mummy?'
'Omie, how are you doing?'
Omie tells her he will return on the 24th, the Saturday after next. 'I will be coming by with someone special I want you to meet, okay?'
'Someone special? Omie, have you found a wife?' Kariba dances with joy.
Omie laughs and tells her that he will be home at 8:00pm.

***

By 3:00pm on the 24th, Omie picks up his bag to leave his quarters on the rig. He and nine others are supposed to be on the 3:05pm boat to Brass. It is a two-hour journey. By his estimation, if they arrive at 5:05pm, he can pick up his car and drive the one-hour trip to Jessica's house in Port Harcourt. There will be plenty time to kill, and they will leave her place by 7:30pm to be at his mother's by 8:00pm The plan seems solid.

They get on the boat, everyone in their mandatory orange coloured life jackets, and it takes off at 3:05pm. The boat is cruising through the sea. He is tired and dozes off. An hour later, he is woken by screams. He sees people jumping overboard. Before he gathers his wit about him, there is a big crackling sound. He sees the fire and tries to make sense of what is going on; it is all happening too fast. He tries to rise to his feet, but the boat is still spinning. He falls to the floor of the boat, manages to pick himself up and as he is about to take a dive into the water, there is an explosion that throws him into the water. Floating and badly hurt, he tries to open his eyes, but he cannot see. His eyes are hurt. He is crying out for help, but no one hears him, because no one is there. The spinning boat moves far away from his co-passengers. He is marooned. Then he smells burnt flesh, and it is so close. He starts to swim. He does not know where he is going, but he just swims. A few yards more and he feels something; he sighs in relief. It could be a board he can rest on; he is getting tired. When he reaches for it, there is an extremely sharp pain in his arm, and he cries out in agony. He is bleeding. What he thought was a board was the spinning boat's propeller. He is stranded in the middle of the sea, without sight and missing an arm. He is losing blood. Before the world goes dark, he only has one thought, 'Mummy', and his breathing ceases.

***

She lifts her head to peak through the open louvres. It is not the grey vehicle she hopes to see. She sits back, sighing. There is a stool positioned in front of the sofa opposite her. There's a food warmer made of stainless-steel on top of it, a bowl of water on the floor, a neatly arranged pile of China plates as well. She looks at the clock for the umpteenth time. It is 8:00pm She runs her hand across the line of her collarbone, smiling and thinking about how she proved the seer wrong. *My son turned out okay, my son became a man.*

A Girl Becomes a Vessel

Kofi Konadu Berko

1

She has tried and failed and tried and failed until today...

The girl's grandmother has been missing for two years and it's her fault. She bends, cups water from the tap into her hands and splashes it over her face. Her middle finger lingers on a pimple under her nose. She lifts her head from the washbasin and stares at the jagged-edged thing that holds her reflection. It's a piece from her father's office. She stole it, hoping that it would force him to barge into her room to claim it. Anything was better than the cold indifference.

Droplets of water from her left eyelid, hang on her lashes, drop to her cheek then down her chin and into the sink with a series of 'kos!' She stares at the thing in the mirror and sighs. The thing has her eyes—red corneas. Its hollow cheeks resemble the depression on both sides of her face. That is where the similarities end. The thing stuck in the mirror doesn't have her ebony complexion that gleams under the yellow bulb hanging from the ceiling, skin that is marked by even the softest of pinches, supple, what Suzy Williams called 'nɔme nɔme' and 'naha naha'. She rubs her left shoulder as the women do in the body cream adverts on TV. She doesn't watch TV anymore. The skin of the thing in the mirror looks like salted fish that has spent years drying in the sun with its left eyebrow gone and a mound rising in the middle of *its* head, ready to give birth to a horn. She runs her hands over the top of her head. Her fingers touch a mound there too. She shakes her head. The thing in the mirror does the same. Her braids fall across her face.

For the past two years, the girl's grandmother has been appearing in her dreams calling to her to come find her. In the dream, the girl is standing on the shores of a beach as strange men and women sing and chant. Feet pounds ground, palm strikes hide and bass melds with tenor. Her grandmother rises from the sea leaving a trail of water as she floats towards the girl, until her face is inches away. In the old woman's irises, the girl doesn't see her reflection but rather a sprawl of glassy buildings. Then the old woman speaks, 'The key is here, girl. Find the key and you will find me. Grant a wish and you will become a vessel.'

When the old woman leaves her dreams, she leaves evidence of her visits. A receipt. Noises that grow in the girl's mind. It teases, rising and rising to a crescendo then gradually recedes into silence. This is how she explains them to her sister:

> It's like the strange songs of men and women on the shores of a beach, chanting and singing and crossing from one end to the other. Feet pounds ground. Palms strike hide. Bass melds with tenor. I stand in the middle. The cacophony rises as they draw closer, deafening when the people surround me and then losing intensity as they move away until the group is gone. In my case, they never move on. It's like a rewind. They go maybe 30 feet and return to drown me in a meaningless song.

The din of the voices is unbearable. The girl steps away from the washbasin. The echo from the dripping water from the tap blends with the throbbing in her head. She is sure of one thing. She will leave the house today. She will find her grandmother today. But first, she needs to find the key from her dream. And for the first time in a very long time, the voices return more quietly. They are gentle, coercing, kind even. The throbbing abates. The near silence reminds her of the time when her mind was quiet. Before her grandmother entered her dreams and left the voices behind. A time she when she had a friend who played with her. A time when she could watch TV. A time when she was normal. She misses the warmth of joy and the heat of laughter rising from her belly.

The girl's stomach rumbles with hunger, but she ignores it. Rather she draws out her phone, wipes it against the towel wrapped around her midsection and taps play on Kwesi Arthur's *Celebrate*.

She opens her wardrobe; dust falls onto her face. She picks the first dress that her hand touches, a knee length dress the colour of eggshells, with long sleeves that cover her wrists. She finds a hat. Then spectacles. In half an hour, she waltzes towards the door.

2

The girl stands by the road. She looks like a sick thing. The sun hurts her eyes. She adjusts her glasses. The voices are kind. It's been months since she has been in the sun, and it makes her skin itch. Red dust rises off the ground as cars, motorcycles and bicycles hurtle down and up the road. Tyres sink and rise from bumps and tiny hills in the road. People gauge the speed of oncoming vehicles and cross from one end to another. Sellers carry their wares on their heads and call out to buyers. The mates of the trotros scream their destinations as the vans get near her. She flags down one trotro. Whilst her arm is outstretched her phone rings. She dips her left hand into the pocket of her dress and puts it on vibrate.

Her grandmother liked her ring tone. It is why she kept it. It was the time before her grandmother's mind had begun to fail. Before the old woman began to ask, *Where am I? Who are you? What am I doing here?* Before the pills, her grandmother told her the story of the tired goddess and a vessel:

> *In the beginning, there was the goddess, a voice and a vessel. A goddess whose ears had grown heavy from listening to the cries of their children. A voice who collected wishes, prayers, desires, wants. Then a vessel who carried them to the goddess to grant them. When the goddess' ears fell*

*off her face, it was the vessel who assisted her. She listened
to the wishes, prayers, desires and wants of the children.
Years later, the goddess would send the vessel to live among
the humans to collect wishes, prayers, desires, wants on her
behalf.*

The girls had stared at the old woman's lips as she told the
story. Admiring the lines that traced their way from the edges
of her mouth and the way her grandmother's back curved into
the couch. The girl's eyes roamed over the many pictures of
her father and grandmother placed on the tables and plastered
on the walls of the living room. In this place, she felt warm,
wanted, worthy. The girl, six, declares:
'I want to be a vessel too.'
'But you have to listen to a lot of voices,' the grandmother replies.
'I don't care, I will grant people's wishes, prayers and desires.'
She scratches her head. *'Wants,'* her grandmother concludes.
She nods.
*'When you are ready. When you grant a wish, child, you will
become a wonderful vessel.'*
The girl's older sister has seen her blood and so her mind has
lost its magic. She mocks the girl, grandmother and the story,
cackling. She bleats into the old woman's face. The girl doesn't
care. She revels in happiness, inviting a swarm of butterflies
into the living room. When she is seven, she teases laughter
out of shadows and lullabies out of flowers. She is still laughing
at nine when her teeth fall out and turns to little golden crabs
that scuttle long the walls of her bedroom. Then she is ten and
the stars make their way into her bed to kiss her good night,
showering her in sparkles and glitter. At eleven, a door opens
in the ceiling of her bedroom, and she spends a day dining with
the moon. When the girl turns twelve, the old woman forgets
how to tell the story of the tired goddess and the vessel. Her
brain turns to soil and the disease grows, sprouting coconuts
and fields of amaryllis, suffocating the woman's memories such
that she can't remember her son's name.

3

'Kasoa!', 'Lapaz!', 'Accra!', 'Spintex!' When the girl enters a car headed to Spintex, the voices begin to rise in her head. She clutches the sides of her head. Finally, the trotro is headed to Accra, and she knows where she is meant to go: the mall. Again. Of course. The dream. She slaps an open palm against her forehead. She has been there before. She didn't find the old woman. What were the voices trying to show her and why now, after two tumultuous years? Was the key at the mall?

The trotro bumps up and down as the vehicle passes buildings and people and birds. Her fingers find their way to the pimple under her nose. The girl's mother has the exact same pimple in the same spot too. She is rubbing it when she first encounters the girl's father. Her father, a widower, is sick, desperate and restless. He begs her for a child before he joins the ancestors. She has told him she does not want children and she does not want a husband. 'Your eggs will shrivel up,' the girl's father says. She is unmoved.

The girl's mother is not that cruel. So, when a man, educated with a scholarship from the village, and now owns his business, sees her rubbing a pimple under her nose on their first date, yet asks her to marry him on their third, she obliges. She has a baby girl. The girl's father is overjoyed and lives four more years. His joy infects his daughter such that she feigns her happiness and hides her growing resentment. By the time, the first daughter is seven, the woman is satisfied.

The first daughter is a star. She has her father's intellect and her mother's beauty. She sweeps awards and stares. Then three months after her eighth birthday, the woman falls pregnant again. She doesn't want it. *Keep it,* her man begs. *If I keep her, I will leave you.* The woman replies. That is how the girl meets the world. When she is born, her mother refuses to touch her; she cannot feign happiness a second time. The first time she attempts to leave, the girl is three, but the man asks her to stay again, to *allow the children to grow*. She stays, until she forgets when it's time to leave. She becomes a shell. Her body is only stimulated by the recklessness of her affairs. The girl's mother has not shared a bed with her father for many years.

When the girl arrives in front of the big cluster of glassy buildings that rises and spreads behind the northwest of the roundabout. She tries to grin. It's the exact one she saw in her dream. Her face doesn't have enough skin to stretch that wide. She misses how it feels: the sweat, the cars stuck in traffic that forms in the parking lots, the trolleys stuck in parking spaces, the security men shooing away taxis, women offloading items into the boots of their cars whilst their children watch. The girl stands for a minute and inhales the scene and the harmattan air. She crosses to the other side of the road. The voices do not protest, she weaves in between cars and lanes and people until she is at the entrance. She enters and is struck by unfamiliarity, Truworth, this wasn't here before. She continues down. Yes, the winery is still there. Playstore, still here. Akpene's beads. Closed. Then she walks to the left wing of the mall and facing her is PansXPans—the store where her grandmother went missing.

***

The girl's grandmother had asked to be taken to the mall. *The new one. The one with the glass walls.* She wanted to buy a new pan for her good son. It was a good day. The girl's mother was in a good mood and agrees to drop them. She is meeting someone there anyway. The girl is surprised. Her mother calls her grandmother 'the woman' in front of her daughters, even before the old woman's brain had begun to fail. *The woman is here, call your sister, go and help her with her bags. Why is the woman using cow's blood to cook? Has the woman told you when she will go back to her house?* Even when she spoke to the girl's father—*The woman disturbs me a lot. Tell the woman to leave me alone I don't want to talk to her...*

The old woman is hesitant until the girl convinces her that she needs to get the pan in time to make food for her father.

The girl's mother parks the car in the parking lot of the mall and asks the girl to send 'the woman' into the store; she will be back in an hour to pick them up. They go to the smallest utensil store in the mall, PansXPans. The girl walks behind the old woman as she browses shelves: she picks up pans, presses them against her cheek, licks the cold metal and knocks the bottom of the metallic containers, then she moves on to the next.

The girl sees a stream of girls in colourful clothes who sing as they walk into the stores nearby. She leaves the store to speak to them. It is not long until she returns, thinking of how to convince her mother to let her join the girls' club – Tiki Tiki Girl's Club.

Then she realises her grandmother is gone. The girl darts through the store, swivelling, ducking, dodging. She glides through the entire length and breadth of the place. She goes to the counter, her chest heaving, about to cry.

'I came in with an old woman. I can't find her. Help me.'

Her legs are shaking. Maybe her mum came and took the grandmother away? She hurries to the parking lot and sees her mother's lips locked with a man. The person she was coming to see. The person who had made her restrain her dislike of the girl's grandmother and bring her to the mall. The girl exhales, 'I can't find grandmother.' The woman sighs as if the girl has only lost her left slipper.

The sun's orange-red hue spreads across the sky. Darkness is imminent and the girl and her mother are still in the store quizzing the staff. Her mother is calm when she asks the staff to check their security cameras. Then sits and stares at her nails. She picks up the phone in intervals to speak to a voice bristling in rage at the other end of the line.

The girl's father strides into the store with his imposing frame and rippling muscles. Darkness has finally swept through the sky.

'There's no footage. The cameras are for show because people like to steal,' the shopkeeper confesses.

He turns to the girl. 'What were you doing?'

He doesn't look at his wife.

The girl's father reports to the mall manager. They find footage. Here is the summary: The old woman entered that shop, but the camera never shows her leaving. The man goes to the police. A search begins. Posters appear on TV, radio announcements, Facebook posts, and tweets. Just like that the old woman has been misplaced.

4

Not a single thing has changed. It looks the same as the day her grandmother had disappeared—the signpost with the two frying pans makes an X to announce PansXPans, the bright and polished glass doors, and the peeling notices on discounts and counterfeits and 'Beware of the security cameras' are still glued along the sides of the door. A cold breeze from the air conditioner greets her dry skin. Only one customer, a woman, who stands before a lone shopkeeper. He's not the one from the last time she had come here to find her grandmother.

She knows she is supposed to be in here but what is she to do? She releases her clenched fists, adjusts her cap, takes off her sunglasses. Her right-hand dives into the pocket of the dress. She pulls out her phone. Thirteen missed calls. Ten from her sister, two from her mother, one from her father.

He called. She gasps. Her father had really called. The last time he uttered a word to her, he called her 'demon' at the memorial for the missing woman.

***

The girl's father had grown up in a small hut in the middle of a village in a place teeming with thick trees and grass. He was twelve when he started school. His mother travelled all the time, and he was left at home with his father, who mocked his skinny frame and his grandmother who stayed silent and spoke to voices only she could hear. School wasn't an option. *No school, cocoa farming until you die*, his father had said.

His mother heard his prayer and guided his feet into a classroom. It was his mother who held his father's raised arm when he ordered him to *put that bag down and hurry to the farm.* It was his mother who told him *pack your things we are leaving* when his father asked her to choose between her son and him. It was his mother who toiled on farms of foreigners for years so the boy could stay in school.

When he starts school, and the big boys and smart girls jeer at him, steal his homework, rip apart his patched shirt and steal his fruits, he endures. He cannot let his mother's sacrifice be in vain. It goes on for two years until he is fourteen – when his body begins to change – a lump appears in his throat, his chest broadens, he has a growth spurt, towering above his mates and his arms bolster. Then he exacts his revenge on every boy and girl who hurt him or stood in his way. With his fists, he punches his way through. At fifteen, he makes a girl's body sing in terror so he can have first place. When he turns sixteen, he breaks a boy's spirit and tosses his soul into a well so he can take his set of pens. At seventeen, he carves a hole into a teacher's back so he can have a scholarship into the city because his mother cannot afford it. At twenty-four, he grips the neck of employees who try to steal from him and sucks their breath from their nostrils. At twenty-five, he falls in love, with a woman who rubbed the pimple under her nose on their first date and agreed to marry him on their third. At thirty-four, the marriage is breaking in bits when he begs his wife to stay. At thirty-nine, he chains her to the marriage when he asks her to *allow the children to grow.*

He settles for any piece of her he can have because he loves her and endures through the recklessness of her affairs. When the second child was born, he was overjoyed, but the girl is different, and he will forget that *he* wanted the girl. The girl doesn't show the intellect and beauty of her older sister. At fifty-two, when the girl loses his mother, by this time the seed has grown from a grudge to resentment to hate. He cannot hide it. The girl has taken his wife and now his mother.

***

The girl's phone vibrates again. She presses silent and swipes her screen until she finds a photo of her grandmother. She approaches the glass counter at PansXPans and admires the intricate arrangement of rows of saucepans and frying pans and casserole dishes and shiny silver lids. The woman, the only customer in the store, argues with the man behind the counter who is clad in an ivory shirt that hangs at his elbow, and black trousers.

'I left my frying pan right by the door. It can't just be gone! I put them right there!'

'I am sorry madam. Once we issue a receipt, we are not responsible for your purchase. And our security cameras don't work. It's just for show because people like to steal.' He smirks.

The woman turns and the girl is struck by her beauty. Her face is plump and her mahogany skin looks like the exterior of balloons filled with water. Her corneas are so white they make the girl jealous. She tugs at the spectacles covering her eyes. The woman's lashes are thick and lush. A set of key-shaped earrings dangle from her ear. Her black hair cascades down her back, twirling as she turns. She is like a real life Mami Wata.

Her eyes meet the girl's. The girl raises her phone.

'What?' She humphs. It sounds like music to the girl.

'Please have you seen this woman?'

The woman doesn't flinch when she sees the girls red corneas. She corks her head towards the screen like an old man trying to see an image better and her eyes widen with recognition. The girl feels an ounce of warmth.

The woman turns back to look at the shopkeeper. Her eyes sweep over him before she saunters toward the door wordlessly. The girl follows.

'I am sorry girl. I cannot help you. You have no offering.'

The girl pauses, then she asks, 'What do you desire?'

The woman's eyes bore into the girl's.

'Whatever is familiar in a strange place. What was almost lost, lost and never lost.'

The girl stops and stares at the woman's back as she turns to leave. Her legs wobble and she steadies herself against the wall of PansXPans. The woman is nearing the exit.

Whatever is familiar in a strange place. What was almost lost, lost and never lost. She repeats.

The girl stands there, and she doesn't know what to do. The mall is cold, and she begins to shiver in her light dress; goose bumps appear on her skin. She is supposed to know the answer to the riddle. Her grandmother told her that to be a vessel she needs to know people's desires. She closes her eyes and tries to conjure an image of her grandmother. Instead, all she hears is the low humming of the voices in her head.

She needs to give the woman something. She turns back and enters the store to find an offering so the woman can help her. She roams the shelves. No, not that. Too bulky. Too ugly. Cheap. She weaves her way up and down until she is in the last corner. Then she spots it. It's black and shiny and it hangs there among the other silver pans. It's just like the one her grandmother had admired years back. Perhaps even the same one. Whatever's familiar in a strange place? This frying pan was familiar. At least the only familiar thing to her here. She digs her hand into her pocket for money as she lifts the frying pan. Her hand comes out empty.

She will have to take it. She holds the pan and tries to walk in an easy gait. She turns towards the counter. Her heart is pounding because she can't say 'Please I have no money. Can I have this?' Maybe she could trade her phone? She falters in her step and the shopkeeper's attention is drawn to her. And as he watches her, she turns and escapes through the door of PansXPans. She doesn't hear: *Hey, what do you think you are doing?* When the shopkeeper screams at her. *Or Thief! Thief!* when he alerts the guards.

But she runs. She rushes down and turns left. A flurry of faces blurs as she whizzes past them. The girl twirls and makes a right for Mr. Xam's Food and runs past Kiddy Clothes and keeps going. She hears the heavy hurried footsteps hitting the ground behind her and she darts to her left and sees the exit into the parking lot. The one reserved for Ubers. She dives for it but a security man materialises, obstructing her escape. Her heart is pounding in her ears now. Her frail body feels a surge of momentum. She waits until she's meters away from him and falls back, slides through his legs and lands on the pavement. The back of her shin burns. But she recovers and bounces to her feet. A car screeches in front of her and the back door opens. She flies in without a thought.

'Hello again.'

It's the woman from the store earlier. The car jerks and speeds out the mall's main exit. The girl drags in breath and presents the pan to the woman.

'An offering.' The woman smiles and receives it.

The girl is glad that she has granted a wish, answered a prayer, fulfilled a desire, satisfied a want, even if it's with a mundane thing like a pan.

'I am Saafe. What's your name child?'

The girl doesn't answer instead she says, 'Key. Your name means key. You are the key from my dreams.'

'Yes, I am the key.'

5

The car stops at the beach and the woman leads her to the water. Her feet sink into sand and more sprinkles on her legs from the little children throwing cupfuls of sand at each other.

'Come!' The woman leads her along the beach until all the people are left behind. The voices in the girl's head are growing louder. The girl grits her teeth and stares at the woman. Her beauty soothes her.

'Does your family know what you are becoming?' The girl doesn't answer. The question reminds of her phone. She takes out her phone. Thirty-four missed calls. Twenty-nine from her sister, four from her mother and one from her father. A memory floats into her head. It was a few weeks after her grandmother went missing. The day the voices burst inside her head, the girl is in her room finishing her homework. At first, she thinks it's from the earphones in her ears. She switches them off, then the TV goes off too, but it doesn't stop. The voices continue to rise in volume. The girl rushes to her mother's room. She meets her mother on the bed with the curtains drawn and the room dark. The girl clutches the sides of her head when she reaches the mother.

'Mummy please make them stop! Mummy please make them stop! Mummy please ...'

'Go to your sister,' the woman drawls and turns and presses her face into the pillow. So, the girl races to her sister's room and she tells her to describe it. The girl's sister sits with her. Humming songs to calm the girl.

Then the girl's father's car honks at the gate. The girl's sister asks her to go to her room. She doesn't want the girl's stain.

'But I am afraid.'

'Go. After I speak to daddy. I will come.' Her sister leaps off the bed to show her father a new medal she has won, leaving the girl in the room.

She stands at the door of her sister's room. Listening to her sister chatter with her father. Then the girl goes to her room to fight the voices alone. She continues to fight the voices alone until today.

6

'You can help me find my grandmother,' the girl says. Rays from the orange red sun touch the edges of the girl's lips.

'I can assist you on your journey,' the woman clarifies.

The woman finds a zip in the back of her yellow flowing dress and pulls her dress off, bra, panties, earrings. The girl imitates her.

'Come.'

She gestures and glides into the water. She and the girl have waded in enough. The woman stretches out her hand and the girl holds it. She mutters words the girl doesn't understand. Then she feels a pressure on the mound on her head, when the water begins to swirl and bubble around her. Then the woman's hands plunge the girl into the water.

The woman drags her out of the water. The girl gasps for breath:

'No! No! No! Think of the voices. Let yourself go, child!'

She resumes her incantations as water swirls and bubbles around the girl and plunges the girl under again.

When the girl opens her eyes, she is on a beach. The one from her dreams where strange songs of men and women are chanting and singing and crossing from one end to the other. Feet pound ground. Palms strike hide. Bass melds with tenor. She is standing in the middle as the cacophony rises as they draw closer, deafening when the people surround her and she cannot move.

This time, she lifts her feet and turns her waist and lifts her hands to the rhythm. She dances with them. She embraces the voices. When her eyes open, she is on the beach. Her braids are wet, but her clothes are dry. She stares out into the sea. The woman is gone. *The strange songs now familiar.*

The girl sets off from the shores following the distant circles of light until she stands in the street. Why has she let the voices unsettle her for so long? Now they feel like her friends. She hears them. One wishes for popcorn and milk, the other desires the death of his employer, another prays for money to start her boutique, a fourth wants a child. She hears the individual wishes, prayers, desires, wants. No longer a cacophony, just a thread of seeking offerings. She chooses a strand, distinct from the other many voices to guide her to her grandmother. She turns whenever the strand hums. Right, left, straight, centre. She continues.

Her phone vibrates again.

The girl pulls her phone from her pocket. Thirty-five missed calls. Twenty-nine from her sister, four from her mother, two from her father.

The girl stares at her phone, her face stretches: an attempt to smile. Then she tosses the phone and watches it fly into the bushes.

Sugar's Daughters

Akua Serwaa Amankwah

Victoria Falls, Zimbabwe.

Patient Name	Nana Yaa Bakoma Poku
Vital Name	11:02 AM (14–11–2016)
Temperature	39.0 Celsius – Axilla
Pulse	92
Blood Pressure	135 mmHg – 94 mmHg
Respiration Rate	30
SpO2	98
BMI	0.00

The patient is in severe distress. A guest from Stanley & Livingstone, on her third day of a week-long vacation. Slipped on the pool coping of the boutique hotel. Lost consciousness initially but regained it. Sustained some lacerations on her scalp. Bruised forehead. Left flank cut. Left fractured wrist. Mild traumatic brain injury—intracerebral bleed ruled out.

The patient has been transferred to the stretcher and is being wheeled to the emergency services. She wears a red dress that ripped while she was being moved from the ambulance. Her husband is shaken, and his light blue shirt spots blood smudges. The patient's eyes remain shut; her face contorted in pain, a tiny cut on her upper lip, and she is still trying to say something.

'Aky...c-call Aky c-t-tell I w-want p-please.' Each word takes an enormous effort, but she is insistent and the husband, though he frowns, understands her.

'Babe, I'll call her, please just hang on for me, okay? I'm calling her now, I promise'.

He tries to calm her down but sees she will not rest until he's made that call. She is mouthing 'please' over and over, and he cannot take it anymore. He steps aside, his fingers scrolling through his phone, tapping on a number, watching it ring. While everyone pretends to be busy with their work, they also want to know what this call which does not concern them is about. If it's drama, they want in too.

**

There was something about Kumasi that enveloped Akyaa in a hug, kissed her welcome, calmed her raging senses and helped her shed off the pressure of just existing in Accra. Yet, she could not imagine living and working in Kumasi. She needed it in small doses, like shortbread biscuits. She contemplated messaging her tenants to announce she was around, but she did not want to be a bother, nor for them to bother her.

She had earned a week away from pediatric neurosurgery and needed to lap up that rare freedom until its last drop. In a week, her colleague Dr Ansong would lay all his burdens on her as she had on him. Only, he would not stop calling her when she was on leave, but he would avoid her calls when he was. The bastard. No wonder Kukua left him; he deserved it. Now, she had to find a way to ward off the Association of Free Consultation Patients, the president being Bema. Her body had become so sensitive that any twitch sent her flailing for help.

'Dr Sarpong, I still feel some sensations on my skin, what do I do?'

'Dr Sarpong, sorry to bother you but the pricking of needles on my fingers and feet won't stop. Should I be concerned? I am, actually. I can't sleep. I am scared.'

'I bought the list of drugs you prescribed for me, but the side effects of Medrol? Wild.'

'One last question, please. The back pain has only gotten worse. What do you recommend?'

Akyaa messaged Bema, including a subtle warning that she was on vacation for a while. She had already turned off all her alarms and set up an autoresponder for her emails. She wished she could put her phone off, but her boss had begged her not to, just in case they needed to reach out. She would manage it, she promised herself.

She had planned her first night: watching *Things We Do for Love* reruns while enjoying limitless Prosecco with cashew nuts. She made herself comfortable on the couch that swallowed her in softness, and draped herself with a fluffy duvet. Nothing could make her unfurl herself from this bliss.

The shrill of the telephone and her mobile phone ringing at the same time yanked her out of her snooze, and she fumbled for her phone which had slipped down the inside of the couch. Seeing the +263 code made her roll her eyes. Scammers were working harder than the devil, but she was not in the mood.

She picked up the telephone, wondering who it was.

'H'llo?'

'Good evening, ma. Sorry to disturb you, ma, but you have a visitor,' Sai, her security guard said.

'Me?' she echoed.

The +263 number was flashing on her phone again, Akyaa muted it and tossed it under the duvet.

'Who is this visitor, Sai?'

'Her name is Madam Nana Yaa Bakoma, please.'

Sai's words hung in the air, and Akyaa pressed the phone to her ear as if it would make him take back his words.

'Excuse me?'

'Madam Nana Yaa Bakoma, please,' Sai repeated.

'Right. Right. Please let, uh, let her in, Sai. Thank you.' She dropped the phone in its cradle as if it were a piece of hot coal. Her little sister. *Bakoma.* Her name was sour and sinful in Akyaa's mouth, and she wanted to spit it out. She was in a trance as she went in search of something appropriate to slip on. It had to be a mistake. How did Bakoma know she'd be here?

Akyaa paused, as if she was now realising just how absurd it sounded, that she had stopped talking to her sister, and eight whole years had passed. In a slip of a moment. She remembered the last time they had seen each other, dressed in black and seated in solemnity in Lawyer Kwesi Coffie's stuffy office for the reading of their father's will. Bakoma and her husband Duke were huddled together like birds seeking warmth from each other—the picture-perfect family. Akyaa wanted it to end as quickly as possible; she felt hemmed in by the stale air and the insane number of books on the shelf, his desk, the floor, that swallowed every space in the room. It did not help that on her way she had snagged her dress on a nail and had to cover it with a book because there was no time to change.

Their father, Kofi Asante Sarpong, had passed away in his sleep months earlier, and death had respected his wishes, for he loathed the idea of being taken in an inglorious manner. He did not want an illness that would twist his insides and make him an echo of his former self before delivering him at death's door, nor some accident that would leave him at everyone's mercy—it was something he could not deal with. He wanted to slip away quietly.

Akyaa and Bakoma had secretly nicknamed him Sugar when Manhyia and Jubilee House appointed him the sole supplier of their sugar. He was now a god in his circles, and there was something about such gods, on the outside they were likeable and sweet and generous and made you want to worship them, but you dared not cross them. Akyaa had.

She had been hopeful that even though she had disappointed her father, he would consider her a deserving candidate to take over Sikyire, his sugar company. She had planned her life around Sikyire and put her medical school education on the line many times. They had sugarcane farms at Kuntanse, Pramso, Titrifu and Kotwi, and she had developed relationships with the farmers and supported them during the planting and harvest seasons. Through the Sikyire Farmers' Fund she created, she took care of the farmers' children's school fees. They called her 'Doctor Doctor', and she knew their names and their children's names and she cared in a way that won their admiration. She was their go-to person, and she went to great lengths to be available, even in the middle of tests and exams. When the centrifuge was acting up or the evaporator needed to be replaced, she knew who to call. She liaised with suppliers and supervised the process of distributing the sugar around the country after packaging. She spent her vacations at the factory in Kaase and mastered the business side of the trade. But it had still not been enough.

She had prayed that her father would not punish her. That his words, 'You will not have peace for disobeying me' would not take a life of its own and taunt her for the rest of her life. That he would have mercy on her, except Akyaa forgot, though her father was generous, he was incapable of granting mercy freely.

Lawyer Coffie pored over every single instruction word by word, and Akyaa wondered if he was stretching things out on purpose. She had cases to attend to at the hospital—a seven-year-old had suffered brain tumour procedure complications, her favourite patient Dede was being prepped for a spinal cord surgery—and she wished she was there, but this man was reading with the speed of a snail. She wanted to scream.

Then it was time.

To his firstborn daughter, Nana Akyaa Prempeh Sarpong, Kofi Asante Sarpong left her the family mansion at Nhyiaeso. His second daughter, Nana Yaa Bakoma Poku, and her husband, Duke Poku, would co-own Sikyire Company at Kaase, his house at Ahodwo, and his guesthouse at Duayaw Nkwanta, close to Sunyani. To his brother, Kusi Sarpong, his orange farms at Kwahu ... Lawyer Coffie's gravelly voice stabbed her with each word, and she had to tune him out to keep sane. She felt a ringing in her ears, then she was on fire, then her teeth threatened to chatter, and then she went numb. Her father had whittled off the biggest deal of her life to her younger sister and *her husband* and left her with bones.

Akyaa used a hospital emergency as a reason to escape, and she staggered toward the door, moving blindly. She did not look back at her sister, Duke or the few relatives who had been invited. She slammed the door and felt her dress rip further as she stomped off to her car, but she did not care.

***

Bakoma was here. Akyaa hesitated at the door and leaned against it, stalling. The doorbell rang, and then again and again until Akyaa flung the door open, ready to pounce.

'How long did it have to take you to get here?' said the familiar voice, a meld of petulance and disrespect. Sai had made no mistake. That was her sister, right there in the flesh.

'Huh?'

'You took a while, that's all I'm saying,' Bakoma shrugged.

'Let me get this right. *You* come to *my* house uninvited and demand when *I* should open *my* door?'

'Courtesy for boys and girls rule one: you don't keep guests waiting.' Bakoma seemed amused, and Akyaa felt pricks of annoyance. She sighed, crossing both arms, leaning against the door, and appraised the firebrand that stood before her. Time had been generous to Bakoma. She was as fresh-faced as eight years ago and she looked like she had passed by on her way to a dinner party. She was glammed up in a red silk dress whose thigh-high slit was ascending to heaven, and neon green heels dramatised with frills and fur. Hair pressed into a sleek bun, bright tomato-red lips and eye makeup that sparkled. Under the balcony lights, she seemed too ethereal to be true. Her perfume was typical of her: floral and fresh with an undeniable patina of old money.

'So? Are you going to let me in?'

It infuriated Akyaa that her series reruns had been interrupted by an entitled sister who didn't know when to shut up, or, at the very least, show some respect.

The old Akyaa would have fought Bakoma pepper for pepper. Three decades earlier, *she* was the fiery older sister and Bakoma was the mousy one. She imitated every move Akyaa made and was comfortable being her shadow. There was one time when they had sneaked out with their bicycles when their parents had travelled for a funeral. Daa Joe the gardener was late for the thousandth time, Aunt Essie was on a telephone call from London, Mamaa was baking up a storm in the outhouse kitchen and Meri had gone to the fish market. They were not to go beyond the gates without supervision, for apart from a few scattered estates, Nhyiaeso was nothing but bushes and budding farmlands. There was more than enough space in their house to do whatever they wanted, but the other side always seemed tempting with promises of better adventures. They rode to the Ntims' banana farms, played with the twins Oppong and Opokua, stuffed their faces with the creamiest banana fritters they'd ever tasted and raced back home. Akyaa, still unsatisfied, longed for extra portions of the creamy, fluffy fritters and decided to go back. Bakoma would go home and wait, hiding her bicycle just in case their parents returned. When Akyaa got back, five minutes later, Bakoma was walking up and down at the front gate, shaking with fear, because their father's anger could dissolve mountains into tiny pieces of gravel. She had laughed when she saw her sister's anguish for just a little disobedience.

After the mouse married well and became the favourite, she transformed into a lion who could not be tamed.

'Akyaa. Akyaa?'

She blinked, only just realising Bakoma had been speaking.

'I'm sorry. I, I ... I know this was unexpected but I had to see you. The kids are with their grandparents, Duke had to attend to something urgent ... this was the only chance I had.'

Her tone had turned softer, as if she realised she was one step away from getting the door slammed in her face. Behind Bakoma, Akyaa now noticed, was a leather holdall. Had she meant to even stay the night, and yet had come attacking like a fool?

Bakoma kept babbling and Akyaa was rather tired of standing in the doorway. She wanted to go back inside, so she relented.

'Fine. Come in,' Akyaa's look was terse as she stood aside.

Bakoma turned to pick up the holdall she'd brought with her. 'Thank you,' and she stepped in.

Akyaa felt a warmth, a feeling, something soft, something sad, wash over her. 'Welcome,' she said, a smile plastered on her face.

'This is such a lovely place.' Bakoma's eyes were everywhere, and she could not help the grudging respect that had crept into her voice.

When Akyaa got over her disappointment over what her father had left her, she discovered she had enough space to build five two-bedroom houses. She would rent out four of them and keep one for herself. The mansion was remodelled to accommodate large families on vacation, and the profits she'd made were insane. She knew she had done well, but seeing her sister's admiration made her smile.

Akyaa's eyes stayed on Bakoma. She was a replica of their mother. She had Eno's rich and decadent mahogany skin and large soft chocolate eyes framed by rows and rows of unfairlythick lashes. Her nose was their grandmother's – straight and stately – and her full lips and smile made fools of men. While Eno had been docile, 'Yes, ma', 'Yes, Daddy', 'Welcome, ma', 'Sorry', 'Please', and allowed their father to run over her, Bakoma had turned out differently. Even now, where she knew she was not welcome, she reeked of chutzpah.

'Do you want me to make you anything?'

Akyaa asked out of politeness and hoped she had not made the mistake of giving Bakoma options.

'If I have to be very honest, I will do anything for a Disco sandwich.'

Their eyes met. Disco sandwich, the soundtrack of their childhood. The sinful club sandwich that their father bought on his way home from Asokwa on Sunday evenings. They knew he had not broken his promise when he came bearing the white plastic bag and the foil that jealously guarded the goodness. One of the girls would scream 'Discoooo', and the other would gallop to where excitement was promised. The bread and its fillings were always squished, for the seller wrapped it tight so the mayonnaise would not leak. But that was the beauty of the experience; they would eat with their hands and lick their fingers, and if their father was not watching, unfold the foil, lift it to their lips and allow the remnants of the mayonnaise, chicken, bits of egg yolk and breadcrumbs to trickle down their throats. It was a messy meal that required messy eating. Even now, she could taste the meld of thinly sliced chicken slathered with mayonnaise on her tongue. Those were the days when they were inseparable and had more than enough love to share.

'They're still open if that's what you're wondering,' Akyaa said with a chuckle.

'What!' Bakoma squealed.

Akyaa had come to Kumasi for a wedding a few months before and left the wedding party to go to Asokwa and satisfy that relentless craving. She had been shaking with excitement when she saw Disco still existed. The club sandwich was as delicious as she remembered it, but she had only been able to nibble on it, because all she kept thinking about was Bakoma.

'Well, I will add it to the list of things I have to try before I leave. Disco, suya, Bantama waakye, boiled ripe plantain and kontomire stew.'

Akyaa wondered when she would leave. It was tricky, especially with that small bag she brought. Bakoma had never packed light in her life.

'That sounds like something we could arrange. But I don't have much at the moment … frozen meat pies, sobolo, some bananas, groundnut soup, I think?'

'Bananas. Tell me you have eggs and flour,' Bakoma's eyes lit up in anticipation.

'Eggs and flour?'

'Banana fritters!'

They both paused for a while and when Bakoma started to giggle, even Akyaa could not resist the laughter that erupted from her lips.

'You were so afraid that day. If I'd stayed away for one more minute, you'd have wet yourself.' Akyaa made a face and Bakoma rolled her eyes, but she was smiling.

'You don't have to do it, though. I can make it. Would you like to eat some?'

'No I'm fine, I had a heavy lunch. Let me get a room ready for you.'

'Thank you. I'm going to make some magic,' Bakoma said in a sing-song voice. She slipped off her heels and disappeared to the kitchen.

The room where Bakoma would stay was already clean, Akyaa only had to move a few things around. She placed two bottles of water on the bedside accent table and turned on the feather lamps so the room was illuminated. She had to find some nightwear for her just in case she did not bring any. She then sat on the stairs with her second glass of Prosecco, taking in everything. How surreal it all seemed, that she had planned her night and the one person she had never imagined seeing had marred it by visiting, and then plaguing her with memories she had tried her best to avoid.

Bakoma climbed up shortly after, holding her plate of fritters.

'It is so good. Want to taste?' She offered, and Akyaa shook her head, mouthing a thank you.

'I just— I can't help but wonder, Bakoma, why are you really here?'

'I can't just visit my sister?'

'No, not really. I mean, no.'

'That's the problem. Two more years and it would have been a decade since we last saw each other. It's not right.'

Akyaa shrugged, turning silent.

'You don't get to play innocent in a one-sided fight you started. You left Lawyer Coffie's office that day and cut all of us off.'

'What did you expect? That I would pretend I was fine that he punished me by taking what I deserved?' She was speaking faster than she had intended; her chest was heaving. She had to close her eyes and calm herself down.

'You act as if you are the only one who was punished. Akyaa, I married a man our father handed over to me. I love Duke with all my heart, but I never got to make a choice.'

'Didn't you get everything already? What are you complaining about?' The conversation was wearing her out already.

'I didn't get *everything*. If you'd stayed to listen to the details of the will, you'd know Duke owns everything. My name was there for formalities. You complain about Sugar, but you're like him in so many ways. You don't get your way and the whole world falls apart. You only see your truth and you stand firmly by it. Eight years, Akyaa Prempeh. Eight!'

'Would you cut your daughter off for getting pregnant and not falling into your grand plan? Would you take her child away from her?'

'I know... listen.' Akyaa faltered, and then she cleared her throat.

'Listen, he had a long list of faults, but don't make it seem as if you were the victim in all of this. He didn't cut you off, you cut yourself off. You appear at the reading of his will expecting him to carry his business and put it on your head?'

'Are you shifting the blame to me?'

'I am telling you to own up to your mistakes too,' her sister retorted, but then she let out a soft yelp and winced while she rubbed her scalp.

'What is it? Are you okay?' Akyaa was up in a minute, peering over her.

'I think. It's uh, a migraine. I just need to get some rest.'

'Sorry,' Akyaa helped her up but was still hovering.

'Is this migraine a constant thing?'

'Oh come on. Don't go all doctorly on me. I just need to get some sleep'.

Akyaa smiled.

'Good idea, patient. Let's see how it is tomorrow, okay?'

'Alright, but this conversation is not over. That's why I came.'

'Fine. Just feel better. Goodnight.'

'Goodnight, Akyaa. See you tomorrow'.

You complain about Sugar, but you're like him in so many ways. You don't get your way and the whole world falls apart. You only see your truth and you stand firmly by it.

Bakoma's words echoed in her mind, and she realised for the first time, she could not deny the truth.

***

In 1997, Akyaa met the first man who made her feel free. She had just turned 21 and was enthralled by Kekeli, the lanky boy whose smile unsteadied her, whose soft afro she wanted to run her hands through, and whose intellect blew her mind. She could not wait to introduce Keli to her father. What was better than one doctor in the family? Two!

Sugar and Akyaa's relationship scared and amused his friends—they did not pin their hopes on their daughters the way he did. They did not allow them to sit through business meetings under the guise of taking notes when he had a perfectly capable secretary, and they did not talk business details with them. This advantage made it easy to strut about as the daughter of Kofi Sarpong, and the future heiress of Sikyire.

She brought Keli to Bakoma's nineteenth birthday party at Piccolo Mondo Restaurant. Bakoma was in her second year at Cambridge and had come home to visit. Their father was swelling with pride and gloated to his friends that his daughters were better than ten sons combined, and they would take the family name to high places. Then, Akyaa had picked up the beautiful blocks of the façade he had built for their family and hurled them at him one by one by one.

It was the first time she had experienced the full heat of her father's anger. He had called her aside to meet him downstairs.

'Keli Agbesi Dumor? Have you gone out of your mind?' He could not stand, nor sit still. She felt the heat emitting from his eyes on her's and she squirmed.

She did not grasp what was going on at that moment, and with her lips quivering, dared to ask, 'I don't understand, Papa, what has he done? How do you know him?'

He had stared at her, shaking his head, as if she had cotton wool for brains.

'What has he done? How do I know him? Oh, my daughter Akyaa.' His laugh was high and dry.

'You don't bring a boy to meet me at a party without bringing him home first, and you certainly do not bring home Agbeli Dumor's son!'

Akyaa felt like hot pins were prickling her. She sank into the nearest chair and knew that she and Keli were in trouble. Agbeli Dumor was the wingman of the chairman of the Armed Forces Revolutionary Council behind the 1979 coup, who had forced her father to declare Sikyire to the government, knowing full well that he would find an excuse to declare it illegal, and then confiscate it. They had done it to many of his friends and their companies – Classic Pilsner Beer, Napoleon Group Restaurants, Myrabia Floral Perfumery and ASE Timbers – had all been seized by the government. Sugar was the perfect target; he was a competitor to the government-owned Komenda Sugar Factory and expropriating his business would allow the government to exercise their monopoly. He closed the factory just in time to escape to a cousin's home in Cote D'Ivoire. The losses he incurred nearly crippled the factory. The Dumors were not just off-limits, they were enemies.

While Akyaa stopped seeing Keli as Sugar had ordered, they always found themselves in the same circles and at some point, continued right where they had left off. Months before she was to pursue a master's in Public Health in London, she got pregnant, and it broke her heart to tell Sugar why she could not leave yet. Before, her father had merely distanced himself, but with the pregnancy, she was as good as dead to him.

***

It was the vibration of Akyaa's phone that woke her up the next morning, and she groaned at the rude interruption. She was not familiar with the number and dismissed it. She could not risk picking up and dealing with an unexpected medical issue at work. For a moment, she wondered if she had dreamt of what happened the day before, but Bakoma's perfume greeted her at the door, and when she opened the next bedroom, there she lay, dead to the world. Her sister was a light sleeper, and so she tried to close the door as softly as she could.

It did not work.

Bakoma opened one eye, her voice laced with sleep.

'How are you feeling now?'Akyaa asked her.

'Better, better.'

'Good. Get some more sleep, I will come to check on you later.'

'No, no come. Sit by me.'

Akyaa sat at the edge of the bed and realised how relieved she was to be home.

***

For the remaining days they spend together in Kumasi, Akyaa puts her phone on mute and decides for the first time to prioritise herself and get some rest. She agrees to listen, but only if Bakoma discards that disgusting chip on her shoulder. They agree to the deal, and they spend their mornings in the mansion, rediscovering the rooms they grew up in, and even though every single space has been transformed, the memories remain the same.

At five and three, they sit at the table in the kitchen where they dine with Sugar and Eno. Sugar looks dapper in his navy-blue suit, complaining about how uncomfortable it is, yet breaking into a smile if he is complimented. He would drink endless cups of steaming Richoco, and if he has the time, go through the latest catalogues from the sugarcane industry, mailed to him from his best friend in America. Eno floats to where they are sitting to fuss over them, asking if they are fine, if they want more of anything, and Mamaa is in the kitchen, working on their requests. Sugar would ask for one thing, and then change his mind, and Eno would respond to each complaint, comment and outburst with so much grace that they grow angry on the behalf of their mother. It is why Akyaa looks at the unlikely match and decides she will *never* marry a man like her father.

In December, they go shopping from UTC Departmental Stores to Kingsway to Glamour and Leventis, loading their car with goodies and singing Christmas carols, laughing because it is vacation, and no one has to remember long division or multiplication and little stories in the Lomond English book. On Christmas day, they wear white dresses as light and fluffy as clouds and unwrap new shoes boxed and shipped straight from Italy. At Christmas church services, they giggle throughout the sermon, forget their memory verses, and use their offertory to buy biscuits.

They watch family members troop in, Mamaa cooking and Meri serving trays of chicken so tender they slide off the bone, coated groundnuts and endless bottles of Coca Cola and Fanta and Sprite, the trinity, and its cousins—Crest and Amstel Malta. After the visit, Sugar shares envelopes filled with money, and they bend and dance and leave with smiles.

They race around the house, slippers slapping on gravel, and when one sister trips and falls and begins to cry, the other consoles her. Bakoma hates braiding her hair, and sometimes they would leave her looking wild and other times she would only allow Akyaa to touch her hair.

Then there was that talent show in Sixth Form where Abigail Zanzama performed with other girls. She shoots one hand in the air and one breast pops out of her loose top, and for days they would call her Abigail Showgirl.

When Akyaa is six and Bakoma is four and attending a British School at Ahodwo, they practise their British accents. Akyaa will try to explain that it is 'strawberry' and not 'strawbebby' and 'cockroach' and not 'ockroach' and they would laugh because Bakoma loves her strawbebby and ockroach, and likes to twirl round, round, round like a merry-go-round.

***

The calls unnerved Akyaa. She scrolled through her call log and text messages and returned the calls of those that mattered. Dr Ansong needed clarification on a patient who had returned after changing hospitals and dealing with a botched surgery by a nonsense pseudo-neurosurgeon. Then there was a missed call and a message from Opokua, which was quite strange. When Akyaa returned the call, Opokua did not respond, and when Opokua called again, she did not pick up. She would call her another time, she only hoped it was not urgent.

***

At 22, Akyaa is shipped off to Nanabaa's house at Duayaw Nkwanta, so she can grow her baby, spit it out, return home and continue as if nothing happened. Akyaa will fight to stay home, but no daughter of Kofi Sarpong will humiliate him in this way. When Akyaa returns, childless and filled with some of her father's anger and her mother's timidity, the world is upside down and Keli won't talk to her. She leaves for Cambridge, but switches from Public Health to Neurosurgery because of her obsession with nerves and how they work, and how they can shut a body down. She also does it to spite Sugar and excels to show him that she can be anything she wants. Her mates call her 'Blade' because of her gift with power drills. She's an artist. When she wraps up her residency, Addenbrooke's, Mayo

Clinic, Nagoya and Sheba Medical Centre wrestle over her, but she will turn away and return to Ghana. They will call her a patriotic fool. She also wants to find her daughter, but Nanabaa is dead, and every lead goes nowhere, and everyone else will act like the baby never existed.

Eno leaves without warning and they are relieved for her after lasting that long in the marriage. Sugar will act like he is alright but they will watch him begin to deteriorate. One day, he feels a pain in his chest and clutches his heart. Akyaa wonders if she should retaliate because he's taken away her child, but she will save him anyway, by barging into the right hospitals and gathering the best surgeons. He will recover and live for two more years, and she will hope that he reconsiders her role in Sikyire and do right by her. Sugar owes her.

***

They spent their afternoons waltzing from one area to another, sampling *alewonyo* and suya and brukina. Bakoma still finds bosoa nauseating because why did blood have to belong with meat and spices, and Akyaa rolled her eyes at her as if she did not know what was good for her. They had Meri to thank, she had introduced them to most of the street snacks, and they wondered which part of the world life had blown her to. Bakoma would not rest until they tried Bantama waakye, and then she spent nearly an hour fanning the inside of her mouth because of all the shito she ate.

They now slept in Akyaa's room because there were too many stories and they wanted to make up for lost time. She encountered her nephews through photographs, and Bakoma made her promise to visit Vevey during Christmas. She said yes, yes, yes. She had not felt such peace in years; the sound of her laughter surprised her, how light and silvery it was, and how sweet and fresh it tasted, like honey that had just been harvested. She felt whole, even though she had not known she needed parts of her filled up. She loved and was loved.

***

The vibration of Akyaa's phone spoiled a perfectly good nap, and by the time she found it, the call had ended. She had been watching a movie with Bakoma earlier and must have dozed off. This time, however, she called the number again, because she needed to tell this person off and thereafter, block them.

'Hello?' The voice was familiar, and Akyaa was thrown off balance.

'Who is this, please?' She demanded.

'Akyaa? This is Duke.' The voice on the other side of the line made her sit up straight.

'Duke?' Something leapt inside of her, and she wondered if the boys were fine.

'I have been calling for days ... I tried to reach you with other numbers but there was no response.' He sounded weary.

'Oh God. Oh God. It was you all this while? I'm so sorry... I just ... I was on break and Bak—'

'Yes. Bakoma, that is why I am calling. She has been admitted to the hospital for almost a week now.'

'How is that possible?' She felt a chill envelope her and she was transfixed to the spot.

He told her about the vacation, the accident, what the doctors were saying and not saying. The whole time, Akyaa felt that surely, Duke was going a little crazy. She felt like she was in a trance when she finally mustered the courage to move up the stairs. One of them was wrong.

Duke was still talking. When she got to the door, she hesitated, and her heart was thumping so hard that she was afraid of what it might do if she held on. She flung the door open.

Empty.

The room was the way the cleaning company had left it the week before. The same light grey sheets without a crease in sight. The peach duvet folded meticulously. All six pillows in place. They had opened one window slightly to keep the breeze coming in, and it kissed the floral curtains into billows.

Empty.

'Duke?'

He was crying now, as if he had been waiting for the right moment, the right person.

'I don't know what to do, honestly. We've been referred and we're now at a hospital in Durban. I am making arrangements to return to Vevey. *A pause.* They want to operate on her brain … you are the surgeon. This is scary.'

'Duke.'

'She was calling your name the whole time,' he continued as if she had not spoken.

Akyaa had walked from room to room and finally stood at the doorway where Bakoma arrived with an attitude and a small holdall. And she stood there because she felt compelled to stay there.

The breeze that came in was very light, and for a moment, Bakoma's perfume stayed and lingered, and in the next minute, there was nothing at all.

***

Durban, South Africa

Referring diagnosis

Mild traumatic brain injury with a fractured wrist. Being managed with anticoagulants, antibiotics and analgesics. Had been at the previous facility for the past five days but complained of persistent headaches and nausea with an episode of vomiting.

Glasgow Coma Scale – 13/15.

Pupils 4mm on the left and 6mm on the right.

Evidence of a raised intracranial pressure. Possible epidural hematoma. Needs emergency CT scan and should be prepared for an emergency craniotomy.

Update*

Blood tests, Chest X-Ray, EKG, and CT scans are normal.
   Glasgow Coma Scale – 15/15
   Possible mix up – to be confirmed.

Homecoming

Akachi Adimora-Ezeigbo

A keke pulled up in front of Ochudo bus station and a man and woman descended from the tricycle after paying for their ride. The keke driver waved and drove away. Okechukwu, the first son after the birth of three daughters, walked into the fenced bus station dressed in *Isi Agu* jumper and black trousers with an *Abiriba* cap. He flinched like someone had hit him, visibly disappointed by what he saw. The park was a replica of the neglect he had observed in bus stations and motor parks all over the country, especially in the South-East. There was chaos and disorder everywhere – vehicles driving in a disorderly manner; one almost crushed a teenager hawking pure water sachets piled up in a green plastic bowl. The ground was rough and dirty like a cattle shed without the shit. There were potholes, some as wide and deep as small gullies.

In his attire, Okechukwu looked out of place in the run-down bus station, but he had an important journey to undertake and no other park in the city had vehicles going to his destination. Carrying his travelling bag, he picked his way carefully, trying to avoid the potholes. His elder sister, Ijeoma, trudged behind him in high-heeled shoes, walking with measured steps like an *Ijele* masquerade. Her rich and embroidered clothes made movement difficult. She was wearing a long skirt and blouse made from brocade material. Her *gele* was the expensive type imported from Switzerland and it perched on her braided hair like a bird about to take off. She carried a bag in her right hand while her left hand held up her long skirt to make her walk easier.

Okechukwu scowled at touts running amok, scouting for passengers. A man wearing an old T-shirt bellowed: *Ekwulobia here, ready to move now, now!* Two young men waved frantically, each calling out in a voice that had cracked from persistent cries: *this way to Awka and Amawbia. Come and enter the bus. Our final stop Onitsha.* What madness is this? Okechukwu thought. Some were bold enough to grip passengers' hands or luggage, pushing them towards empty or half-empty buses without asking for their destinations. A skinny middle-aged man grasped Okechukwu's travelling bag and urged him to follow him to a bus he pointed out, saying, '*O na-apa apu kita, bia banye*, the bus is ready to move now, come on board!'

Okechukwu pulled his bag away and glared at the offender. 'Did I ask for your help? Leave my bag alone or I'll show you what I can do.' He hissed like an enraged cobra.

The man looked at his face, took in his well-built strong frame; releasing the luggage, he quietly walked away. The little tip the man would get from the driver for this passenger wasn't enough to risk a beating. Okechukwu turned to his sister, who was watching the scene, and they laughed.

'These people will never change,' he said, shaking his head. 'Look at him, he's going to harass that poor girl now.'

'It's their only means of livelihood,' Ijeoma observed, still laughing. 'It's a matter of survival. Tell me, if a hen abandons her accustomed clucking sounds, with what would she raise her chicks? Leave these *ocho* passengers, that's their life. They know no other.'

Ijeoma was walking beside Okechukwu now. 'The other day I was going to Nnewi and one of them held my arm so fast you would think I was his wife or sister. He was pulling me towards the bus he was loading. My protests meant nothing to him.' Her ringing laughter caused a few heads to turn in her direction.

'It's not a laughing matter,' Okechwkwu said, shaking his head. 'I tell you, they need to be checked. They cannot be allowed to harass passengers in this atrocious manner. I blame the state government and the local government that fail to regulate their activities. Every motor park in Nigeria is a war zone, thanks to these unscrupulous men.' He thought of buying a car for himself for the umpteenth time since he had returned home some six months ago. He told himself that he could no longer afford to delay getting a car to protect himself from these annoyances. The transportation system in Abakaliki was inadequate and hazardous. Okechukwu was fed up with their pranks and insults. Since he could not avoid travelling frequently, returning home often on account of his job and his social engagements, he decided to get his own car to save himself from these impositions. 'Enough was enough,' he breathed.

He searched carefully and saw a sign a little further away announcing the section of the park where buses heading to Ekwulobia were parked. He strode towards it, closely followed by the stressed Ijeoma. He wished he didn't have to embark on this journey, but he had no choice. He and Ijeoma had to be in Ekwulobia for the traditional marriage of their eldest sister's second daughter. It was a family affair and so could not be pushed aside. He remembered their octogenarian mother's admonishing words when he voiced his reluctance to attend the wedding because a more urgent engagement had come up. Of course, there was not really a serious engagement stopping him, that was just a convenient excuse. The truth was that after he lost his girlfriend, Uchechi, whom he had intended to marry, he did not want to have anything to do with marriage – either someone else's or his. However, the eighty-five-year-old imperial matriarch had commanded: 'Okechukwu, you and Ijeoma must go to support your sister and her family. Remember, you are all she has, having lost her twin sister, our Onyinyechi, to breast cancer three years ago. Don't forget that *nke ayi bu nke ayi* – ours is ours. If you, her only brother, and Ijeoma, her only sister, don't support her with your presence, who then would?' That was the end of the argument.

Okechukwu reached the place where Ekwulobia buses stood, waiting for passengers. 'Can we hire a Sienna bus to take us to Ekwulobia?' he asked a stocky man with premature grey hair who seemed to be in charge.

The man looked at him, sizing him up. With eyes as red as palm nuts, he gave the impression he had not slept well, or at all for a week. After that frank stare, he turned his gaze on Ijeoma and smiled. He seemed even more impressed by her rich attire. 'We have only two Sienna buses to Ekwulobia today. One has loaded and left, and only this one is left.' He hit the corner of the Sienna's roof nearest to him to emphasize his point. 'You can buy your tickets, the Sienna bus will soon fill up. You can see there are three people already in the vehicle and if you join them, we will need just three more.' He stretched his right hand for their fare.

'No, we want to hire it. We are travelling for a special purpose and want the vehicle to ourselves as we would need to stop to buy a few things on the way.' Okechukwu hoped the man would transfer the passengers to another bus or perhaps help them find another Sienna bus. The man spoke again, shaking his head.

'I'm afraid there is no other one. You have to join this one that is loading now. But there are these other 14-seater buses, you can hire one of them.' He pointed with his right hand and Okechukwu saw his long nails, like an eagle's talons.

He could not hide his disappointment and frustration. The need to buy his own car and his regret that he had delayed it for so long flared up again and oppressed his mind. He hissed and turned to Ijeoma. 'I don't want us to ride in any of these 14-seater buses. They are not comfortable, and the drivers are often reckless. Shall we join the Sienna that is loading? When we get to Ekwulobia, we can hire a taxi to take us to Ugomma's house. It's really a pity we do not have taxis or car-hire companies in Abakaliki, we could have taken one.'

'That is okay by me,' Ijeoma replied, shrugging. 'Let's join the Sienna. Hopefully, other passengers will join us soon.' She climbed into the Sienna bus while Okechukwu paid and collected their tickets. He followed the driver to the boot of the car and watched as he stowed away their bags. Returning to the vehicle, he took the seat next to Ijeoma.

Two hours later, they were still sitting in the Sienna, waiting for passengers that would not come. The sun was high and hot by this time and Okechukwu was beginning to sweat. The only reason he had remained was the affirmation the driver gave him that, if he paid the right amount, he would take them to where they were going after dropping the other passengers at Ekwulobia Motor Park – and even bring them back to Abakaliki before dusk. He thought the driver looked decent and reliable, judging from his neat clothes and gentle mien.

More and more people, especially traders, had arrived at the station and proceeded to display their wares. *Okirika*, second-hand clothes sellers, cucumber and gala hawkers presented their items and waved them in front of the passengers, tempting them to buy, pleading with them to open the market and be their first buyers – *Biko, gbaa m aka ahia*, they cried. Okechukwu stared, pained at the sight of so many young people chasing passengers and passers-by in a bid to sell their wares. He wondered and grieved at the level of child labour he had observed since returning to his roots.

Disenchanted with the entire situation and fed up with watching the antics of *ndi ocho* passengers and the hawkers, he got out of the vehicle to stretch his legs. His mind turned to the research project that brought him home to the South-East, his geo-political zone, on a visiting fellowship. He and two other Nigeria-based researchers were working on Igbo women's history, culture and economic development in colonial and post-colonial Nigeria. His tenured position as the Wilson Wren Professor of History and International Relations at Dominican University in River Forest, Illinois, USA, gave him the opportunity to develop his lifelong ambition of becoming a cutting-edge, well recognised and effective researcher in history and international relations. By occupying such a prestigious position, Okechukwu brought several bright students from his community and other parts of the country to study at Dominican University. Some of them were on scholarships awarded by the university and other organisations, a few of them were retained as assistant professors at the highly rated university. Okechukwu was satisfied with his success in the

US and even went further, organising conferences to which scholars from Nigeria were regularly invited. He dreamed of organising similar conferences in his country.

His current visit to Nigeria as a Fulbright Scholar in the Department of History and Strategic Studies at Alex Ekwueme Federal University Ndufu-Alike was, indeed, the fulfilment of a dream to give back some of the knowledge and resources he acquired from America, a country that had received and embraced him. America had also wiped away his unending tears and sorrow after he lost his first and only love to rampaging Fulani herdsmen one terrifying morning at Umucheke village near Ngwulangwu. It was the year after he completed his compulsory National Youth Service Corps (NYSC) and got a job in an oil and gas company in Port Harcourt as a public relations officer. Uchechi had served with him in the one-year national programme, and she found a teaching job in a prestigious private secondary school in the same city.

It was a love that consumed him and redeemed him. Uchechi was a friend and a lover for all time. Okechukwu thought no woman was her match when it came to beauty and character. At the NYSC camp where they met, everyone had called her black beauty because of her exquisite complexion and pleasant smile. Not only was she beautiful, outgoing, vivacious and energetic, but also responsible, honest, forthright, sensitive, supportive and caring. Okechukwu's plan was to get married as soon as he settled down in his new job. As fate would have it, their plan was never realised.

Thinking about Uchechi still brought a sharp pain to his heart – though not as piercing as before. She had died at the farm where she had gone to help her parents during a short visit to her hometown. He learnt of her death in the most brutal way. He had returned from work that day and was relaxing in his room, thinking of her return from her village when his phone rang that bleak evening.

'Okechukwu, prepare yourself for bad news,' his friend, Amos's voice had said, 'Uchechi and her parents have been slaughtered like goats. Their lifeless bodies were discovered in their cassava farm...'

Life completely lost its meaning. For years, he wondered why Amos broke the news to him in that callous manner. The remembrance of those acts of savagery that led to the beheading of Uchechi's parents and the sexual violation and eventual stabbing to death of Uchechi by the killer herdsmen remained a nightmare for Okechukwu. It eventually drove him to migrate to America to seek refuge from the demons that pursued him day and night. Twenty years after the terrible incident, Okechukwu had remained single – to his father's bewilderment, his mother's despair and his sisters' eternal sorrow. An only son delaying taking a wife and raising children to keep the family's forge warm and glowing was an aberration among his people. The ancestors must be grieving and mourning, everyone in the family had said. No one seemed to be able to convince him to marry. Talking to him about the matter was like tilling a rocky ground. The image of Uchechi fanned the fire of his love and devotion, night and day. He could not forget her. His mother had written hundreds of letters to him in the United States, pleading, crying, feigning sickness and finally threatening to invoke a curse on him. All to no avail. His father had disowned him before he passed away five years ago. His reply to his parents and sisters was consoling to him: *O huru mmuo ma ere isi ya ha*, one who has seen a spirit knows how big his head is. No one dared speak to him about the issue again after he intoned this enigmatic and unfathomable proverb that meant 'only one who has had the audacity and the fortune to love deeply knows the hopelessness, the irretrievable nature of a lost love; the ache in the heart that can never be healed'. His knowledge of local proverbs, idioms and aphorisms dated back to his primary school days when they had contests in the mastery of Igbo proverbs.

Ijeoma, his confidant in the family, stopped badgering him to get married and she admonished their parents to make them stop by telling them: *Ukwa ruo oge ya, o daa*, when the time comes, *ukwa* will ripen and fall to the ground: what will be, will be.

One of the passengers, a fat woman sitting at the rear of the Sienna, called out to the driver, interrupting Okechukwu's sad thoughts and musings. 'Driver, will this journey still take place today? We've been waiting for almost three hours.'

'We will set out as soon as we fill the bus. We can't move until all the seats are taken and paid for.' The driver, a patient man dressed in *Ankara* shirt and brown trousers turned to her and rewarded her concern with a sympathetic nod.

The woman sighed and sat back, probably resigned to her fate and hoping that passengers would appear soon enough to end her ordeal. She turned and placed her hand on the left knee of the elderly man sitting close to her who probably was her husband. His face was stolid as he returned her gaze but said nothing.

'Let me find something for us to eat,' she said to him, heaving her bulky body up as she struggled to climb out of the bus.

Okechukwu realised that it might take much longer to get passengers, and this would ruin his plan for the day. The idea came to him that he could pay for the three empty seats so that the journey could begin. He was about to present this proposition to Ijeoma when she spoke first.

'Let's also find something to eat,' Ijeoma suggested, as she got out of the vehicle. 'This delay is something else. We never anticipated it, or we would have had breakfast before leaving your house.' She had left Afikpo the previous day to join Okechukwu in Abakaliki for the journey to Ekwulobia.

Okechukwu nodded. 'You have a point. With this long delay, the traditional marriage ceremony is bound to start before we arrive in Ekwulobia.' Looking at his wristwatch, he continued, 'We might as well have breakfast here, for whatever it's worth. I hate eating in places like this, but I'm famished.' His eyes roamed the bus station in search of a decent place to eat. A tall young woman in a pink catsuit arrested his gaze. She was arranging plastic plates and bowls on a plastic table under a makeshift shelter at a corner close to the park gate. Next to the table was another like it with three huge food warmers on top. Some five or six plastic chairs were arranged in a semicircle and behind one of them stood an empty, rusty wheelbarrow. Okechukwu was fascinated by the dark-skinned and attractive young woman. As he watched her, he thought there was something in the way she carried herself that seemed familiar. Turning to Ijeoma, he blurted out, excited. 'Ije, look at the girl standing over there under that canopy. Does she not look like my Uchechi?'

Ijeoma followed the direction his hand was pointing and stared at the girl for a while. 'Yes, she does. She has a figure like the Uchechi I knew and moves like her.'

'Let's go there, I want to meet her,' Okechukwu said walking to the young woman's shed. A familiar but long-forgotten emotion tugged at his heart. As he got closer, he could hear the beating of his heart: *kpuu, kpuu, kpuu*. As he entered the shed, he was trembling, for the resemblance had become even more striking– the same oval face, dark flawless skin and a well-shaped nose, like that of a female masquerade, *agbogho mmonwu*, found among the ancestral masquerade cult in his community. The swell of her breasts ignited a fire inside him that he had thought he would never experience again in his lifetime. No woman had succeeded to do this since he lost Uchechi.

Ijeoma hastened her steps to catch up with him, worried by his manner and the unnatural gleam in his eyes. 'Okey, what's the matter?' she whispered, standing close to him at the entrance of the shed. When he said nothing but continued to gaze at the young woman who was serving food to a customer, Ijeoma whispered again, fiercely, 'My brother, when will you learn to forget Uchechi. For crying out aloud, she is dead. She died over twenty years ago. You must move on with your life. The girl you're looking at means nothing to you.' She tugged at his hand as if to bring him back to earth, to reality.

The young woman waved them to two plastic chairs in the shed. 'I'll attend to you soon,' she said, flashing them a smile that increased Okechukwu's heartbeat. It seemed to him that his heart would run away from its chamber and latch onto the young woman's body. The girl was back shortly. 'What can I serve you?' she asked, looking at them with a gracious smile. 'There is white and jollof rice and beans and stew. There is *moin moin* and cooked vegetables. I also serve assorted meat – beef, chicken, snail and fish.'

While they ate rice and beans garnished with vegetables and fried chicken, Okechukwu watched her every move like one in a trance. He recalled, as an eleven-year-old primary school pupil, the story his father told him about a woman who had died in Afikpo and was sighted some years later by their townsman in Nkwere, living a normal life. The story had not meant much to him then but now it got him thinking. Was this young woman his Uchechi living a different life in Abakaliki? Who knew what the dead were capable of doing, especially those who suffered untimely deaths or died by violence? She was too young to be Uchechi, but the resemblance was striking – like a reincarnation.

Okechukwu's attention did not go unnoticed by even the young woman. She glided to his side and asked sweetly, 'Sir, I hope you like the food? You seem to have stopped eating.' Okechukwu was happily conscious of her nearness. A smile played at his lips and then touched his eyes. She was probably in her early or mid-twenties – about the age Uchechi died.

'The food is okay,' he admitted, smiling at her. 'By the way, what's your name? You look very much like someone I used to know.'

'Ujunwa is my name. But my family and my friends call me Uju,' she said.

'Where are you from? Are you related to someone called Uchechi who died many years ago? She was from Umucheke, near Ngwulangwu.' His voice was gentle, tremulous.

'Why do you ask, sir?' she asked, trying to protect her identity. Then she said in a voice that implied she did not want to be asked personal questions. 'I don't have a living or dead relative named Uchechi, and I'm not from anywhere near Ngwulangwu. I'm from Nsukka in Enugu State.'

Okechukwu nodded, striving to hide his disappointment, his sadness. He had half-hoped she was Uchechi's relative, if not her reincarnation.

Ijeoma, who had finished her food stood up and said, 'OK, let me find out if the bus has filled up. We don't want to miss it, do we?' She waved to Uju and walked away, saying, 'My brother will pay the bill.'

Uju turned to collect the empty plates and cutlery to wash them.

'One more question, Uju.

She stopped and gave him a quizzical look. Then she smiled again, and Okechukwu felt his heart beat faster.

'I want to ask you a personal question,' he began. 'Is this really your best choice of profession, the food vendor business? You seem to be well-educated.' He smiled, as if to assure her that he meant no offence.

Uju hesitated, shrugged, and said, 'I'm a graduate of Computer Science. After national service year, I couldn't find a job for three years. So I decided to do anything available to keep body and soul together and help my mother take care of my brothers and sister. My father died while I was in the university.'

'Computer Science and no job three years after graduation?' he asked, incredulous. 'What class of degree did you graduate with?' He felt she might consider the question disconcerting, but he asked anyway.

She replied, 'I graduated with a First Class from Alex Ekwueme Federal University Ndufu-Alike. We were the second graduating set from the university.'

Instinctively, Okechukwu clapped his hands, beaming with smiles and pride. 'Wow! Great!' That was all he was able to say, for in the next second, a rusty bus on reverse gear crashed into the shed upsetting the plastic table, the food warmers and everything else in the shed. Luckily Okechukwu was facing the road, so he saw the menacing vehicle before the final impact. He had got up hastily, pulled Uju towards him and whisked her away to safety through the back of the shed. There was an uproar and people ran to help or record what had happened with their smart phones.

Uju pulled away from Okechukwu and ran back to her shed. Her plastic tables, chairs, broken food warmers, damaged plastic plates and spilled food destroyed on the ground. Stupefied, she howled like a demented woman. '*Chi m egbuo m! Obu gini ka m mere*? My Chi has killed me! What did I do wrong?' She collapsed and lay on the ground thrashing about, rolling from one side to another.

Okechukwu ran forward and gathered her in his arms. 'Please, take it easy, Uju. Do not harm yourself. It's okay.'

Uju did not try to pull away from him, she was too distraught. All she thought about was her ruined business – the shed, equipment, plates and food warmers. She wept.

'It's okay...' Okechukwu said again, holding her close, loving the closeness of her and wishing to hold her like this forever. For the first time in two decades, he felt a desire to press a woman's body to his and even to kiss her lips.

'It's not okay, it can't be okay,' she wailed. 'What do I do now? I'm finished! How do I repay the loan I took to start this business? I borrowed fifty thousand naira from Mazi Okorocha to start the business. How do I pay him the loan?' Crying bitterly, she tried to pull away from Okechukwu's embrace.

He released her. 'Don't cry anymore, I'll help you. Don't worry, you'll be alright. I'll help you repay the loan.' He talked to her as if she were a child, but all he wanted was to take care of her and take her to the United States to continue with her studies. It would give him the greatest satisfaction to assist her to migrate to the United States, if she was willing.

At last, his words penetrated Uju's consciousness. 'You'll help me repay the loan? Did you say you'll help me?' She wiped her tears and rubbed down her dishevelled and dirty clothes.

'Yes. And I'll help you move to the US and continue with your studies if you allow me. I'll take care of everything, don't worry.'

'But you don't know me? I don't even know you?' she cried. 'How then can you help me?' She stared at him, wanting to believe him, but fearing it was futile to believe and trust such promises.

The crowd surged forward. Some people tried to salvage the wreckage, including the bus driver, who came to survey the damage he had caused. Holding his clean-shaven head in his hands, he was in a daze and looked defeated.

Meanwhile, Okechukwu was still standing close to Uju, consoling her, when a yam seller approached and watched them for a moment. 'Chief, please help her if you can,' the woman pleaded, 'she is a well-behaved and hardworking girl. I buy food from her when I come to Ochudo Park to sell my yams.' She adjusted her load and sighed.

'I will. Thank you, madam,' Okechukwu replied, amused by the thought that the *Isi Agu* and the *Abiriba* cap he wore raised his stature among these people.

It was at this time that Ijeoma returned to tell him that the Sienna bus was ready to set out for Ekwulobia. 'We must go now before we lose our seats,' she said.

'Wait here for me,' Okechukwu said to Uju. In a minute he was back. 'Here is my card, and here is money to repay your loan. I'm going to Ekwulobia now, but I'll see you tomorrow after I return. Don't worry, you'll be fine.'

'Thank you,' Uju said softly, wiping away her tears with her bare hands. She smiled at Okechukwu who reluctantly left her.

He turned one more time, smiled and said, 'Let me have your phone number, I'll call you.' This time she did not hesitate, she gave him her phone number and waved gently at him as he departed.

A Spruced up Young Man

Andrew Aidoo

i

It was morning assembly. The headteachers, teachers and three head boys stood on the platform, taking turns behind the lectern. The students were arranged according to their houses. OJ was a diplomat's son in Prempeh College. He was also a freshman.

He stood at ease in the Opoku Ware line, wearing chino trousers and a white shirt with French cuffs. Methodist hymnbook in right hand, left hand in pocket, head tilted up and eyebrows slightly raised over heavy-lidded eyes, he was as proud as his father had been twenty-five years ago in the Butler House line.

Even though OJ towered over many boys behind him, he insisted on staying in his position on the assembly line. Because, after the dry sermon and addresses of the headteachers, Kwame would climb up the platform, read the announcement and dismiss the assembly. From the first time he saw Kwame, OJ was compelled to speak to him.

As his father once said while they waited for drinks at an antiquated rooftop in Corinthia, 'If you see it and you like it, go for it. Nobody can resist your charm, my boy.'

OJ saw Kwame first at the official welcome Sunday Service for freshmen. They were expected to wear any wax cloth or kente wrapped around the torso and thrown over the left shoulder, leaving the right bare. The venue was the Osae Assembly Hall. OJ sat on a chair in the front row. His kente was so sturdy and his mien so regal that none of the seniors questioned his place in the front row. Three minutes later, a timid usher moved him to the third row.

They sang hymns, danced, and then sat for the plain sermon that was pallid like the Anglican wafer. The priest's voice droned. OJ's eyes grew heavy. His head dropped forward and soon saliva leaked down his open mouth onto his kente. The thundering sound of claps through the hall, from the balcony, the nave and the high table, made him gasp sharply and suck in his saliva. The service had ended. OJ looked around with red eyes, confused; later, embarrassed. Then he saw Kwame rising from the first row, adjusting his black-green kente on top of a loose, short-sleeved lace shirt before ascending the stage. When he began to speak, OJ shivered.

He remembered his dark skin, the way Kwame gripped the edges of the lectern with his wiry arms as he leaned into the microphone, the expensive black wristwatch, and the deep voice. OJ wanted to walk up to him and ask, 'What is your name?' His father would have told him to do it. Somewhere on the stage, the piano was playing. The teachers and prefects were rising from the high table, walking through the aisle to the door in one pompous file. The students stood as they passed. Kwame was behind a preacher in a tab collar and a black clerical gown. Kwame's head was up, his right hand holding his kente to prevent its train from dragging on the floor, while the left held his hymn book and KJV Bible. OJ trained his eyes on Kwame's face in profile till Kwame stepped out of the hall.

In his bed later that night, OJ imagined how pleasant it would be if Kwame was his friend. And how if Kwame needed something from him, he would do it and not expect gratitude. When he fell asleep, he dreamt about him. OJ began to idealise Kwame. He was no longer the pretty prefect, but the perfect boy who did not need anybody's friendship. With this, his heart closed against Kwame.

But OJ felt the smile of fate.

It happened on an October morning. The day was bright and softened by rain from the previous night. It was assembly time and Kwame, searching for an example of a well-dressed freshman, pointed to OJ.

'Like our spruced up young man over here.'

The students in the front row turned and craned their necks to see OJ in his green shirt, brown shorts and darker brown wingtip Oxfords that matched his socks and belt. Their stares made him conscious of being watched. After assembly, he went to the Post Office to buy an envelope and letter paper to write to his close friend, Blewu.

Later in the evening, while changing from his uniform into the house jersey, he wondered for how long Kwame had noticed him. Had Kwame noticed him all this while? He remembered all the times he saw Kwame turn and glance at him. Was there meaning in them? When Kwame stood at the podium on that first Sunday, OJ was certain that Kwame had glanced at him at least three times. The third time, there had been a glint of admiration in his eyes. The same glint as when he said: *like our spruced up young man here.* Such a charming expression. OJ could see his father saying that.

It thrilled OJ to feel seen by Kwame, but it made him nervous too. From that day forward, whether during Presby-Methodist Student Union (PMSU) meetings on Friday evenings or during Sunday evening services, OJ anticipated where Kwame would be in the hall and sat where Kwame would not see him.

During assembly, he began to stand at the back, bending forward slightly to block his view of Kwame with the heads of other students. His awareness of Kwame intensified. He expected Kwame where he was not and hoped the footsteps he heard were Kwame's. When he sat in class or on his bed, he'd remember Kwame's fingers gripping the edge of the lectern and the third glance. *Our spruced up young man!* In the shower that evening, OJ felt someone standing behind him. He turned sharply and swiped the running water from his face. It was not Kwame. He dried his body while his heart swelled with sadness.

He cut a steely image of a brooding prince, but his heart was tender, hurting as the days went on, such that he felt that his heart would break if he did not tell somebody how he felt. So one Friday evening after the PMSU meeting, he responded to Blewu's letter and unburdened all his troubles. She had replied to his previous letter, which he read before he tucked it under his pillow.

Then it happened. Kwame appeared at the gate of Opoku Ware House the next day. In his right hand was a folded exercise book, a pen in the left. He was the prefect on duty for inspection. He went through the dorm rooms, checking the bedsheets and corners of bunk beds and ceilings, sniffing the air, feeling the surfaces with his delicate fingertips to check for dust or grease on the shutters. From the ground floor up, dorm room after the next, he inched nearer to OJ. Kwame kept a flat face and his deep-set eyes stayed focused. His shirt and trousers were so white that the students felt it was the state of their souls and not their dorm room that was being inspected.

OJ had been holding his breath since the seraph had entered their dorm room. Kwame's Windsor knot was shaped like a rolled tongue. With the help of a false-emerald pin, the college tie maintained a gentle curve above the neck of his lintless sweater vest.

Kwame was close; OJ smelt his soft lavender. Kwame signalled OJ to step aside and bent to closely look at the bedsheet and raise the mattress to check the floor through the palette. Then standing, he ran his index finger across the sill above OJ's bed with an undecipherable expression on his face. When he bent to observe the bed, OJ had observed that Kwame's vest had pulled over his black belt. The small fold caused a tremor in his heart. Then OJ looked down and saw that a trouser leg was caught in the elastic loop of a Chelsea boot. Couldn't Kwame feel it?

Kwame scribbled in his book. The room was quiet. The dorm rooms that had completed inspection on the ground floor bustled with students preparing for breakfasts of capitals and dough. Kwame was turning slowly, head lifted, taking in the corners of the ceiling. OJ watched Kwame's feet. He wanted to pull the hem of his trouser out from the elastic loop. It was like an itch lodged where the nail could not reach. The prefect sighed, his back facing OJ, and ordered the four boys to clap for themselves. But OJ did not clap and he watched Kwame walk out the door in long strides. He moved to the open shutters and saw Kwame enter the next dorm room across from theirs. Kwame had come into his room. He had touched his mattress. Lifted his pillow. Did he see the envelope?

OJ had not forgotten Blewu. He sustained a steady correspondence with her. He added a Prempeh College dog tag and lapel pin to one of his letters to her. Blewu's reply was sweet, with the sticky, *I love you more than you can ever imagine, OJ,* leaking through the text. She reciprocated his gesture by including in her letter a stainless-steel Holy Child bracelet and a customised brooch made of amber encrusted in silver, with his name *Oppong Junior* engraved underneath it. This bold expression of her love moved OJ to pour out his heart about Kwame in his next letter to her. He was going to post it that weekend. But when he arrived at the Post Office, the content of the letter felt inappropriate. It was so sacred to him that he shuddered at the thought of it passing through the hands of strangers before touching Blewu's. He folded it and pushed it down into his pocket. He would tell her during Christmas break. Later in the day, he crumpled it, tore it into pieces and threw the confetti into a bin.

Prempeh College vacated the students. Christmas events filled OJ's house. First, his father always held a pre-Christmas party with ambassadors and consulates staff as guests. Then the main event, on Christmas the next day, brought in the extended family members, including OJ's uncle, the flagbearer of the party that had lost the general election that month.

OJ also played host as the only son. Therefore, he had no time to sit with Blewu. He went up to get the singer, his cousin twice removed, to perform the musical interlude for the desserts and indoor games. Blewu was in the game room and bar, talking to a Turkish boy in a three-piece suit. Her right leg dangled from the barstool, her head supported by her right hand and elbow. The boy, from the back, looked like Kwame. OJ turned, almost choking, and left before she saw him.

At the end of the party, he walked around to thank guests and family for coming. His cousin, Samuel had had such a good time, that he praised him: 'Such an excellent host, OJ. See you in London, next year.'

The guests began to leave in groups. Blewu fell asleep in OJ's bed. He'd imagined he would find time to speak to Blewu and he would only tell her after they had said everything and had nothing more to say to each other. Kwame was the last thing to talk about.

ii

When OJ completed Prempeh, he enrolled at Cambridge. His father was the high commissioner of Ghana to the UK and Ireland. On the weekends, his father and his cohorts took him jet-setting around Europe, tasting wine and exotic food.

Distance would separate OJ and Blewu for the next four years while he was in Cambridge. Before he left Ghana, Blewu found a paid internship at the Ministry of Foreign Affairs. She was taking a gap year to learn about the world and corporate Ghana before she entered university. In the beginning, they stayed in touch and sent messages frequently, but after the first three months, she stopped initiating the conversations. She hoped he would get the hint, but he forgot about her.

When he arrived in Ghana on the 20th of April 2018, he remembered Blewu. Her house shared a fence with his. He remembered when he was eight and she was six, how they fought over his console and his mother had snatched it from him and given it to her. He had refused to set up the game and watched her flounder with the menu and settings.

The security recognised him and greeted, 'Good day, honourable!'

OJ smiled. 'Baba. OJ o.'

OJ went through the first living room, then up the corkscrew stairs to the first floor. He greeted the domestic help who was ironing in the hallway, humming *He lives in me*. She curtseyed. OJ's half-shoes knocked on the wooden floor, he turned the corner and knocked at Blewu's door.

It opened and shut in his face, then reopened.

'I was naked,' she said, covering herself with her negligee, before letting him in.

He removed his tweed jacket and left it on the coat hanger beside the door, dropped his flat hat on the nightstand and slumped into the bed.

She was in the other room, rummaging for underwear in her wardrobe and found some red lace panties. She was surprised to see him but was determined not to show it. It was not the first time he had left her for a long time, but she acted like it did not matter.

'What brings you here today?' she said, pulling her underwear up her thighs.

She turned in the mirror, checked out her butt, and gently bounced on her toes to see if it shook. She threw on a turquoise tank top because of the heat.

'I don't know,' OJ said and laughed. 'I never used to have any reason. What kind of question is that?'

Blewu returned in the doorway. 'For four years, OJ, that was too much.'

OJ could see through the lace, the trimmed bush, and a faint trace of hair rising to her navel, the sunny complexion of her body. It was unlike Kwame's, which was firm, ribbed and dark.

'Nice breasts,' he said, squinting.

The first thing that startled her was OJ's voice. It was deep and commanding. Timid OJ no longer existed. He laughed too, a rich boom travelling around her room. She sat a little distance from him in a lotus position, her fingers fidgeting. He looked out of the window in the opposite direction.

'I worried about you, you know? Your mum said you were sick in Munich.'

'It was Berlin,' he said, turning to her. 'I wasn't sick. I died. Almost. Munich was where the hotel was. We flew from Munich to have fun in Berlin.'

His emphasis was on the 'er' in Berlin.

'You're following your dad around.'

OJ shrugged and leaned forward to take her hand. 'What do you say I take you out to dinner? We need to talk.'

OJ had become a man. His trimmed moustache stood out. When he arose, she was dwarfed beside him. His plumpness spread out well to match his big frame and broad chest, so he did not appear overweight. He looked confident, but Blewu could sense his sadness.

'You look like an older man.'

OJ laughed, slapping his knee. 'Funny thing. Baba greeted me 'Honourable' and I told him that it's me OJ. At the tarmac too this woman greeted me as 'Your Excellency.' My father was climbing down the jet. He laughed.'

'What's with the old people clothes? You went to the UK and decided to stop being fashionable?'

OJ took offence and Blewu saw it. She doubled down.

'Yes. You look like a sugar daddy.' And shot a peal of laughter through the room.

He stepped off the bed ready to leave. Blewu lifted her tank top to cover her cleavage. On his way out through the hallway, she felt him up, squeezed his buttocks and laughed and agreed to have dinner with him. OJ only shook his head. Some things never changed.

At dinner, OJ was glib and charming. Blewu thought he acted like a gentleman. He ordered three bottles of wines that were not available, so Blewu ordered a bottle of vintage champagne. They reminisced about old times. He shared his plans for the future; he wanted to run for president in twenty years. Blewu laughed. As they drank wine, and it got to her head, Blewu let out that she was still single and confessed that she missed OJ.

She lay her head on his shoulder on the way back and it made him remember Kwame, and it filled him with grief.

That date helped to melt the coldness between them after four years. Blewu had resumed flicking his cheeks. Even though OJ made her heart flutter, she refused to own up to how she felt for him. He would always be that timid balloon with long limbs during their childhood. It had turned to a habit now to squeeze his butt for her pleasure, but he treated her as a girl who wanted something she did not know.

Two weeks before he returned to England, Blewu came to his home. After talking to his mother, she stole into OJ's room where he lay in bed, covered with his blanket and eyes closed. He daydreamed about what it would be like if Kwame were with him in his bed at Prempeh. But it could never happen: OJ was in Opoku Ware House and Kwame was in Serwaa House – they slept far from each other. That was what he told OJ when they reconnected on Linkedin.

The room was dark. The streetlight appeared through his open windows. The doorknob turned and Blewu stepped in. OJ knew she was there. He felt her breath on his ear. Then he twisted, grabbed her by the upper arms and pinned her on his bed. She was breathing in short bursts near his face. She had been chewing peppermint gum. Just before he let go of her to laugh at how surprised she looked, she kissed him on the lips. He pulled himself away and Blewu dashed out of the room.

For three days, neither of them visited each other. Their texts were stilted, and the replies were few and far between. But it was OJ and not Blewu who made the first move. The sky was bright and the clouds were stagnant through his open window and he was tired of playing video games. He rang up Blewu and asked what she was doing.

'Trying to sort out my clothes. Actually, I need some help. Wanna come over?'

He was bored so he went. Blewu was wearing a strapless red dress. It was elastic. She bounced on her toes, 'What do you think?' the breasts bobbing.

'Turn around,' OJ said.

She did. The back was cut low, and the hem of the dress had a slit that was thigh high.

'Risqué, I'd say,' he said and nodded.

OJ sat down on the bed.

'So how can I help you?'

She went into her wardrobe and wore a brown jumper. She went over to OJ, her back facing him, standing between his open legs.

'Help me with the zip.'

He could see her face in the vanity. It was calm, even innocent. He drew up the zip but stopped. He brought his head near her back and pulled the zip down. His pulse quickened at the scent. The two dimples at her waist pulled him forward. Since when did Blewu wear lavender? He pressed his lips against the small of her back. It tensed. Then he kissed it again, with tender wetness like that night, in the dark cubicle, when Kwame had asked him to sit on his bed, while he removed his singlet. OJ's heart ran wild. He pressed his face against the groove of her arched back, his hands gripping her waist, tightening.

'Let me guide you, baby boy.'

Blewu took OJ's hands by the wrists and sat on him, cupping her breasts with them. He was still and tense, a gentle tremor of dread passed through him. He made to push her away, but Blewu was already grinding against his crotch, her soft ripe breast in his dark hands. In the vanity, her nipple was peeping out of his knuckles.

She threw her head back while grinding. OJ's penis was hardening and softening. Her eyes were closed. She brought her hands down his abdomen, searching for an entrance to prise off his trousers. She grew frantic when she felt the pubic hair.

She sucked in air, exhaled softly, yes. What was she doing? That was not how Kwame had done it. Kwame had turned, sat astride him, held his head in his velveteen palms and kissed with hunched shoulders so soulfully that the pleasure coursed through OJ's body. OJ had let himself fall back into the bed, felt Kwame bearing down on him, kissing so fiercely that their teeth ground and threatened to spark. Nobody was in Serwaa House. All of them were at the Osae Assembly Hall, singing, dancing, and listening to sermons. But he was with Kwame, breathing hotly on his neck, pressed against him till sweat gathered and glistened on their bodies. OJ's head hung at the edge of the bed, eyes glazed with intoxication; Kwame issuant upon him, and that was when OJ said to him, 'Please, kiss me again.' Blewu turned, bent over and kissed OJ.

iii

They married on the 14th of September 2019. On the day of the marriage, OJ wore the immortal kente of his great-grandfather, a kingmaker at the time of Agyeman Prempeh I. It was a triple-weave of gold, lime green and cream yarns. Its sturdy fold gathered on OJ's left shoulder. A brooch of amber encrusted in silver was tacked on it. He wore a round neck shirt made of golden lace under the cloth. His hands were held fingertip to fingertip across his curved belly, a gold chain gleaming on his left wrist. His expression was serene as he stood before the pulpit looking out the open door. For the first time since he had returned from Cambridge, he was happy.

His father, the honourable, and his mother were seated in front on the right side. His mother's right hand, covered in his father's hands, rested on his father's knee. OJ's uncle, His Excellency the president, sat next to OJ's father, smiling, nodding and whispering.

Mr Apenyo emerged through the door with his daughter's arm hooked in his. He was in a slate suit, with his Windsor knot rolled like a tongue. It reminded OJ of Kwame, but he only blinked and smiled.

Blewu wore the traditional Ewe kente of gold, royal blue and cream yarns, sewn into a dress whose train dragged along the red carpet about half a metre behind her. Kwame had carried his to prevent it from dragging on the floor.

The congregation watched her with rapt attention. Behind the blusher, she was looking down at her feet. She climbed the stage and stood facing OJ. She lifted her eyes and they shone. Kwame appeared in the crowd in OJ's periphery. This moved him and drove moisture to his eyes.

'I, Nana Kwesi Boamponsem Oppong Junior, take you, Blewusi Apenyo, to be my lawfully wedded wife and to continue to hold you for better, for worse, in sickness and health, as I have always done since our shared childhood, and not even death will cleave us asunder.'

He had read with conviction, with such raw honesty in his glistening eyes, that the maid of honour had rushed up to prop Blewu at the waist, who was shaking, threatening to cry. OJ smiled at her, head tilted and a tear running down his eye over the bridge of his nose. When she looked up at him again, she broke into a chuckle.

Later, at the table, OJ leaned to Blewu and whispered 'I almost said, wawfully ledded life' into her ears.

Blewu burst out a peal of resounding laughter. 'Oh, OJ! Please!'

Their parents gifted them a five-bedroom apartment with two living rooms. It was secured at Dzorwulu ten years ago. They moved in right after the wedding. Blewu's office was on the east wing of their new home, furnished in mahogany and granite. She was a consultant for Agribusiness. OJ had an office in the west wing, but he preferred the summer hut on the rooftop, where he smoked cigars and gazed listlessly into the distance.

On the night of his wedding, OJ stayed up on the rooftop till eleven smoking and sky gazing. The garden view below was illuminated by the white floodlight. He pulled a drag from his cigar and held it. This would be his last. He remembered the clear night when he climbed over the balcony of Serwaa House overlooking the dining hall. He had been wearing only his boxers. He had looked up to the sky that spread like a black velvet cloth sprinkled with glitter, the bright sickle of the moon glinting, just like this night. He was liberated when the wind beat his bare chest. Kwame had been inside his cubicle, not daring to come out. OJ had been happy then.

Blewu climbed up to find him blowing a cloud of smoke. She took the cigar from his knuckles and screwed its lit end into the ashtray.

Land of Prophetic Women

Rafeeat Aliyu

The smell of raw meat assaults my nostrils. I hold my breath, suppress a grimace, and resist the urge to pull away. Over Celestina Godlove's shoulder, my vision blurs. I count backwards in my head, *ten . . . nine . . . eight . . .* and try to focus on a framed picture on the back wall. Brown polished wood wraps around three children, all shiny foreheads, bright eyes, and wide, toothless grins. *Seven. . . six . . . five . . .* My head is beginning to swim as Celestina breaks the hug and steps away. She smiles. Beady eyes gleam behind thick-rimmed glasses.

'How I've longed to meet you!' she says, holding my hand as though we are old friends.

I'm itching to pull my hand free, but I offer an awkward smile in return. *Four . . . three . . . two . . . one. . .* That stench – the one that brought to my mind the abattoir near my childhood home – I can't smell it any more.

'See how shy you are!' Celestina trills. Round shoulders exposed in the boubou she's wearing shake as she laughs. The gold embroidery of the gown sits at the curve of her shoulders, the rest is a sea of blue.

I don't laugh and can't meet her eyes. Instead, I crane my neck for Olivia. She's the reason I'm here. Celestina closes the front door and leads me into the sitting room. I hear the hum of a sewing machine, though I can't see it. It must be coming from one of the rooms in the back. Olivia sits on a grey sofa on the right-hand side of a room cluttered with ramshackle furniture, placed haphazardly. She's staring down at her palms folded demurely on her lap. A lump rises in my throat.

It's been a week since Olivia told Abba and me that she was moving out. We'd offered her shelter from Thomas, but she said she found a proper one here, at the Land of Prophetic Women.

'Come, sit down.' Celestina releases my hand, places her palm on the small of my back and steers me towards the sofa. She pushes me down next to Olivia. I'm relieved to see my friend and glad to be free of Celestina's touch. 'Olivia, won't you greet your friend?'

Olivia glances at me sideways, tilting her body in my direction. 'Hey Hamida, thanks for coming to see me.'

I frown at this robotic greeting, so unlike the friend I know. 'Olivia . . .' I whisper, but Celestina cuts me off with a snap of her fingers. She looms over us like a lighthouse does the sea.

'Tell me, my dear, what will you eat?'

'Nothing . . . ma.' I add the 'ma' as an afterthought. While Celestina does not appear old enough to be my mum, she merits being called 'aunty' out of respect.

'Nonsense!' Celestina says. 'You must eat something. Prudence!'

A petite young woman appears at the doorway, her chemically straightened hair pulled back in a thin ponytail.

Having sent Prudence to the kitchen to prepare the pounded yam that I won't be eating for sure, Celestina sinks into one of the armchairs opposite us, her form overflowing its bounds, blue dress hanging over its sides. I give her another small smile and watch Olivia. She doesn't move. *What is wrong with her?* Now she's staring at the TV mounted on the south wall, where an Indian serial is showing. A bride sits, surrounded by women who take turns applying a yellow paste to exposed skin. Upstairs, a man is arguing with a woman and she pushes him down a long, curved stairwell. A slow montage ensues: wide-eyed faces, mouths agape, hands raised in horror.

'I don't understand the point of these shows,' Olivia had said when I made her watch Zee World when she was at mine. Yet here she is, eyes glued to the screen, inconscient.

'It's so kind of you to come to visit,' Celestina's grating voice pulls me away from my thoughts.

'Yes, ma,' I reply.

You're not the one I came to see.

I take in the room: frayed, mismatched chairs; watermarked, wooden centre-table; the plastic tablecloth atop the rickety dining table in the far corner. This isn't a shelter for women, it's a two-bedroom flat nestled on the third floor of a suite of apartments. Beads of sweat prickle my scalp. I blurt out, 'How long have you been here?'

'It's been three years of God's grace,' Celestina coos. 'I started this ministry to take care of vulnerable women and their children.'

'So . . . this is like a church?' I reach up to pat my hair beneath my head wrap.

'In many ways,' Celestina says, smile widening. I wonder if her cheeks hurt. 'Women and children are beloved by God. We also have a school: Godlove Academy for Blessed Children.'

I turn away from Celestina's smugness to face Olivia again, placing my left palm on her thigh. 'Livvy O, na you I come greet o. Wetin dey sele now? Talk to me.'

Pidgin sputters from my mouth like water from a broken faucet. Olivia always laughed when I tried to speak pidgin. After calling me ajebo, she would say 'Mida, be posh and proud. Never attempt speaking pidgin again'. She's quiet now.

'She's fine,' Celestina answers. 'Thomas somehow found out she was here and caused a disturbance just this morning. Nothing I couldn't handle, of course.'

Thomas, Olivia's ex-husband. The reason she was moving house. I can't recall a time he triggered this kind of reaction in Olivia. Then again, things can break you. What was that proverb about water wearing down rocks?

'And she hasn't said anything since?'

'She just greeted you, my dear,' Celestina points out.

I wish I could speak to my friend alone. My eyes are once more drawn to that picture on the wall. I see now that there are more photographs surrounding it. Three children, different to the last, this time standing in front of a brick building with rose bushes rambling along its side. A dozen or so women in what looks like a classroom, smiling up at the camera over the sewing machines in front of them. There is a solitary child, her curly hair styled in pigtails, holding a flower; she's wearing blue overalls.

'Where is Regina?' I burst out, turning from Olivia – still entranced by the TV – to Celestina. I expected to see Olivia's daughter, to have her run to me, begging me to carry her in my arms as always.

'Ah, here comes the food.' Celestina's eyes are on Prudence as she shuffles towards us, carrying a round metal tray laden with two plates. From afar, I can make out fried rice on one and, on the other, what seems to be asun. Prudence drags a centre table towards me with one foot – I wince as it scrapes against the polished floor – and places the tray before me. I was right – the fried rice is mixed with vegetables and liver. The goat meat on the other plate is cut into bite-sized pieces and liberally stained red with pepper.

As Prudence straightens up, her belly presses tightly against the tank top she is wearing. I suck in my breath, masking it with a cough, as if to clear my throat. Prudence is pregnant. When the aroma of the food wafts up, I don't smell fried rice. I'm back beside the abattoir – raw meat, the metallic stench of spilled blood. My stomach lurches as I leap to my feet.

'Ahahn, what's the matter?' It's Celestina.

'I've been sick,' I say, suddenly desperate to leave this place. If Olivia won't talk to me, what's the point in staying anyway?

'What about the food?' Celestina says. There is disapproval in her eyes as they study me.

'I can't eat it,' I say, 'not right now.'

'Prudence, go and bring a plastic container.'

'Don't worry about that, ma,' I bend my knees in a curtsey, 'I'll come again when Olivia is better.'

With that, I stumble to the door. Why is Celestina going on about food when Olivia won't say a word? Olivia hasn't so much as glanced at me since I arrived. *And where is Regina?*

'It was nice meeting you,' I call out as my hand touches the greasy doorknob.

I hurtle down the darkened stairway, my stomach quivering. Women mill about the space outside the apartment. Sitting with their backs against the wall, they are knitting, stringing beads together, carefully clipping at paper with scissors. They don't acknowledge me as I rush by. They work mechanically, eyes fixed on their tasks; no sound of singing or idle gossip in their mouths; no laughter in the air. I have already made it downstairs to the courtyard when I hear Celestina calling my name.

'Hamida!' she shouts. 'You forgot the food.'

I look up to see her leaning against the rusted railing, all the way from the third floor. Her blue gown billows around her, glasses perched on her nose. I spin around to see Prudence lumbering towards me, seemingly without any concern for the extra weight she is carrying. Instinctively, I step back, but her approach is determined. Prudence pushes the plastic bag – rumpled with use and reuse – into my hands. I glance up again and Celestina is still watching.

In the back of the Taxify cab heading home, my stomach growls. It's forty minutes till home and the bag is at my feet. I reach for it and pry open the top of the container. Prudence threw the food in here in a hurry, the meat is underneath the rice, the sauce is peppered throughout the food. Slowly, I bring the bag close to my nose and sniff. Instantly, I draw back, repulsed. The car is still speeding as I toss the bag and its contents out the window.

***

Rafeeat Aliyu 303

It's two days before Abba returns from his official trip to Yola.
He joined the police force because his dad and grandfather had
been policemen. It was a job guaranteed to lift him up through
the ranks due to networks, but Abba also loved listening to
Grandpa's stories of solving crime in colonial Nigeria. It doesn't
take much to convince him to help. It never does.

'So, tell me more about Olivia,' he says, when we're done
talking about his trip.

'Something didn't feel right,' I say. We'd already talked on
the phone as soon as I got back home from meeting Celestina
Godlove. Yet as I tell him everything again, Abba nods as
though he's hearing the story for the first time.

'I sent one of my boys to watch over that place,' he's telling
me, as he moisturises his skin. 'He noticed several women
passing through its doors. There are photos on my phone.'

I grab his mobile from where he left it charging. Soon, I'm
scrolling through his photo gallery. The quality isn't great and
I have to zoom in often. There are women standing at the
door of the Land of Prophetic Women. Women emerge from
the building's entrance; they stand at the front gate and wait
to cross the street. Their stomachs bulge, some at half-moons
and others full. My mouth falls open at a detail I'd missed
before. The women in and around Celestina's apartment are
all pregnant.

'We stationed a roadblock on the street,' Abba explains.
I don't dig in too deep. On American TV shows, they have
warrants and crime labs. Here, we have connections. I try not
to think about the people who have had justice slip through
their fingers because they couldn't make one phone call, or
were not married to the right person. I also push aside thoughts
about the corporals grumbling when their superior made them
get into a blue Hilux Jeep and park outside a nondescript block
of apartments. Instead, I think of Olivia, staring at the TV, only
speaking at Celestina's prompts. I think of the fact that Regina
was not at the so-called shelter. I remember Celestina's tight
hug. My nose cringes at the memory.

'Why are all these women pregnant?' I've swiped through photo after photo and it's like a pregnant-women's pageant. Diverse women pushing forward with extended abdomens of varying widths.

'Haba, it's a home for women,' Abba shrugs. 'What's for dinner?'

He's at the last stage of his coming-back-home ritual. It starts like this: salaam-salaam, a kiss to my lips, wudu-salat, a shower, then moisturiser and now food.

'Tuwon shinkafa and miyan kuka,' I reply. My eyes are glued to the phone as I follow him to the kitchen.

'Again?' Abba sighs. He's probably as tired of cooking as he is tired of eating my miyan kuka. The tart taste of the ground baobab leaves used to make that soup is my latest food craving. I don't even need the rice balls that accompany the soup; I can slurp up miyan kuka all on its own.

I'm still scrolling through the image gallery when Abba settles at the dining table. I opt for the armchair in the adjacent living room, folding my legs beneath me as I stare at the phone.

'Just how many photos did your boy take?' I ask. I hear Abba rinsing his hands in preparation to start eating. I've seen throngs of pregnant women, but no sight of Celestina yet. Or Olivia, come to think of it. The only recurring familiar face is Prudence's – she's escorting practically every woman out. I recall the way she ran towards me, and shiver. When I finally spot Celestina, I rush to Abba's side.

'This is her,' I say. 'She's the founder.'

Abba takes the phone with his left hand, the fingers of his right hand buried in the oily green soup. He scrutinises the photo and nods.

'I'll send it to the DoI,' he says. 'Daddy has a friend there. You remember Uncle Mukhtar? He'll let me know if there's anything to worry about.'

'Thank you, Baby.' I kiss his forehead.

'Haba, for what?' he replies.

For involving the Department of Investigations in this unauthorised investigation based on your wife disliking someone's body odour.

The first time Olivia really confided in me about the trouble with Thomas was when he burned all her clothes and threw her out naked in the middle of the night. We've all done things for men – Abba was my doorway to a new religion – but I hated the way Olivia fiercely stood by Thomas with a passion. She'd swallowed a stone and kept his maltreatment of her well hidden, until that night when he exposed her shame. Olivia had found refuge with a neighbour and later, with us. I had spoken to Abba about it. It really would not have cost much to round up a few constables to teach Thomas a lesson. Maybe throw him overnight in a dark, filthy cell for good measure. But Olivia had said no. Sometimes, I wonder if he would have continued to sniff around Olivia if she had given her consent and let us do it.

***

Thursday, I'm driving to meet Temi at her cafe. Back in the day, it used to be Temi, Olivia and me raising a storm at youth camp. I can't wait to tell Temi about what's currently going on with Olivia. At the traffic lights, before the cab driver makes a right turn, a red Honda swerves in front of us. I lift my head up from my phone in time to see that the person driving is wearing glasses and a blue gele.

'Yeye woman!' the driver curses.

'See her ugly head wrap,' I mutter in agreement.

Seven Cafe is quaint, with second-hand furniture: long picnic tables and car tyres upcycled and painted in bright colours. I meet Temi in her office and, wolfing down a shawarma while a slice of cake for dessert waits on the side, I don't waste time downloading the gist.

'What did you say her name was again?' Temi's eyes are on her laptop screen, fingers poised above the keyboard like a virtuoso.

'Celestina Godlove,' I say, waving my hand. 'I already searched, it was useless.'

'Did you say she had a school?' Temi presses on.

I frown at first, then I remember the name. Godlove Academy for Blessed Children has a website. Leaning over as Temi scrolls through the photo gallery, I can see heavily edited pictures of school grounds, rows of smartly dressed children, smiling teachers pointing at blackboards. There's even a sunburnt white man running with older children along a football pitch.

'This looks legit,' Temi shrugs.

A familiar image pops up of three children, the smaller girl with pigtails and overalls. She looks about seven – Regina's age. If I squint, she even resembles Olivia's daughter. Cold air whistles down my back.

'It's not legit,' I insist, shaking my head. 'Check the contact page.'

'It doesn't show any physical address.' Before Temi can add to that, my mobile buzzes from within my bag.

'She's not who she says she is,' Abba says, once I click accept and we've exchanged salaams. He has always preferred to talk over messaging.

'I knew it!' I whisper into my phone. I gesture at Temi as well. *I told you so.*

'I'll tell you more when I get home,' Abba continues, 'but yeah, the woman in the photo is Elizabeth Bababipoi. She used to live in Port Harcourt, also running a ministry dedicated to helping women. A woman brought a report to the police station there. She accused Elizabeth of stealing her baby.'

'Of what?' I yell into my phone. I've abandoned the citrus cake on the plate in front of me, half-eaten.

'Stealing her baby,' Abba repeats. 'Rumour around the neighbourhood was that she was using the children for money rituals. Her neighbours said she used to pound babies to mash in mortars. The police had to stop a mob from lynching her.'

Saliva floods my mouth. I reach forward to grab a paper napkin from the stack in the middle of the table. Across her office desk, Temi is looking at me, her eyebrows pinched together in concern.

'Oh no, Olivia!' My voice breaks as I spit into the paper napkin.

'It's okay, gimbiya.' Abba only reminds me that I'm his princess when he's trying to calm me down. 'The police never found any concrete evidence.'

'But . . .' I feel sick to my stomach. I'm already on my feet, direction bathroom. I feel giddy with my mobile pressed against my ear, 'they must have been onto something. Who makes up things like that?'

'Listen, we'll talk more when I get home, okay?' Abba says. 'I've got to go.'

I'm barely inside the bathroom before I yank up the toilet lid with such force it slams against the cistern. I'm heaving everything I just paid to eat. I see the cake and bits of sausage from the chicken shawarma. The acrid taste remains in my mouth even after rinsing with water from the small basin in the bathroom.

On any other day, such details wouldn't bother me. Abba has told me of sorting out charred arms, legs and heads after car accidents – this was before his transfer and promotion. But none of them had to do with Olivia. I flush, rinse my mouth again and the next thing I do is call Olivia. No one answers.

Temi knocks on the door. 'Are you good, Babes?'

I'm drumming my foot hard against the linoleum floor as I tap out and send a WhatsApp message.

Livvy, let's meet for lunch at Temi's cafe.

It's a while before I receive a reply – to my text, not my phone call.

We'll see – maybe near Banex tomorrow, there's a good joint there.

Temi is standing guard when I emerge.

'You sure you're okay?'

I nod. 'I'm meeting Olivia tomorrow.'

'That's great – but you should take it easy.' Temi's eyes are saying what her words won't: that I'm overreacting, overstepping my bounds.

'I'll keep you posted.'

The restaurant smells. There's an open gutter right outside where days-old rainwater, sewage and urine float bits of discarded plastic and other trash. I arrive early and sit in wait for Olivia. I have not told Abba I'm coming here. The last time we spoke he advised me to hold on while he continued to push our secret investigation forward. But if something is up with Celestina – or Elizabeth, or whatever she calls herself – and she is indeed a witch, I can't just leave Olivia like that. I've stood by her at every turn, from the time we met at youth service to her marriage to Thomas, *through* her marriage with Thomas, and now this.

I can't hold my breath as I wait. This restaurant's odour is not coming from outside, it's coming from inside. It's that abattoir again, the one beside the home I grew up in. I try to forget ever being there. Aunty Julia wasn't pleased when I was sent to Minna from the village – her husband's younger sister, an extra mouth to feed and a responsibility she didn't care for. Now I'm no longer there, I can see we lived in a slum. Yet Aunty Julia never trusted me to stay alone in the same house with *her* gold. As if it was not our family who gave the set of earrings and a necklace to her as dowry! What did she think I would do – steal it?

Brother Shedrack worked at his mechanic shop all day and Aunty Julia kept the front door sealed with a gleaming silver padlock while she braided hair at the market. With the few hours of freedom after school, I'd play with friends and rush home in time to help prepare the evening meal. One day, the owner of the abattoir saw me holding my nose as I ran past and cursed me.

'Yarinyar banza! Every living thing bleeds.'

That night pains in my stomach, which had been mild during the day, intensified with a vengeance. I thought they had come from eating too many wild fruits with my friends. Then I saw the blood. Waking Aunt Julia was risky but I had no other choice. Under the sole bulb in the bathroom, Aunt Julia spat in disgust at the sight of my stained pyjamas. She left me standing there, grumbling through the dark room where my brother slept.

'Use that,' Aunt Julia said, throwing a piece of blue cloth at me.

It would have to do. I shifted from squatting to prostrating in pain, smelling not just the blood from the abattoir but the dark mass coming out of me, weighing down my underwear.

I'm still sitting at the booth after half an hour. Olivia's not picking up her phone, it's become a habit. My chosen booth offers a straight view to the door. It opens and a tall woman wearing a blue gown and glasses enters. My heartbeat quickens as she walks straight to the counter and places her order. As she waits for her meal, she peers over her shoulder at me. I ignore her.

I'm relieved when I see Olivia pass through the greasy glass door, but my smile drops as she approaches. Her eyes are glazed over, her pupils big and black. Her arms hang limply at her side when I pull her into a hug. The silence is awkward. I never have to sit in silence with Olivia – conversation always comes easily. It feels like she cannot function on her own.

I clear my throat. 'How are you feeling? Are you all right?'

She shrugs, her eyes fixed somewhere above my head. Over my shoulder is a TV locked behind iron bars. Another Zee World serial. So, like before when Olivia hid things from me, I hunt for physical signs. She looks the same: long neck, curved shoulders, clavicles poking through her skin in the dress she's wearing. Her hair, usually adorned with a weave, is braided all back. Her skin glows golden.

'We should eat something,' Olivia blurts out.

'Right!' I leap at the opportunity. There are no waiters here so I have to walk over to the counter. While I'm not sure about eating in this kind of place, I want to spend more time with

Olivia. Rice and stew is easy enough, there's nothing to get wrong. I keep glancing back at Olivia while the server piles the hastily prepared food onto chipped plates.

'Livvy, where's Regina?' I ask, after I've collected the order.

Olivia flinches, then pauses, as if to steady herself. 'She's fine,' she says, but her voice wavers.

She's staring out the window now, tracing a finger up and down her left arm. 'Celestina is taking good care of her . . . of us.'

'Where is she?' I probe further.

'In a better place,' Olivia says. 'Better than I could provide on my own.'

She might as well have stuck her hand through my chest and squeezed my heart. I swallow. 'What do you mean? Is Regina dead?'

Olivia shifts her eyes away from the window and the busy street and onto me. Is that pity or contempt in her eyes? The hairs on the back of my neck prick up. Her eyes are like black holes sucking me in.

'Say something, Livvy!' I'm desperate.

'You just love putting your nose in everything,' she smirks, 'but you can't even notice what you're carrying.'

It's the most she's said since she left for Godlove's sanctuary. Her cryptic words feel like an attack. What does she mean?

'I'm just concerned,' I stammer.

Olivia ignores me, looks down at her food and begins eating. As if on cue, my stomach grumbles, surprising me. The stew on top of the rice is too pale. It probably has more tomatoes than tatashe and atarugu. I clean my plastic spoon using a tissue from the pack in my purse and wipe my hands.

The food is sour. I can't eat more than a spoonful. My stomach is turning again and I'm close to the bathroom when I bump into a woman wearing a cap pulled down low. She immediately turns her back to me, but not before I notice that she's pregnant. When I apologise, she grunts, keeping her head down. I've seen her before. Nausea now gone, I reach for the woman before she can walk out the door. I spin her by the shoulder as I tear off the cap. Prudence. She ducks down, then twists out of my grip.

'Hey!' I yell. 'Hey, Hey! Wait!'

But Prudence is out the door, her hand on Olivia's back, pushing her into the sunshine. Her cap hangs limply in my hand. Was Celestina spying on us through Prudence? I snap into action.

The sun warms up my head and the back of my neck outside the restaurant. There's a crowd, as expected – this area is busy in the afternoons – but I can't spot either Prudence or Olivia. I call for a cab on the Taxify app and the driver calls me shortly after we've been connected. I tell him to meet me in front of the LG office. It's big and red, hard to miss. As I cross the street, I steal a glance at the restaurant. A tall woman wearing a blue gown bustles towards me. At the bus stop near the LG office, I stumble onto one of the hard, grey benches; my knees are shaking. The back of my jeans will be dirty when I get up, I just know it.

My Taxify cab is seven minutes away. Suddenly, I feel a heavy weight land on my shoulder. It's Olivia. She rests her head on me like she often did on movie nights at Temi's flat. Now though, she's looking up at me with those dull eyes. Her mouth is twisted into a sneer.

'You want to know what happens?' she growls, her voice both guttural and otherworldly. 'I will take your baby. We're going to take your baby.'

'What . . .?!' I leap to my feet.

Olivia points at my flat belly. Tremors run through my body. I don't know that I have been screaming until the crowd appears like a flash flood: mostly unemployed men, muscles straining as they direct cars to park in front of the multiple shopping centres on both sides of the streets. They just want to make money. Others are just looking for any excuse to have fun or to release their frustrations. This is Banex, after all.

A man in a brown T-shirt is holding Olivia by the cowl neck of her dress. Another is standing in front of me.

'Wetin you talk now now?' he grunts, red-rimmed eyes burning into me.

I can't form the words, I just gasp. Someone I can't see says, 'That girl be witch o!' Another agrees, 'She fall from sky, she dey try kill our sister here.'

'She say she wan comot her pikin.'

And before I can take another breath, I see the man that's holding Olivia slap her. It's so hard her head snaps back. Random acts of violence burst forth like a flame sparked when you've had the gas running for too long. There is a gas station close by. My hand is shaking as I reach for my phone, I need to call Abba, get the police.

They won't come if I'm not married to one.

The crowd has engulfed Olivia – I can't see her any more. My voice is still trapped in my throat. I need to tell them that Olivia is a victim, the real witch is this Celestina-Elizabeth woman – whoever she is.

My free hand pressed to my tummy, I can smell the fresh blood of countless animals spilled on the abattoir floor again. I look up, and standing apart from the crowd is Celestina, wearing that same boubou – blue with the gold trim – looking first at me then at the melee. Prudence materialises by her side.

'Ku dena,' the switch flips on and my voice returns. 'Kar ku saka mata taya. Don Allah, don anabi.'

Something is happening, the crowd has stilled. Strong hands push me forward and when I see Olivia I barely recognise her. I throw myself over her bloody body.

'Ku dena!' it is now a mantra. Stop it. Just stop it!

***

In this hospital, the floors and walls are white and white. The Turkish doctor tells me that the amount of sedatives they had to flush out of Olivia's body could kill a horse.

'Any idea why she was using the drugs?'

'No. I only know that it's the handiwork of a woman who told me her name was Celestina Godlove and her accomplice, Prudence.'

'The drugs alone were enough to harm the baby she was carrying, but it's the trauma that caused the miscarriage.'

I swallow my scream. In my bag, my phone is ringing. It's Abba.

'How is Olivia?' he asks.

'She's still passed out.' I say. 'Doctor says she'll be fine.'

'And how are you?'

'Fine,' I say, but my lips won't stop trembling. 'No. It was horrible.'

'I'm coming to the hospital now,' he says.

'Did you check on the shelter?' I demand. 'Have you arrested them?'

I hear the sharp intake of his breath. 'Gimbiya na . . . the flat was empty.'

'It's a lie!' I yelp, and a passing nurse shoots me a dirty look.

'It's just . . . the neighbours say they didn't notice any activity,' Abba says. 'But I think they must have hurriedly packed out . . .'

I suck in air through my teeth. The thought of Celestina setting up shop in another city makes my head spin. At least my friend is safe and the police are actively tracking Regina. My black shoes cut through the hallway as I make my way to Olivia's room. Looking at her now, I can't bring myself to touch her hand. I keep seeing her eyes, the way she stared at me at that bus stop. Then I blink and she's lying on the dusty street covered in blood because there's a fuel scarcity.

'Hajiya?' It is the doctor from earlier. 'Your test results are ready. You can pick them up at the lab.'

As I wait for my results to be printed, my eyes tug over the technician's shoulder to the back room. It must be a staff room of some kind – a bank of grey metal lockers runs along one wall, a row of coat hooks lines another. I count the hooks to pass the time, my eyes skimming along the crisp white doctors' coats draped over the first nine. I stop at the sight of a piece of cloth hanging loosely from the tenth, my breath catches in my throat.

It is a gold-embroidered blue scarf.

Please, Please

T J Benson

Nse did not marry Brother Faustus for love, even though such marriages were becoming fashionable. She knew she had to get him because Constance had her kohl-lined eyes on him. Constance was a better catch. Constance had finished primary school with the White men. Nse's education was aborted at Form Two because she was beautiful, and thus considered valuable; would fetch the right caliber of suitors when it was time. Constance was plain, in looks and in carriage, the way a child is plain during those first years of life before it becomes a girl or boy; so she continued on to St. Tansi College undisturbed. The people of Ala sent their undesirable children to missionary schools – the plain ones, the last-borns or abomination children born from incest. But now that more men were starting to prefer educated girls who would not embarrass them once they had established their city lives, Nse, who had her eyes on the bright lights, wished her father had let her stay on at St. Tansi.

**

Brother Faustus was not the most attractive man in Ala. Constance had settled for him at last, after abandoning her other loves to Nse. There had been Shagba, who worked in the Taraku Mills factory and had brought Constance new slippers and dresses whenever he visited the village. Then there was Mvendaga, with his full afro and moon-white teeth, who zoomed down from Gboko every market day on his motorcycle. Each time Nse only had to smile at them and they were hers. Constance must have been sure Nse would leave her with this one, since he was 'sickle-celled', as the White men said. Nse did not. She believed even though Brother Faustus was carrying death, there must have been something valuable in him for Constance to have set her sights on him.

So she married him and he was grateful. As were his people. From this gratitude sprang genuine love of her, potent enough to make him forget her friend Constance, with whom he'd first made acquaintance. It was Constance he'd approached after the St. Agnes Parish Christmas carol rehearsal to enquire whether she would make it to the main event. When she didn't show and her body was found, he was there to comfort Nse out of her numbness after Constance's burial. Her grief swallowed his, and before long he was in love with her with an extravagance people believed would kill him first. After coercing permission from his father, Brother Faustus evicted all the tenants living in their second compound next to the Parish. Then he made sure his mother sent vegetables, tomatoes and peppers every market day and a chicken on Easter Day. His elder brother, who worked in a plastic-manufacturing factory in Lagos, sent the latest kitchen appliances and a crockery set, and his father sent a goat at Christmas. These, along with his Latin recitations in the evenings and the size of the compound, captivated Nse. He taught English in the new government school and he began teaching her too. What was this, if not the gloss of city success right in here in her own compound?

**

Nse unties the knot of her wrapper, brings out a stick of Benson & Hedges and a lighter. She props the cigarette in one corner of her mouth, cups a weathered hand over the lighter and scrolls up a flame. She takes a small puff and exhales, chokes a little, chuckling through her cough at the image of his face, his pity-filled eyes, his praying lips pinched and disapproving. 'Ah, Constance,' she mutters, tucking the lighter into her bra, 'if he could see me now . . .' Brother Faustus would detest her smoking. He had, like the rest of his family, been as firmly rooted in the

Roman Catholic Church as the old mango tree in the center of their compound. Nse, whose parents had somewhat abandoned the gods of the land, yet never allowed themselves a new religion, had followed along as best she could, joining the choir and going to weekly Mass – in the end committing everything but her heart. 'Constance . . .' she whispers again, but the chirping birds and gentle rustle of leaves are her only answer.

Nse sighs into the breeze.

Picturing Brother Faustus on his knees, reciting a prayer to St. Michael to deliver her from this ungodly habit, tickles her now. She knows he meant her well. But her memories are sore; the smoky haze about her head a salve. She takes a drag and laughs again, staring up through the plume of smoke and the ceiling of forest leaves and ponders the years behind her. 'Yes, women smoke as they like these days, Constance – can you imagine?' she says, sensing her old friend again. Constance. Nse still talks to her as if she were here. And for Brother Faustus, she still wears a white rosary around her neck.

***

Brother Faustus didn't live as long as her in-laws had promised. He didn't even die from sickness as everyone feared. Nse had been squatting over the pit toilet, isolated from the living quarters, sometime after midnight in the first year of their marriage, when she heard the front door crash. She perceived the brutal, pungent stench of male arrogance, a kind of steel smell in the air that mummified you, made your head throb and your heart wince. Heard their rabid yells in the night. His anguished plea: 'Don't kill me, please . . . I have a wife!' The rap of gunshots. Then the silence that held her until cockcrow. Nse never allowed herself to return to the tenderness of those words, throughout the burial ceremony, throughout her other husbands, throughout her life: *Don't kill me, please...I have a wife.*

***

Lying on the grass with Constance now, Nse shuts her eyes
against the green leaves filtering the sunlight. She sucks on her
dwindling cigarette, daring herself to return to that night. She
flinches as she replays the *ka-ka-kpa-kpa* of the gunshots and
forces herself to confront the sentence: *Don't kill me, please . . . I
have a wife!* She exhales, whispers to the assembly of trees, eyes
still shut: 'And a baby.'

Nse opens her eyes and sits up. She knows Constance would
think she has come to pick a quarrel. She turns to where she
imagines the dead woman must have been buried years ago
and scolds, 'I just came to rest!' before lying flat on her back
once again. This was the small portion of land Ala people had
given the white missionaries to bury their dead. It had been
rededicated to their Ala, the ancestor who brought them
here and now it was a forest no government knew to touch.
Constance was here; Nse could feel her. 'I need to rest,' she says
again.

But how does one rest from 85 years of living? What kind of
rest would placate a body worn out from the years, if not death?
She lifts her hands like the musical conductor of their school
choir did in the fifties, studies them briefly before cupping
them beneath her head. How she envies Constance. How happy
she must be wherever she is, without the burden of having to
bathe, eat, sleep, wake up, think of enemies, or think of death.
It cost too much, this business of being alive.

'I didn't kill you, Constance.' She has to say it out loud. This
is the first time she has ever said it in the absence of people.
Of course, she had said it to her parents, to Constance's
mother, to the local government police, to Brother Faustus –
even swearing on the lives of her future children – and to the
community, but never to herself. She always feared the words
would fall flat, turn and mock her. Self-deceit is impossible, no
matter how successfully one deceives others. She tries it again,
louder this time: 'I didn't kill you, Constance!' A startled flock of
birds descends from the ceiling of leaves and branches, before
flying up and out, their shrills echoing in the forest as they soar.

'I. DIDN'T. KILL. YOU!' And because now she is sure of it – surprised, but sure – she begins to weep.

***

Constance had always aimed for an easy life. She had four younger ones from her mother and since she had to nanny them, she became their friend to avoid the trouble of disciplining them. She was usually first in line to have her hair braided at Mamfe's house, but would quickly stand aside, hair half-plaited, yielding the stool to Nse, or whoever came with a mind to displace her. She avoided fights at the stream by waking up to fetch water before the sun lit up the sky. At first Nse thought it was cowardice, but when Constance reached the age of 14 without a single scratch from childhood brawls, she began to reassess her judgment of the girl and they became friends. This is what Nse was thinking about when she looked at her hands before placing them beneath her head – Constance's hands.

It was customary for the girls in the village to go to the edge of the stream to collect the fine sand they used to glaze their arms and feet till they reflected light. They usually did this to prepare for festivals, and when Christianity came, they did it on the day before Christmas Eve. If they could no longer parade their gleaming limbs before men in the name of their local deities, at least they still could in the name of the White Man's God. This was how the Christmas carol service held in St. Agnes on Christmas Eve came to be one of the most populated annual events in the entire region. Young men would come from nearby villages and towns, as much to be in the presence of these women whose skin shone like glass in the night as to mark this precious night before the Savior was born.

That Christmas Eve, the year they turned 15 and the day of her death, Constance was using a wand dipped in kohl to line her eyes – the only cosmetic procedure she allowed herself – when Nse noticed her hands. Then her skin. Constance never went for the fine sand beauty ritual, not just because she didn't want to pick up a fight, but because she didn't need it – would never need it – Nse realized. Her dark skin was even throughout the backs of her palms, up her hands to her shoulders, her neck then to her spotless face. The mahogany skin was rich enough and needed no artificial shine.

'Why are you looking at me like that?' she stopped suddenly, staring at Nse with big, bewildered eyes.

'Me ayam riking your eyes o. Maybe when merchant bring lat poison from Kaduna I tell my father to buy this your thing for me. I rike it vely wer.'

'It is "like" not "rike", and it is "rat" not "lat" – you this beautiful Tiv girl!' Constance chided, giggling. She beckoned her over. Nse moved to her, mesmerized by this quiet girl's secret power and charm, hidden till now. 'Besides, the merchant has already passed our village yesterday. Open your eyes, copy copy.' she said, and laughed, revealing her front gap tooth. Nse boiled inside. This was the most beautiful girl in the village besides her – perhaps even more so. And clever too! Constance tilted Nse's head in the mirror to place the wand of kohl at the upper lid of her right eye. Nse flinched and she chided her again. 'I won't blind you, just close your eyes so that your eyelids will press the thing. Ehen. Yes.'

When they were done they admired each other in the mirror for a moment – the moment Nse would dedicate her life to outdoing Constance in everything – until Constance reminded her that they would be late for the carol service.

'Yes o, your boyfriend is waiting for you!' Nse jumped up, giggling. Constance looked away, her voice low.

'We are just friends.'

Nse shrugged and went to get the boiled yam, which was already burning on the fire. She doused some red oil onto the large chunks after peeling the softened skin. On her way back to her room she paused, then turned back into the kitchen hut to sprinkle some salt onto Constance's share, knowing her friend's distaste for anything bland. She brought the plate to her room, fetched a small bowl of water to wash their hands, and they sat on the floor and ate.

'Chop quick-quick,' urged Nse, 'or you want us to do latey-latey for carol?'

But Constance, careful in everything, wanted to take her time. Rushing a meal might upset her stomach at the carol service. Nse had no such concerns. She washed her hand in the bowl of water and stood up to re-apply some charcoal to darken her eyebrows and spread some extra pomade on her lips. Satisfied, she shouted, 'Till you come,' behind her as she rushed out.

All through the walk to the church Nse fought back a smile so broad that people paused to wonder what had made the most beautiful girl so giddy. The priest was sharing a few words for the Christmas season, so she hastened to the front where the other choir girls sat. After the mass she had the confidence to walk up to the man who had been looking at her while she sang and explain Constance couldn't make it. When she returned home after that magical night, Nse found Constance on the floor, eyes locked open, and screamed for her mother.

⁎⁎

She knew people always wondered, even if they didn't tell her, why she put so much effort into being alive. They must have admired the zeal, if not the deviousness with which she ensured her survival. She juggled trades to keep afloat, rejecting aid from her in-laws after the death of her husband, alms that really were gifts of guilt – through them Nse had become a young, childless widow. They begged her to remarry and when – after three successive, childless divorces – her own parents gave up on her, they became her parents, eventually leaving her with the compound. She rented out a portion of the house to Peace Corps members from Sweden, then to soldiers during the war. The whole village knew she picked lovers amongst her tenants in the Force but they forgave her for it, wondered why she would even seek any pleasure at all, why she would make any effort to keep her flesh aflame. Who was she living for?

There was a lecturer who had just returned from Cambridge and promised to leave his family for her once he got a new job and help her further her education if only she would marry him. When the church secretary announced in St. Agnes Parish that Sister Nse had gotten admission at the newly established University of Calabar, the Catechist decided to intervene. He visited her home after mass and received her hospitality with God's blessings, sitting on the chair she had placed beside her stool on under the mango tree. 'Sister, I heard your announcement during mass,' he said.

She beamed at his sandals. 'I wish to better myself, Brother. I stopped school in Form Two, small time I married. So you see–'

'Which is beautiful, very beautiful. You see, even the Almighty tells us in the book of Hosea, and I quote: "My people are destroyed for lack of knowledge." See this war that just finished eh, will it have happened if the north and south had knowledge?'

'No, Brother Paul,' she shook her head violently, 'at all!'

'So it is good that you are going back. However, have you thought of devoting your life to heavenly causes? Something that would make your life more . . . *meaningful?*'

There were orphans dropped in the church almost weekly now that the war was over. There were several displaced children who had wandered from their homes till they ended up in Ala. What if she decided to be a mother to them? The church would assist her, of course. They would offer her the finance to enlarge her compound and deploy some Sisters to assist her. Nse told the Catechist that she would think about it. During the week she managed to find tenants who would rent the other half she had occupied, where she had made her first baby with her husband, and by the following Sunday she had already said yes to the lecturer and moved with him to Calabar to start her registration.

Everything she was, everything she had tried to be, was for Constance. She had husbanded her beauty up to her late fifties to spite the dead woman. She had taken lovers from the village, people's husbands, Swedish Corps, another lecturer at University of Calabar (who she dumped the first lecturer for and had four dead babies with in the late seventies) and – to her delight – as she approached middle age, a young pastor from one of the Pentecostal churches springing up everywhere.

She had survived all kinds of ridicule and name-calling; the second lecturer's mother had come to chase her from their staff quarters' apartment, flogging her with a broom, calling her a child-eater. When she ran for local government chairman for her constituency, to make Constance quiver in the grave, her long history of deaths was brought up and stories were shared about how she had harnessed the energy from all the babies and husbands she'd murdered to win the election. She won. Two terms. She accepted the honors which all testified to her hard work, but she knew that if she examined herself, she would find she accomplished all these things to show Constance that she was greater. Surely by now she was greater – wasn't she?

***

Constance won in the end, she realizes now. Rather than grow old and grow fat and labour and disfigure her body with children, she had chosen instead to die beautiful and remain forever young. And as for Brother Faustus, this understanding has finally come to Nse: she had not won him by seduction or any such manipulation after all. For him, any choir girl with gleaming skin and a cherubic voice would have made a suitable wife, not because of the carnal pleasures such a girl would bring to his bedroom with her naiveté, but for her potential as a conduit to healing and heaven; for surely to behold such a woman each morning, to listen to her recite the *Angelus* or sing holy hymns would be to touch the hem of the Lord's garment and to see God in the flesh? Any girl in choir would have brought him that.

Constance was always born to win; how couldn't anybody see this? How couldn't anybody see she was the consummate deceiver, this Constance – for while Nse was dusting her face with powder and thickening her eyebrows with eye pencil and cutting new wrapper, Constance was busy blooming in the dark.

Nse frees one hand from under her head to pluck the cigarette from her mouth. She cackles again but she catches herself in her delirium, examining her heart for any leftover rivalry. She is grateful to Constance, her one great excuse for being alive. 'I did it all for you,' she says, and it is the truth.

**

There was a baby that stayed long enough in her womb to be born full term. She can't remember whose it was, probably one of the tenants'; those years she was desperate enough to bring even what the village would call a sin into the world. Like the other babies she couldn't convince this one to breathe air, so on the same bed she had conceived her first dead fetus she forced her nipple into its mouth. 'Take breast. Ma atumba wan wam,' she begged, as the sympathetic nurses tried to wrestle the warm corpse away from her. She felt so alone when they left her in her room with no one in the world to belong to her that, for the first time, she almost questioned the rigor of her commitment to outdo Constance and longed for death. Then Constance came to her. Not as the friend who had helped her with English and make up, but as the secret nemesis who was better than she was. Nse hardened her resolve, buried the baby and sought another lover.

**

She married her soldier husband after the war. He had nothing so he moved into her dead husband's house, but he didn't like it one bit. He tried to move her out of the house, take her to Jos with him to live in the barracks. Of course, she refused. She had already left her second lecturer husband and had moved back to Ala for teaching practice. One day he came home drunk and brought up the issue of leaving the house. She took his face in her palms and tried to sweet-talk him out of it but he slapped her, kicked her until she was malleable enough to carry to the pit toilet outside where she had been nursing a stomach upset the night she heard the gunshots that took Brother Faustus from her all those years ago. He locked her in and went to pack their bags so that they could leave with the trailer drivers who moved sacks of beans some hours before dawn in the village bus park. When he opened the toilet door at first light she threw the excess raffia rope that had been used to fix the thatch roof over his head and pulled hard. Once he fell, head lurching forwards in the direction of the pit toilet, she passed another coil of rope over his head, squeezed past him and dragged him out by the neck towards the back of the kitchen, muttering furious things in Tiv. When the story rose with the sun later that day no one could believe the petite woman could drag her hefty husband like that but it was true – she dragged him to the back of the kitchen and pointed at the ground. 'You know how many children I've buried at this spot?' she spat, but he was fighting the rope with his hands and struggling to breathe. She tugged at it, and he yelped a hoarse 'NO!'

She dragged him to the other end of the L-shaped compound and pointed to the flowerbed. 'You know how many I buried here?' She wasn't shouting or quarreling now, her voice was calm. When she tugged the rope and he jerked his head up to see her face pinched with anger he became truly terrified. 'Do you?'

He shook his head and clasped his hands together.

'I am not going anywhere,' she said, and entered the house. No matter how far she went from that house – even for the marriages that took her away from it – she would always return. She locked the door behind her, leaving him outside to recover. The next time she opened the door, he was gone.

***

'How many babies have I buried?' she asks Constance now.
Constance has been dead with them so she should know. She
used to keep count, but memory can be fragile you know. Like
how she would never ever know for certain if it had been the
merchant's rat poison or salt she had sprinkled on Constance's
share of their boiled yam that Christmas Eve. The kitchen hut
was too dark for her to be sure. She remembers the days she
began to forget. It had been during those years when she got
admission, before she married the lecturer and she had come to
expect her miscarriages like the seasons. One of the soldiers had
been redeployed so she was staying in his room and when the
other saw her digging behind the house to bury a half-formed
fetus at dawn she had challenged him: 'Wetin you dey look?
Ehn? You sabi how many pikin I don bury?'

She crosses her arms over her breasts and stares at the stars
of light between the leaves and thinks of how thoughtful her
only friend Constance was – Constance who had once taken
such care of her own siblings, going into the ground to mother
Nse's dead children. She imagines them in an oneiric afterlife,
playing and dancing round her and she stifles a flare of jealousy.
'You were a better mother anyway,' she shrugs. Nse takes a last
long drag of her cigarette and exhales at the afternoon stars.
'You loved children more than I did,' she says.

The dying stub of cigarette burns her finger and she yelps in
surprise, flicking it away. She is about to sit up and light another
when she remembers a phrase she heard amongst the women
in Port Au Prince in response to a greeting. It was a year before
her mother in-law would come to chase her out of her lecturer-
husband's house; that husband had been a visiting lecturer in
the languages department of Universite d'Etat d'Haiti and had
taken her along for the one-year sabbatical. She smiles and
scratches the white hair at her temples, smiles at how fitting
the phrase is now that she has come to the full revelation of
Constance's victory over life, now that it is clear who really was

more beautiful. For when she thinks of Constance, she sees that quiet 15-year-old girl with kohl-lined eyes and perfect hands, perfect complexion the shade of new water yam skin, while she, Nse – ha! She doesn't bother with mirrors these days. She would be no match for the dead woman.

'Nou led, nou la,' she recites, but her chest is heavy and it is hard to breathe. She feels the weight of all these years so she places her palms flat on the ground to feel those perfect brown hands, to feel her Constance. She tries the words again, in English this time: 'We are ugly, but we are here.'

Biographies

Chair of judges

Okey Ndibe chaired the Judging Panel for the 2022 AKO Caine Prize for African Writing. He is the author of two novels, *Foreign Gods, Inc.* and *Arrows of Rain*; a memoir, *Never Look an American in the Eye* (winner of the 2017 Connecticut Book Award for nonfiction); and *The Man Lives: A Conversation with Wole Soyinka on Life, Literature and Politics* He earned MFA and PhD degrees from the University of Massachusetts Amherst and has taught at various universities and colleges, including Brown, St. Lawrence, Trinity College, Connecticut College, and the University of Lagos (as a Fulbright scholar). His award-winning journalism has appeared in major newspapers and magazines in the UK, Italy, South Africa, Nigeria, and the US—where he served on the editorial board of the Hartford Courant. He writes a column on the substack platform titled "Offside Musings," and co-hosts a podcast of the same name.

Editor

Anwuli Ojogwu is an editor and the co-founder of Narrative Landscape Press. She has edited the works of Chimamanda Ngozi Adichie, Petina Gappah, Binyavanga Wainaina, Uzodinma Iweala and more. She served as a consultant to the Rivers State Government on the landmark UNESCO World Book Capital in Port Harcourt. Anwuli is a co-founder of Society for Book & Magazine Editors of Nigeria (SBMEN). She is the editor of the stories from the 2022 AKO Caine Prize Writers workshop.

2021 Shortlisted writers

Doreen Baingana is a Ugandan writer. Her short story collection, *Tropical Fish*, won the Grace Paley Prize for Short Fiction and the Commonwealth Prize for Best First Book, Africa Region. Two stories in it were nominated for the Caine Prize (2004 & 2005). She has also published two children's books as well as stories and essays in numerous international journals. Other awards include a Miles Morland Scholarship, a Rockefeller Bellagio Residency, a Tebere Arts Foundation Playwright's Residency, and in 2021, a Sustainable Arts Foundation grant. She co-founded and runs the Mawazo Africa Writing Institute, based in Entebbe, Uganda.

Rémy Ngamije is a Rwandan-born Namibian writer and photographer. He is the founder, chairperson, and artministrator of Doek, an independent arts organisation in Namibia supporting the literary arts. He is also the co-founder and editor-in-chief of *Doek! Literary Magazine*, Namibia's first and only literary magazine. His debut novel "The Eternal Audience Of One" is forthcoming from Scout Press (S&S) in August, 2021. His work has appeared in *The Johannesburg Review of Books*, *American Chordata*, *Lolwe*, and many other publications. He is the Africa Regional Winner of the 2021 Commonwealth Short Story Prize and was shortlisted for the AKO Caine Prize for African Writing in 2020. He was also longlisted for the 2020 and 2021 Afritondo Short Story Prizes. In 2019 he was shortlisted for Best Original Fiction by Stack Magazines. More of his writing can be read on his website: remythequill.com

Meron Hadero is an Ethiopian-American who was born in Addis Ababa and came to the U.S. via Germany as a young child. She is the winner of the 2020 Restless Books Prize for New Immigrant Writing. Her short stories have been shortlisted for the 2019 Caine Prize for African Writing and published in *Zyzzyva, Ploughshares, Addis Ababa Noir, McSweeney's Quarterly Concern, The Iowa Review, The Missouri Review, New England Review, Best American Short Stories,* among others. Her writing has also been in *The New York Times Book Review, The Displaced: Refugee Writers on Refugee Lives,* and will appear in the forthcoming anthology *Letter to a Stranger: Essays to the Ones Who Haunt Us.* A 2019-2020 Steinbeck Fellow at San Jose State University, she's been a fellow at Yaddo, Ragdale, and MacDowell, and her writing has been supported by the International Institute at the University of Michigan, the Elizabeth George Foundation, and Artist Trust. Meron is an alum of the Bill & Melinda Gates Foundation where she worked as a research analyst for the President of Global Development, and holds an MFA in creative writing from the University of Michigan, a JD from Yale, and a BA in history from Princeton with a certificate in American Studies.

Troy Onyango is the founder and editor-in-chief of *Lolwe.* His work has appeared in Prairie Schooner, Wasafari, Johannesburg Review of Books, Nairobi Noir, Caine Prize Anthology and Transition among others. The winner of the inaugural Nyanza Literary Festival Prize and first runner-up in the Black Letter Media Competition, he has also been shortlisted for the Short Story Day Africa Prize, the Brittle Paper Awards, and nominated for the Pushcart Prize. He holds an MA in Creative Writing with distinction from the University of East Anglia, where he was a recipient of the Miles Morland Foundation Scholarship.

Iryn Tushabe is a Ugandan-Canadian writer and journalist. Her creative nonfiction has appeared in Briarpatch Magazine, Adda, and Prairies North. Her short fiction has appeared in Grain Magazine, the Carter V. Cooper Short Fiction Anthology, and in The Journey Prize Stories 30. The winner of the 2020 City of Regina Writing Award, she's currently finishing her debut novel, *Everything is Fine Here.*

2022 Shortlisted Writers

Joshua Chizoma is a Nigerian writer. His works have been published or are forthcoming in Prairie Schooner, Lolwe, AFREADA, Entropy Magazine, Anathema Magazine, Agbowo Magazine, and Prachya Review. His story, 'A House Called Joy' won the 2018 Kreative Diadem Prize in the flash fiction category. He won the 2020 Awele Creative Trust Short Story Prize with his short story *Their Boy* and was shortlisted for the 2021 Afritondo Short Story Prize. He is an alumnus of the 2019 Purple Hibiscus Creative Writing Workshop taught by Chimamanda Ngozi Adichie.

Nana-Ama Danquah was born in Accra, Ghana and immigrated to the US as a child. She is the author of the memoir *Willow Weep for Me: A Black Woman's Journey Through Depression* and editor of the anthologies *Becoming American, Shaking the Tree, The Black Body* and, most recently, *Accra Noir*. Her work has been widely anthologized and published in magazines and newspapers such as Essence, the Washington Post, the Village Voice, and the Los Angeles Times. She has taught at Otis College of Arts and Design; Antioch College; University of Ghana; and, NYU in Ghana.

Hannah Giorgis is a staff writer at The Atlantic. The daughter of Ethiopian immigrants, she lives in Brooklyn by way of Southern California. Her criticism and reporting have appeared in publications including the New York Times magazine, The Guardian, and Pitchfork. Hannah's short stories have appeared in the *Addis Ababa Noir* anthology, the Lifted Brow literary journal, and SPOOK magazine. She was the recipient of the 2018 Yoojin Grace Wuertz Writers of Immigration and Diaspora fellowship at the Jack Jones Literary Arts retreat and the 2021 Writer-in-Residence at Syracuse University's S.I. Newhouse School of Public Communications. Most recently, Hannah co-wrote *Ida B. The Queen: The Extraordinary Life and*

Legacy of Ida B. Wells, a dedication to the pioneering American journalist and advocate, with Wells' great-granddaughter, Michelle Duster.

Idza Luhumyo is a Kenyan writer. Her work has been published by Popula, Jalada Africa, The Writivism Anthology, Baphash Literary & Arts Quarterly, MaThoko's Books, Gordon Square Review, Amsterdam's ZAM Magazine, Short Story Day Africa, the New Internationalist, The Dark, and African Arguments. Her work has been shortlisted for the Short Story Day Africa Prize, the Miles Morland Writing Scholarship, and the Gerald Kraak Award. She is the inaugural winner of the Margaret Busby New Daughters of Africa Award (2020) and winner of the Short Story Day Africa Prize (2021).

Billie McTernan is a writer and artist who experiments with literary and visual art forms. She has an MFA from the Kwame Nkrumah School of Science and Technology in Kumasi, and has published many articles and essays from her travels in West Africa. As a storyteller, she is drawn to the ways that stories are manifested, be it through the body in dance and performance, or through literature, sound and visual arts. She has been published in TSA Art Magazine, ARTnews, Artsy, Financial Times Life & Arts, Contemporary And, ARTS.BLACK and other independent artist-run platforms. She is currently working on a piece that falls somewhere between a short story and a novel.

2022 Workshop Participants

Elizabeth Johnson is a writer and researcher. She works with the Writers Project of Ghana and Pa Gya! A Literary Festival in Accra. She writes short stories and poetry and her works have been published both online and in various anthologies. She won third place in the Kofi Awoonor Literary Awards (2018) and was guest editor for the Random Prize Anthology, *Identity during the*

Pandemic (2021). She is currently a resident with Oroko Radio where she produces and hosts a show dedicated to Highlife Music and works as a Faculty Intern at Ashesi University.

Audrey Obuobisa-Darko is an author from Ghana. Alongside her books, The Magic Basket, and Wahala Dey, Audrey has short fiction publications in Kalahari Review & The African Writer and in anthologies for African writers. She's a 2020 K&L Prize shortlistee and 2020 Wakini Kuria Prize longlistee. Wahala Dey has been awarded at the Ghana Association of Writers Literary Awards and the Osagyefo Kwame Nkrumah African Genius Awards.

Audrey is studying Computer Science at Ashesi University while nurturing her passion for writing.

Sally Sadie Singhateh is a Gambian writer. She is the author of *Christie's Crisis, Baby Trouble, The Sun Will Soon Shine*, and *Stories From The Gambia*, Sally is a recipient of the International Poet of Merit Award by the International Society of Poets. She currently lives and works in The Gambia as a Communications Expert, developing and implementing both Communications and Fundraising Strategies.

Victor Forna is a Sierra Leonean writer based in his country's capital Freetown. His short fiction and poetry have been published in Fantasy Magazine, Lolwe, Short Story Day Africa Anthology: Disruption, Bad Form, the Nami Podcast, Brittle Paper, and elsewhere.

Onengiye Nwachukwu is a writer and a graduate of Nnamdi Azikiwe University, Nigeria. He is an alum of the 2022 AKO Caine Prize writers workshop

Kofi Konadu Berko is an MA student at the Department of Adult Education and Human Resource Studies. His story *The Sun is White* is published in the Afroyoung Adult Anthology by the Goethe Institut titled Waterbirds on the Lakeshore. His writing has been featured in Kalahari Review, Writers Space Africa, Tampered Press and other places.

Akua Serwaa Amankwah is a writer and academic. Her stories have been published in The Mirror and Flash Fiction Ghana, as well as the *Kenkey for Ewes* and *Resilience* anthologies. She won the Inspire Us Writing Contest by Worldreader in 2019, and the imagining Early Accra competition in 2021.vShe was a participant of the Tampered Press Fiction Workshop 2021, as well as the AKO Caine Writers' Workshop 2022. She is currently undertaking an MPhil degree in English (Literature) from the University of Ghana, Legon.

Akachi Adimora-Ezeigbo is a multiple award-winning writer of more than fifty books and a Professor of English who has taught at the University of Lagos and Alex Ekwueme Federal University Ndufu-Alike, Ebonyi State, Nigeria and has had Research Fellowships in the United Kingdom, South Africa and Germany. Adimora-Ezeigbo writes across genres: she is a novelist, poet, short story writer, playwright and children's author. Her literary awards include The Nigeria Prize for Literature (2007) and Fonlon-Nichols Award (2022).

Andrew Aidoo is a Ghanaian writer, an alumnus of both the Mo Issa and the AKO Caine Prize workshops, and an Ebedi Fellow. His work has appeared in literary magazines including Jalada Africa. He's currently working on a novel in which he is the main character.

Rafeeat Aliyu is a writer, editor and documentary filmmaker. Born and raised in Nigeria, she is a currently studying for her MFA in Creative Writing at North Carolina State University. Rafeeat is a graduate of the Clarion West Workshop for Science Fiction and Fantasy Writers (2019). Her short stories have appeared in Nightmare, Strange Horizons, FIYAH and Omenana, among others.

TJ Benson is a Nigerian writer and visual artist whose work explores the body in the context of memory, African Spirituality, Africanfuturism, mythology, migration, utopia and the unconscious self. His work has been exhibited and published in several journals and shortlisted for awards. His Saraba Manuscript Prize shortlisted Africanfuturist collection of short stories 'We Won't Fade into Darkness' was published by Parresia in 2018.

His debut novel *The Madhouse* was published in 2021 by Masobe Books and Penguin Random House SA and his second novel *People Live Here* was released in June 2022. He has facilitated writing workshops, more recently teaching a class on magical realism and surrealism within the context of African literature for Lolwe Magazine. He is a Moniack Mhor alumni, IWP University of Iowa Fellow and Art Omi New York Alumni. He currently lives in an apartment full of plants and is in the danger of becoming a cat person.